After the Fire

Felice Stevens

After the Fire (Through Hell and Back – Book 2)
February 2017
SECOND EDITION
First Edition published in 2015
Copyright © 2017 by Felice Stevens
Print Edition

Cover Art by Reese Dante
www.reesedante.com
Cover Photography by Alejandro Caspe

Join my newsletter to get access to get first looks at WIP, exclusive content, contests, deleted scenes and much more! Never any spam.

Newsletter:
http://eepurl.com/bExIdr

A single bullet destroyed the dreams of Dr. Jordan Peterson. With his lover dead, Jordan descends into an endless spiral of self-destruction that nearly costs him his friends, his career and his life. When Jordan finds himself working closely with the aloof Lucas Conover, the investment banker's mysterious past and unexpected kindness shocks him back into a life and emotions he'd thought lost forever.

The betrayal by the foster brother he'd worshiped, taught Lucas Conover never to trust or believe in anyone. Living a solitary life doesn't free him of the nightmare of his youth; it reinforces his belief that he would never fall in love. When the death of one of his clients forces him to work closely with Dr. Jordan Peterson, he meets a person whose suffering exceeds his own. Though Jordan rejects his effort to help, something within Luke pushes him discover more about the first man to ever get under his skin.

As Luke lets down his guard and Jordan lets go of his pain, desire takes control. Each man must come to terms with past struggles if they are to create a future together. And learning to trust in themselves and love again after tragedy and a lifetime of pain, may be the only thing that saves them in the end.

Dedication

To my children: thank you for your support and encouragement. You make me proud every day.

Acknowledgment

To Hope and Jessica of Flat Earth Editing, thank you for putting up with the craziness-I couldn't do it without you. And bottles on the floor. To Dianne Thies of Lyrical Lines, you are the best.

But it all comes down to the readers. I love you guys. Every day you make the dream a reality. I couldn't do it without you.

Join my newsletter for sneak peeks of Works in Progress, exclusive content, contests and more! No spam ever.
http://eepurl.com/bExIdr

Chapter One

ONLY THE PAIN in his heart eclipsed the ache in his head. Bleary-eyed, Dr. Jordan Peterson sat slumped at his kitchen table and stared into the void of his house. Empty bottles of vodka littered the table, alongside half-full takeout Chinese food containers.

Still alone.

Each time he awakened, Jordan prayed the nightmare that played consistently in his head would cease. It was like that annoying song repeated on the radio every hour you wanted to forget but couldn't.

"I'm sorry, Jordan, but Keith didn't make it."

How do you move on from the finality of the death of your love when you've promised him the rest of your life? After almost nine months Jordan still didn't have the answer.

The doorbell rang. Groaning with the effort it took to move his protesting body, and with his head pounding from another vicious hangover, he grabbed the bottle of aspirin sitting on the countertop and popped two pills, aided by a handful of water directly from the tap. Then, swallowing his nausea, he shuffled to the front door of his town house. Jordan massaged his temples and squinted through the peephole, grimacing at the sight of his best friend Drew, with his lover, Ash.

Jordan's chest tightened at the happiness on his friend's face as Drew kissed Ash's cheek, unaware he was being spied upon. Smothering the bitterness he'd felt toward Drew these past few months, he yanked open the door to greet the two men.

"Damn, you look like shit." Ash's sharp gaze raked him up and down. "Ow." He rubbed his arm when Drew elbowed him. "Don't get mad at me, baby. You know he does. Look at him."

"Can we come in, Jordy?" Drew's kind smile only made him feel worse, not better, considering the enmity Jordan carried inside.

He said nothing and pulled the front door wider for his friends, leaving them to trail behind him back through the house and into the spacious kitchen. Sunlight poured onto the terra-cotta floors and glinted off the glass-fronted maple cabinets. The kitchen was his pride and joy, and when he and Keith bought the brownstone, it had been the only room he cared about decorating. Jordan had always loved staring out of the large bay window at the garden and the sky as he relaxed with his cup of coffee in the morning, Keith beside him reading the paper. Now he saw nothing.

"Did you have a party?" Drew tipped his head to the table, still cluttered with vodka bottles.

"Party of one, more likely."

Despite a throbbing head and a roiling stomach, Jordan lashed out at Ash's muttered remark.

"Shut up, Davis." He and Ash never had the easiest of relationships; the man still irritated the hell out of Jordan no matter how happy he made Drew.

"Why, Jordan? The truth hurts?" Ash's voice, oddly enough, neither condemned nor derided him. Instead, it held an overall note of sadness mixed with empathy that pulled Jordan up short. "You sit here, night after night, refusing our dinner invitations, as well as Rachel and Mike's, or even Esther's. Don't think we don't know what you're doing and why."

Jordan winced. *Shit.* A kindhearted, sympathetic Ash Davis was almost worse than the sarcastic, overly confident man Jordan was used to. "I'm not in the mood for company; that's all."

"And I call bullshit on that. You're still mourning Keith, and I get that, but it doesn't mean you don't go on living. When your only company since he died has been a bottle of vodka, you're heading for disaster."

"Jordy," Drew entreated, bracing his hands on the kitchen island. "I'm worried about you. You've lost weight, skipped days at the hospital, and I was told that during surgery last week—"

"Are you checking up on me?" Shaking with anger, Jordan fisted his hands at his side. "What the fuck, man? You're not my goddamn keeper." Humiliation, shame, and a sense of despair tore through him as he turned away from his two friends to sit at the kitchen table. He ran his hands over the battered wood of the long farmhouse table, recalling how happy he and Keith had been to find it in the small Pennsylvania town they'd stumbled upon one Saturday. The memory of making love on top of it after lugging it up the stairs of the brownstone was forever etched in his mind. He gripped the edge of the table to steady himself.

For over thirty years he and Drew had been friends; the man knew him better than anyone. People might think Drew Klein a sweet and easygoing pushover of a man but Jordan knew the core of steel within him. Drew refused to back down if he thought he could help. True to form, Drew dropped into the chair right next to him, challenging and direct.

"Jordan. Look at me."

It took great effort to tear his gaze away from the tabletop but he inhaled a deep breath and smiled into Drew's face. "What is it?"

He didn't fool Drew. "Don't give me that fake-ass smile. I'm not checking up on you. It's common knowledge that you showed up to your first surgery since Keith died and had to wait an extra hour to start because you had the shakes." Drew's mouth thinned to a hard line. "Are you crazy, showing up drunk for surgery? You could lose your fucking license, for God's sake."

"I wasn't drunk. I was overtired and hadn't eaten since lunchtime the day before."

Behind him he heard Ash snort with laughter. "Are you fucking kidding me, Jordan? You can come up with a better one than that."

"Fuck off, Ash," he shot back. "I couldn't care less about your opinion."

"How about mine? Don't lie to me." Drew's stare remained unflinching, his eyes soft. "I know you're still having a hard time moving on from Keith's death but it's going to be a year soon."

"It's only been nine months. God almighty, did you expect me to forget him already?" Horrified, Jordan swept his hand across the table, sending the empty bottles and food containers crashing to the floor. "Keith and I were together for almost four years. You haven't even been with Ash a year; could you forget him so easily? Stop pressuring me to move on with my life. It's over for me. There will never be anyone else."

"So you plan on drinking yourself into an early grave, losing your job and quite possibly your friends along the way?" Drew placed a hand on his arm. "I don't think Keith would expect you to mourn him forever."

"I didn't expect to have to mourn him at all. He was supposed to be here, with me." The tears, always threatening below the surface, spilled over, coursing hot and fierce down his cheeks. It seemed he hadn't stopped crying since Keith had been murdered. "I can't get past it. No matter what I do, he's always there with me, and I can't let him go." All the fight and anger left him deflated like a balloon several days after a party. An ineffable weariness stole through him, and he laid his head on his arms on top of the table. "Go home, you two. Leave me alone."

Without a word, Ash found the broom and dustpan and began to clean up the broken glass while Drew remained seated next to Jordan at the table.

"Look, I understand what you're feeling. But destroying yourself isn't going to bring him back. We know you miss him."

"You don't understand." Jordan shook off Drew's attempt to comfort him. "I'm beginning to forget him. Not only his voice but also the way his arms held me. The way the sound of his breathing calmed me so I could fall asleep every night." His breath caught in his throat, and a shudder racked his body.

Jordan couldn't reveal the worst—that he could no longer recall the press of Keith's lips on his or the sweet sweep of Keith's tongue in his mouth. The warmth and smoothness of Keith's skin, once as familiar as Jordan's own, had begun fading to a cold and distant memory. Sometimes he'd sit in bed late at night and play his voicemail messages simply to hear Keith's voice. How fucking disloyal a love was he? It had only been nine months, yet Keith's touch, something he'd longed for every day of his life and sworn he'd never forget, had slipped away like fog in the summer wind. Gentle and swift, leaving no trace behind that it had ever existed.

"Shouldn't I remember? I lived with him and loved him with my life." He lifted his head to stare into Drew's eyes, seeing the sympathy and pain that had resided there since Keith died. Hating Drew for that. He didn't want anyone feeling sorry for him, perceiving him as weak. He preferred the way Ash treated him, with stark truth and harsh reality. At least with that he could get angry and curse. But when Drew treated Jordan with kid gloves, all sweet and sympathetic, he couldn't strike back.

"It has nothing to do with loyalty. It's merely the way the passage of time allows us to accept what's happened. After my parents died, I raged over not saving their voicemails." Drew's green eyes glimmered with tears. His parents had been gone now for well over ten years, killed in a horrific car crash, and Jordan knew Drew still mourned their senseless deaths. "To be able to listen to their voices might've brought me some comfort. I knew they were really gone when I couldn't hear their voices in my head anymore. But in a way, it finally allowed me to move on with my life."

Jordan watched as Ash placed his hands on Drew's shoulders, bending down to brush a quick kiss on his cheek. That was what he missed. The support, the small gestures letting him know someone loved him enough to care.

"What if I don't want to move on? Or can't?" Unbeknownst to Drew, he was part of Jordan's problem, though Jordan couldn't bring himself to tell Drew that salient fact. It would crush him. Jordan pushed himself up from the table and took the broom. "There's nothing you or anyone can do. I'm doing the best I can, so leave me alone. Go bother someone else."

"You're such a bad liar." Ash leaned his hip against the kitchen counter. "This"—his hand swept at the debris littering the floor—"is the best you can do? Day-old takeout food and empty liquor bottles? Where's the Dr. Jordan Peterson I knew—stylish, arrogant, and always in control?" Ash quirked a brow. "Even before you met Keith, you were a proud bastard. This is far, far from your best."

A knot twisted in Jordan's stomach. That was the point. He didn't want to go back to the way he'd been before. There'd been other relationships, but none had mattered. Only Keith had seen through him right from the start. No one knew how badly Jordan needed Keith to anchor him. Jordan knew he could be that proud bastard, as Ash called him, to the outside world, because he had Keith at home, loving him, flaws and all. With Keith gone, the soft part of Jordan, vulnerable and needy for comfort and love, was dying.

"Go away, both of you, and leave me alone." He continued to sweep up the floor, unwilling and unable to meet his friends' eyes. The *thunk* of the mail falling through the slot gave him the perfect excuse to leave them. As he made his way to the front door, the bell rang.

Christ, was he to get no peace today? The weekend was supposed to be for resting.

He answered the door to see his mailman on the stoop. "Hey, Bill. You have something for me?" Jordan and his mailman were on a friendly basis since Jordan had operated on the man's knee the previous year with excellent results.

"Yes, Dr. Peterson. I have a certified letter you need

to sign for." He held out the green card, which Jordan signed and returned. "Thanks, Doc."

"See you in a few months for your checkup." Jordan smiled at the mailman and watched him walk away, noting with a professional eye the even gait and freedom of movement of Bill's knee as he descended the steps of the brownstone. Jordan turned away and closed the door behind him. As he scanned the letter, he saw with a sinking heart it was from Lambert and North, the financial consulting firm Keith had used to set up his accounts.

Most people hadn't known the extent of Keith's wealth. The man truly had a Midas touch when it came to having his money make money, and he'd been intimately involved in the investment of that money. When Keith died, he left Jordan as his main beneficiary. He'd also created a trust for charities dedicated to LGBT inner-city children.

Upon the reading of the will a month or so after Keith's death, Jordan learned Keith had created a foundation to prevent gun violence among the city's youth population. He'd coordinated it with the police department so that the teens would be taken to Riker's Island to see what happened to men and women who chose to get involved with crime and illegal guns—a sort of *Beyond Scared Straight* program. But there was much more to it. There were after-school sports programs to be set up, music lessons for kids, computers—anything to keep them off the streets. It was mainly centered around Keith's precinct and the schools in the area. Keith had arranged for several corporate sponsors to keep the money coming, but the hope was that more private funding would flow into it once they publicized the charity.

Jordan had been named president of the foundation and administrator of the trust but had been putting off meeting the financial adviser since the reading of the will. He didn't have the heart or strength to get entangled in the endeavor, even if Keith had wanted him to. He was so tired of it all and wanted only for people to leave him alone.

"Who was that?" Drew asked. He and Ash both looked up from the floor, where they had recommenced cleaning. All the glass had been swept up and put in the recycle bin, Jordan noticed, and Drew had wiped the tile floor with some wet paper towels. He really did have some good friends, even if they came with pain-in-the-ass boyfriends.

"It was the mailman. Nothing important." Jordan knew better than to tell these two how he'd been blowing off meeting the foundation's financial adviser. Drew's own cause, the medical clinic he'd set up for abused teens, was his whole life, and his and Ash's dedication to it was extraordinary. They wouldn't take kindly to him dodging his responsibility. For a brief moment, shame coursed through him, and he decided he'd call Monday morning to set up an appointment.

"Don't think you have to babysit me. I'm going to take a shower and run some errands." He needed to refill his liquor cabinet and some prescriptions but they didn't have to know that.

Ash shot him a hard look, disbelief apparent in his eyes while Drew merely shook his head. "Is that what you think we're doing? You're my best friend, yet I barely see you anymore." Drew's inscrutable expression unnerved Jordan. Seeing Drew so guarded and hurt, shame once again pricked Jordan's conscience. Keith had been his lover, but Drew and their other friend Mike were his brothers in every sense of the word. He'd never hidden anything from them. Until now.

The past few months had made him an expert in masking his feelings. So with a smile he hoped didn't look too fake or forced, he slapped Drew on the back, trying to lighten the mood. "You're right. And I promise to make an effort to get out more and get a handle on my life." With a small prayer of thanks, he watched as his two friends prepared to leave.

"Don't be a stranger. My grandmother misses you." Drew hugged him, whispering into his ear, "I miss you." Guilt cramped his stomach.

"Seriously, Jordan. Come by for dinner this week. Maybe you can distract that cat from attacking my ankles every time I walk by." Ash grimaced, but his eyes crinkled with amusement.

Even Jordan laughed at Ash's running battle with Drew's cat, Domino. Seemed the cat resented Ash's place in Drew's life and took his displeasure out on him every chance he got.

"I can't help it if the cat has good taste, Davis." Jordan smirked and ducked Ash's friendly punch before he followed Drew out the front door.

Jordan couldn't help but notice how, when they were halfway down the block, Ash stopped, grasped Drew around the neck, and kissed him hard. They continued to walk, Ash's arm snug around Drew's shoulders to tug him close. A pain sharp and deep knifed through Jordan, and he caught his breath. There was no one left to hold him. Not anymore.

Grief-stricken and unwilling to face more loving gestures between his friends, Jordan turned his back and reentered his house. He picked up the certified letter and opened it, scanning the brief paragraph.

Dear Dr. Peterson:

I have tried, unsuccessfully these past few months, to contact you regarding the foundation the late Keith Hart created. As you have failed to respond, I will take this as your decision not to participate in this worthwhile endeavor. Please consider this as formal notice that I will be asking the other members of the board to remove you from this position, and we will begin the process of acquiring a new president of the board.

Very truly yours,
Lucas Conover, Platinum Account Services
Lambert & North, LLC

Jordan's eyes narrowed as the burn of anger rose in his face. *Fucking snotty bastard.* Who the hell was this Conover to talk to him like that? Jordan stormed into the bathroom and opened the medicine cabinet. The bottle of pills sat there, mocking him. Jordan grabbed it, wrenched the top open, and swallowed the last two. If one was good, two were better. Antidepressant? Shit, make it more like anti-feel anything at all. The way Jordan liked it. He slammed the door and faced himself in the mirror, wincing at his too-pale skin and bloodshot, sunken eyes. Once the pills kicked in and he took a shower, he'd be good as new. The languid sense of well-being from the drugs began to seep into his body. He couldn't wait until Monday morning when he'd come face-to-face with that little prick, Lucas Conover.

Chapter Two

*M*ONDAY MORNINGS SUCK. At the alarm's incessant blaring, Lucas Conover rolled out of bed with a grunt and shuffled into the bathroom. He relieved himself, brushed his teeth, and started the shower, all without pausing to glance in the mirror.

The heated spill of water pouring over his face and body revived him somewhat. To save time, he shaved in the shower and, as an afterthought, stroked himself to a quick release that rushed through him, leaving him less tense but feeling no better off than before. Sad that sex had become merely a shower-time ritual for a thirty-year-old man, but considering his hand had been the only thing giving him any pleasure in his life for years, he wasn't surprised. Better safe than sorry. And being safe was the only thing Luke wanted from life.

That's what happened when you grew up eating fear for breakfast, hoping the man who pretended to be your father was still so drunk from the night before, he'd sleep like the dead so you could grab your little brother and run to school before the drunken bastard woke up. And then there were days Luke and Brandon didn't bother to wait for their cereal, choosing to get to school early rather than hanging around their house, hearing their "father" bellow in anger. Unwilling to start his day with unpleasant and unwanted memories, Luke squeezed the water from his hair and stepped out of the shower.

After drying off, he ran a comb through his wet curls then returned to the bedroom to dress. Barely looking in his closet, he pulled out a pale blue shirt along with a navy-blue suit. He picked out a tie but didn't put it on. Bad enough he had to wear the damn thing all day long, he could at least enjoy his coffee without choking. Slinging the tie around his neck, he left the bedroom and headed to the kitchen.

It had been a typical New York City galley kitchen when he purchased the apartment, but hating that feeling of being cramped, he'd knocked down the wall separating it from the living room to open it up, creating a bright expanse of space. Doing that allowed the light from the living room to reach all the way into the apartment. The wide counter doubled as his table, and his white cabinets and black granite countertops gleamed where the sunlight struck them. But right now, only the shining stainless coffeepot drew his attention. He took his giant-sized mug out of the dish rack and poured himself a large, bracing cup.

Occasionally he wondered what it might be like to share his life with someone, to not wake up alone every single day, but that farfetched idea never lasted long.

He sipped his coffee, thankful for all he did have now, never forgetting what he'd been through to get to this point. It had been something he'd learned to live with after the long, hard years alone. Since Ash—the foster brother he'd worshiped—ran out on him and their younger brother. Since his last night at home with his foster father, Munson. Since he woke up in a hospital and discovered he'd been abandoned by his family. A decade, in fact, of him with only his wits, learning to survive.

His hand tightened around his coffee cup. Not again and not today. Mondays were bad enough without thoughts of those two ruining his day before it even started. It had taken him years to come to terms with Munson's actions. Ash's betrayal clung to him like a second skin, impossible to remove without further damage.

He threw the cold dregs from his cup into the sink and filled his stainless-steel travel mug with more coffee. After placing the mug on the table in the hallway, Luke faced the gilt-edged mirror and knotted his tie. A brief grin flickered on his lips as he smoothed his hands over the small Winnie-the-Pooh faces on the dark blue silk.

His ties were always the talk of the secretaries. Serious in everything he did and not known for having a sense of humor among his colleagues, Luke allowed himself a brief outlet for amusement in his ties. They always had cartoon characters on them—Bugs Bunny, Flintstones, or Pokémon figures.

He slipped on his suit jacket, shrugged on his wool-lined raincoat, and left his apartment. No one knew that those ties were a sort of homage to his young brother, Brandon, whom he so desperately missed. The Saturday mornings they'd all spent snuggled up on the couch watching cartoons were among the happiest times of his childhood. Brandon would always sit on Ash's lap, doling out fistfuls of some disgusting sugary cereal until Munson woke up and stumbled into the living room where they'd congregated. Then Ash would find some excuse to leave, sliding Brandon next to Luke.

Even then, the bastard had run away from them.

In the elevator, he checked his phone and saw a calendar entry for a new meeting his secretary had scheduled for him at eleven o'clock with the elusive Dr. Jordan Peterson. Well, well. Finally, he'd flushed the rat out of his hole. Luke couldn't prevent a small smile from breaking out across his face. After all these months, it figured threatening him would be the only way to ensure the man would make an appearance.

Keith was a good man, and his senseless death had devastated Luke. He'd dealt with Keith's money for years, even before Dr. Peterson came into the picture, and Luke and the detective had become somewhat close—as close as Luke allowed anyone to get. When Keith informed him he was going to marry Peterson, Luke tried to warn him about giving the man control over such a sizable estate.

In his natural, good-natured way, Keith had

laughed. *"Luke, my man, I trust Jordan with my life. He already controls my heart. My money doesn't really mean much to me if he isn't there with me to share the ride."*

Luke's chest tightened at the memory of the big blond detective laughing without a care in the world. Not two months after that, he lay cold in his grave. Life was so fucking unfair. A piece of shit like Munson remained alive, while someone as good and decent as Keith…damn. Luke rubbed his suddenly damp eyes and then flagged down a cab on the corner of 19th St. and Eighth Avenue.

"Fifty-Sixth and Lex." The cabbie nodded and took off, jolting Luke back into the seat. A year or so ago, Keith had shown him a picture of his partner. Luke remembered Peterson as an incredibly attractive man, tall and lean, with sculpted features and a somewhat arrogant smirk. Waves of golden-blond hair fell over his brow but failed to hide the intensity of his pale blue eyes. When he'd teased Keith about his boyfriend's elegant looks, Keith had chuckled.

"He has a big enough ego, Luke. Don't ever tell him that if you meet him, please. But in spite of what people may think of him, he's the best friend I've ever had."

Luke had laughed along but couldn't relate to the obvious love in Keith's voice for Peterson. He'd steered clear of most friendships and all relationships. Occasionally he'd go out after work with a few people to grab a beer, but he never accepted their invitations to go to clubs or play golf on the weekends. On the rare occasion when the nights got too lonely for him to bear, he'd venture to a bar for anonymous sex. A hot mouth on his cock was all it took to obliterate the darkness in his mind, but it wouldn't last longer than the night. Casual was the best he could do. Most weekends found him at home, holed up in his apartment, or volunteering at one of the homeless shelters on the Lower East Side. It killed him to see the families with young children, their eyes full of hopelessness and despair. No matter how many left the shelters, it always seemed the space was filled again immediately with another family looking for help.

Nothing had changed from when he'd lived there, alone and afraid. Only the kindness and determination of Wanda, who ran the shelter, to see him get off the streets and back into school saved his life.

Shit. Reminiscing was one big fucking mistake. With a subtle brush of his fingers, he wiped away any trace of wetness in his eyes. Uttering a silent prayer of thanks for the quick ride uptown, he ran his card through the machine and took his receipt. Luke jumped out of the cab, and with brisk strides he shook off the past and entered the glass-and-steel skyscraper, exchanging pleasantries with the guard. He still got a secret thrill knowing he belonged here.

A top financial firm, Lambert and North was newer than the old warhorses that had their names carved into the history of Wall Street, but Luke never regretted his decision to work there. It had a younger, more modern vibe, and he knew that his being gay would've been looked down upon at the older, more established firms, no matter that it was the twenty-first century. Here, it was no big deal.

He nodded at several colleagues in the elevator, listening to them talk about their weekends. When the door opened on his floor, he spotted his secretary already working at her desk. He loved Valerie. She was efficient and organized, and never tried to become overly personal like some of the other secretaries did. From the first day, he'd made it clear his work and personal life were separate, and she controlled his professional life perfectly.

"Good morning, Luke." She smiled and handed him his messages and mail.

"Morning." He glanced at the papers for a second, then stopped and turned around. "I see Dr. Peterson scheduled a meeting today at eleven. When he comes in, make him wait a bit." Sure, it was childish, but the man pissed him off. Peterson's procrastination did a disservice to all Keith had tried to accomplish. He deserved a little setdown.

To her credit, Valerie didn't miss a beat. She merely blinked her big brown eyes and nodded. "Yes, sir."

He entered his office and immediately got to work. After the usual Monday morning directors' meeting with his boss, he began to wade through the various e-mails, phone calls, and questions that required his attention. He picked up his head only once, and that was to acknowledge the delivery of his bagel and cream cheese.

"Hey, Orlando, how's it going? You and your family get settled yet in the apartment?" Orlando Hernandez, his mother, and his twin sisters had been in a shelter when Luke first met them. He'd not only assisted the family with navigating the confusing world of food stamps, Medicaid, and Section 8 low-income housing but had gotten Orlando a part-time job in the deli down the block from Luke's office building while he studied for the GED.

It was all about paying it forward.

Thinking back, he recalled all that Wanda had done for him when he'd first stumbled into the shelter that cold night. She'd cleaned him up, given him warm clothes and a hot meal. But more than that, she'd given him hope. Hope he could survive through the trauma of his flight from Georgia. Hope he could ascend to heights he'd never thought possible during the blackest time of his humiliation.

It began with his education and determination, but the common thread running through it all was her love for him. He'd vowed to make her proud and never let her down.

The young man's teeth flashed brightly. "Yes, Mr. Conover. Mama is thrilled to have a place to cook again and wanted me to tell you she expects you over to dinner one night soon."

Luke took the bag with his bagel and third cup of coffee of the morning and placed it on his desk. "I'm sure she loves cooking up a storm."

Valerie buzzed from outside. "You have a phone call. Mr. Davis again."

His heart accelerated. *Shit.* When was that bastard going to get the hint that Luke didn't want to talk to him? "Same as before, Valerie. Tell him I'm busy and let security downstairs know not to allow him access to the building to see me, please."

"Yes, sir."

He gave a rueful smile to Orlando, who stood waiting before him. "Someone from the past I have no desire to see now. You know how it is."

Orlando's lips quirked in a smile. "Of course."

Luke paid him, adding a hefty tip, and watched him leave, pleased he'd accomplished at least one good thing in his life so far. The phone calls and e-mails never stopped as he devoured his bagel and drank his coffee. It seemed everything this morning demanded his immediate attention.

At precisely eleven o'clock, Valerie buzzed him. "Dr. Peterson is here. Do you want him to wait here or in the conference room?"

"Here. Let him sit for ten minutes, then bring him in."

"Yes, sir."

Luke left his seat to stare out of the window. Much as he hated to admit it, the call from Ash still upset him. He didn't want memories banging their way back into his head like an incessant woodpecker. The past was called the past because it was over and done with. There was no forgiveness in his heart for Ash Davis. His brother. *What a joke.*

As far as he was concerned, he was as alone as ever.

A rap at the door brought him back to awareness. "Yes?"

Valerie opened it part of the way, effectively blocking anyone outside from seeing in. She was worth her weight in gold.

"Are you ready for Dr. Peterson, sir?"

He smiled and stood at his desk, hands clasped together. For some inexplicable reason, a shower of nerves prickled his skin. "Yes, send him in, please."

Luke remained standing as Valerie opened the door, and he got his first look at Jordan Peterson.

"Mr. Conover? I'm Dr. Peterson."

The man greeted him head down, as if its weight was too heavy for him to bear. All Luke could think of was how different he looked from the picture Keith had shown him last year. Where Peterson had been laughing into the camera, holding up a wineglass, his face alive with joy, the hollow-eyed person who stood before him bore little resemblance to the photograph, though vestiges of beauty remained in this shattered, emotional wreckage of a man. The blond hair no longer lay as neatly trimmed and styled as it had been and the pallor of his skin left little doubt he hadn't seen the sun in months. His expensive, well-tailored suit hung loose on his skin-and-bones frame.

Against his better judgment, he took pity on the man and mustered up what he hoped was a sympathetic smile. As difficult as it was for Luke to show emotion, Keith's death nonetheless had hit him hard. He couldn't fathom Peterson's anguish.

"I'm sorry for your loss. Keith was a wonderful man."

He raised his gaze from his study of the floor to meet Luke's. Empty, sad, and bloodshot, the devastation in his eyes hit Luke like a slap to the face. What would it be like to love someone so intensely? From the way Peterson looked, Luke was better off not knowing.

"Yes, he was, and I don't know why you thought it necessary to threaten me. Who the fuck are you to write me a letter like that?" The handsome face twisted in a sneer.

So much for sympathy. "I've tried to contact you for months, and you've ignored me. Anyone would think the same thing I did. You weren't interested in the position."

"Bullshit." Peterson's pale skin flushed red with his obvious outrage. "I was mourning my fiancé's death, goddamn you. Can you understand? Haven't you ever lost someone who meant everything to you so that nothing else mattered?"

Heat rose in Luke's face as his heart slammed hard against his chest. Fuck, yes, he had. Not a lover, never a lover. But God, Brandon. *Where the hell did you run to?* His eyes widened with surprise as Peterson advanced on him. The distraught man stood so close, the heat of his breath touched Luke's cheeks.

And then he smelled it. The scent was faint, but he'd know it anywhere. "You've been drinking, haven't you?"

A slight hitch in the other man's breath gave it

away. "You don't know what the hell you're talking about."

Luke sneered right back at Peterson. "I grew up with a drunk. I know what I smell. It's only eleven in the morning, and you've already been drinking enough that I can tell." Then it hit him. "Are you operating today? Christ, you'd better not be going to the hospital like this."

At least Peterson had the grace to look ashamed. "I only had rounds today, early this morning. No surgery or office hours."

Luke released a relieved breath. "Thank God for that at least." His eyes narrowed. "Maybe you really shouldn't be involved with the project. I'm sure Keith wouldn't want—"

"Don't you dare think to lecture me on what he would've wanted. You're a fucking nobody in our lives. I lived with him. We were going to be married. You barely knew him." Peterson's voice rose with each word spoken until he was yelling in Luke's face. His door opened, and Valerie, as well as Dave, an analyst whose office was next door, stood there. Luke waved them back, never taking his eyes from the man in front of him.

"Look, Peterson. Why don't you go home and sleep it off?"

"Go home?" Peterson's laugh rang bitter and hollow. "It's not a home anymore. The walls are closing in around me. Everywhere I am, I see him there or hear his voice." Peterson gripped his arm, and it surprised

Luke to feel the power in his grasp. "I think I might be going crazy."

Unaccustomed to people touching him, Luke forced himself to ignore the searing pressure of Peterson's hand through his suit jacket and listened to the man, as close to a total breakdown as he'd ever seen anyone before.

"I have to do this. To prove to him that I was worthy of his love. Don't take away the last thing he ever asked from me." Peterson's long fingers curled around Luke's bicep, digging in through Luke's shirtsleeves. "I can't bear the thought that I'm disappointing him."

Shit. He didn't expect to feel sympathetic toward Peterson. Here he was all prepared to hate the man, and yet something deep within him, frozen solid for years, shifted and cracked, exposing a soft core not visible since he left home. Luke needed to put some distance between himself and this troubled man whose mere presence sent such confusing signals to both his mind and body.

He wrenched away from the hand on his arm, waiting until his own breathing slowed, and his heart settled back to its normal rhythm. "Then don't behave like an asshole. If you're going to take on this responsibility, get your shit together. We'll be working closely, and I won't stand for working with someone who's loaded all the time." He folded his arms, again in control.

Peterson had dropped into a chair in front of his desk, pale and defeated looking. "I never had more than one or two drinks before—before it happened. I can do it."

Luke could see the effort it took for him to admit his failing. "You'll have to."

"I said I would." Anger flashed across Peterson's face, a hint of the initial arrogance creeping back into his voice. "I don't need you to be on my back." Those pale blue eyes flicked over him, cool and dismissive. The son of a bitch dared to pass judgment on him?

"I know what you say." Luke sat and leaned back in his chair. "Make sure you do it." The look of outrage on Peterson's face was priceless. "Now let me explain what we are dealing with here."

He handed over the thick bound book of the business plan and began to outline the details of everything they'd done so far to set up the after-school programs and the trips to the prisons. After approximately an hour passed, he tossed his pen aside. "I think we can stop there. You have a basic understanding of what we've accomplished and still need to do."

Peterson nodded. "I do. How involved are we planning to get with the teenagers and young kids in the shelters? They need protection from people preying on them." His lips tightened. "I want as many guns off the street as we can get."

"As do we all, Peterson."

"I think by now you can call me Jordan." The tight lips softened to a tired smile. "You're Lucas, correct?"

Shit. A shiver trickled down his spine at the sound of his name on Jordan's lips. Maybe he was coming down with something.

"Yeah." He cleared his throat. "Well, um, I've got another appointment, so…" His voice trailed off, the lame excuse floating in the air as he failed to meet Jordan's eyes.

"No problem." Jordan stood and shook his hand. "We'll talk soon." He turned and walked out the door. The faint scent of his cologne lingered after he left.

For the rest of the day, whether in meetings, on phone conferences with major clients, or on the cab ride home, Luke's thoughts strayed to Dr. Jordan Peterson. The elegant, cultured voice, piercing blue eyes, and firm mouth didn't surprise him; he knew Jordan was an extremely attractive man from the pictures Keith had shown him. The physical reaction he had toward the man troubled Luke and he vowed to keep his mind on the job they had to do. It shouldn't prove to be too difficult for him. Luke had made a point of never allowing anyone to get too close. Jordan would be no different.

Chapter Three

J ORDAN SLAMMED INTO the town house and threw
his keys at the hall table but missed, sending them
skittering along the wooden floor. He didn't break
stride, continuing until he reached the kitchen. The last
few hours had been torturous. Gearing himself up to
get dressed and presentable for rounds had required a
pill. Making it through rounds at the hospital then the
meeting with Keith's financial adviser had been
arduous. So what if he had a couple of drinks beforehand to settle his nerves and dull the pain? The Xanax
he'd taken in the morning hadn't done the trick; his
body hummed, tight as a high wire. He needed another
pill or drink; it didn't matter which. Nothing truly
helped anyway.

"Fuck him," he muttered to himself. He sloshed
some vodka into a glass and took out a bottle of tonic
water and a lime to mix it with. "There's nothing
wrong with a drink in the afternoon with lunch." Or
two for that matter. Hell, he imagined those hedge
fund guys did it all the time.

For Conover to lecture him was laughable. Those Wall Street moneymen were parasites, contributing nothing to the world. He was a doctor, for Christ's sake. He helped people. So what if he took the edge off sometimes, with a drink or one of his happy pills? The stress was tremendous, and he deserved a little relaxation.

The cool glide of the iced vodka down his throat settled him. It wasn't like he needed the drink or anything. Another swallow and it was gone. He'd better get something in his stomach before he really did get drunk. He hit a preprogrammed button on the phone and placed an order for a roast beef sandwich and fries to be delivered from the diner down the block. Checking his watch, he saw there were still several hours before he had to leave for Drew's clinic.

Drew had set up a treatment center for abused young adults, and he, as well as Ash and their other friend Mike, volunteered there as much as they could. Drew's sister, who also happened to be Mike's girlfriend and had her PhD in adolescent psychology, ran the suicide prevention line. Ash, along with two other lawyers, helped with the legal problems, and Mike, the resident dentist, took care of the dental problems. They'd received enough publicity by now to enjoy a steady stream of funding and had hired other doctors, lawyers, and dentists to assist them, but neither he, Drew, nor Mike ever considered giving up their work there. Jordan believed Keith had envisioned the foundation he wanted to set up to have the same type of success.

The doorbell rang, and he retrieved his food from the delivery guy. For the first time in a while, his stomach grumbled with hunger, and he attacked his fries. Beer-battered and crunchy, they were exactly the way he liked them. Once he'd eaten a few bites of the sandwich, he took a bottle of water from the refrigerator and gulped it down.

Except for a few sporadic visits, he hadn't been to the clinic to see patients since Keith's death. His chest tightened at the thought of spending time there this afternoon, but he knew he couldn't bail on Drew again or the kids who came for treatment. They needed him and his skill, and no matter his anger, he would be there to help them. As he bit into the second half of his sandwich, the resentment bubbling under the surface broke free, cracking through the shield he'd built up over the past nine months. How could he explain his anger toward his best friend? Who would understand it?

Irritated at himself, he tossed the sandwich aside. One day, when he had his emotions sorted out and more under control, he would talk to Drew. For now, he'd put on his game face and do what he had to do. A noise from the backyard drew his attention and he got up from the table to investigate.

A dog had somehow found its way into the yard. Instead of growling or barking like he'd expect, the animal's tongue hung out of its mouth, and the stubby tail wagged furiously. The sun gleamed against its

short, shiny fur. The dog looked to be a Rottwei-
ler/shepherd mix, and would normally possess a strong,
muscular frame. Instead, the sun gleaming against its
coat highlighted the outline of its ribs.

Jordan had always wanted a dog, but with Keith's
allergies, he'd put that wish aside. The dog appeared
mild mannered and not growly; Jordan approached the
animal with care. It sat on its haunches, head cocked,
an inquiring look on its face, and seemed to be
assessing him as well. Jordan knelt down, and with
warning bells going off in his head, he held out his
hand.

"Hi there." Stupid, he knew, because if the dog
went after his hand, his career as an orthopedic surgeon
would be over. The dog stood and inched closer until it
offered a warm, wet swipe to Jordan's fingers. Jordan
petted the dog, who immediately rolled over on her
back for a belly rub.

"Good girl…nice girl." He gave her a few pats and
could feel how thin she was. With no collar, it was
obvious she was a stray, and probably a hungry one at
that. "Come with me." He stood, and she followed at
his heels as he returned to the kitchen table and his
leftover sandwich. A low whine came from her throat.
"It's okay, girl. Take it." He placed it down for her, and
in two bites it was gone.

Keith had always told him he was too impulsive
and made snap decisions, but he wanted this dog with
every fiber of his being. Something to love, that might
love him back. Having finished the food, she sidled up

to him and rested her muzzle on his knee, a contented sigh huffing out of her. The feel of her warm, sleek fur against his hand as he petted her soothed his earlier anger. "You want to stay with me, sweetheart?" Her answer was a lick of his hand.

Jordan checked his watch and saw he only had about an hour until he had to be at the center. Not enough time to take her to the vet and the pet store for supplies. He had to leave her in the yard, not knowing how she'd react to being locked inside a strange house without him.

Now that he'd made up his mind to keep her, he got out a bowl and filled it with cold, fresh water. As soon as he placed it on the ground, near the glass door that led inside to the kitchen, she lapped at it with gusto, the water slopping over the sides of the bowl. After she finished, the dog lay down in a patch of sunlight and closed her eyes.

"I have to go to work, girl, but I'll be back in a few hours. Stay here, okay?" Jordan rubbed behind her ears, and that stubby tail wagged. She stretched out, the picture of contentment. He went inside, showered, and got dressed. When he was ready to leave, he glanced outside to see if she was still there. His heart sank when he saw the sunlit space where the dog had lain was now empty. *Shit.* Nothing in his life went right. Even a stray dog didn't want to stay with him. His hands shook as wrenching loneliness slammed into him.

He strode back into the bathroom and shook out two pills. Without bothering to use a glass, Jordan swallowed them with a handful of water from the faucet. Unable to look at himself in the mirror, he squeezed his eyes shut while he gripped the edge of the sink. It took several minutes until the familiar lassitude of the pills seeped into his bloodstream and he could relax.

The image staring back at him in the mirror after he opened his eyes presented a man in control, happy, and without a care in the world—the man he used to be. Only the darkness in his eyes and the tightness around his mouth indicated the pain he held inside. Whatever it was, he'd make sure to hide it better when he got to the center; otherwise he knew Drew would be all over him, and Mike as well.

He wished people would leave him the fuck alone.

Once he'd hailed a cab to take him to the clinic in Red Hook, Brooklyn, his thoughts strayed to the meeting he'd had with Keith's financial adviser, Lucas Conover. Keith had always been a good judge of character, so he must've seen something in the man to trust him to handle the foundation. To be honest, the man pissed him off with his know-it-all attitude and sanctimonious talk. But the vacant expression in Lucas Conover's eyes struck Jordan as being at odds with his hard-ass behavior. Before he started working so closely with a stranger, he wanted to find out a little bit more about him.

In a flash of inspiration, he pulled out his phone and called Keith's old partner, Jerry Allen. They'd kept in touch after Keith's death, and Jordan trusted the detective to be discreet and honest.

"Allen here." The deep voice sounded brisk and efficient.

"Hey, Jerry. It's Jordan. How're you doing?"

"Jordan." Jerry's voice softened, and Jordan could hear him tell someone to hold on, he needed to take the call. "How are you? I've been meaning to stop by, but we're working this illegal gun-ring detail and time gets away from you."

Jordan appreciated Jerry's directness. "I understand. I haven't exactly reached out to you either. But listen, I'm calling for a favor." He outlined what he wanted from the police detective.

"This shouldn't be too hard to find out quickly. Who is this guy again?"

"It's Keith's financial adviser, the one I'll be working with to set up his foundation to keep guns off the streets and away from the kids." The cab entered onto the ramp for the Brooklyn Bridge. Jordan squinted in the sunlight as he took in the expanse of the East River and the skyline of downtown Brooklyn. The pills he'd taken earlier dulled the nerves that would normally kick in at the thought of entering the center and having to face his friends. He made a note to himself to refill the prescription with his therapist when he got to the center.

"So why are you checking up on him, if Keith used him?" An honest question and one Jordan had no real answer to.

"Well, you know Keith was way more trusting than

me. And he may have known the guy but I only met him today for the first time. I'm not asking you to do anything wrong, am I? Tell me something about him; that's all." Jordan frowned into the phone as a vision of Lucas Conover's face came to mind. His chestnut-brown curly hair and deep-set hazel eyes were so different from Keith's golden-blond looks. Not unattractive, but not Keith. He swallowed hard around the lump in his throat. What the fuck did he care if the guy was good-looking or not?

"No problem, I'll get the info for you, and maybe you'll come over for dinner one night soon? I know Marie misses you." Jerry's calm, unruffled manner brought Jordan's thoughts back to the phone call and away from Conover.

"I'd love to. Your wife, aside from being gorgeous, makes the best eggplant parmigiana." He chuckled. "If I weren't gay, I'd steal her from you."

"If you weren't gay, she'd go in a second."

They both laughed and agreed to a date and time for dinner the following week before ending the conversation. Jordan's good humor remained, thanks to the conversation and his happy pills, until he entered the clinic. Nodding hello to Marly, the girl who manned the front desk, he smiled faintly as she hugged him and whispered, "I'm glad you're back."

Jordan suffered the hellos and welcome backs of the rest of the staff. Their excitement at his return touched him, but his reality was altogether different. Every-where he went, Keith's memory waited, lurking around each corner. In his office, he visualized Keith lounging back in his chair, eyes glinting with desire, those powerful legs spread wide, a seductive smile curling his lips. Love, regret, and loss slammed into him with a force so strong he swayed, then grabbed on to the doorframe.

"This was a fucking bad idea," he murmured to himself. "How am I going to get through this?"

"We'll help you, man."

He turned around to see Mike and Drew standing behind him, their solemn faces pale and strained. Unable to speak, he held out his arm, and Mike grabbed him, tugging him into a bear-like hug. Drew took his other arm, and as they'd done since they were kids on that playground long ago, they held each other, healing their hurts.

"It'll be all right. Every day might seem impossible, but look how far you've come." Drew wiped the wetness from his cheeks. "Take it as slow as you need, but I think coming back on a schedule and keeping busy will help more than you know."

Jordan desperately wanted to believe Drew's words as truth. He needed to believe it because his grief was slowly strangling the life out of him. Realistically, he understood. Life went on. Keith wouldn't want him to mourn forever, and he was young enough that he might meet another person to share his life with.

That was reality.

Emotionally, however, the thought of touching someone else and having another man's lips on his made him want to curl up into the fetal position. The sudden brutality of Keith's murder and the fact that he never had the chance to say good-bye crippled Jordan. But he couldn't go on like this any longer. Only the knowledge that it would kill his parents stopped Jordan from swallowing a whole bottle of his pills before he went to bed at night. To think he was the one who used to make fun of overly emotional people, calling them weak and failures. Keith had always called him out on his cavalier snobbery and coldness, telling him people fought battles he couldn't understand because he'd been lucky to live a life untouched by hardship or pain.

I didn't know what you meant until now. I've been a selfish fuck. If Drew and Rachel could make it, I can too.

"I'm going to try. I went to the financial adviser today, and we discussed the foundation Keith set up." He pulled away from his friends and straightened his tie. "Have either of you ever met him?" Once again the recollection of Lucas Conover's sad eyes gave him pause for thought. What battles had he fought to hide his pain? Jordan made a mental note to pay more attention the next time they met.

Mike shook his head. "Not me. What about you, Drew?"

"Nope. Don't see why we would've, either." Drew stretched, groaning as he reached upward. "God, I think I need a massage. I had early morning rounds at the hospital, then came here and had a bunch of girls walk in with lacerations on their faces and chests." He grimaced. "A goddamn fistfight because one poor girl talked back to someone who called her fat. I've been stitching all morning."

Jordan pushed the disturbing thoughts of Luke Conover out of his head and turned his attention to the files on his desk. The center had two young orthopedists who'd been hired in the past six months, and Jordan was impressed with their work as he viewed the X-rays. "These two are good. The breaks they've set are healing nicely."

Drew cracked a smile. "High praise coming from you, who never thinks anyone's work is good enough."

Jordan twirled a pencil around and around his fingers to keep his friends from noticing how they shook. "Things change, right?" His smile stretched thinly across his lips. He wanted a drink. He needed two. Anything to settle his nerves. Christ, he could feel his heart slamming so hard it was ready to explode through the bones in his chest. Before he forgot, he needed to refill his Xanax prescription.

"I have to call Dr. Meyers, and then I'll look at whoever is here."

Drew shot him an unreadable look. "Are you still seeing him?"

"Yeah. Once or twice a month now." Better than the three times a week right after Keith had died.

"Are you"—Drew took a step forward, then seemed to think better of it and stopped in front of the desk—"are you dealing with it better now at all?"

Jordan watched Drew gnaw at his lower lip, and his

hostility escaped for a moment. "Sure I am. I'm learning to deal with how senseless his death was, why I have to move past my anger."

"Who are you angry at?" Drew's pale green eyes stared unflinchingly back at him.

Another reason he'd been unable to move forward with his life was his unresolved resentment toward Drew over Keith's death. Up until now, Jordan hadn't thought Drew understood his fury and pain. But the way Drew looked at Jordan right now? The time for that talk was fast approaching. He couldn't do it. No matter that he wanted to verbally flay Drew until he broke, Jordan didn't have it in him to hurt Drew like that. One day, there'd be time enough for the two of them to sit down and have that talk, but until they did, Jordan knew he'd never be able to resolve the divide in their friendship. It was his problem.

"Myself." True as well, and a much safer answer. Besides, he really needed to call Dr. Meyers and get another bottle of pills. He picked up the phone and, with a raised brow, waited until Drew took the hint.

Red patches streaked Drew's pale face. "Talk to you later." He turned on his heel and left with Mike.

Jordan got through to the doctor right away. "Hey, Wes, I need a refill for the Xanax."

A heavy sigh filled his ear. "No can do, my friend. The time has come for you to wean off the pills and stand on your own. I told you last month it was time, and I meant it."

The pencil he'd been holding snapped in his hands.

Jordan welcomed the pain of its jagged edges digging into his fingers. "Come on, Wes," he pleaded. "I've gone back to work and I need—"

"No, you don't need them, Jordan. That's what I'm telling you. You're using the pills as a crutch to keep from dealing with your emotions and anger over Keith's death." Wes's voice gentled. "Talk to Drew. Tell him how you feel, and I promise you the anxiety will diminish."

He huffed out a dry laugh. "Sure. No problem. Talk to you soon." Ending the call, he tossed the broken pieces of the pencil across his desk in disgust. *Shit.* What was he going to do now? He only had enough left until the end of the week. An idea formed in his mind, one that never would've occurred to him a year earlier.

With precise, even steps, giving no indication of the tumult inside him, Jordan approached the supply room. It was also where they kept their locked inventory of prescription drugs. Impatient at his failure to find what he needed, his gaze traveled over the glass shelves until finally, on the bottom shelf, he saw them. Several bottles of medication Mike, and even he, prescribed to some of their patients when they needed to ease the pain from their broken bones or dental work.

He curled his hand around one of the bottles when a noise from behind startled him. When he turned around, he came face-to-face with Drew's sister, Rachel.

"Jordan? What're you doing?"

With an ease he didn't know he possessed, Jordan placed the bottle back on the shelf. His stiff, cold fingers shook only slightly. "Hey, sweetheart, I didn't know you were here. It's great to see you." He smiled and gave her a hug and a kiss.

"Yeah. I came to pick up Mike." Her suspicious, knowing eyes glanced at the drug cabinet, then back at his hands. "What are you doing in here?"

"I was checking inventory."

"We have people to do that. And you've never cared before. Is there a problem?" She squeezed his arm.

Her sympathetic tone grated on his nerves, but he tried not to let it show. "No, of course not. I have to get back; I have patients waiting."

Rachel opened her mouth as if she wanted to say something, then snapped it shut. She pushed back the dark, wispy strands of hair that had escaped from her sleek ponytail, and grabbed his hand in hers. "Promise me if you need to talk, you'll call me." Her wide green eyes searched his. "Please, Jordan."

"Sure." The lie tripped off his tongue so easily he almost believed it himself. But he knew he wouldn't. "I gotta go." He pecked a light kiss to her cheek and, with a casualness that surprised even him, walked out of the supply room and into the waiting area.

Two people sat in the chairs, a teenage girl with her mother. "I'm Dr. Peterson. How can I help you?"

The girl bit her lip. "After the fight, they pushed me down and my wrist hurts so much I think maybe it's broken."

"Let's see," he said. She followed him into the examining room, where he sat her down and chatted with her for a few minutes as he assessed her wrist. While her daughter was being x-rayed, he talked with her mother, trying to ease her nerves.

The X-rays read negative, and he diagnosed it as a very bad sprain. He wrapped her wrist up, accepted the thanks of her mother, and collapsed in the chair of the examining room after they left. Thank God they were the only ones waiting for him this afternoon. Seeing patients again was harder than he'd expected. Baby steps, Wes had told him in his therapy session last week. Every small step would lead to something bigger. He filled out her chart and went through some of the other charts of patients the new orthopedists had seen, remaining impressed with the quality of their work. The clinic was lucky to have these doctors.

He splayed his fingers against his chest, the rapid beat of his heart playing against his fingers. He needed something, anything to calm him down. Maybe a drink before he went home. Not like anyone was waiting for him there. He said good night to Marly at the front desk and walked out into the early twilight. The setting sun painted a peacock's tail of color across the lavender-gray sky. Charcoal snuffs of clouds drifted above the buildings in lower Manhattan. Wandering aimlessly down Van Brunt Street, he decided to head over to the Fairway supermarket, where he could catch a quick bite on their outside deck, then go home and have a drink.

Or two.

After purchasing his sandwich and bottle of water from the café, he sauntered out onto the deck, looking over the twinkling lights of the city. He drank his water and stood, enjoying the cool, early-evening breeze playing against his face. A young man, probably no older than seventeen or eighteen, stood next to him, shoulders hunched, fingers drumming a beat. He eyed him curiously.

"I ain't lookin' to rob you. You want anything? I got Xannies, Molly, X, and Oxy."

Fascinated, Jordan watched as the kid's hand slid into his jacket pocket and pulled out several plastic baggies filled with different colored pills. His nerves escalated at the sight of the familiar yellow pills.

"Whaddya say, man?" The kid nervously licked his lips.

Jordan smiled slightly.

Chapter Four

INEXPLICABLY NERVOUS ABOUT meeting Lucas Conover again, Jordan scowled at his reflection in the mirror. The youth center, he needed to remind himself, wasn't Lucas's to control. Keith had intended him to be in charge and Jordan vowed to follow through on Keith's dream. Considering how he was failing miserably in every other aspect of his life lately, the least he could do was not let Keith down.

The idea sounded brave and strong but the mirror told another story. No wonder everyone who knew him looked askance when they first laid eyes on him. The pallor of his skin and slightly red-rimmed eyes didn't paint a picture of a man anyone would willingly put their faith in. They should only know he hadn't much faith in himself. Not anymore. One more pill to settle his nerves—he didn't want to take a drink and risk Conover coming down hard on him again like the first time they met. Jordan straightened his tie and threw back his shoulders. Time to buoy up the confidence and take charge. Let Conover see he wasn't a man to be pitied.

They'd agreed to meet at a restaurant in the Meat-packing District to begin ironing out the structure of the Center. Unused to going out to clubs or the party scene in general the past four years, Jordan wondered as he got into the cab if Conover picked the restaurant to make it easy for him to go out with his friends afterward. He knew the man was gay from discussions with Keith, but he didn't get the sense he had a steady partner.

The area had changed since he'd last been here. Gazing around at the swarms of well-dressed people, trendy restaurants and art galleries, once again it hit Jordan how life continued its ruthless merry trek despite a person's inner hell. People were born, died, and fought wars in distant countries, yet here the search for the perfect martini to go with their hundred-dollar steak went on as if that were the norm and the most important thing in life. Had he also been as shallow as these people? Dismay rolled through him, leaving him deep in thought.

A car door slammed, jolting him back to the job at hand, and Jordan promised himself not to become mired down in blackness and misery. Time enough for that when he lay awake at night with regret his only bedtime companion. Keith's legacy, his dream, had been to help kids stay off the street and, Jordan swore as he walked into the restaurant, the Center would be the only thing on his mind tonight.

"Good evening, sir. We're fully booked for reservations tonight." The tall woman, hair in a severe chignon, greeted him with a brief, assessing glance Jordan knew all too well, one that debated whether you belonged. Knowing he didn't measure up to his best, anger simmered inside him at the hostess's snobbish behavior basing his net worth solely on his appearance. He recognized that look, as it was one he used himself occasionally only to have Keith scold him on it.

Who was there to stop him from falling down, now?

You know better, babe. You can do it. Keith might not be at his side, but his spirit rested within Jordan.

Defiantly, he glared at the woman. "I'm sure you are and yes I do. The name is Conover and no need to check. I see him at the table now." With long, purposeful strides, Jordan walked to the back of the restaurant where he'd spotted Lucas. In his dark suit, stark white shirt and bright blue tie—was that Bugs Bunny on there?—Jordan found Lucas a hard man to ignore even in a sea of equally well-dressed men. A look of something wild and dark—untamable was the word Jordan fumbled for—came to mind when he assessed Lucas Conover. Without being told, Jordan knew the man had a past with a story.

"I hope you weren't waiting too long." Jordan sat in the comfortable chair directly across the marble-topped table. The restaurant was lauded for a casual, home-style cuisine, but Jordan had spent enough time in Italy in his youth for the truly traditional places where he could sit with a simple glass of house wine and an enormous plate of pasta.

"Not at all. Only long enough to get my beer. Do you want a drink?"

Luke's assessing eyes met his across the table and over the flickering candles.

"I'm fine with sparkling water with lime, please. Thank you," Jordan said to the waiter who'd appeared silently at their tableside. "So," he said, directing his attention back to Luke, "what have you come up with in terms of space?"

"We've already leased the space; that was done prior to you joining us. We have a real estate developer on the board, and he was able to secure a location not far from the precinct but more important, close to several schools."

"Perfect."

The waiter returned and Luke ordered stuffed clams and chicken parmigiana while Jordan ordered grilled artichokes and chicken marsala. He figured whatever he didn't eat, he'd take home for tomorrow. That had become his life; where once he'd loved to come home and cook for Keith, himself and their friends, he now subsisted on takeout food and coffee. And his pills. A brief throb of despair rose within him. He needed someone to scream at him and tell him he not only hurt himself, he also hurt the kid he bought his pills from and assisted the people who'd contributed to Keith's death. He didn't have the strength to do this alone anymore, but his pride wouldn't allow him to ask for help.

They sipped their drinks in silence and Jordan could appreciate Lucas's reticence. Handling vast wealth must require discretion and the ability to listen more than talk.

"I bet you do this a lot; take people out to high-priced restaurants and woo them to invest with your firm." Jordan broke a breadstick in half and clutched it to keep his hands from trembling. "I imagine it must be nice to eat at all the trendy places." He personally never liked that shit; nothing satisfied him more than coming home, stripping off his clothes, and relaxing. Lucas was different. A single, good-looking guy could have the city at his feet if he wanted. With a pang, Jordan remembered he too was single, and the thought of going to a club or a bar made him break out in a cold sweat.

Looking up from the piece of bread he'd buttered, Lucas's lip curled in a faint sneer. "I have no time for that. I don't like crowds and never saw the appeal of the clubs. And as for the food?" He tossed the piece of bread onto his little plate and picked up his glass of beer. "I'd rather be home on my sofa watching the Yankees, drinking my own beer than be here paying twelve dollars for something with a cute name." His lips curved in a teasing grin. "No offense."

Hit by Lucas's unexpectedly charming smile, Jordan returned one of his own. "None taken. I was thinking the same thing. These kinds of places aren't my thing. Never have been."

Their appetizers came, and in between bites, Lucas

sketched out the plan for the next few weeks. "We have a board meeting next week to decide if we want to accept sponsorships or not. I'm all for getting companies to donate as much as they want."

Pushing his artichoke around the plate, Jordan chewed his bottom lip in thought. "I understand, but I don't want this to become something they crow about and take credit for. It isn't about them or us. It's about what Keith wanted and helping the kids of the community so they have a safe place to come to every day if they choose. We have to make them want to come. So for sure we'll try and get the computer companies to donate their computers and the libraries to donate children's books. But this is always going to be The Keith Hart Center for Youth. Not XYZ Corp Center. I'm doing this to help Keith's dream become a reality."

Noting Lucas's silence, Jordan quirked a brow. "Did I surprise you? You're awfully quiet."

The chatter from the cavernous dining room filled the silence, while he awaited Lucas's response.

"I agree. For the record, I never intended to acknowledge the corporate sponsors any more than having maybe a plaque in, say the computer area, stating, Computers Generously Donated by…whomever we choose. As you put it so very well, it isn't about them." Once again, he flashed that charming grin that lit up his normally austere face.

A tug of desire hit Jordan low in his belly and the breadstick crumbled in his hand. For almost a year he'd barely thought about sex. In the cold hours of the dark, he'd awaken from dreams where he'd been making love with Keith, and his body's natural urge had led him to finish off with his hand. But not until this moment had he felt a pull toward another man. Disturbed, Jordan studied Lucas from beneath lowered lashes, pretending to concentrate on his food.

For God's sake, what was he even thinking? Shaking his head, angry with himself for having those traitorous urges, Jordan drank down half his sparkling water, his hands shaking so badly he feared Lucas might comment. Lucky for him, the waiter approached to take away their dishes, engaging Lucas in conversation so he saw nothing.

Lucas wasn't even his type. Jordan ran a critical gaze over the enigmatic man sitting across from him. Sure, he had the broad, muscular build similar to Keith but personality-wise, the two men were nothing alike. Keith's friendly, joyful personality drew people to him; they couldn't help but want to be his friend. Totally unlike the quietly serious Lucas Conover whose lone-wolf persona and hands-off attitude screamed, *Don't ask, don't touch.* Jordan excused this inexplicable physical reaction as his first time in months being in close proximity to a man.

"You okay, Jordan? You looked kind of sick for a moment."

As far as he knew, there wasn't yet a cure for being heartsick and heartbroken.

"I'm fine."

Fine as he'd ever be.

LUKE DIDN'T BELIEVE Jordan for one moment. He'd bet his last nickel Jordan was reminiscing about Keith, and in an odd way it made him respect the man more. He remembered clearly Keith's loving expression whenever he spoke of Jordan. Luke had his doubts about Jordan Peterson at first, especially after he'd ignored the firm's repeated requests for a meeting. He'd assumed the man hadn't cared one whit for Keith and ignored his letters because the Center meant nothing to him.

How wrong he'd been. Seeing the private hell Jordan lived in proved the adage to never judge a book by its cover—and for the first time in his life, Luke took pity on another person. Of course, Keith's tragic death upset him terribly and Luke had shed private tears, but he couldn't fathom allowing another person to intricately tie themselves up with him so that their lives became bound together. Luke knew he was meant to be alone. Alone meant safety, where no one could hurt him.

"Okay. Let's move on to the people working at the center. I had the idea to use people from a homeless shelter I volunteer at on the weekends. Who better to know the community and its needs than the people who grew up on the streets?"

A thoughtful expression entered Jordan's eyes.

"That's an excellent idea." He shuddered and Luke's fingers tightened around his knife and fork. "I can't imagine the hell those people live in. Keith and I would occasionally drop off clothing and furniture to donate at various shelters and no matter how the directors spun it, they were all depressing places."

"They are."

The waiter arrived with their main courses and eying him sharply, Jordan opened his mouth as if to speak but Luke focused his attention on his plate, effectively shutting down any further discussion. Nothing he could say would enlighten Jordan. Luke could speak from today until next month about the shelter system; how once you're in it, it sucks the life out of you until it seems impossible to break free. How the nighttime opens you up to unspeakable horrors so that you'd rather sleep outside in the warm subway station and take a risk, rather than be a sitting duck in your bed in the dark.

In the rich, prep-school life of dinner parties and cashmere sweaters where Jordan grew up, he could never relate to people like Luke and the others. People who didn't know where their next meal was coming from or where they'd lay their head to sleep that night. How easy it must be to drop your bag of unwanted clothing and leave to go to your fancy brunch and sit around a table, flush with the knowledge that you did something good for the "poor unfortunates."

"I think," Jordan said carefully after several minutes had passed with no conversation, "the training they

FELICE STEVENS

receive might help them to find work, so they can leave the shelter. So not only can we give the kids a safe space, we can give the adults a workable skill to market to potential employers."

Surprised because he hadn't thought about that aspect, Luke set his cutlery down on the white damask tablecloth and stared at Jordan. "That's a really good idea. There's so much they can be taught."

"Right," said Jordan, excitement creeping into his voice, animating him for the first time since they'd met. "Let me think what we could have them do." He pulled out his phone and began to make a list, his tongue caught between his teeth.

Luke couldn't help but watch, fascinated with the change in Jordan. This vibrant man before him must've been who Keith fell in love with, and for the first time since they met, Luke could understand what drew Keith to Jordan. Jordan's eyes sparkled and his pale cheeks flushed as he sat thinking. When he caught his lower lip between his teeth, an unfamiliar throb of desire rolled through Luke and he wondered how Jordan's mouth would taste and what his skin felt like underneath his clothing.

"The computer work alone is a skill any employer would be grateful for." Jordan's smile reached his eyes and Luke couldn't look away from that burning gaze.

"Huh? I mean, yeah. Good point." Furious with himself for getting distracted, Luke stabbed at his chicken parmigiana. No longer hungry, he still made the pretense of eating so as not to draw attention to his unusual case of nerves. "Uh, I also think they could talk to the kids who might be at-risk, you know? Give them firsthand knowledge of the danger they face becoming entangled in that life."

"Yeah," said Jordan distractedly, staring out into the distance. "People often get on the wrong track and without proper guidance, they can fall by the wayside."

Something else lay behind those words, Luke was certain of it, and it frustrated him that he was unable to pick up on the hints staring him in the face. In their brief acquaintance, Luke had seen many sides of Jordan, yet the man before him remained an enigma—first, the haughty, attractive man in Keith's pictures, laughing without a care in the world, the broken, pitiful man who sat before him in his office several weeks ago and the snidely sarcastic, caustic man, lashing out in anger. And tonight, yet another persona of Dr. Jordan Peterson presented itself, perhaps the most puzzling one of all. A thoughtful, caring man, one whom Luke might like if he gave himself the opportunity.

And that scared him enough to climb into his foxhole and hide, willing himself with all the strength he possessed to ignore this impossible attraction to Jordan simmering in his blood. Impossible because Luke knew for certain Jordan would never love another man like he loved Keith. And while he respected that, he had no desire to be a stand-in lover, even for a night.

"So, uh, I think we're onto something. I can talk to the people at the shelter and get it started."

"I admire you. Most people, especially in your field don't see the need to do charity." That faraway look in Jordan's eyes returned. "When I joined Drew's clinic, Keith and I talked about the Center and doing work in conjunction with it. It was always our plan. I just never thought it would come to fruition so soon."

"Life doesn't always work out as we plan."

Chapter Five

L UKE RETURNED HOME late Friday night, completely drained. It had been a hellish week, full of
conference calls and long meetings that sometimes
extended well into the evening. In addition, because he
dealt with international clients, he had to hold
meetings in the middle of the night to accommodate
their schedules. He never complained, as the pay more
than made up for any inconvenience, and he banked
the majority of his salary, his only major expenses being
the apartment and the gym. No wonder so few people
in his firm had long-term relationships. What spouse
could put up with hours like these?

Jordan had seemed in a much more lighthearted
mood over the phone when they'd finalized additional
plans for the Center. Hopefully it wasn't the liquor
talking, but Luke was neither the man's keeper nor
babysitter. Everyone had, at some point in their lives,
lost people precious to them. The man had to learn to
deal with the shit life threw at him.

Luke stripped off his work clothes and pulled on a

pair of sweats and a long-sleeved T-shirt. A Bruce Willis movie played on the TV. Luke settled down with a beer but spent more time thinking than watching the screen. Though he'd never known his parents, growing up in foster care had given him Ash and Brandon. Neither he nor Ash had overtly displayed his sexuality, yet they were often the targets for homophobic bullies, and on more than one occasion, Ash had been suspended for getting involved in bloody fights with members of the football team, almost always saving Luke from being hurt.

How could he ever forget Ash saving his ass in the boys' bathroom when two members of the football team held him around the neck, inches from shoving his head down the toilet? Or the time he was jumped as he cut across the field so he wouldn't have to walk past the team hanging out in front of old man Beamer's candy store? Once again, Ash had rescued him, and they'd escaped with only some minor cuts and bruises. That's why he couldn't believe or understand how Ash had left him and Brandon. Ash pleaded with Luke to leave with him and take Brandon, but Luke had known that would be impossible, as Brandon was too young. Instead he'd begged Ash to stay, but Ash was adamant.

"You don't understand. I gotta go. Take care of yourself and watch out for Brandon. I'm gonna make sure he don't hurt you. When I get settled, I promise to come back for you."

Fucker. Ash never came back, never did anything to make sure Luke didn't get hurt. Now for some reason, when Ash had decided it was time to make an appearance, he was expected to drop everything for him. Maybe once Luke would have. But those days were gone. Luke finished his beer and placed the bottle on the coffee table. He wasn't the scrawny kid any longer who needed someone else to be his white knight. Training at the gym had given him hard muscles so that he could take care of himself. As a boy, he'd always looked up to Ash because of his size, but he now knew bigger didn't always mean better.

At the commercial, he went into the kitchen and rummaged around the fridge until he found some Chinese food that still smelled okay from a day or so ago and decided to heat it up. Waiting for the microwave to ping, Luke decided to pay a visit to the shelter the next day and see if any candidates wanted to work with the kids. Thinking about the foundation focused his thoughts back on Jordan Peterson. Pale and thin as he was, the man exuded sexuality. Blond hair and blue eyes had always been Luke's weakness in men. Add to that a cockiness Luke admired and Dr. Jordan Peterson was one dangerous package. Not that he'd ever act on it or that Jordan would have any interest in him, considering how deeply he still mourned Keith.

His food ready, he grabbed another beer and headed back to the sofa to watch the movie. The second beer hit him hard, and as he ate he remembered he'd had no lunch that day. His body slumped against the sofa cushions while his mind wandered from the television screen back to Jordan. That arrogant mouth and blue, blue eyes heated his blood, and he shoved his hand beneath his sweats, freeing himself to the air. The image of Jordan's pink lips wrapped around his cock sent him thrusting into his palm, the wetness of his precome enabling his hand to slide down his shaft, creating a delicious, torturous friction.

"Fuuuck." His groan bounced off the empty walls of his apartment, mingling with the sounds of the gunfight from the television. Fast and rough, he stroked himself until his balls drew tight and his dick jerked, once, twice, and he came hard, ejaculating onto his shirt. White light burst behind his eyes as he gasped for air, perspiration drenching the curls that lay on his brow. He sank back into the sofa, the cushions beneath him damp with sweat, his body boneless and utterly spent.

With a heavy, fumbling hand he pulled off his sticky shirt and threw it on the floor, then dragged a throw blanket lying folded on the sofa over his naked chest. On the one hand, his body lay pliant, sated, and drained. He groaned and stretched. On the other, he hadn't jerked off to the thought of anyone he'd known in years. And why Jordan Peterson, someone he didn't even particularly like? The answer eluded him, and before he drifted off to sleep, Luke found the remote next to him and clicked off the television set.

"GOOD MORNING, LUKE." Miranda, the security guard

at the Bowery Homeless Shelter located on the Lower East Side, greeted him with a smile. New York City had over fifty thousand homeless people, and the shelters were all bursting at the seams. He'd called this place home when he first arrived in the city, and it became as familiar to him as his own skin. The hallways hadn't changed much in all that time, and Luke shivered slightly from his memories on his way to the offices in the back. The same dank smell of unwashed bodies and fear permeated the air and the walls, despite the stinging scent of disinfectant and air freshener the cleaning crew left behind. The sense of despair was palpable. It was a place where hope came to die if you let it grab hold of your soul.

Groups of children untainted as of yet by the cruelty of their situation played in a community room. He passed by vast rooms filled with rows and rows of beds that looked comforting yet provided no safe haven once the dark of night settled in. When he'd lived here, he'd taken evening classes at City College and worked two jobs during the day. The less time spent in this depressing atmosphere, the better. The half-opened door to the director's office allowed him to peek inside and see Wanda Grant, the director of the shelter, roll her eyes in disgust at whatever story the person on the other end of the telephone tried to feed to her. She caught his eye, and a grin burst across her face.

"I gotta go. Talk to you later." Her accent, a curious combination of Southern and Brooklyn, became more pronounced whenever someone or something got her annoyed or excited, which was most of the time. After she hung up the phone, she beckoned him inside. "What are you standin' there for? Come on in here."

Wanda barely gave him a chance to move before she pulled him to her well-endowed chest and gave him a big, smothering hug. Luke remembered the very first night, after he'd arrived at the shelter from his painful trip up north. Wanda had taken one look at him, shaken her head, and led him straight to the kitchen. In between bites of roast turkey and mashed potatoes, she managed to get his entire life story, something he had sworn to never tell anyone. Lonely and confused, Luke held back at first, but Wanda, motherly and comforting, had proved hard to resist, and the words poured out of him. It had been years since anyone had listened to him or paid him attention.

"How are you doing? It's been so hectic. I'm sorry I haven't been by in the past few weeks, but I've been working on the gun violence prevention foundation. Thanks for setting up today's meeting with the volunteers." He pulled away from her jasmine-scented embrace to sink into the chair in front of her desk.

Wanda nudged the other chair closer to his and sat next to him. "I'm fine, baby doll. How are you doin'?" She ran a critical eye over him, and he flushed as if she could see all the secrets inside of him. "You're lookin' too thin, like you haven't been eatin' proper." A scowl twisted her mouth. "They're workin' you too hard at that hellhole, aren't they? I told ya, they'll eat your soul for breakfast if ya let them."

He shook his head. "I'm fine, and I am eating." If you counted takeout and leftovers. But if he told her that, she'd be over at his place with enough Tupperware to have a party for the entire borough of Manhattan. Luke shuddered.

"Humph. So you say." Those fathomless black eyes narrowed. "You meet a fine young man yet? I can't stand to think of you all alone night after night." Her well-worn hand reached over and took his, giving it a gentle squeeze.

Mother of his heart. If ever anyone could claim the title, it was Wanda. She'd never judged him or looked down on him when he'd told her he was gay, even though she was a churchgoing woman.

"You know me. I'm not looking for anyone. I'm fine the way I am." With his hand and his dirty thoughts. That was all he could hope for, anyway. What did he know about relationships? The only people he'd ever been close to had betrayed him, left him swimming against the tide, only to be flung back to the shore, more battered and helpless than ever.

"It's not right for a man like you to be by himself. It gets you thinking about things too much. You're young. You need to live a little."

"I am living. That's what I'm here about. I finally met the person in charge of the foundation, and now we can move ahead with the men and women you've chosen to work with us. People who've lived through the violence have a better understanding to talk to the people in the community." What a shame Keith had to die for something like this to come to fruition. At least Jordan had finally come to grips with his loss and proven himself worthy of Keith's trust.

Back to business, Wanda handed him a folder. "They're all waitin' for you in the big conference room at the end of the hall. Inside you'll find the names and background checks for the people I feel will be best for the job." For a moment, the gleam in those dark eyes dimmed. "Each one of them has had experience with drugs and gun violence, either personally or by losing someone close to them. I wish I'd have been able to meet the detective who died. He sounds like he was a wonderful man."

"He was."

Startled, Luke almost dropped the folders as he swung around to face the door. "Jordan?" Surely he must be seeing things. Dr. Jordan Peterson would not be at a homeless shelter on an early Saturday afternoon, looking casually elegant in jeans and a cashmere sweater as if he'd stepped out of the pages of a men's fashion magazine. Yet here he was, and he'd made an obvious effort to pull himself together. The paleness of his skin contrasted with the luminous blue of his eyes, and he'd cut his hair so that although it wasn't short, it no longer lay in waves against his collar. A shame, Luke mused, imagining the thick silky strands sliding between his fingers.

Also obvious and altogether unwelcome was this unholy response his body had whenever the man was in his vicinity. That needed to stop immediately.

"In the flesh. I thought I should also meet the people who are helping to make Keith's dream a reality." The slight arrogant drawl of that prep-school voice normally grated on Luke's nerves. He heard it plenty in the halls and meetings in his office. But somehow on Jordan, each word echoed sensuality and promises yet to come. Watching that wicked mouth, his appeal was clear. Jordan radiated charm, sex, and class. The man was out of his league, and Luke was out of his mind for even thinking about him.

"Hello, I'm Wanda Grant." A smile tugged at her lips as she introduced herself. "I run the shelter. So nice to meet you finally." Her voice softened. "I want to extend my sympathy for your loss. Luke tells me Detective Hart was a wonderful man."

And like that, the light flickered out of Jordan's eyes. "Thank you. He truly was one of a kind."

As Wanda murmured more comforting words to him, Luke wondered if he'd been wrong in thinking Jordan had begun to recover and move past his loss. It would be criminal for a man like him to live the life of a monk. His gaze traveled over Jordan's lean but more than appealing tight body, stopping only when he met the dancing dark eyes of Wanda.

Shit. Busted.

Even the fierce, dark scowl he directed at Wanda did little to detract from her smile. Best to get Jordan out of here now and speak with Wanda later. "So, um, why don't I take you around, and you can meet the people Wanda selected to work for the foundation.

Then we can sit and explain what the day-to-day activity of the center we're planning will be like."

"What a lovely idea. You two go ahead and do a little meet and greet with the folks. Luke, baby, I'm a little busy right now, you know?" She directed her wide-eyed, innocent gaze at him. "Why don't you and Dr. Peterson have some lunch afterward and talk. You know you love that little seafood place across the street." Her arm slipped into the crook of Jordan's elbow as she whispered loudly in his ear, "If I don't push Lukie, he'll never eat."

"Lukie?" Amusement lit Jordan's eyes as they walked down the hall.

"Wanda loves to tease me." It took the strength of Luke's willpower to keep his face a study in grim determination. Why did this man, with his presence alone, get under Luke's skin? His mood blackened, driving away the optimism and good cheer he'd enjoyed earlier.

"How long have you known her? You two seem like long-standing friends." Jordan sounded curious, as if he couldn't understand how a man like Luke and a woman like Wanda could know one another.

The devil on Luke's shoulder won out, if nothing more than to hear Jordan's response. "I lived here for a few years when I first came to the city." There. He'd said it, and he couldn't take it back.

Luke slanted a quick, furtive glance to the side. Looking for something, anything that might give away Jordan's reaction to that bit of startling news. But aside from a slight falter in his step—which admittedly Luke could be mistaken about—Jordan said nothing.

That irked him even more. Was Jordan so startled that he couldn't speak? Or maybe he was looking for a way to back out of the project, or would he replace Luke? His imagination spun out of control.

The silence festered between them, deepening like a thorn embedded in the skin, until with uncharacteristic emotion, Luke blurted out, "Well, aren't you shocked or surprised by the news? If you don't want me to work with you, let me know now."

Jordan halted his steps and gave him a brief smile, its unexpected sweetness transforming his tired, too-pale face. "Don't be an idiot; why would I think that? Now come on. I want to meet everyone." He continued walking down the hall, leaving Luke to scramble after him.

"Here, this is where they are." Luke shouldered past Jordan into the room, where a group of nervous-looking men and women sat on metal folding chairs. A large desk, folders and binders stacked on its surface, took up the far side of the room beneath a bank of tall, narrow windows, double plated, with chicken wire between the glass. No way in, no way out, Luke observed, his own memories playing havoc with his senses.

Get a grip. You made it out, and you're helping them get out as well.

Jordan stepped aside, in obvious deference to Luke's familiarity with the people and the place. "Go on," he murmured. "But don't think I'll always let you be the one in control."

A rush of heat swept through Luke at the amused yet slightly mocking tone in Jordan's voice. For a brief moment he wondered if Jordan was as cool and calm in the bedroom. A vision of that long, pale body spread out underneath him filled Luke's mind, and he could almost taste the heat of Jordan's mouth. Not in a million fucking years would that happen, and with his usual ruthless intensity, Luke slammed the iron door shut on his disturbing thoughts.

"We'll see about that, Doctor." Luke bit out his words, allowing no smile to soften the anger in his voice. He was determined to quash any sexual interest he might have for this man, knowing it would only end in a disastrous blaze of fucking epic proportions. And if it culminated with Jordan disliking him, so be it.

"Good afternoon, everyone." Luke granted a smile to these people whom Wanda had chosen. They were the ones who would make the program successful since they'd be on the front lines, so to speak, dealing with the day-to-day issues that would crop up.

"My name is Lucas Conover, and I'm the chief financial officer and director of The Keith Hart Foundation. The man to my left is Dr. Jordan Peterson, the president. Keith Hart was a detective with the NYPD whose life mission, aside from protecting the people of New York City, was to rid the streets of drugs and illegal guns. Tragically, he was killed last year by one of those guns, trying to save the life of a friend."

Jordan drew in a shuddering breath and in deference to his emotions Luke waited a moment, then continued.

"Detective Hart dedicated his life to the people of New York City. He knew being a police officer meant risking his life every day, but to him it was worth it if he was helping his fellow man. He created this foundation to stop the never-ending spiral of violence and told me that even if something should happen to him, his desire to make New York City a safer place for all men and women but especially the children, the most vulnerable in our society, must continue. The funding he has provided, along with the corporate funding we've secured, has allowed us to set up an after-school center that we hope can be a model for other neighborhoods."

The disinterested, dubious faces of the people suddenly sparked to life. One bald, hulking man Luke knew as Troy spoke in a gruff tone. "So we'd be helping at the center? How, man? I'm no teacher."

"And I ain't no snitch, neither." That came from a young, skinny man named Andre, sporting long dreads, his arms covered in tattoos. "Don't ask me to tell on who's doing what with who."

All legitimate points. "First, let me assure you, we aren't asking you to snitch or tell the police anything. What we are asking is to help us with our project. Learn to work the computers, help out in the library or with art projects. Once a month we will be running a Grins Not Guns program, where for every gun brought into the precinct, no questions asked, the person will be given a twenty-five-dollar gift card from MasterCard or Visa. So, in addition to you helping the youth in the neighborhood stay out of trouble, we'd like you to help spread the word."

A sense of interest and acceptance sparked a discussion. The two main questions on everyone's mind seemed to be, if the people turning in the guns could be sure they wouldn't be arrested, and whether there was a limit on the number of guns brought in on one day.

"Does he talk at all?" A young woman Luke remembered as Juanita gestured toward Jordan. "If he's the president, shouldn't he have something to say, or is he one of those rich, white do-gooders who wants to save the poor?"

Before Lucas had a chance to answer, Jordan stepped forward. "I'm not here to save your lives or make excuses for mine. You don't even have to pretend to like me. I don't care." Jordan's blue eyes flashed. "Detective Hart was my fiancé, and I loved him. He lost his life, and that's the only reason I'm here. To make sure that not another person loses theirs to an illegal gun."

Way to make friends, Jordan. Luke opened his mouth to try and soften Jordan's harsh words but was cut short by Juanita.

"Okay, man. And I'm sorry about your boyfriend. I heard he was a cool dude." The other women in the group, as well as the men, expressed similar condolences to Jordan in friendly, almost warm tones.

Luke stood, mouth open. Had he heard right? Had Jordan been accepted by this group of people, who'd taken months to warm up to Luke?

"We'll talk to you all again soon. Thank you for agreeing to become a part of this."

Luke couldn't help but stare at Jordan as everyone filed out of the room.

"Didn't anyone ever tell you not to stand with your mouth open? You'll catch flies." Jordan smirked. They stood alone and Jordan folded his arms, leaning against the door.

Anger pulsed within him in deep, thrusting jabs. Anger at himself and at Jordan for getting under his skin. "Shut up, asshole."

He heard Jordan's inelegant, derisive snort. "Let's go have lunch, like Wanda said."

"I'm not hungry." The words flew out of his mouth, making him sound like a growly, petulant child.

It didn't seem to matter to Jordan in the least, as he raised a blond brow and drawled in that infuriating prep-school voice, "But I am. And Wanda said—"

"I know what she said; however, you don't have to do what she says." But all of a sudden he wanted to have lunch with the man. Otherwise it would be another boring Saturday at the gym and on his sofa, waiting for night to fall.

Perhaps Jordan saw Luke's needy desperation, but more likely the man wanted to get his own way. "I never do what anyone tells me to unless I want to.

Would you mind if we picked something up along the way? I have to go home, but I"—for the first time today, Jordan looked vulnerable as he bit his lip—"I wouldn't mind some lunchtime company." He raked his hand through his hair.

That's when Luke noticed it. The dull gold shine winking through the thick, pale strands of Jordan's hair. A band, not too wide but still substantial, encircled the ring finger of his left hand. It hadn't been there the other times they'd met. So, although Jordan had physically attempted to move on with his life after Keith's death, the emotional reality remained.

Even so, Luke wondered in the back of his mind, *How do the flawed and damaged living ever measure up to the perfection of the dead?*

Chapter Six

CHRIST, THE MAN was touchy. Jordan blinked in the bright, cold sunlight as he and Lucas stepped outside. Traffic flew by them on First Avenue, cars and taxis filled with busy people with busy lives.

Lucas's bristling reluctance to be there with him forced Jordan to offer a way out of lunch. "Look. If you really don't want to hang out with me, you can take off. But I'm offering lunch at my house. I have to check on something; otherwise I'd be happy to try the seafood place Wanda suggested." Before he could stop himself, he blurted out, "Rain check on the restaurant?"

Jordan didn't know who was more startled by the invitation, him or Lucas. It presupposed there'd be more opportunities to spend time together. Somehow that didn't upset him as he thought it might. His eagerness to share his time with the relative stranger instead of the friends he'd known all his life confused the hell out of him.

"I'd like that. I, um, don't have any plans for the rest of the day."

Unaccustomed happiness settled in Jordan's chest, and, more content than he ought to be, he broke into a full-fledged smile. "Then come on. There's someone I'd like you to meet." He hurried down the steps, anxious to hail a cab back to his brownstone in Chelsea. One pulled up to the curb, and he held open the door, ready to climb inside when he realized Lucas wasn't there next to him. When he looked back over his shoulder, Lucas still stood on the steps of the shelter, an unreadable look darkening his face.

Motioning to the cabbie to wait, he ran back. "What are you waiting for? Come on."

Lucas slanted him a funny look. "Who do you want me to meet and why?"

"Come on, stop being so stubborn." Jordan yanked on Lucas's arm, dragging him into the waiting cab. "It'll be fine. Everyone I know has been nagging me to move on and start living my life again, so that's what I did." The cab took off, whizzing in and out of traffic in typical frantic fashion, and their bodies slid toward each other, then moved apart. For the first time in close to a year, blood heated Jordan's veins. Perhaps it was the press of his arm against the hardness of Lucas's, but he hadn't touched another man since Keith. A ridiculous surge of excitement had him grinning at Lucas in spite of the guy's strained expression. "Why do you look so unhappy?"

"I'm not." But the words came out gruff and somewhat hostile.

Admittedly, Lucas's life story made him curious,

and wrapped up in his own personal misery as he was, even he could tell Lucas not only had walls around him, he had a fucking moat complete with piranhas swimming in the water, ready to rip anyone to shreds if they dared to get close enough.

There was nothing Jordan enjoyed more than a challenge, and Lucas Conover was nothing if not a challenge.

Mercifully, the cab slowed, then stopped in front of the brownstone. Jordan tossed some bills over the divider and opened the door. "We're here. Come."

This time, he wasn't mistaken; a flicker of something dark yet hesitant shadowed Lucas's eyes.

"Come on. It'll be fine, promise."

Finally, Lucas slid out of the cab and joined him on the sidewalk. "This is a nice place. If I remember correctly, you haven't lived here that long, have you?"

A throb of sorrow pulsed in his chest, but Jordan had vowed not to be dragged down today. *Time to start living, Jordan. Take everyone's advice. Move on, move on.* "We bought it about two years ago. It was a total wreck and took over a year to renovate, but we had a blast doing it." They trudged up the steps, and Jordan swung the black wrought-iron gate closed behind them with a *clang*. A large golden pomegranate gleamed above the glass panes of the front door, under the stained-glass fanlight.

Jordan unlocked the door and waved Lucas to follow him down the hallway. "You want a beer or anything?"

"Nah, I'm fine." From the corner of his eye, he could see Lucas craning his neck to look into the spacious rooms as they passed by. It was a typical twenty-five-foot-wide brownstone, with the staircase on the left, the polished mahogany newels of the banister marching up toward the second story like wooden soldiers. The parlor had a beautiful bay window overlooking the front garden. A wide window seat curved around, with his mother's colorful needlepoint pillows piled high, offering an inviting place to curl up and watch the world go by.

Jordan viewed his home with pride. They'd had the original tin ceilings beautifully restored, and the inlaid polished wood floors gleamed with the obvious care he'd lavished on them. Each fireplace had intricately cut copper gates fanned out in front of them, and pictures crowded the mantels, evidencing that happier times once took place in the house.

Lucas wandered to the photographs. Jordan didn't need to look; he knew them all by heart. There was one of their only Christmas here together, a towering spruce tree in the background, lit by dazzling lights. His parents and him on the day of his graduation from medical school. A picture of him and Keith the night they got engaged, as well as pictures of him with Mike and Drew as young kids, through life's milestones, in their high school and then college caps and gowns, up until about a year ago.

Sunlight streamed in through the front window, creating waving patterns on the floor from the sheer, lacy curtains. The beams hit the back of Luke's head, highlighting the gleam of his chestnut curls. Pictures floated through Jordan's mind, like a vintage movie from the silent era. Highlights of his life played in flickering images, and he lost himself in memories.

Thanksgiving dinner with all their friends and family together. A strong, warm arm slipped around his waist.

"I've waited a long time for you."

Jordan smiled and kissed Lucas on his mouth.

A cold sweat broke over him. *What the hell was that about?* Blinking rapidly, Jordan glanced around, fearful Lucas could read his mind and see what he'd imagined. The room spun, then tilted, and he needed to lean against the doorframe to keep from sagging to the ground. His mouth dried, and the panic set in.

I can't do this.

Kissing Lucas. He didn't want that, not at all. A quick scan of the room found Lucas still studying the photographs, and Jordan breathed a sigh of relief. Best to forget that confusing image and get on with the business of lunch.

A bark sounded from the back of the house. Luke turned and stared at him, a small smile of delight breaking the stern line of his mouth. "Is that a dog?"

Jordan shared the smile, happy to see Lucas obviously liked dogs. "Yeah. She appeared in my yard a few weeks ago, left, and then just as quickly reappeared." A brown-and-tan four-legged body hurtled through the hall and jumped up on him, wriggling and trying to lick his face. "Meet my newest sweetheart, Sasha. Down, girl." He knelt to pet and scratch behind her ears and accepted her licking his face with her wet tongue. "Come on. She won't bite. I've taken her to the vet and gotten her all her shots."

Lucas approached and knelt next to him, reaching out his fingers for the dog to sniff. Sasha immediately licked them, then flopped on her back to present her belly for a rub. Lucas sat back on his heels, and for the first time, Jordan saw him laugh. Shoulders shaking and eyes squeezed closed, Lucas tilted his neck back and let go with abandon. Fascinated, Jordan couldn't tear his eyes away from Lucas in such an unguarded state. Then he froze.

It hadn't happened in months, but it was undeniable. An ache in his groin. What he'd thought dead and buried, locked away with the love he'd lost, came roaring back to life at the sight and sound of this walled-up man enjoying a moment with a dog.

"Let's go to the kitchen. We can order some lunch and play with her." He jumped to his feet. Sasha scrambled upright, yet Lucas remained crouching on the floor, his laughter gone. Jordan caught a yearning in his eyes, a glimpse of sadness, as he stared after Sasha padding down the hall toward the kitchen. "Lucas?" Their gazes locked, and at the undeniable hunger in Lucas's expression, the floor seemed to drop out from under Jordan's feet. There was no denying his body's reaction now as every nerve ending tingled, and he could sense the blood rushing through his veins, watering his soul, drenching his parched insides. Like a plant long denied the sun, his body stirred with the long-ago remembered warmth and stretched toward its source. To Lucas.

"Lucas." Jordan wet his lips, his heart racing with fear. This wasn't attraction; it couldn't be. He loved Keith still. His skin crawled with nerves. It must be time for another pill. Or two. But first he had to get away from the close proximity of Lucas Conover. "Come on. The kitchen's this way. It's time to feed Sasha." Without looking behind to see if Lucas followed, he almost ran down the hall to the kitchen.

Although she'd only been with him for a few days, Sasha had already settled into a routine, one that naturally revolved around her eating. Jordan, excited to have another living creature in the house, lavished all the love he had bottled up inside on her, taking her for long walks, spending time with her in the backyard, and even letting her sleep in his room. Her dark, expressive eyes followed his every move as he filled first a bowl with fresh water, then another with food. As she ate, Jordan went to the refrigerator and took out a couple of beers. Now that he'd removed himself from Lucas's disturbing closeness, his scrambled wits had settled. Still, he opened a beer and drank half of it in several quick swallows.

"Uh, Jordan? Is everything all right?" Lucas stood at the entranceway to the kitchen, his arms folded, worry clouding his eyes. "Did I do something to make you want me to leave?" He entered the kitchen, which suddenly seemed too small for them both.

Shit. Now even Lucas's voice, sounding all rough and sexy, set him on edge. Throwing up a silent prayer to get control of his sudden raging libido, Jordan managed to face Lucas with a forced smile. "Of course not." He tried not to focus on Lucas's face, but it didn't help quell Jordan's emotions to have Lucas standing so close in his tight shirt over a pair of dark-rinse jeans. Jordan's heart began to slam in hard, powerful beats.

"I, uh, I'll be right back." Before Lucas could answer, Jordan sprinted up the stairs to the bathroom and opened the medicine cabinet. With shaking fingers, he fumbled for the pill bottle. After several attempts, he popped it open and shook two yellow pills out. He scooped up a handful of water from the faucet and swallowed them, barely able to choke them down his dry throat. He gripped the edge of the sink and closed his eyes, waiting for his heart to settle.

Several minutes passed before the room steadied enough for Jordan to return downstairs. First, he checked his reflection in the mirror, and after smoothing his hair, he attempted a smile. *Hmm. Perhaps not.* He didn't need to smile anyway. Time to go back and pretend all was well. Descending the steps, he heard Lucas's quiet voice murmuring to the dog. Silently, he peeked into the kitchen.

Lucas sat cross-legged on the floor. Sasha's head lay in his lap, and he smoothed his hand over and over the silky part of her head, scratching under her ears. Straining but keeping as quiet as possible, Jordan could just make out Lucas's words.

"Sweet baby girl. You're so lucky to be here. He's gonna take good care of you." In this unguarded moment, Jordan detected a slight Southern accent. Sort of like how Ash sounded when he spoke so lovingly to Drew. Regardless of the pills he'd taken, Jordan's heart once again began to ricochet against his breastbone.

God, he was fucked. No matter how he tried, his body betrayed both his mind and his heart. It was merely getting so close to another man, any man since Keith had died. Absently, he rubbed the wedding band on his finger, its smooth warmth centering him. Remembering the day they'd picked out their rings didn't bring the usual stabbing pain. A gentle calm descended on him. He'd buried Keith with the matching ring on his finger. It seemed only right that if they couldn't be married in life, Keith would be wedded to him in eternity. Bringing his hand to his face, he stroked his finger against his lips, as if it were the kiss of his lover.

"You all right?"

Jordan jumped at the sound of Lucas's voice. He'd been lost in such a strong daydream he hadn't even realized the man had stood up. The pills, along with the beer, made him a bit woozy. "Uh, yeah, fine. Why don't we order some lunch?" He gestured with his hand at a stack of takeout menus on the counter. "Pick whatever you like. I don't eat much these days."

They decided on pizza, the easiest thing, and Jordan called it in. Delivery was always quick, and he and

Lucas had just finished their beers when the doorbell rang with their food. Jordan placed the pizza box on the wide center island, creating a safe barrier between him and Lucas.

"Can you take two more beers out of the refrigerator? I'll get the plates."

"Sure."

They might have been any couple sitting and enjoying a Saturday afternoon lunch, and perhaps that depressed Jordan the most. If he didn't choose to remember, Keith might have never lived here. Everyone nagged at him to start living again but for what? Before Keith, no one had touched him or opened him up to face his truth. Why bother to take the chance to start fresh, when pain waited in the wings? He nibbled on the edge of a slice of pizza.

He hadn't heard anything from Jerry concerning Lucas's past and decided the time had never been better to ask questions on his own.

"Why don't you tell me about yourself?" The warm garlicky pizza smell should have set his mouth watering but his appetite had yet to return. "Did you grow up in New York?"

"No." Lucas bit into a slice and chewed, his eyes suddenly wary.

"So where are you from?" Getting this man to talk wouldn't be easy, but Jordan had all day.

"Down south."

A brief smile curved Jordan's lips. "I thought I detected a bit of a twang. Where about?"

"Why all the questions?"

If you didn't want to answer a question you asked one of your own. Jordan had learned that when Keith would discuss interrogation techniques. But Jordan was a persistent bastard and had every intention of finding out as much as he could about the enigmatic man in his kitchen.

"Why're you being so defensive? If we're going to be working together we might as well get to know each other better." He swiveled his chair so he faced Lucas and quirked a brow. "I've got nothing to hide."

Lucas snorted. "That's bullshit. Everyone has something to hide. It all depends on how good you are at faking it." Gazing down at the half-eaten slice of pizza in his hand, Lucas's expression sobered. "And some things remain better off buried deep." He tossed the pizza on the plate.

Watching Lucas lost in his own mind, Jordan wondered what secrets Lucas had buried that caused him to keep people at a distance. He wondered why he cared. The man had pushed him away and been nothing but rude, yet instead of it putting him off, Jordan remained intrigued.

"I wonder if that's true," said Jordan, thinking of his feelings toward Drew. "Isn't it better to put things on the table and talk it out? That's what my therapist says."

"I don't know." Lucas said nothing further and Jordan decided to drop the topic. After all, he'd been hiding a shit-ton of stuff from people and the last thing he needed was for Lucas to get curious and prod him to reveal his own secrets.

Lucas bent to murmur soft words to Sasha who, sensing an easy touch for food, sat patiently by his stool. Watching the man's long fingers stroke the dog's ears, the earlier warmth rekindled deep within Jordan. He ached for the life he once had and now feared was lost forever. People thought him cold and superior but it was all an act, one he used to cover up the fear he'd never find anyone to love. Falling in love had lulled him into a false sense of tranquility that his life would always be as perfect as those moments spent with Keith. Now it all seemed like tunnel vision, far away and beyond his reach. How long could he exist without being touched or touching someone else? And why did he think these thoughts only when Lucas was around? Troubled and confused, he pushed away the pizza and drank his beer instead.

Lucas stopped petting Sasha and studied him instead. "You're way too thin."

Jordan bristled at the criticism. "It's no big deal."

Lucas's mouth quirked up in a slight grin. "Not if you don't mind looking like a skeleton. You have no strength." He folded his arms. "You're weak. I could take you down in a second."

A vision of him and a sweaty, naked Lucas, rolling around on his bed, lips fused together, flashed through Jordan's head. His mouth dried. Face burning, he stood and turned his back, mumbling, "Yeah, so what the hell, I'm out of shape."

"I could help you." Lucas slid off his stool and stood by his shoulder.

Unused to such close proximity from another person now, Jordan's shoulders stiffened and he spun around. "Help me what?"

"Train you, get you back in shape." Luke came closer. "You're a bag of bones. You're pale, and you have no strength or muscle tone." His voice gentled. "You've had it rough, but I know if you worked your body, it would help your mind."

Jordan took a step back. "Maybe you're right. We could go running and take Sasha with us." At the sound of her name, Sasha whined. Jordan was amazed she'd learned it in such a short time, but she was proving to be highly intelligent.

Lucas agreed. "Yeah, but you also need to do some weight training. Lifting, leg presses, that kind of stuff. You need to build your upper-body strength." His large, warm palm descended on Jordan's shoulder. "All I feel is bones."

And all I feel is you. Jordan's knees almost buckled at the touch of Lucas's hand on his body. For the first time in almost a year, his body's response to being touched nearly overwhelmed him. Hadn't he sat at this very table not too long ago, in total despair, vowing never to feel again? How could it be then that this man's hand on him had him nearly shivering with a need so violent and intense, he thought he might break apart if he moved?

His breath caught in his throat as Lucas's hand slid

from his shoulder to his back and turned him around so they faced each other, and he could see the dark uncertainty in Lucas's eyes.

"Lucas."

Jordan's whisper was lost in the tentative brush of Lucas's lips against his trembling mouth. It should have shocked him, but Lucas's lips felt so soft against his own and so warmly alive he couldn't help but melt into his touch. So gentle. So sweet. Lucas's hesitant fingers traced a trembling path along Jordan's cheek, then down the cords of his neck. Dismayed at his body's reaction, Jordan stood frozen, unable, and God help him, unwilling to move. The shock of another man's touch bringing him pleasure both scared and excited him.

Emotionally he might not be ready to move on but physically his body ached for this contact, for Lucas to touch and hold him. And without allowing himself to fall into self-analysis, Jordan wound his fingers around the curls resting on the nape of Luke's neck, and arched into the kiss, as eager to give as to receive.

Good, so good. Jordan's mind spun in fuzzy circles as he sucked Lucas's thick, wet tongue into his mouth. How had he lived so long without the touch of another person? No wonder his life had become an emotional wasteland. He slid his hands down Lucas's broad back, only to freeze at the feel of the man's erection prodding him. Kissing was one thing, but was he ready to take the next step?

Lucas's cock thrust upward into the cradle of Jordan's hips. The reality of Lucas's desire broke through the fog of Jordan's mind, and he pushed away from the circle of Lucas's hard arms.

"I-I can't. I'm not ready for this." He fixed his gaze on the floor, embarrassed at letting down his guard, angry at what he thought of as his betrayal of Keith. Terrified at having to start his life over again. It hadn't hit him how lonely he really was until now, and how afraid and unprepared he was to take this first step back to normalcy.

Lucas's harsh, raspy breath slowed. "Jordan?"

There was no way Jordan could have a conversation right now or even look Lucas in the eye. "It's not your fault. It's me. I'm sorry I led you on."

"You didn't. I shouldn't have done that. It was wrong, and I apologize. It won't happen again." To his surprise, Lucas's voice, normally so deep, sounded uncertain and strained.

Jordan still couldn't bring himself to look at Lucas even though the intoxicating taste of the man remained in his mouth. He couldn't admit he wanted more. Heartbreak, loss, desire, and lust twisted and warred with each other inside his mind. It wasn't until he heard the *click* of the front door that he realized Lucas had left.

What the hell had he done?

Chapter Seven

THE WEEKS FOLLOWING the debacle in Jordan's kitchen were brutal for Luke. Even though he'd barely had time to breathe between conference calls and meetings, the way he'd left Jordan standing so devastated in his kitchen weighed on his conscience. Twice he'd called to apologize, but each time, Jordan had sounded like he did the first time they met: polite, distant, and cold.

Many nights were spent attending to the start-up details of the foundation, and only because it was absolutely necessary as chief financial officer did he attend. Jordan would come in after everyone had already arrived, and leave as soon as the meeting was over. His pale blue eyes flickered over Luke without a hint of recognition or friendliness.

If Luke tried to catch his eye, Jordan averted his head, refusing to meet his gaze. Maybe Luke shouldn't have kissed him, but Jordan's extreme reaction pissed him off. After all, Luke didn't kiss himself. Jordan had been a more than willing participant.

Very willing, as Luke remembered the push of Jordan's smooth tongue into his mouth and how his long fingers dug into Luke's hair as he held him tight. The scrape of Jordan's slight stubble against his jaw and the light, teasing scent of his expensive cologne lingered in Luke's mind.

He wants me but can't admit it.

His body tightened at the recollection. Dr. Jordan Peterson could turn out to be one of the biggest challenges of his life, and Luke loved challenges. It was how he'd pulled himself up from nothing when he first came to New York City. Someone only had to tell Luke no, and that was all the impetus he needed to make it a yes. It was why he was so successful in business.

Dispassionately, Luke stared out of the window of the cab as it traveled through the streets of the city toward home. As attractive as Jordan was, Luke didn't have time to deal with the man's baggage. Luke's infrequent sexual encounters were little more than a meeting of bodies in the dark and a quick release. The effort had grown depressing and tiresome, so he'd stopped trying altogether. One thing he didn't need was a conflicted, overly emotional man. As attractive and sexually appealing as Jordan was, Luke had no desire to get sucked into his world.

In the end, Luke decided Jordan might be the one challenge he wasn't willing to accept.

Yet...from the moment Jordan stepped into his office weeks ago and rocked his world with his cocky attitude and arrogant airs, Luke had thought of little else. Now that he knew him slightly better, Luke realized Jordan's pride and superiority masked a well-hidden insecurity. A shield he used to protect himself. Men like Jordan didn't respect anyone who bowed down to them too easily. They pushed everyone away, to find out who was genuine and also to keep their own secrets close to their hearts. Because Luke sensed Jordan had secrets of his own. Those dark shadows in his eyes weren't only caused by grief. Whatever Jordan hid had the possibility of blowing up his world.

Luke never bowed down to anyone. But then again, he wasn't looking for a relationship with Jordan. He'd meant what he said. Jordan needed some time at the gym to not only get physically stronger but to mentally work through his problems. Luke had done that very thing for himself. Normally he wouldn't give a shit, but if the two of them would be working closely on this project there was no need for it to be uncomfortable. They'd be work partners, nothing more. The weirdness of the kiss would fade, and life would go on.

Satisfied with the way he'd worked everything out in his mind, he exited the cab, anxious to get inside and out of his suit and tie and relax. As he watched the cab pull away, an unbidden image of Jordan popped into his head and Luke realized he didn't live all that far from Jordan's town house, maybe six or seven blocks at the most.

"Hi, Arthur." He nodded to the gray-haired doorman. "Anything doing tonight?" Arthur and the daytime doorman had been instructed to tell anyone not on his approved visitor list that he was either away on business or not at home. That took care of his foster brother Ash's attempts to see him at home when he couldn't get through to him at the office.

"Not tonight, sir. Nice and quiet." The doorman handed him some files that had been messengered over from his office. Because it was the weekend didn't mean the workload ended.

"Thanks." Luke glanced at the files, then got his mail and took the elevator up to his apartment. Ever since he'd found out that Jordan had taken in a stray dog, he'd debated getting a dog himself, or even a cat. Something living to come home to, that would be waiting for him. Something that would care if he lived or died, even if it was only for their own creature comfort. But with his insane hours, it wouldn't be fair to leave an animal cooped up all day and half the night alone.

He unlocked his door and flipped on the light, hating the darkness. Immediately, he turned on the television to keep him company. He had it programmed to one of the business channels so he could keep up-to-date with the foreign markets. The only benefit to working late at his firm was the full dinner spread they always provided to the staff, so he didn't have to worry about food. Beer, on the other hand, he always had in full supply. He opened a bottle and took a deep, satisfying swallow.

Carrying the rest of the six-pack, he trekked into the living room. With a tired grunt, he flopped onto the sofa, not even taking the time to remove his shoes. A glance at his watch showed the time as well after midnight. Most of his co-workers had headed off to a club in Tribeca after they'd left the office, but Luke had zero interest in standing around, chatting up some random guy. Not even the thought of an easy blowjob could tempt him. His health wasn't worth it. Drugs flooded the clubs these days, and he knew many of the regulars who hung out at those places did them; even some of the guys at the firm indulged. Drugs and the people who used them disgusted Luke. Only the weak let themselves get pulled into that world. He'd seen plenty when he ran away and had been offered a variety numerous times but avoided it at all costs. Unless he had no say in the matter.

Shaking from those haunting memories, Luke forced them out of his mind. He wondered what Jordan did in the evening to pass the lonely hours, and completely on a whim, pulled out his cell phone, found Jordan in his contacts, and pressed the call button. He set the bottle on the floor next to him and closed his eyes as he lay back on the sofa. The phone rang once, twice; then Jordan's voice, low and rough from sleep, answered.

"Dr. Peterson."

Oh fuck. Yeah, he'd probably think it was an emergency call. "Um, Jordan, it's Luke."

No answer.

"Lucas Conover? Jordan, are you there? Did I wake you?"

A deep sigh filled the phone receiver. "Give me a moment."

Luke heard sheets rustling and movement. While he waited, he pulled off his tie, unbuttoned his shirt, and toed off his shoes. Settling back again on the pillows of the sofa, he closed his eyes.

"Why are you calling me? Don't you know it's after midnight, for Christ's sake?" As usual, Jordan's irritated voice only made Luke smile. He did love to push the guy's buttons. And the fact remained he had no idea why Jordan piqued his interest. Maybe it was in how hard Jordan loved Keith; Luke respected the hell out of the man who took his relationship so seriously.

"Maybe if you'd talk to me during the day or at the meetings these past few weeks, I wouldn't have to track you down and wake you from your beauty sleep." Luke chuckled at the outraged breath that hissed in his ear.

"I wasn't aware we had anything else to say to each other." That frosty, pissed-off tone was pure Jordan. He had that prep-school asshole thing going on, yet Luke wanted to hold onto the thread of friendship he'd sensed beginning those nights in the restaurant and in Jordan's kitchen. "You apologized, I accepted, and that's it."

"Look. I know I fucked up and I'm sorry for the kiss but I did mean what I said. I think you'd feel much better if you built up some strength, and I can help. Besides," he teased, trying to lighten the mood, "Sasha was pretty sweet on me, and I wouldn't want the dog to mope around, nursing a broken heart."

"You're an asshole, you know?" Jordan's growl only made him laugh.

"Yeah, but animals and little old ladies love me."

"Why are you bothering me, Lucas?" The resigned tone reentered Jordan's voice. "I'm fine as I am."

Back to that challenge. "Bullshit. Come on, Jordan. What's the matter, afraid you'll fail? Won't be able to keep up with me?" For some indefinable reason, a wicked smile curved his lips. "I'll go easy on you, considering you're so much weaker than I am."

"Don't be ridiculous."

"Then meet me tomorrow at Power Fitness on Eighth and 17th. We'll start on a regimen to get you back into shape." Luke dropped the joking tone and turned serious. "Eleven o'clock?" He held his breath waiting for an answer.

"Pushy bastard." Jordan's annoyance came through loud and clear. "You aren't going to leave me alone until I show you you're wrong. I'll meet you then and prove I'm fine and don't need your help."

The phone clicked off. Luke grinned to himself as he got ready for bed, ridiculously happy.

Challenge accepted.

AT FIVE MINUTES to eleven the next morning, Luke strolled into Power Fitness—the gym he'd belonged to for the past several years. He gave a perfunctory greeting to the young woman who checked him in at the front desk; then he scanned the waiting area. No sign of Jordan yet.

Luke decided to change in the locker room first. He liked to take a shower and have a change of clothes so he didn't have to walk home all sweaty from his workout. After pulling on the thin T-shirt and light sweatpants he normally wore, he slung a towel around his neck and returned to the reception desk. Jordan sat on the bench, looking out of sorts and out of place. As he did each time he saw the man, Luke sensed something wasn't right, but he couldn't place his finger on it.

"Good morning."

There it was. That blue-eyed stare that had caught his attention the first time they'd met. As hard as he tried, Luke was unable to dismiss this man from his mind. Admittedly he hadn't tried too hard.

"What's good about it? You woke me out of a sound sleep and made me come here, when I could've been home—"

"Doing nothing as usual?" Luke cut off Jordan's grumbling. "Stop bitching and start moving." He walked past Jordan and waved him to follow. "Put your stuff in a locker, then we'll hit the weights first, and you can show me what you've got."

Luke waited while Jordan did as he suggested, then they walked in silence until they reached the weight room. For a Saturday morning, it was relatively empty. A few other guys, headphones in place, sat at the machines, their concentration solely on their workout.

Luke scanned the room and indicated to Jordan they should approach the bench press area.

"Come this way. What was your usual workout like?" The bar was set with one-hundred-pounds total weight.

Jordan's eyes darted off to the side, and he shifted on his feet. "I, ah, I wasn't ever a lifter. I'm not the muscle-bound type. I ran mostly and did some yoga." At Luke's smile his voice rose, becoming defensive. "I did it for stress relief, after long days of surgery."

"Hey, I'm not one to judge." But his smirk grew broader. "Of course, if you don't think you can do it—"

"Screw you. I can do anything I want to." Jordan threw down his towel and lay back on the bench. "Spot me."

Luke had to bite back a laugh at Jordan's angry growl. "All right, Prep School. Calm down." Jordan lay down on the bench and reached for the bar, and Luke stood behind him to give him instructions. "Lift it slow and even on both sides."

"I know." The words came out through gritted teeth.

Right away, Luke could see Jordan was barely able to lift the bar. It wouldn't do any good to call him out on it, as Jordan was the type who'd rather hurt himself than admit defeat. The man was way too stubborn.

"You know, we should probably have started out with some sit-ups and stretches first, to warm your body and loosen up." That sounded plausible to him and not too obvious that he didn't think Jordan could lift the weight.

Jordan pushed through five more lifts before setting the bar back on the rack. His flushed face shone with a damp sheen of perspiration, and his breath puffed out heavily. "I could've handled it." But he looked happy to get off the bench.

"I saw, Prep School. But I'm running this show, and I say to the mat now." He strode over to the workout mat and sat down. "Sit-ups. Let's do fifty of them."

Jordan stood over him for a minute, and Luke couldn't help but stare. The man had a perfect ass, the thin nylon shorts he wore leaving little to his imagination. Against his will, Luke's cock hardened.

Focus, buddy. You're not here to score. "Hands behind your head. Keep your core tight and your legs straight. Look up at the ceiling and lift, using your stomach muscles, not your neck."

"I've done sit-ups before. I know how to do them." Jordan's black scowl only spurred Luke to goad him further.

"You may think you know, Prep School. Now I'm showing you the right way." He placed his hand on Jordan's abdominal muscles to make sure he was doing it right. At his first touch, the man nearly jumped away from him. "Calm down. I need to check your form."

Uncertain blue eyes met his.

"Do a set of twenty-five for me now."

Jordan blinked, then jerked a nod and lay back. Luke kept his palm flat on Jordan's stomach as the man rose, then lay back. Underneath his fingers, the slippery fabric couldn't hide the tautness of Jordan's muscles or the heat from his body. As he counted in his head, Luke could hear Jordan's exhalations and feel the clench of his stomach muscles. The man's body was all lean, sinewy muscle, with very little mass to him. Luke wondered how the softness of Jordan's bare skin would taste, and lost himself in the thought of licking down Jordan's—

"Lucas."

He blinked and jerked his hand off Jordan's body. "Why do you call me Lucas, when everyone calls me Luke?"

Jordan shrugged. "I don't know. I decided Luke sounds like a cowboy, and you're a city boy."

Not really, but what the hell. Luke nodded. "So your form is decent. I'd have you do three sets of twenty-five sit-ups to build up your core. What you need to do is concentrate on strength. As I suspected, you have little to no muscle mass."

"I'm not built like that. Keith tried to build me up and failed." His gaze dropped to the mat, and his fingers twisted the edges of his shorts.

"I'm not trying to build you up, Prep School. I want to make you stronger." Luke watched him carefully. Now that he was so physically close, Luke noticed the slight tremble in Jordan's fingers and the occasional twitch of muscles in his arms and legs. "Hey, are you all right? You're shaking."

As if he hadn't heard him, Jordan remained staring

at the ground.

"Jordan, man. Are you all right?" A bit afraid that he'd pushed him too far between the lifting and the sit-ups, Luke shook Jordan's arm. "What's wrong?"

"Huh? What? Nothing." Jordan blinked and rubbed his eyes. "I must've zoned out for a moment."

Something was definitely off, and it frustrated Luke that he couldn't figure it out. "Well, let's do some stretching, and then we can see about some free weights." He paused. "Does that work for you?"

"Yeah, sure."

He took Jordan through a routine of free weights and noted in his phone the weights and reps. "So do you think this is something you can handle? I think if you do this three times a week and eat properly, you'll regain your strength. Maybe even become stronger."

"Sure, it's fine." Jordan's phone buzzed. As they walked back to the locker room, he checked it, and Luke saw him bite his lip and hesitate over returning the text.

"Bad news?"

They entered the locker room, and Jordan slumped down onto the bench, indicating Luke should sit next to him. Jordan rested his elbows on his knees, bracing his head in his hands, obscuring his face from Luke's view.

"No, merely another obligation I've been ignoring for months that I shouldn't have." Jordan's eyes met his through the fall of his hair. He blew out a gusty breath and sat up straight. "See, for years, we all visited Drew's grandmother, Esther, on Sundays. We've known her all our lives. She raised Drew and his sister, Rachel, after their parents were killed. Esther's close to ninety and still going strong, but we like to keep an eye on her."

"Sounds nice, if you're into all that family stuff." He wasn't, since you can't want what you never had. Luke leaned back on his hands and continued to listen.

"She's a special lady, and loves having a house full of young people." A smile flickered on his lips as his eyes softened. "She especially loved Keith since he'd bring her chocolate all the time."

"You didn't mind going?" Strange that the cool, indifferent Jordan Peterson would care about someone else's relative.

"Of course not. I love her like she was my own grandmother. But I haven't seen her in months, and that text was from Drew, pleading with me to come tomorrow. It's her birthday this week, and they'll all be there. Drew and his boyfriend, his sister Rachel and Mike." His fingers twisted together. "They want me to come."

Once again, Luke noticed how his hand shook. "So go. They're your best friends."

Jordan balled his hands into fists. "You don't understand. They're all paired up now, and I'm alone. I sound like a fucking wuss, but I don't think I can face walking in there by myself, without Keith. Seeing all that happiness. Shit, I thought I was past it but..." He shrugged. "It fucking sucks because I hate the thought of disappointing Esther." They sat in silence for a while; then Jordan's face brightened. "I have an idea."

Luke, tired of sitting for so long, had gone to his locker and fiddled with the combination. "Yeah? What, Prep School?"

"What the fuck is with that name?" Jordan shot a scowl at him.

Luke couldn't help but grin. "It fits you perfectly, and it pisses you off."

Jordan gave him the finger, a wicked smile curving his lips. *Uh-oh.* Luke didn't like the look of that smile.

"Come with me."

Luke froze and huffed out a nervous laugh. "What?"

"Come with me. Keep me company. Eventually, you'll have to meet the guys anyway since they're going to be involved with my work at the foundation. I can pick you up tomorrow morning. It's only a few hours." Those pale blue eyes gleamed. "Besides, Esther's an amazing cook."

"Look, it's nice of you to offer, but I don't know you guys, and I'd feel weird going to some old lady's house for her birthday." Luke's fingers fumbled with the combination, and mercifully it opened so he could hide from those piercing eyes.

With a swiftness Luke didn't think he possessed, Jordan appeared at his locker, crowding him into the small space. "Esther would flay you alive if she heard you call her old." That arrogance dropped from Jordan's voice, replaced by a warm, almost intimate tone. "Please, Lucas. I'm as close to begging as I've ever been. I don't think I can do this alone."

Lucas. Jordan's seductive voice curled around Luke's spine, and he closed his eyes. The scent of Jordan's cologne mixed with the sharp tang of their sweat and heat, creating a dizzying need within Luke he'd never before experienced. He imagined Jordan underneath him, begging in that same sexy tone. His cock stiffened and he stood still, keeping the lower half of his body hidden behind the open locker door.

He didn't belong in Jordan's happy family nucleus. Badgering Jordan to join him here was the wrong idea; he should've left things alone and let Jordan continue to avoid him. Luke needed to put some distance between them. This was what he got for letting himself get too close.

"What are you so afraid of? Am I good enough to hang out with at the gym but nowhere else? I'm only asking for some company, goddamn it. Why do you have to make me beg?" To his utter shock, Jordan pushed him into the locker, his angry face only inches away. "Just fucking forget it. And forget this gym bullshit. I don't need you for anything." He stalked off into the bathroom.

Luke raked his hand through his sweaty hair, guilt now coming into play. He hadn't meant to come off as such a bastard. What would be the harm in spending a few hours with the guy? It was hard having your life ripped away in a moment while everyone else continued with their own as if nothing had happened.

He knew what it was like. Shame coursed through

Luke. Had he forgotten about his promise to pay it forward? This was no different. He might have been able to make it alone, but it didn't mean he couldn't help Jordan try and overcome his own demons. The man had a life to get back to, after all. He closed his locker and found Jordan in the bathroom. Luke saw him pop something in his mouth.

"Headache," Jordan mumbled under his breath.

"Look, Prep School. You're right. I was being a dick." Noticing Jordan's raised brows, he rushed to finish his train of thought before he changed his mind. "I'll come with you. Keith always talked so much about you all, I feel as if I know everyone already."

Luke's heart jolted at the faint smile and relief in Jordan's eyes.

After showering and deciding on a time for Jordan to pick him up in the morning, they parted ways at the front of the gym. Unable to keep his eyes off the lean form of the man walking away, Luke knew he was doing the right thing by going with Jordan, even if it would be a boring way to spend his afternoon.

Chapter Eight

AT PRECISELY NOON the next day, Jordan pulled up in front of Lucas's apartment building. All morning Jordan been expecting a text or call from Lucas with an excuse to cancel, but to his surprise, his phone remained silent. He hadn't told his friends he was bringing Lucas. He didn't want them to make the mistake of reading more into his invitation than having someone to walk in with and spend time with at Esther's while everyone else was paired off. Additionally, they needed to get to know Lucas since the foundation was primed for opening, only a few weeks away, and he had ideas about integrating their work with Drew's clinic.

Nervous about the day to come, he popped open the pill container and swallowed three tablets. Lately they hadn't been working as well, and he wondered if the kid selling them was giving him low-quality pills. He drank down half a bottle of water and willed away the slight shaking he'd begun to notice in his hands.

A low whine from the back seat broke the silence

inside the car. "Quiet, girl." The dog was excited to go for a car ride, as she knew from previous times there were usually treats involved somewhere along the line. Jordan reached for his phone to send a text to Lucas that he'd arrived, when he saw him exit the building. Jordan's heart rate increased.

Lucas's chestnut curls lay in their usual disarray over his brow, and his hazel eyes glinted with amusement. He wore a beautiful green cashmere sweater, with a black scarf tossed around his neck and tucked under a well-worn but soft-looking leather jacket. Dark jeans molded tight against his muscular legs. Irritated with himself for noticing, Jordan squeezed his eyes shut for a moment, then unlocked the car doors.

After Lucas slid into the front seat, he grinned at Jordan. "You brought Sasha?"

At the sound of her name, she barked and pawed at Lucas's arm. That had the desired effect, as he petted and scratched her until she was satisfied and lay back down.

"Why not? They all love animals, and she needs the day out. Esther has a nice backyard, and she can play Frisbee with us out there." Jordan pulled his SUV out into the traffic, and they sat in companionable silence as they traveled downtown.

"Tell me, did you let your friends know I was coming with you?"

He shot Lucas a quick glance, then turned his attention back to the cars entering the Brooklyn Bridge from Chambers Street. "Well, I did say I was bringing a surprise, but I kind of meant Sasha when I said it." He smirked at Lucas's scowl, then realized the guy was seriously pissed when he didn't come back with one of his usual smart-ass retorts. "I told you before, it'll be fine. Esther's like my own grandmother; she loves having people around and you should meet the guys and Rachel."

"I don't like walking into situations I'm not prepared for." Lucas slid farther down into the leather seat, arms folded, lines of disapproval etching deep furrows between his brows.

"We can never be prepared for everything in life. The best we can hope for is to be able to handle whatever is thrown in our path without going crazy." Jordan maneuvered onto the highway after exiting the bridge, and soon they were wending their way through the tree-lined streets in Brooklyn.

"Whoa, man. That was some serious shit you laid down."

Jordan could feel Lucas's stare and smirked. "I can be deep."

For the first time since getting in the car, Lucas smiled. "So I see." He turned down the radio. "Why don't you tell me a little about everyone so I have an idea who they are at least before I meet them?"

That made perfect sense. "Well, Drew and Mike are my two best friends. We've known one another since our moms became best friends at the playground when we were little. I'm a few years older than both of them and sort of looked out for them, like a big brother."

"How old are you, Prep School?" Lucas grinned at him, once again relaxed and at ease.

"Thirty-five, asshole. How old are you?" He was actually curious. He knew Lucas was younger.

"I turned thirty this year."

This area of Brooklyn boasted Victorian homes with wide lawns and leafy old oak trees. Jordan had always enjoyed visiting Esther. All he wanted was to hug her and have her tell him everything would be all right again like she had when he was a little boy.

Blinking back against the burning in his eyes, he made the familiar turn down her block and pulled into her driveway. Only Mike's car was there—Drew and Ash hadn't arrived yet. "This is it." He turned off the engine.

"Yeah, Captain Obvious. I figured you wouldn't pull into some random person's driveway for no reason." Lucas unbuckled his seat belt.

Rolling his eyes, Jordan snapped a leash on Sasha before opening the door, as she had a tendency to jump out of the car and take off. "Come on, girl. You too, Lucas."

But Lucas had already stepped out of the car, his face an unreadable mask. After Jordan let the dog take care of her business at the curb, he approached him. Whatever Lucas had said the other day, Jordan did feel as if they'd become friends. Putting aside the strangeness of that shattering kiss they'd experienced in his kitchen, Jordan could admit to himself he enjoyed spending time with him. One minute Lucas could be sarcastic and charming, yet other times, like now, for instance, his defensive walls came up, rendering him untouchable.

But no less unforgettable.

Swallowing hard against the unexpected but not wholly unwanted emotions swirling through him, he leaned against the car, where the man remained rooted to the spot. "What's wrong? You look as though you're ready to bolt."

In that hard, almost deadened voice Jordan hadn't heard in a while, Lucas responded. "It was so easy and perfect for you guys, huh? Growing up like this." He swept his arm wide, indicating the house and its surroundings. "Intact families who loved and sheltered you from all the big, bad problems of the world. I bet your biggest problem growing up was deciding what to watch on television or which cereal to eat in the morning."

Jordan had opened his mouth to respond when the front door opened and his friend Mike Levin stuck his head out. "Yo, Jordy, are you gonna stand out there all afternoon? Come inside and say hello." He walked out onto the porch, Rachel at his side as usual. His eyes widened, and Jordan could see him staring at the dog. "You got a dog?"

Rachel detached herself from Mike and came tripping down the stairs. "Oh, Jordy, she's beautiful, aren't you, sweetie?" She put out her hand for Sasha to sniff.

He knelt beside Rachel and kissed her cheek. "Her

name's Sasha, and she adopted me, showed up in my backyard one day." Sasha wriggled on the ground from all the attention, and both Rachel and now Mike, who'd joined them, were petting and rubbing her belly, to her obvious doggy delight.

When they'd finished with the dog, Jordan stood up and introduced Lucas. "Lucas Conover, this is Rachel Klein and Mike Levin. Rachel is Drew's sister, and Mike is, well, Mike." He looked with affection at his old friend, who, as usual, held on to Rachel. When Mike had come back from Iraq with injuries that left him, among other things, deaf in his left ear, he'd gone through a wild phase where it seemed to Jordan he'd bedded almost every eligible woman in New York City. Then Rachel came back into his life and centered him so that he could deal with his disability. They shared a deep, strong love, and Jordan couldn't be happier. Both had suffered enough.

They walked up the steps to the wide front porch, Jordan keeping a tight hold on Sasha's leash. Luckily, Esther's house had a fully fenced-in backyard, so he'd be able to let the dog out and keep an eye on her from the kitchen, which was where they always spent their time whenever they came to visit Esther anyway.

They entered the center hall colonial, and Jordan breathed in the familiar scent of sugar, vanilla, and Esther's sweet rosewater perfume. The house smelled of his childhood—comfort, and love. From the moment he entered he'd become ten pounds lighter, the weight lifting from him, freeing his soul, enabling him to breathe for the first time since that horrific night Keith had died.

"Is that my darling boy, Jordan? Where is he?" Esther's faintly accented voice carried down the hallway as he heard her quick steps tap on the highly polished parquet floors. She might be almost ninety, but nothing could slow her down.

"Esther, Happy Birthday, my love." He saw her then, thin and beautifully dressed, her silver hair set in simple waves about her face. Those bright blue eyes snapped with life, lines etched deeper in her fine, pale skin that hadn't been there the last time he saw her. His heart skipped. *She's gotten older.* "Still the loveliest lady in Brooklyn." He held out his offering. "I know how much you love your chocolate."

Her radiant smile was all he needed. "Oh, you sweet young man. You shouldn't have." Her eyes twinkled as she sneaked a peek into the bag he'd brought her from her favorite chocolate shop in New York—Li-Lac Chocolates. "But I'm glad you did." She set the bag on a small side table. "Now come here and give me a proper hello."

He handed the leash to a silent Lucas, who stood off to the side, then walked into Esther's open arms. "I've missed you." He gathered her into his arms, careful not to squeeze her too tight, but she was stronger and fiercer than he remembered and pulled him close.

"Oh, my darling boy. Not a day's gone by since that horrible night that I haven't thought about you."

Her tears wet his sweater, but he didn't care as he rocked her against his chest.

"It's been so hard, you know?" he whispered into her hair, but she heard him and nodded, saying nothing. "I'm trying, though. Not to forget, never to forget him, but to live with the loss. That's good, right?"

Esther tipped her head back and wiped her tears as she gazed at him. She'd lost her whole family in the Holocaust before she came to this country, so Jordan figured if anyone knew how to deal with senseless death, she did. "You'll never forget. You shouldn't, sweetheart. But you must go on living to prove that their death wasn't meaningless and that your life was made better for knowing them. That you learned and grew from having shared your time on earth with them." She reached up and stroked his cheek. "He would've wanted that. Your young man would never want you to live a cold and unremarkable life. You were made for better things than that, my darling boy."

Without thinking, he caught Lucas's eyes and held them for a moment, then returned his attention to Esther. "Thank you. It's one day at a time, still."

She patted his shoulder. "I understand. Now who do we have here?"

Jordan slipped his arm around her slender waist as she turned in his arms to face Lucas and the dog. "This is Sasha. I adopted her a few weeks ago. I always wanted a dog, and now, well…" He let the sentence die off.

Sasha licked Esther's hand and sat at her feet as if she understood how important Esther was.

"She's very sweet, but I wasn't talking about the dog. Who is this handsome young man?" From over her shoulder she fixed him with a funny smile before facing Lucas again. "I know I've never seen you before."

"Hello, ma'am. My name's Lucas. Lucas Conover. Jordan and I work together on the foundation that Keith set up." He held out his hand, and Jordan was amazed to note how nervous Lucas looked. He didn't miss the assessing smile that curved Esther's lips either. "I'd like to wish you a happy birthday as well."

"Oh, how lovely to meet you, Lucas, and thank you. This may be one of the best birthdays I've had in years." She tucked her hand into his arm and tugged him. "Why don't you come with me to the kitchen, and I can get you something to drink and a snack? Coffee, tea? A beer, perhaps? Do you like chocolate chip cookies?" They walked down the hall, Esther's light voice doing most of the talking, only occasionally interrupted by the deeper, smooth tones of Lucas.

Sasha, off her leash now since she was inside, followed Esther and Lucas to the kitchen as if sensing where the good stuff was. Jordan took off his jacket and hung it over the banister. Mike and Rachel stayed in the hallway with him.

"He seems nice, Jordy. How long have you two been together?" Rachel gave him an encouraging smile.

"We're not together; we're friends, Rach. That's it. He was Keith's financial adviser and CFO of the foundation. Plus we go to the gym together." He shoved his hands into the front pockets of his jeans, rocking back and forth on the balls and heels of his sneakers.

Mike barked out a laugh. "You, going to the gym? That's funny."

Jordan bristled. "Why? What's so funny about me at the gym?" His hands ached, and his mouth tasted like dust. He needed a drink or another pill. Or both. He'd taken three this morning, and already the effect was wearing off. Brushing aside the thought that maybe he was becoming too dependent on the pills, he growled again at Mike. "You don't see me as able to work out?"

Mike held up his hands in self-defense. "Whoa, don't take my head off. It's only that you never went before. I never knew you were into working out."

"I'm using it as a sort of therapy. Work your body and you'll feel better about your life."

Rachel smiled and placed her hand on his arm. "That's true, you know. I fully believe that the body and the mind need to be in tune."

"Speaking of bodies, where the hell is your brother? He's usually never late." Jordan checked his watch, noting it was twelve thirty. "Davis is coming as well, right? They're still together?"

"Yes, Jordan. They're still together." Rachel shook her head, giving him an exasperated look. "I don't know why you still have such a bug up your butt about Ash. He and Drew are insanely happy."

At my expense. His heart dropped to his stomach as the mind-set he'd been unable to let go of echoed in his head. He'd never voiced his anger to anyone, never could, but it remained there, as deep and wide as the ocean.

Because of Drew's stupid, impetuous behavior, Keith had died, and Jordan didn't have the guts to talk to Drew about it or even fully face it in his own mind.

"Whatever. The guy annoys the shit out of me." Jordan looked up at the sound of the front door opening, and as if on cue, in walked his nemesis, Asher Davis.

His large, imposing presence filled the room. The hard mouth and glittering ice-gray eyes that caused opponents to quake in their shoes when he faced them in court were nowhere in evidence whenever he was with Drew. Instead his face radiated happiness, warmth, and love.

What Jordan once had and now was gone.

"Who annoys the shit out of you, Peterson? Not me, I'm sure." Ash's smirk showed he knew exactly whom Jordan had been speaking of.

Choosing to ignore Ash, Jordan greeted his friend. "Hey, Drew, what's up? How's the clinic going?" Jordan might've shown up and taken on several easy orthopedic issues, but the thought of going back to a full surgical schedule sent him into a panic. His thoughts strayed to the yellow pills he had in his jacket pocket in case the day became too overwhelming for him.

Drew hugged him, then took off his jacket and tossed it over Jordan's on the banister. "It's great. The donations keep coming in, and the new doctors are working out great, although the orthopedists keep asking for you. They'd all hoped to be working with you." Drew's calm green eyes held his. "Do you think you might put in more regular hours in the near future? You don't have to answer me today." Drew rushed onward before Jordan had a chance to respond in the negative. "Promise you'll give it a thought, okay?" His kind smile had Jordan nodding in agreement. He rarely could refuse Drew.

"Glad to see you've come out of exile to join us all, Jordan. For some reason, Esther's missed you." Ash looked around. "Where is she? We brought her birthday cake."

"She's in the kitchen with Jordan's dog and his friend." Rachel volunteered that helpful bit of information before Jordan could even open his mouth. "We should all go into the kitchen where Esther is now that you're here, Drew."

"Finally, I might add," Jordan grumbled but didn't miss the soft kiss Ash gave Drew. His mood, already spoiled by Ash's presence, grew even blacker at the sight of the man's happy face. His irrational mindset didn't help the situation, but as his mother always said, *"It is what it is."*

"You got a dog, Jordy? You never said you planned on getting a dog." Drew sounded surprised.

"I didn't plan on it. She sort of found me."

Rachel cut in. "She's adorable. And so sweet too."

They all trooped into Esther's homey kitchen, where platters of fruit along with Esther's favorite foods—corned beef, roast beef, and pastrami—sat on the table. She must've spent the whole morning baking, as cake plates piled high with her famous chocolate chip cookies, brownies, and other assorted goodies sat waiting to be devoured.

Lucas sat at the table, a plate of apple strudel in front of him, along with a big mug, which Jordan knew would have coffee. The man basically lived on caffeine. Sasha sat at his feet, her muzzle resting on his knee as he stroked her head. Esther spotted them, and her eyes lit up.

"There they are; there's my darling grandson." She got up to hug Drew.

"Happy Birthday, Nana." Drew kissed her cheek. "We brought you a cake, but I should've known you'd bake up a storm."

She laughed. "Yes, you should, but who am I to deny another piece of cake in the house?" She peered behind him. "Where's that scoundrel of yours? Asher, where are you, darling?"

"Esther, my love. Happy Birthday, darling lady." Jordan watched with disgust as Ash charmed Drew's grandmother with his old-fashioned, courtly gesture of kissing her hand.

"Come, you two. Come have some coffee everyone, and Drew, Asher, come meet Jordan's friend and his sweet dog." As she approached the table, she took

Lucas's hand in hers. Jordan moved over to make the introductions, but Lucas stood abruptly, dropping his fork so that it clattered on the plate. Sasha jumped up to stand by Esther, whining.

"Luke?" Ash's voice cracked. "Is that you?"

Instead of greeting them, Lucas stepped backward, his face locked into a mask of indifference, but Jordan, knowing him now as he did, could see how affected he was; his normally olive skin paled, his eyes narrowed, and a muscle jumped in his tightly clenched smooth-shaven jaw.

"No, you aren't dreaming. More like a nightmare."

By now, Sasha had placed herself in front of Lucas, growling at Ash. Smart dog, Jordan thought to himself. *Good girl.* "Do you two know each other?" He looked over at Lucas in confusion, and the bitterness and hatred on his face rivaled any Jordan had seen in his life. "Lucas?"

Drew had come to stand by Ash and take his hand. "Ash, is this—"

"It's my brother, my foster brother Luke." Ash took a step toward him. "Luke, please, let me talk to you. I've been trying for months."

Sasha barked, growling deep in her throat at Ash as she pressed against Luke's legs.

"You're no brother of mine. You lost that right when you walked out on us." Lucas snarled in Ash's face as he brushed right by him as he would a stranger. "Now watch me as I walk out on you. I hope it hurts you as much as it did Brandon and me."

Jordan stood and watched as Lucas, with Sasha at his heels, strode out of the kitchen and the house, the front door slamming behind him.

Chapter Nine

*F*UCK. WITH A heavy thump, Luke sat on the bottom steps of Esther's front porch. Sasha crowded in next to him, and he wrapped his arm around the dog's solid warmth, hugging her close. Spots danced before his eyes, blurring his vision. Nausea threatened, then receded. Eight fucking million people in New York City and he had to find the one person who somehow had a connection to his brother.

No. Not his brother. Not any longer. Never again.

But he knew it wasn't true. Because the mere sight and sound of Ash thrust that yearning he thought he'd buried years ago back to the surface. A yearning to once again have a family, have his brothers back in his life. *Goddamn it.* He couldn't handle it. He needed to leave.

"Lucas."

He glanced up at Jordan's stricken face. "What are you so upset about? Go back inside with your friends. I didn't mean to break up your party."

As usual, Jordan ignored what he said and sat next to him on the step. "Don't be stupid. This is more important." Jordan placed his hand on Sasha, smoothing the fur on her head. "So, Ash is your brother?"

"My foster brother. It was the three of us—Brandon, Ash, and myself." A trembling began deep within him. This exposure was what he'd feared the most—strangers pitying him, looking down at him, thinking him weak. "Ash left right before he turned eighteen, ran away in fact."

"That must have been rough for him, leaving home all by himself." Jordan's thoughtful voice had lost its usual patronizing tone.

"It was rough for us to stay."

He'd ceased petting the dog, who wandered up the stairs and back into the house. Jordan's warm, dry palm slid over the top of his hand, entwining their fingers together. A frantic pounding began in his heart, resonating in his head and chest. It took a supreme strength of will to draw a breath deep enough to reach his lungs. Their linked hands rested between them on the steps.

"Do you want to talk about it?" asked Jordan.

"Not here...." A squeeze from Jordan's hand startled him. To think he might have an ally, or someone he could confide in, after all his isolated years, overwhelmed him. "I can't talk to him now. I won't. He left me to live with a monster. It's been fifteen years since I've seen or heard from him. He can't expect me to—"

"Hey, hey, relax." The grip on his hand tightened. "You don't have to do anything you don't want. If you want to go, I think everyone would understand." Jordan's soothing voice flowed over him, his thumb circling over the top of Luke's hand. "I'll make our excuses, and we can go."

Shocked, Luke swiveled around on the steps, drawing closer to Jordan, their knees touching. "I can't let you do that. It isn't fair to Esther. She told me how much she looked forward to you coming today." He leaned closer to Jordan, who never took his steady gaze off him. "She told me all about you. How you always stood up for your friends and tried to protect them, even when you were boys."

"Nice try, but this isn't about me, for once. It's about you and your pain." Jordan's leg slid closer, hard and warm against his thigh. Luke froze.

Their mouths were mere inches apart, lips poised to touch. He heard nothing save for their mutual breaths and the rush of blood through his veins. Something dark and deep unfolded within him, exposing his heart. And for the first time, Luke needed someone, wanted someone to hold on to. Loneliness had been his companion for so long, he'd never imagined there could be anyone else to share himself with.

Gone was the arrogant demeanor Jordan carried around with him. In its stead was a man whose blue eyes gazed upon him with a tenderness he'd never seen.

"Let me help you for once, Lucas."

An unknown emotion coiled in the pit of Luke's stomach as Jordan reached up to brush aside the curls falling over his brow. Not content, however, to stop with that brief touch, Jordan's hand trailed down his face, coming to rest against his cheek. Jordan whispered, "Please."

In Jordan's eyes, Luke viewed a yearning, a hunger so fierce and bold it robbed him of all capacity to speak. Desire, hot and thick, flooded through him, and no longer willing to remain passive, he brushed his lips against Jordan's. The immediate soft gasp of satisfaction played like music to his ears. The kiss stayed sweet and light, but the promise of more remained. Luke sensed it in the ripples racing under the fine skin of Jordan's neck and the trembling hand that remained on his face.

And he wanted more, God help him.

Luke slid his tongue against the seam of Jordan's lips and he opened his mouth, granting entrance into its heated depths. Their lips slanted together, and his breath grew short. Jordan's mouth fit over his, locking into place like the last missing piece of a puzzle Luke had been searching for his whole life.

Like he'd never been kissed before.

In matters of the heart, Luke was a virginal schoolboy in uncharted territory. Except there was no fumbling or missteps, no embarrassment or rushing. Kissing Jordan was like getting swept up in wave after wave of sensation, every nerve ending awakening for the first time, fresh and new.

He drew back, reluctant to stop kissing but fearful of exposure should someone come outside. Jordan's eyes remained closed for a moment; he opened them and gave a tentative smile.

"I'm not sorry this time." Jordan raked his hands through his hair, to smooth it back off his face. "It felt good to offer you comfort, for once."

The smile froze on Luke's face. He made sure to speak very carefully so as not to break down and lose control. "So that's all it was—a pity kiss?"

"Are you serious?" Jordan's horrified expression mollified Luke somewhat. "Why would I pity you? Aside from knowing Ash, that is."

That set Luke to thinking. "Why do you hate him so much?"

Jordan leaned back, bracing his hands on the steps and stretching his legs out in front of him. "Hate is a rather strong word." Even though his voice remained calm, Luke could see pain in those troubled eyes. "I don't trust him, no matter that he and Drew have been together all these months. Before he met Drew, even when he first met him, Ash was a player. He'd screw anything on two legs. He even made a pass at me, years ago."

Whoa…not what he'd expected to hear. "Um, so did you ever get together?" For the life of him, he didn't want to know, yet he had to find out the answer all the same. His stomach soured at the thought of Ash's hands on Jordan's body.

The look of distaste on Jordan's face sent all of Luke's misgivings out the proverbial window. "Christ, no. I would never be interested, and I told him so. He didn't want to believe me and wouldn't leave me alone.

I almost had to threaten him with a restraining order." Jordan broke out in a huge grin. "Took the wind right out of his sails."

"Yet your friend had no problem with his past?" Of course Ash's life interested him. Now that they'd been face-to-face, sooner or later he knew he'd end up speaking to him. Better to find out his whole story ahead of time. "I'm surprised at the two of them. Drew seems pretty nonthreatening. Not the tough, strong personality I'd always figured Ash would go for."

Sasha had come outside through the half-opened front door and down the steps, looking for some attention. Jordan let her lick his hand before continuing. "Don't let his size fool you. Drew may not be physically big and overpowering—but he is one of the strongest people I know. He had to be after his parents were killed. But he's also the nicest person you'll ever meet and sees the good in everyone. In many ways, he's like Esther. I think that's what drew Ash to him."

That made sense. Ash would want to surround himself with people who made him feel good since he was such a miserable son of a bitch.

"To be fair to Ash," Jordan continued, "he's never given me one reason to doubt his feelings for Drew. He's been nothing but faithful to him from the time they met. I know he loves Drew."

"Yet there's something else, isn't there?" Luke hugged his knees to his chest and clasped his arms around his legs. "Something about their relationship that goes beyond the way you feel about Ash?" Jordan's face tightened and turned away, and Luke knew he'd hit a nerve. When it became apparent Jordan didn't plan on answering him, Luke left his side and returned to the porch. "I think we should go back inside. I feel bad Esther's party had to be interrupted because of me. You were right. She's a special lady and doesn't deserve this."

Jordan stood up, Sasha at his heels. Luke looked down at them and wondered why this man above all others had insinuated himself into his life and his mind. Here Luke was, breaking all the rules he'd set in place to prevent it from happening—encouraging it even, by wanting to drag Jordan up against him to kiss him again and hold him close. And maybe, just maybe never let him go. There wasn't anything he could do to stop it, he admitted, watching Jordan and Sasha walk up the steps to meet him.

Sometimes you walk into a room and meet someone, and though you know you've never seen them before, they're no stranger. Your body recognizes them, even if your mind doesn't. Right from the start, Luke's body had recognized Jordan.

Releasing some of the inner strength he'd worked so hard to acquire to keep people away, Luke shocked himself by putting his hand on Jordan's shoulder, kissing him on the cheek, and opening his heart for the first time. "Thanks for coming out here, Prep School. You barely know me."

"You're wrong." Jordan covered his hand. "I know you. I know you're kind but like to hide it for reasons you can't yet share. I know you've been hurt and have walls up to keep people out. Maybe one day we'll find that trust between us."

Luke remained silent and unmoving as Jordan leaned over and kissed him, a mere brush of their lips, yet it set off a glow of fire in his belly. "I also know you shouldn't be alone to face Ash for the first time in years. Now let's go back inside and confront your brother. I'm on your side." He held out his hand, and Luke took it, then followed him back into the house. No one had ever been on his side before. Having an ally made facing Ash easier, but having that ally be Jordan meant everything.

Upon their reappearance in the kitchen, Luke glanced at the clock, shocked it had only been half an hour since his entire world had been rocked to its core. Mike and Rachel had disappeared, Luke noticed, but Drew remained seated next to Ash, their entwined hands a symbol of their united strength.

With a start, he realized he still held Jordan's hand. He tried to pull away, but Jordan held tight, squeezing his fingers as a warning he shouldn't let go. Luke cleared his throat and spoke directly to Esther.

"I'm so sorry I messed up your birthday celebration. I know you're aware of what a shock this has been to me. Please forgive me, and I'll understand if you'd rather I left so you can share this afternoon with your family."

Jordan's hand once again squeezed his tightly. It was then that Luke caught sight of the pile of crumpled tissues on the table at the place where Esther sat. It wasn't right that a woman should cry about anything on her birthday. He finally pulled free from Jordan's hold and sat down on the opposite side of the table from Ash and Drew. He still didn't understand what Ash saw in the pale, green-eyed man, but there was no accounting for taste. His gaze flickered for a moment back to Jordan. Who would think he'd be attracted to a man with an ego the size of the Grand Canyon? Yet he was.

"I want to thank you for your hospitality, Esther, and—"

"Oh, you mustn't go. Please. You've only just gotten here. You must stay. Jordan, darling, make him stay." Esther grabbed Luke's hands in hers, showing surprising strength.

But Luke didn't need Jordan to make his decisions for him. "I don't belong here. This day is for your family and friends. Strangers don't belong."

"Oh, young man. Strangers are merely the friends I haven't met yet. And at my age, I don't have time to go out and meet all the friends I don't yet know." Her blue eyes twinkled, and he couldn't help but get drawn into her warmth. "I think you must be a very special friend for our Jordan to have brought you here today."

"Now, Esther, don't start." Jordan settled into the seat next to him.

"I don't know what you mean." Esther sniffed.

"Nana," Drew interjected. "I think Ash and Luke might want some time to themselves to talk. I'm sure they have some things to say that only need to be shared between the two of them."

Luke met Drew's frank stare across the table. *Huh.*

"I don't have anything to say to him that can't be said in front of all of you."

Ash, his mouth a tight, grim line, sat quietly while Drew took over.

"I'm sure, Luke, if you gave Ash a chance to explain, you'd change your mind."

"Considering you know nothing about me, Drew, you shouldn't be so sure about my state of mind." He gestured toward Ash with a brush of his hand. "Go ahead"—he pinned Ash with a glare—"explain. I'm all ears, *big brother*. Tell me why you left and never came back when you promised you would. Tell me why you never wrote one letter to see if we were even still alive." He crossed his arms. "Go ahead. I'm waiting."

Ash paled, and his eyes glittered with wetness. He opened his mouth to speak, then shook his head and lowered his gaze to the floor.

This wasn't turning out as he'd dreamed all these years. It gave him no satisfaction to witness Ash's pain. From his reaction, it seemed obvious Ash had suffered too. Shame replaced the anger flooding Luke's body.

A thin, warm hand covered his. "Lucas, dear boy. May I speak with you in private for a moment?" Esther's bright eyes held his.

"Esther, I know you want me to listen. But you're Drew's grandmother, so of course you want Ash and him to be happy." The words stuck in his throat. In another place and time, he might have belonged at a table like this, with a family who cared about him as much as they did Ash.

"Come, please." She stood and left the room, and because he respected her age, he followed her. She led him into a beautifully furnished living room and indicated he should sit. "Now, while it's true I want my grandchildren to be happy and I consider Asher like my own grandson, I never turn a blind eye to their faults. I understand it's a shock for you to come here and have him thrust back into your life." She pulled a small handkerchief out of her sleeve and wiped her eyes, then wrapped it into a tight little ball held fast within her fist.

"You are wise not to speak to each other tonight. Emotions are running high, and you both need a chance to cool down."

Luke sat and listened.

"But you need to talk. There are things that happened to Asher you aren't aware of, as I'm sure there are things you should tell him about your life." Her shrewd gaze held his. "You've suffered greatly as well, haven't you, dear boy?"

Before he realized what he was doing, Luke found himself answering her. "Yes."

A cloud passed over her face, dimming the light in her eyes. "I'm sure Jordan will help you through it, as my Drew helped Asher with his demons. Love teaches you to give of yourself." She patted his hand. "I can't tell you how wonderful it is to see Jordan has finally decided to move on and find love again. You've made him happy."

"We're friends, nothing more."

"Very well, dear. If you say so." She patted his hand again. "I've known these boys since they were in diapers, but you know better, I'm sure."

Luke couldn't hold back his grin. She was very cute.

"So you'll stay, and we'll all eat dinner together and have my birthday cake, right?"

How could he say no to her? Ice water would have to run in his veins, and by now, after all that had happened, he hadn't the strength to say no. "All right. Thank you, Esther, for opening your home to me."

They returned to the kitchen, where Jordan, Drew, and Ash sat in uncomfortable silence. Luckily, Rachel and Mike rejoined them, and soon the discussion turned to the foundation where Luke felt more comfortable and before he knew it, he outlined what they'd accomplished so far. Over the past month, he'd done a lot of behind-the-scenes work, and an unfamiliar glow filled him when everyone at the table congratulated him on having the after-school center up and running earlier than anticipated. It was the warmth of acceptance, of belonging.

Esther slid a piece of her birthday cake in front of him after dinner had been cleared away. "I can't think of anything better to do with your life than helping others. And to carry on sweet Keith's dream?" She patted his hand. "You're a mensch."

Jordan laughed, but Luke didn't understand. "What is that? What does that mean?"

Esther poured his coffee and explained. "It's a Yiddish word, meaning someone who does good for others without expecting anything in return."

Drew interjected, speaking for the first time. "It's a compliment, Luke, and my grandmother doesn't give those very often."

Luke stared hard at Drew. Was Drew kidding, trying to get Luke to react, so he and Ash would start a conversation? His gaze flickered to Ash for a moment, and his heart gave a funny thump. The intensity of Ash's stare, the yearning in those clear, bright eyes threw him. He didn't look angry or bored to be there. Sadness lurked along with a look Luke had become all too familiar with when living at the shelter. Defeat and fear. Luke couldn't help but wonder what Ash had lived through when he'd left home. Then Luke remembered how rich Ash was with his Park Avenue address and successful law practice, not to mention this wonderful family who loved him unconditionally, and he tamped down any sympathy for Ash. Obviously he'd managed fine.

But the sight of Drew holding Ash's hand, their fingers laced together, surprised him. Once again he wondered how they'd met. He'd have to get Jordan to tell him their story.

"Thank you, Esther. I appreciate it."

Jordan stood. "Esther, it's been wonderful, but I think we'll be heading out now. I have to feed Sasha, and I'm sure Lucas has things to do as well."

When Luke glanced at his watch, he was shocked to see how the afternoon had fled. It was past dinnertime, almost seven o'clock.

After saying his good-byes and promising Esther he'd come again with Jordan, they left. Luke settled in the cushioned seat of the SUV and blew out a breath. Jordan didn't say a word; he drove away, heading toward the city. It was one of the things Luke appreciated. Jordan never had a need to fill the empty spaces with incessant chatter about crap. His cheeks grew warm as he recalled their kisses earlier. *Shit*. He hadn't intended for it to happen, but to himself he'd admit it felt good to have someone to talk to and spend time with. Even though it went against everything he'd trained himself to be, he never stopped yearning for affection. He'd merely learned to live without it—a punishment for the pain of losing Brandon.

A cool hand took his. "Stop thinking so much. Sit back and enjoy the ride."

Startled, he looked over at Jordan, then down at their clasped hands. His mind flashed back to Drew's and Ash's hands, entwined together to give each other strength, and another little piece of his heart broke open. Was he ready to let Jordan in?

Chapter Ten

WAVERING BETWEEN NERVOUS anticipation and fear, Jordan kept silent for most of the ride home. That seemed to work fine for Lucas, who sat huddled in his seat, staring out the window. Jordan knew that look of shock and how it could render you numb to all outside interference. He'd felt that way since Keith's death. Only now, there was the stabbing pain, like the pins and needles of blood rushing back into a limb regaining its feeling. Lucas's reality of finding his brother after so many years could be nothing less than devastating. And Jordan's heart, shriveled for so long, suddenly bloomed back to life, crashing through the shield he'd erected to keep from falling apart and shattering into a thousand pieces after Keith's murder. He'd finally found someone to take care of and nurture.

"You know, Lucas, it's okay to feel happy you finally found him. Even if you're still angry at Ash, at least you know he's alive."

Lucas darted a glance at him, his beautiful hazel

eyes glinting with pain and anger. "I don't know what I'm feeling. It seems he has the perfect life, right? Money, a happy relationship, and a wonderful family." The emotions struggling within Lucas played out on his handsome face; Jordan could see the effort it took for him to keep from breaking down. "It all turned out so well for him. And God only knows where Brandon is and what he's gone through."

Drew had told him and Mike something of Ash's background but glossed over anything about his childhood. From Lucas's reaction and the hints he dropped, Jordan surmised there must have been some form of abuse. As an only child who was doted on, secure in his parents' love, Jordan couldn't imagine the pain and suffering Lucas and his brothers had gone through.

What was real and unimagined, however, was the anticipation thrumming through his veins, awakening the dormant desire he'd ignored for weeks now. Jordan knew he waited at a crossroads. By now, Keith would want him to move on. They'd talked about it, as it was a daily thing they'd lived with, what every spouse of a person who worked for the NYPD feared most. One day, they might kiss their husband or wife good-bye and never see them again.

Discussing it and living through it were two different things. Keith had made Jordan promise, if Keith died, to find someone to love again. Of course Jordan had said yes, however, it was an offhand promise—one made without a thought or belief that it would ever come to pass. Promises made to the living weren't as easy to keep after death. And now, even with Lucas's overwhelming presence next to him, the idea of letting another man into his life scared the hell out of him. Yet somehow Jordan sensed an inevitability about him and Lucas. That since they'd met, it had all been leading up to this point in time.

Jordan drove onto the Brooklyn Bridge, thankful for the stop-and-go traffic to keep his mind occupied. Lucas remained a silent presence, obviously caught up in his own memories. He couldn't imagine what Lucas must be feeling right now, seeing his brother after all these years. Resentment, certainly, as there were obvious unresolved issues between the two. But despite what Lucas said, there had to be happiness as well, knowing Ash was safe. Perhaps even nostalgia for the way their life used to be.

Except, Jordan remembered, life wasn't always about happiness. It must've been lonely, for sure, being a foster child without parents who loved you. His grip tightened on the wheel, and he forced himself to pay attention to the road and not his inner thoughts. He swung onto the West Side Highway. Add to that possible abuse or neglect, and it was no wonder Lucas remained leery of friendships. Still, he'd agreed to spend the day together and had offered to train him at the gym.

"Lucas?"

"Hmm. Yeah?"

So he wasn't asleep. Still ruminating. "Want to

come back and hang out? I know you've got work tomorrow, and I've got to go into the hospital, but"— Jordan took a breath—"I wouldn't mind some company. It gets kind of lonely eating by myself. We could have a drink if you don't want to eat and—"

"Hey, Prep School." Lucas touched his arm, then gave it a gentle squeeze. "It's good. I'm fine with hanging out for a while." He blew out a breath, and Jordan gave a quick glance over to see him rub his eyes. "It's been an eventful day to say the least."

He struggled to hold back his relief. "Great. We can order in some food and relax."

"Um, not exactly." Looking more animated than he had in quite a while, Lucas grinned at him. "I think it's a good night to hit the gym. What do you say? You up for it?"

Denial sprang to his lips; then Jordan thought about it. Maybe it would be a good thing to keep out of the house and from being alone with Lucas. If they were in the gym, they'd be surrounded by people and nothing would happen between the two of them. Now that they'd kissed, he couldn't get the memory of Lucas's soft mouth out of his mind.

"Sure." He pulled up in front of the parking garage on his block. "Do you want to meet me back at my house, and we can go together?" It wouldn't take him long to change his clothes and feed Sasha.

"Sounds good." Lucas grunted as he hopped out of the SUV. "I'll come right back after I change."

Jordan handed his car keys to the valet and took

Sasha by her leash. "Okay, I'll leave the front door unlocked. Come in and make yourself comfortable."

"See you in a few." Lucas walked away.

Sasha whined, but Jordan held on to her. "Hey, you belong to me, remember?" She sat on the sidewalk and barked at Lucas's retreating figure. "Yeah, he's becoming kind of a hard guy to say good-bye to, huh?" They walked down the block, and she followed him up the stoop and into the house, making a beeline for her water dish while he shed his coat. After giving her fresh food, Jordan unlocked the doggie door he had installed in the kitchen, allowing her access to the now-enclosed backyard, then hurried up the stairs to take a quick shower. Even though he knew he'd need one after his workout, he wanted the soothing heat and the feel of the pounding water on his body.

After dropping his clothes onto the chair in his bedroom, he walked naked into the bathroom. Without a second thought, he opened the medicine cabinet and took three pills, downing them with a glass of water. By now, the pills he'd taken in the morning had worn off. Glancing at the little clear bags he'd parceled out, lined up on the middle shelf, he briefly thought of giving them up. After all, it was going on a year since Keith died. Surely he didn't need the crutch anymore.

Tomorrow, he thought, as he turned on the taps to his shower. *I'll stop tomorrow.* The hot water sluiced over his body, and he sighed, stretching his arms up to the ceiling. He loved his extra-large shower with the rainfall showerhead and jets pulsating into his body from all sides. The tenseness in his back and shoulders melted away, and his mind wandered back to the afternoon.

Kissing Lucas. A low, snaking heat rippled across his belly, settling in his groin. His cock hardened, and a hot puff of breath escaped him.

"God." Long-denied arousal rose hard, deep, and strong, almost bringing him to his knees. Unwilling to hold himself back, Jordan stroked his cock with long, firm pulls. After spreading his legs, he leaned his head against the wall and closed his eyes, fisting his cock harder and faster. Images flashed before his eyes, but for the first time they weren't of him and Keith making love. His hand faltered for a moment before his body demanded he continue.

It was Lucas he saw. And God help him, but Jordan wanted the man. He wanted Lucas's lips against his, that thick, smooth tongue in his mouth. His dick ached as the water beat onto his body, and he reached down to tug at his balls. Jordan didn't know whether it was from the drugs or his excitement, but it took only minutes before the pressure built and sparks shot through his body. He continued to stroke his cock harder and faster until he was moments away from coming in a glorious, all-encompassing burst of joy. The bathroom darkened and Jordan faltered and his hand dropped to his side.

A figure stood by the half-closed door.

"Jordan."

He swallowed his fear once he heard Lucas's voice. "Yeah?"

"Just letting you know I'm here."

The thought of Lucas right outside the bathroom door while he jerked off to thoughts of him ratcheted up his pleasure. He returned to sliding his hand up and down his full cock, spreading his legs wide to get solid footing.

"Thanks. I'll be done in a moment."

He knew how pathetic, how clichéd it was, to jerk off in the shower, but it was his home and he could do whatever the fuck he wanted. Thinking of the dichotomy between Lucas's heavy, muscular body and gentle soft mouth, Jordan braced himself against the marble shower wall as his hand flashed up and down his dick until, with a choked groan he hoped the rushing water masked, he came, shooting hard into his hand. A sigh of pleasure escaped and he closed his eyes.

"You okay?" Lucas's voice rose over the water.

A bit embarrassed, Jordan bit out a retort. "Of course I am. Go downstairs; I'll be there in a few minutes."

Without a response, Lucas left, shutting the bathroom door behind him.

TOWEL-DRIED AND FULLY dressed in shorts and a T-shirt, Jordan hesitated at the top step, then, deciding he had nothing to feel ashamed about, he ran down the stairs and headed into the kitchen. He couldn't help but smile as, predictably, Lucas was on the floor with Sasha's head in his lap. A powerful surge of lust and longing rolled through him. This was what he'd missed—the companionship, the mundane daily activities to share with another person. It seemed so natural for him to come to the kitchen and find Lucas there, playing with the dog.

Like he belonged.

"Hey." Jordan spoke softly, but it wasn't necessary. Sasha must've heard him and jumped up to greet him. She shook her head, jingling the tags on her collar, and stood at his feet, waiting to be petted.

Lucas opened his eyes. "Hi."

No longer interested in the gym, Jordan joined Lucas on the floor, his back to the cabinet doors. "You seem awfully quiet. I don't want to force you to spend time with me if you'd rather be alone."

"I've been alone my whole life. This is all new to me, having someone to talk to."

How sad. Like earlier on the porch, Jordan slid his hand over Lucas's. "I hope you know you can always talk to me. We may not have started out on the best terms, but I think we've moved beyond that now, am I right?"

Lucas shrugged. "I don't know anything anymore. I thought I wanted to be left alone, yet today I'm finding it hard to leave."

The raw honesty in Lucas's confession touched Jordan. "Then don't. Not yet, at least."

"Upstairs before, when I was in the bathroom…"

"Yes," said Jordan, the heat of desire once again flooding through him. "What about it?" Had Lucas seen him?

"I came inside and heard the shower running upstairs." A sideways glance revealed a glint of something in those changeable eyes.

Jordan's breath stilled, yet his heart thumped in his chest. "And?"

Lucas swallowed. "It was wrong of me but the thought of you upstairs, naked and wet, turned me on like crazy. I wanted to see you, touch you"—Jordan's eyes closed at the touch of Lucas's palm to his face—"taste you." Lucas's heated breath whispered over Jordan's cheeks. "After this afternoon I felt so close to you, closer than I ever have to anyone in my life."

"I did too, Lucas. For the first time in almost a year, I felt alive." Jordan opened his eyes and smiled.

His heartbeat slowed as Lucas's strong fingers caressed his jaw. Something had shifted earlier when they'd sat together on Esther's porch. It frightened him yet reminded him of what life had to offer, and maybe it was time to take that first step. He breathed in the subtle scent of Lucas, thoroughly male and completely intoxicating.

The look on Lucas's face, one of hesitant yearning and desire, sparked an answering throb in Jordan's chest. It hurt for a moment, this realization that he was moving on with his life, going forward and leaving pieces of himself behind. But those broken and damaged pieces weren't meant to be salvaged and reused. They belonged in the past, to a memory so sharp and beautiful he didn't need to replicate it. What he needed were new, fresh memories. Clean, unbroken lines.

A new life and, perhaps, a new love.

"I want you." He'd kept his heart quiet for too long.

Lucas froze, halting his soft strokes.

This time Jordan reached out and took the initiative. He stood and, with his hand curled around Lucas's bicep, pulled Lucas up with him. Swaying together, their bodies barely touching, was exquisite torture. He repeated himself. "I want you. I may not be ready for everything, but I want to hold you and touch you."

After a few moments of silence, Jordan's nerves escalated along with his rising embarrassment. Had he so grossly misread the situation?

Acting on emotion alone, Jordan drew Lucas into his arms and breathed a sigh of relief when Lucas gripped him tighter. Their cheeks touched, and Jordan could feel Lucas's lips against his cheek, so warm, so soft.

So alive.

"I want you too. I've never wanted anyone else in my life the way I want you." Lucas's voice rumbled against his jaw, deep, calm, and comforting.

Several moments passed, and the only sound was their mutual breathing. Even the dog understood their need for solitude and had left. Without hesitation,

Jordan took Lucas's hand and mounted the stairs, leading him back up to the second floor. At the doorway to his bedroom, he stopped and squeezed Lucas's hand. "After Keith died, I couldn't bear to sleep alone in our bed, so I moved it to the other bedroom and bought a new one." Waves of Lucas's chestnut curls fell over his eyes, and Jordan couldn't help but brush them back. Any excuse to touch.

He led Lucas across the bedroom to the king-sized four-poster bed and sat. Jordan patted the space next to him. "You're the only person, aside from myself, to ever be in this bed. I wanted you to know that, so you wouldn't think there are any ghosts between the two of us." He pulled the thin T-shirt over his head and Lucas followed his lead, stripping off his own shirt, then joined him on the bed.

"I'm glad you told me." Lucas smiled and touched Jordan's face, then tangled his hand in Jordan's hair, pulling him close. "Because when I kiss you and touch you, the only one I want you thinking of is me." Lucas bent his head and took Jordan's lips in a bruising kiss, claiming him.

And Jordan knew right then, he was Lucas's.

Chapter Eleven

SWEET. SO DAMN SWEET. Dizzy with desire, Luke spun out of control as he fell back on the bed. He still held on to Jordan's tight, slim body, their lips never breaking contact until Luke murmured, "Are you nervous?" He hoped the answer was no, though the pounding of Jordan's heart resonating against his chest answered that question. "You don't need to be. We don't have to do any more than this if you don't want." Jordan's heady scent, a mix of his light aftershave and warm, soft skin, filled Luke's senses. "It's all up to you. Whatever you want to give to me is what I'm willing to take."

Jordan blinked, pale blue eyes shining like twin flames in the glow of the early evening twilight. "I have everything I want right here with me now. All I want is you."

Luke swallowed hard as unfamiliar emotions swelled in his chest. He'd never had to concern himself with feelings—his own or others. He didn't want to remember what he had to do after he'd been released from the hospital and left Georgia, but couldn't help it as the memories flooded through him. The truckers and the men who had offered him rides up to New York City were friendly as all get-out when he first joined them. Then they became blatant about their expectations. At the first request for sex and his refusal, the trucker merely dumped him by the side of the road. The next time, Lucas was forced to take drugs that left him sick and shaking, unable to resist when the trucker pulled his pants off and flipped him over. That night he was left in the dark of the woods along the highway.

A few days later, when an expensive car pulled over and the well-dressed man, with a smile and a kind face, offered him a ride, he'd jumped. *James, call me James* was a pharmaceutical salesman and spent half the year on the road. Several hours later they pulled off into the woods, and the man had faced him and calmly stated that Luke could either blow him voluntarily or be shot full of whatever concoction he'd come up with and get fucked. His choice. Luke had complied, tears running down his face.

Each experience had caused him to build up a little more of a stone facade around his heart until he'd decided it was no longer worth the effort or the risk. When he made it to Washington DC, he'd resorted to begging on the streets for money rather than giving another blowjob, ever. As soon as he raised the fare for one of those cheap buses and some extra cash for food, he'd left that life behind, determined no one would take advantage of him again. Once he reached New

York City and met Wanda at the shelter, he knew he had to make something of himself and get an education so he would never be dependent on anyone again. He never touched drugs, no matter how many times they were offered. Even an aspirin was off limits as far as he was concerned.

"Lucas, where'd you go?" Jordan rolled off him, resting by his side.

Without the warmth of Jordan's body, Luke felt bereft, as if he was missing something of importance. "Don't. I like the feeling of you on top of me." He reached around and snuggled Jordan back onto his chest, giving him the opportunity to bury his lips in the man's silky golden hair. When he was young and still dreamed of love, he'd ached for a time like this with a lover, skin to skin and heart to heart.

"You seemed so far away, like you were thinking of something unpleasant." Jordan's lips moved against his shoulder. "Can I ask, was it about Ash?"

Shit. This wasn't supposed to happen. He should be making love to Jordan, not thinking of his mistakes. With a quick twist of his body, Luke rolled over and caged Jordan between his arms, his knees braced on either side of Jordan's slim hips. The man's eyes widened, but he didn't move.

"I'm not here to talk about him." That bastard would not invade his time with Jordan. A deliberate slide of his groin over Jordan's left them both shaking with desire. "I don't want to talk at all."

Another bump and grind of their bodies and Luke

couldn't keep himself from groaning out loud. As Jordan writhed beneath him, Luke stroked him, then yanked down the thin gym shorts, along with Jordan's briefs. Jordan's cock sprang out, pale and thick, surrounded by a nest of springy golden curls, the large flushed crown pearled with wetness. It took all of Luke's resistance to keep from pouncing on the man. He looked so sweet and vulnerable.

"Lucas." Jordan's hand reached out and touched him, brushing the front of his shorts where his own cock, woefully neglected, jerked and strained against the thin nylon. Their gazes locked on one another. A gleam of amusement entered Jordan's eyes. "I refuse to be the only one naked here." With a firm pull, Jordan slid the shorts and briefs past Luke's knees until Luke wriggled them off and tossed them onto the floor.

Finally, wonderfully, they were naked before one another, hot skin touching. Luke bent and kissed Jordan so hard, so deep they gasped for breath when they broke apart. The fervor with which Jordan returned his kisses surprised Luke. He'd thought with the prolonged abstinence, there would be some hesitancy. Instead Jordan's tongue pushed into his mouth, thrusting as if they were performing a mating ritual. Their cocks bumped and slid against one another, and Luke reached between them, wetting his hand with the precome leaking from both their erections.

At his touch, Jordan snapped his hips up hard. "God." Luke clenched his jaw and continued to rock back and forth. Normally Luke preferred to take control, but this time belonged to Jordan. It would be a gift for Jordan to rediscover his life and the passion he'd thought died forever with his lover.

And a gift for Jordan would be a gift for him.

"Go ahead, darlin'. Give it to me. I want it all." He brushed the hair off Jordan's face, the strands sliding between his fingers, as silky as he'd imagined. Luke's thumb trailed over Jordan's elegant cheekbones, coming to rest on his full lips. When Jordan drew Luke's thumb into the wet cavern of his mouth, twirling his tongue around it, pulling and sucking hard, Luke nearly came apart. They continued to rock together, sliding and rubbing their cocks, the sweat and slick building up on their straining bodies.

Jordan's pink lips clung to Luke's thumb as it slid in and out of Jordan's mouth. It was as erotic a scenario as Luke had ever been lucky to see. Electrified at the sound of Jordan's soft moans vibrating against Luke's finger, his body buzzed, flooded with unaccustomed desire. Jordan finally let go of Luke's thumb and thrashed his head back and forth on the pillow.

Luke thrust his hips against Jordan's, their slick fluids providing ample lubrication for his hand to slide up and down their lengths. Jordan's cock swelled, and he came, sending warm splashes of liquid across their stomachs.

"Ahhh, God," Jordan cried out, his hands clutching at the sheets by his sides. "Lucas."

With his eyes squeezed tight, teeth bared in an

almost primal grimace, and the strong cords of his neck standing out as he arched his body backward on the bed, Jordan's face was stunning in his orgasm.

A tingling in the root of Luke's cock curled around the base of his spine. Heat flushed through his body, pooling in his groin. He reached down to give himself several hard strokes, but Jordan got there first.

"My turn." Jordan's strong hand grasped him, and the man's long, elegant fingers encircled his cock. Spots glowed behind his closed eyes as Jordan rubbed faster and faster, thumb teasing his slit, fingers dancing up and down the sensitive shaft.

"Jordan, please." Luke found himself begging for release.

"Don't you like the way I'm touching you?" Jordan's hands never ceased their firm, deliberate movements.

He opened his eyes to find Jordan's clear gaze on him. "Yes. I like the fact that it's you." Where the hell had that come from? Lucas couldn't believe those words were coming from his mouth. He never talked to his partners during sex. It was all about him coming and then going, leaving as fast as he could. But now, he didn't want to leave. He yearned to know what it might be like to wake up in a lover's arms.

"Come on, Lucas," Jordan whispered in his ear, hands slippery yet sure and deliberate as he stroked and rubbed Luke's cock. The caress in Jordan's soft voice set off goose pimples up and down Luke's arms, and he moaned, his entire body tightening in anticipation.

Like a fire searing through his chest, incinerating whatever fortress he'd created, Luke's orgasm hit him hard, and he erupted all over Jordan's hands, overflowing as if he'd been holding back forever. Exhausted from the stress of the day, he collapsed on top of Jordan.

Minutes passed, and they remained locked together, their raspy, mingled breathing the only sound in the room. Jordan shifted, and Luke recognized he must be crushing the man.

"Hey, Prep School." He loved teasing Jordan with that name. It was too perfect for his haughty looks and superior airs, even though Luke knew better than that now, having spent enough time with Jordan to see his true, giving nature. "I'm going to take a shower; then don't think you're getting away without a training session from me."

"I thought I'd proved my staying power just now." A lazy smile curled Jordan's lips.

Luke's heart did a funny somersault when Jordan reached up and brushed the curls off his forehead, and for a moment, he found it hard to breathe. He couldn't resist grabbing a quick kiss, their tongues twisting and sliding against each other. After almost losing his resolve to leave the bed, he pulled away from Jordan's hungry mouth. "I consider this cardio. I can't have you thinking I'm letting you get off easy."

Jordan's eyes danced with amusement. "You got me off pretty hard, I'm thinking." Then he smiled and stretched. "I'll let you have the first shower." Jordan fell back against the pillows and lay still, the smile remaining on his face.

"I won't be long." Luke picked up his clothes from the floor and headed into the bathroom. The thought of Jordan in bed all alone—and wonderfully sleep disheveled—set his body humming for a possible repeat performance. He jumped into the shower and quickly rinsed off the evidence of their lovemaking. Not five minutes later he turned off the taps and dried himself off. Damn, he'd forgotten to bring antiperspirant. He always forgot something when he went to the gym.

"I'm gonna use your deodorant, okay?"

"Sure. No problem. I'll be there in a minute." Jordan sounded content and happy, not regretful or, even worse, silent and uncommunicative as Luke feared after the man's first sexual experience since Keith's death.

Luke opened the medicine cabinet and reached inside, but he faltered before he could take the stick out. "What the fuck?" His brow furrowed as he stared at the shelves and tried to make sense of what he was seeing. The entire middle shelf was filled with glassine baggies of pills. Little yellow pills. As if in slow motion, he plucked one off the shelf and held it in his hands. The pills rolled between his fingers, and he traced their shape as if he couldn't believe they were real. Xannies. Not prescription grade.

From his time on the streets of DC and at the shelter here in the city, Luke knew exactly what those pills were and what all those bags meant. Jordan bought on the streets. His mouth tightened, lips twisting in disgust. Drugs. An involuntary shiver ran through him. Why would Jordan be buying drugs off the street? It didn't make sense. Why?

"Hey, what happened? You're so quiet—" Jordan burst through the door, a smile on his face until he caught a glimpse of what Luke still held in his hand. He turned pale, and Luke watched fear replace the happiness in his eyes. "Lucas, it's not what you think."

Fucking liar. "Yeah? Go on, then. Tell me what I'm thinking."

Jordan advanced on him, but Luke would be damned if he'd let the man touch him in his pathetic attempt to prevent questions. He sidestepped away and moved toward the door. Jordan grabbed his arm.

"Lucas, please."

Disgusted, he shook off Jordan's hand. "Don't touch me. You, a doctor no less, buying drugs off the street. Probably from some poor street kid who's on something himself. How dare you?" His voice shook, breaking on the question. "You're helping these kids dig their own graves by supporting what they're doing. And you have the nerve to work at a foundation to prevent drugs and gun violence?" Luke couldn't help but laugh, but there was no happiness in the sound.

"Let me explain, please." Jordan's gaze clashed with his, and for a moment Luke relented. There was true remorse in Jordan's eyes. Afraid of what Jordan might say, Luke remained silent.

Jordan crowded close to him, so close Luke could feel the puffs of Jordan's breath against his cheek. The only thing Luke wanted to do was close his eyes and wrap his arms around Jordan, and it took an enormous strength of will to hold himself back.

"Ever since Keith died, I haven't been able to sleep. I didn't want to leave the house or see anyone." Jordan licked his lips, then bit down on the bottom one, worrying it between his teeth.

Luke crossed his arms. "Yeah, I know. Remember I had to threaten you to honor your obligation to the foundation."

Jordan dipped his head, his gaze trained on the floor. "I wanted to die. The pain crushed me and my will to live."

Luke had to lean forward to hear Jordan's words. Pain squeezed his heart at the anguished sound of Jordan's voice. Would Jordan ever forget Keith? What a fool he was to think Jordan might have started to move on.

"But then I got that letter from you about the foundation, and once I became more involved, I knew I needed to live again, if for nothing else than to make sure Keith didn't die in vain." Jordan swallowed, and a shudder racked his body. He lifted his gaze from the floor, and Luke's resolve almost faltered at the absolute devastation in Jordan's eyes. Almost.

"I'm not hearing anything I don't already know, Jordan."

"I know you're mad when you don't call me Prep School," Jordan joked, but when Luke refused to play along, he raked his hand through his hair and continued. "My doctor prescribed Xanax for me, to deal with the anxiety and depression. It was as if the clouds had been erased. All the blackness disappeared once I took the pills."

Luke growled at him, angry at his naïveté. "Dumbass. You traded one problem for another. And you got hooked, didn't you?"

When Jordan hesitated, Luke couldn't hold back, answering for him. "You did. And it became like water to drink and air to breathe. After a while one pill wasn't enough. It became two, then three, right?" Once again, Jordan didn't answer, but Luke became ruthless and unrelenting.

"How many do you take a day, Jordan? Tell me, goddamn it."

The man had gone mute. Luke grabbed the baggies out of the medicine chest and began throwing them at Jordan. "I bet you'll take six or seven at least, right?" His voice rose as he continued clearing out the shelves, the pills spilling from the bags to bounce on the floor, scattering all over. *Little yellow bullets of death.* "And it's not enough, that craving, that *want*. You need more and more." He waited for a denial, to hear Jordan tell him he was crazy. There could possibly be some crazy, outlandish reason why there were hundreds of Xanax pills in his medicine cabinet.

"I can stop if I want to." Jordan's attempt to sound defiant came off as weak and pathetic.

"That's what every addict says." Luke's harsh voice echoed off the tiled walls of the bathroom. This was a nightmare, his nightmare. It was everything he swore he'd never become involved with. His life had been fine until he'd fucked up and fallen for a man he barely knew. This was why he never did relationships. The pain circling his chest tightened like a vise, threatening to crush his heart. Unbearable.

"I'd already decided tonight, before you came, that I wouldn't take anymore, I swear."

"Yeah, sure." Lucas laughed, the taste of betrayal and heartbreak bitter, like ash in his mouth. "You can stop anytime you want to, right? You're a bigger fool than I thought if you believe that."

"I'm not an addict because I need a little help coping."

"You're an addict because you can't stop taking these pills. Are you that fucking clueless? Because this"—he picked up the prescription bottle—"this is the only legal way to get what you need, but your doctor obviously doesn't think you need them. But you want them. So you took it on yourself to get them illegally. That's not coping."

Jordan sank to the floor and rested his head against the wall. "You can't imagine what it was like. One minute he was there, the center of my world, and the next, he was gone. And without me ever getting a chance to talk to him. To hear his voice again." Grief creased his face, the tears trickling down his cheeks. "Without a chance to say I loved him and say goodbye."

Luke knew he was meant to be alone, but it was his

choice. Jordan had his whole life taken away from him with one fatal shot. "He knew how much you loved him. He felt the same way."

The sweet, vulnerable smile that broke across Jordan's face nearly undid Luke. "He told you that?"

Luke nodded and wondered again if Jordan had fooled himself into believing he could move on. Shockingly, a desperate need grew within Luke to have someone think about him, dream about him, love him the way Jordan loved Keith. He wanted that look on someone's face when they thought about him.

He wanted to see it on Jordan's face.

Once again, Jordan clutched at his arm. He could almost smell the panic rolling off Jordan's skin. "Then you can understand why I needed something to chase the demons away. If I didn't, I might have killed myself. There were days I thought about it, and the only reason I didn't was the knowledge of how much it would hurt my parents." Another long shudder rolled through Jordan's frame.

Jordan needed serious help, beyond what Luke could offer. "Drugs aren't the answer, though. You're heading for disaster. I-I care about you, Jordan. I don't want to see you addicted. Buying drugs off the street is dangerous. You could get hurt or die." From the highs of today to this absolute low, Luke felt emotionally drained and at a tipping point. This was, however, a line in the sand he wasn't willing to cross. "You need to contact your doctor, get into more intense therapy, and give them up."

A weaker man might have crumbled at the discovery of such a humiliating secret. Not Jordan, however. The pale blue gaze held his, and Lucas saw not weakness but strength and determination. "I know. But you can't go cold turkey off this type of pill or you can die. I promise I'm giving them up and will start weaning myself off them." The vulnerability was back in his face, in the arch of his brow and the curve of his mouth. "I care about you as well, Lucas. I feel as though I've let you down somehow."

"Does anyone else know? Drew, Mike, or your family? Perhaps we could strategize and come up with a plan to help you." But he should've known Jordan's pride would forbid such a revelation to his friends.

"God, no." The vehemence in Jordan's voice surprised him.

"I just thought, since they are your best friends—"

"Can you imagine Ash finding out? That bastard would hold it over my head for the rest of my life." Even as he pleaded with Luke, the distaste for Ash dripped from Jordan's voice. "I don't want their pity or for them to worry about me. Promise you won't say anything to them. Please, Lucas."

As he stood contemplating the damaged man crouching on the bathroom floor, something unfamiliar rose within him. It might have been as innocuous as pity, but Luke didn't think so. He'd never pitied anyone for the choices they made. Growing up, he'd had no choices—being placed in foster care, Ash leaving them; nothing in his life had been within his control. Until he'd been forced to make it on his own when he was abandoned by his foster family. Even then, the men who'd picked him up when he hitch-hiked up north controlled his body.

And if it had been anyone else, he'd have walked right out and never looked back. There'd never been room in his life for second chances before. But this was Jordan. Maybe it was the slight tremor in his voice as Jordan pleaded with him, or how his tousled hair fell over his eyes like a little boy's. Or, as Luke sank down next to Jordan on the bathroom floor, it might have been the flutter of those gold-tinted lashes against his pale cheeks. Lucas didn't want to think of what else it might be. The need to touch Jordan whenever they were together. To hold him close and feel his warmth, smell his skin. To taste him. To hear his name cried out in passion and desire as Jordan climaxed underneath him.

"Lucas, I couldn't bear it if you left me now. I need you. Help me? Please?"

Whatever held him to this man, as he took a trembling Jordan into his arms, Luke couldn't imagine leaving him. Ever.

And that scared him more than anything else.

Chapter Twelve

AFTER THAT EXPLOSIVE evening, Jordan barely saw Lucas over the next month and a half. Work on overseas clients' portfolios had him traveling to Europe and then Asia. He called frequently, their conversations revolving mainly around how he was glad Jordan was doing his best to give up the pills. There was nothing personal, no indication that Lucas thought about him or might be missing him.

Maybe as much as Jordan missed him.

Perhaps he was being too needy, too self-absorbed and foolish, but his heart controlled his head, and he wanted Lucas to call and talk to him about, well…the two of them. Like that first breath of sweet springtime air after a miserable winter of slush and snow, Jordan wanted to embrace it and revel in the rebirth of his feelings and the reawakening of his heart.

Lucas's only concern, it seemed, was Jordan's pills.

JORDAN STOOD IN his backyard, listening to the breeze sigh through the leaves, and sipped his drink. Sasha snuffled through the grass, bounding this way and that, happy to be outside in the cool evening air. Every once in a while, she'd come running back up to the deck looking for a scratch or a treat.

It was one of those rare evenings when an earlier rain had washed the air clean, and even in the city he could see the stars, winking faint in the darkening sky. He tipped his head back and studied their glittering cobwebs, spreading across the night.

"What am I supposed to do?" He spoke to no one in particular, as Sasha had returned to the bushes, investigating a particularly tantalizing rustle. The iced vodka slid down his throat, cool and numbing, but did nothing to ease the ache of loneliness. These past few months had seen a change in him as he settled into his routine from before Keith had died. Surgery and rounds at the hospital in the morning, then Drew's clinic three afternoons a week. Where he'd once spent his free time with Keith, Drew, or Mike, his friends now had separate lives that didn't include him. Not that he'd even asked. Once or twice he'd thought about approaching Drew to talk, but the nausea rose, thick and powerful, to twist in his stomach, and he'd chickened out. Instead he spent hours with Sasha or, to his own surprise, working out at the gym.

And he continued to take the Xanax. He went back inside to refill his drink and his hand tightened around the liquor bottle as he poured more vodka into his empty glass. Sure, he'd cut down, but no one realized how hard it was to wean himself off the pills. Not that anyone knew, since he chose to do it alone. The thought of telling anyone of his addiction caused panic to rise in his chest, once again making it difficult to catch his breath. He knew he was making it doubly hard by doing it alone, but pride wouldn't allow him to reveal his weakness to his friends and colleagues.

You're such a fucking coward.

"I am not," he answered the taunting voice inside his head, speaking only to the wind. He gulped his drink and stroked Sasha, who, tiring of her play, came to lay at his feet. Thank God for her. She made him feel wanted and needed again. Her warm tongue bathed his bare ankle. His hand shook a bit when he raised his glass to his lips.

Have you tried to stop? And replacing pills with booze isn't what Lucas meant.

"Fuck him…" He wondered if Lucas understood how hurt he was by the phone calls that only concentrated on the pills. Having sex with him, simply getting naked with another man had changed the dynamic of the relationship for Jordan. He'd never been one to give his body any more easily than he gave his heart. Both were sacred to him. It was why he couldn't understand Ash and his man-whore ways before he'd met Drew. Was that all Jordan was to Lucas, a quick fuck? He'd always been a decent judge of character, and Lucas certainly behaved like a man who cared. And if he cared, why couldn't Lucas say he missed Jordan?

So, though Jordan had cut down a pill or two, he'd replaced it with vodka, hoping to push back against the gnawing panic inside of him. While it didn't help much for the loneliness, it numbed him to everything else. One thing he made certain was never to drink or take pills before he operated. If his hands shook a bit more lately, he'd been using the residents on his team more and more to do the actual surgery. Once or twice one of the doctors looked at him a bit strangely, but he ignored them, his normal arrogance reappearing to keep away any questions.

He felt a bit guilty, knowing he'd promised Lucas to cut down, but as the days stretched into weeks, the other man's lack of intimate, personal conversations fed Jordan's insecurity. Maybe it was time to talk to Drew and settle things between them. Thirty years of friendship should stand for something after all. They should be able to speak to each other about anything. Before he could think too hard about it, he picked up his phone and pushed the speed-dial number he'd set for Drew.

"Jordy? What's wrong?"

Well, what did he expect? The fact that he hadn't called Drew in almost a year would account for the guarded and wary tone in his friend's voice.

"Nothing. I-I wanted to talk to you and was wondering if we could meet." The words tumbled out before he had a chance to think too carefully.

"You do? When, now? I could be there in twenty minutes."

Jordan couldn't help but smile into the phone. Drew could never hide his feelings. His heart shone like a beacon from everything he did and said. No wonder Ash had fallen for him. "Yeah. I do. But it can wait until tomorrow. I have rounds at seven, but can we meet for breakfast afterward, say nine thirty?"

"Sure, of course. The diner across from the hospital? Like we used to, remember?" Drew's excitement strengthened Jordan's resolve to make amends. Nothing positive happened while holding on to his resentment. It was killing him to be cut off from the people he loved. And deep inside, he knew his estrangement would anger Keith, who had also loved Drew and Mike.

These were the people who made his life, not men with whispered promises who broke apart his dreams.

"Yeah, the diner. Sounds good."

"Okay, great, I'll see you then. And Jordy?" Drew's voice softened.

"Yeah?"

"I'm really glad you called."

"Me too, Drew. I'll see you tomorrow."

He hung up and smiled. Step one to forgetting Lucas Conover was on track.

AT NINE FORTY the next morning, Jordan pushed open the glass-fronted door of the Ticktock Diner. As interns and then residents, he and Drew had spent innumerable hours here, drinking endless cups of coffee and eating their enormous breakfasts. They'd meet whenever they could to catch up during the week, when life was so crazy back in those early, sleepless days of their medical careers.

"Dr. Jordan, welcome. So good to see you again." Peter Stavros, the owner, greeted him, a wide smile on his face. The gray-haired owner and his wife, Elena, came out from behind the counter filled with delicious, home-baked desserts to shake his hand and, in Elena's case, give him a hug.

"We've missed you." Elena looked him up and down with a critical eye. "You're too skinny. You haven't been eating, have you?" Her keen brown gaze missed nothing.

"I'm fine, both of you. Stop worrying." He accepted her kiss. "Is Drew here? I'm supposed to meet him."

Peter pointed to the booth they normally sat in. "Yes, he's been here awhile. Does he have a secret? He looks so happy."

Holding back his own grin, Jordan shook his head. "Not that I'm aware." But he knew it was the fact that he'd called, and he took it as a good sign. Jordan only hoped it would turn out with them still remaining friends. "I'll see you later."

This place had been his second home ten years ago, his steps taking him past the tables and the long counter, behind which the harried waitstaff called out orders. Most of them had been there for years, and they shouted out greetings to him as he walked by. All of them had shown up for Keith's funeral, and Peter and Elena had closed the diner for the day, something they never did.

Drew sat in their usual booth, checking his phone.

"Hey, D, how's it going?" Jordan stopped by the table before sitting down. The smile on Drew's face told him everything he needed to know. It would be all right. He simply had to get it out, and they could move past this.

"I'm good, great. How are you? You look better than the last time I saw you." Drew shot him a quick look before slipping his phone in his pocket. "Do you still have the dog?" He pushed his hair back and shook his head. "This fucking sucks, man."

Jordan slid into the booth. "What does?"

The waitress approached to refill Drew's coffee, pour Jordan a cup, and take their orders. They waited until she left to start their conversation again.

"We're talking as if we're strangers, like people who barely know each other. Jordy, please talk to me. I'll make it right. I can't stand this." Drew's eyes glittered with unshed tears, while his pale skin flushed red.

Jordan steeled himself for what he knew would be the hardest conversation he'd ever had with his best friend. Shit, even coming out to him hadn't scared Jordan as much.

"It'll be a year next week that Keith's been gone." He watched as Drew's face softened in sympathy. "I've changed so much I hardly recognize myself anymore, and not all of it has been for the better."

The waitress approached with a refill of their coffee and their orders. After dealing with condiments and buttering bagels and toast, Jordan began again. "I want to apologize for cutting you out of my life. I was in a bad, dark place, and I blamed you for it."

After swallowing his eggs, Drew set his fork down on the table. "Tell me."

Here goes nothing. He gulped down his coffee, then set the cup on the table. "I-I blamed you for Keith's death. Let me finish." He held up a hand as Drew opened his mouth, whether to defend himself or protest, it didn't matter. Jordan needed to say what was in his heart and head.

"I tried not to think like that. It destroyed me. Here I'd lost my lover and I couldn't turn to you, my best friend, because I blamed you. If only you hadn't run after those kids. If you'd only waited for backup at your apartment, things might've been different." He glanced up to see tears running down Drew's face. *Shit.* He knew this was a bad idea. "D, I'm sorry." He reached over the table and covered Drew's hand with his.

"I remember that night, replayed it in my mind a million times, wishing I'd behaved differently." Drew managed to speak finally, after wiping his tears away with his napkin. He grabbed Jordan's hand with both of his. "I knew it was the reason you were angry with me. Jordan, please." He stopped, his voice breaking.

"D, it's okay, really. It'll be all right. I promise." The anguish on Drew's face was almost too painful for him to watch.

"No, no, now give me the chance. You have every right to feel that way. I told Ash you'd resent me. I tried to come to you and talk it out but you wouldn't speak to me. I didn't blame you. It was all too fresh. But I should've pushed harder after a few weeks, and I do blame myself for that. Now it's been festering almost a year." Drew squeezed his hand. "Let me have this time to do what I should've done right away."

Jordan remained silent and nodded.

After inhaling a deep breath, Drew blew it out with a gusty sigh. "I'm sorry. I fucked up so badly and I've beaten myself to death with my guilt over the very fact that if I'd done as you said, Keith would be alive. It was my fault he died, and I let you push me away because it was easier to have you hate me than face what I'd done."

"No, now you have to stop. D, please." Jordan shook off his hands. "Look at me." A moment passed before Drew picked up his head, anguish etched in his face. "I could never hate you. I'm the one who's sorry. I never should've let this happen. It's true I resented you at first, and I let that take over whatever good sense I had left at the time." His mind chased briefly to the pills he'd taken this morning and how already his anxiety had come fluttering back to life, beating against his chest, blooming through his bloodstream. This wasn't the time to think about his craving to make the panic disappear. Forcing his mind back to Drew, he squeezed his eyes shut for a moment to re-center himself.

"I was wrong. It more than likely would've happened the same way whether you waited or not for backup. Keith wasn't wearing his bulletproof vest—why would he when he was off duty and attending a party? He should never have gone there without it on." Jordan took Drew's hands in his. "I'm sorry for shutting you out and resenting you. I should've handled it better, and I know we can't go back, but can we start again? The thought of losing you—and Mike and Rachel as well—is killing me."

He bit his lip, watching the play of emotions flicker across Drew's face. Then, to his eternal relief, Drew's sweet smile broke out, wiping away all traces of fear, grief, and hurt.

"It should be me asking you, but if this helps, of course. And you could never lose us. My life this past year sucked, even with all the good things that happened to me. Nothing was the same without having you there to share it with me."

They sat and grinned at each other, and Jordan could almost hear Keith's voice in his head. *I'm proud of you, babe. You did the right thing.*

Jordan motioned the waitress over, who he knew had kept away from their table as their conversation unfolded. She now approached, Peter and Elena on her heels.

"Can we both have some more coffee, please?" She poured, her lips curled in disgust, and left in a hurry. Whether it was because she couldn't handle two gay men who obviously had some sort of personal issues to work out, or the fact that her bosses were standing right on top of her, Jordan had no idea, nor did he care. He had Drew back in his life, and that's all that mattered at the moment.

"You two are fine now? We missed seeing you here together. It wasn't the same when it was only you and your good-looking man, Dr. Drew." Elena teased, and Drew's cheeks stained red, but Elena continued. "He certainly loves you; that's for sure. Breaks the girls' hearts in here all the time when they find out he's not interested in them, only you."

Jordan couldn't help but chuckle to himself as Drew and Elena continued to chat. Drew and Ash. Still a couple he couldn't fathom. Ash was one of the few men to set him on edge every time they met. Maybe Jordan couldn't get past knowing the man and his reputation before Ash had met Drew, yet here Ash was, a year later and stronger than ever with Drew. He'd never believed Asher Davis had the desire or ability to be faithful, but for once it pleased him to be proven wrong. And Drew had never looked happier.

Ash's place in Drew's life as his lover and partner caused part of his own resentment, he could admit to himself, if no one else. Jordan's subsequent displacement as the person Drew turned to for help and guidance left him somewhat adrift in their relationship. This past year and their separation forced him to come to terms with the fact that he wasn't responsible for Drew's well-being. They were no longer on the playground with him defending Drew and Mike against the bigger kids; it wasn't the first day of school when he walked with them to class, showing them the way so they wouldn't get lost. They didn't need his protection or help any longer. It had taken him long enough to realize, but the time had come for him to stop running their lives and try and manage his own.

Peter and Elena had finally withdrawn, after enthusing again how happy they were to see them both together. He and Drew sat, drinking their coffee, when his phone buzzed with a text. He pulled it out of his pocket, and his day darkened when he saw who it was from.

> I'm back. Getting settled in. Looking forward to seeing you. How's the center shaping up? Maybe we can talk later?

Lucas. His body quickened and grew tight at the thought of him. The memory of his strong mouth and teasing hands instantly had Jordan craving his touch. His traitorous cock grew hard, pressing against his trousers.

Angry at his body's response to a mere text from the man, no matter that he hadn't seen him in almost two months, Jordan shoved the phone back into his pocket. Guilt slammed into him as he recalled his promise to Lucas about cutting back on the pills. He'd barely cut back and was drinking more to compensate for the crushing loneliness that surrounded him when he came home to his empty house. A dog could give him only so much.

"Who's that? Not that I'm trying to pry or anything, but you looked like you wanted to throw the phone across the room." Drew finished his food and sat back in the booth.

"Lucas." He reached for his cup, but it was empty.

"Are you two, um, involved?"

Involved? Jordan didn't know what the hell they were, and that was his problem. He'd never behaved like this before, jumping into bed with a man, letting his body overrule his mind. With Keith, it had never been a choice. They'd shared something special right from the start. Their relationship had been passionate, sweet, and tender. Love should be peaceful and calm— a serene feeling of trust and caring. It's what he craved. He'd fallen in love with Keith as easily as breathing. If Keith had lived, Jordan knew he would have loved him forever.

But time was an evil thief of dreams. Keith was gone, taking their plans for the future with him. The ricocheting emotions from Jordan's days spent with Lucas kept him constantly on edge, never knowing what was about to happen, wanting something, unsure of what. It was volatile and explosive, the kind of passion that spoke of twisted, sweaty sheets and walls echoing from the cries of lovemaking.

"I have no idea. For the past month and a half he's been away on business, traveling through Europe and Asia, seeing clients. We've kept in touch." Jordan could hardly tell Drew the truth. *If being involved means getting some amazingly hot sex, then yeah. But then he found my stash of pills, and that's all he cares about really. Me getting off the drugs, not him and me together.*

He signaled the waitress to bring the check. She scuttled over, not meeting his gaze, and dropped it on the table, retreating immediately. Definitely not happy with her gay customers. *Screw her.*

"Those financial companies will suck the life out of you. Ash has some clients whose families barely see them. Sometimes all it can take is a bad investment decision or losing one high-profile client and the company lets them go immediately. No room for error." Drew pulled out his wallet and dropped a ten-dollar bill on the table. "Take that."

"Don't be an asshole. I'm paying. You'll get the next one." Jordan pushed the money back and saw a smile tug at Drew's lips.

"There's my Jordan. Glad to have you back." He pocketed the money. "Well, I think you two make a good couple if you're ready. But he's nothing like Keith, am I right? He's very serious and quiet. Ash said he was like that even as a boy."

Ignoring Drew's not-so-subtle prying, Jordan chose to satisfy his own curiosity. "Why did Ash leave home? I'm sure you know. Lucas refuses to talk about it, but I know it's the reason he's walled himself off from everyone. He's so resentful of Ash."

Shutters rolled down over Drew's face, eliminating his good humor, surprising Jordan. "I can't say; it's not my story to tell. What I can say is that Lucas is wrong about Ash's feelings and past behavior. Once he was in a position to do so, he never stopped looking for his brothers—Luke or Brandon. It's all he thought about, and it almost killed him. He still has an investigator looking for Brandon, even now."

"You saved him, didn't you, like you always do. You're a rescuer, Drew. It's what makes you so special."

Drew shrugged. "I don't know about that. He saved me too, from living a life without passion, and never taking chances, always allowing other people to tell me what to do."

"Like me, right?" Now that they were being totally honest with one another, Jordan couldn't help but ask.

"Yeah. I said it before. You had to let go and let me make my own choices. Being with Ash is the best thing that ever happened to me. I only hope you open your own heart again and find someone. There's so much love in you; there always has been. You need someone who can appreciate you. And if it's Lucas, then we'll all somehow work it out together, like a family."

Jordan's head whirled as they left the diner. He and Drew made plans to meet again, and he watched his friend walk away. He should've told Drew about the pills. If he was ever to try and have a real relationship with Lucas, he needed to give them up. Who knew if that was even a choice anymore? Fear spiraled through him at the mere thought of doing without them. As a doctor, he knew the incessant cravings, the slight shakes, and loss of focus were signs he was heading toward disaster. There was only so much Jordan could have other doctors cover for him. Maybe now with Drew back in his life, Jordan could talk to his friends again and ask for support. For the first time, he was the weak one, the one who needed help.

But if he didn't stop now, sooner or later his heart would give out from the strain of the drugs. He no longer wanted to die; that had been the grief and anger taking over. Spending time with Drew again was all it took for him to remember how good life had been, what he'd been missing out on.

Determination rose within him, fierce and hot within his blood, to take back his life.

"Drew," he called out, and Drew, who'd only made it halfway down the block, stopped and turned around. Jordan jogged over to him. "Could you call Mike and come over tonight? I need to tell you guys something."

Chapter Thirteen

C HRIST, IT FELT good to be home. Luke pushed his suitcase into the living room, then slammed the door behind him. After being away so long and living in so many hotel rooms, his apartment seemed enormous. He was a little afraid to open his fridge, remembering too late, when he stepped on the plane over a month and a half ago, that he'd forgotten to throw out whatever food he had.

A quick toss into the trash remedied that situation. He'd deal with the rest of the cleanup later. First he needed a shower, then a power nap. Funny, he'd never received an answer from the text he'd sent Jordan earlier after the plane had landed. Hmm. Maybe Jordan was in surgery or with a patient. Shedding suit jacket, shirt, and tie as he walked to the bathroom, Luke gazed with longing at his bed. He couldn't wait to relax, but he first needed to wash away the travel dirt and feel clean again. Then Luke would call Jordan and see how the final arrangements for the center had worked out and how Jordan was feeling now that he had given up the pills. Surely by this time, he'd made significant progress. After all, Jordan was an incredibly strong-willed person, and he hadn't been taking them that long.

After his shower, Luke settled into bed, relishing the smooth sheets and familiar comfort. Nothing like your own bed after a long trip, even if he slept alone. His mind wandered back to that afternoon with Jordan. The sex had been nothing short of amazing, but that wasn't what kept his interest piqued. Something about that man, all skin and bones and blazing arrogance, had intrigued him from the moment Jordan had walked into his office. Secretly, he'd been a little envious of Keith since he'd first seen a picture of Jordan. Luke had always had a thing for the blond-haired, blue-eyed Nordic type, but it was more than his looks that intrigued him so about Jordan.

Self-confidence with a touch of ego was a huge turn-on for Luke. He never went for the helpless type or a man who needed to cling tight. When they were young, Ash, fearless and arrogant, had been Luke's hero. He shook his head angrily. No way would he allow Ash to intrude on his thoughts, especially where Jordan was concerned.

Even from their first meeting, when Jordan lived in his darkest, most sorrowful place, his natural leadership qualities and pride had shone through, making him a damn sexy man. Luke thought about all the times he'd wanted to call him this past month, simply to say hello or maybe engage in a little transatlantic raunchy phone sex, but hadn't found the right moment. Later, after his nap, as his mind was too clouded now by sleep to think anymore, he'd call Jordan and arrange to get together. He turned over on his side and hugged the pillow close as his eyelids drifted shut.

THE ROOM CAME into focus, shrouded in darkness. A quick glance at the luminous dial of his bedside clock showed the time at nine thirty. *Shit.* He'd slept for almost eight hours. He rolled out of bed and stretched. Damn, he'd really needed it, though. Energy now hummed through his body, and his stomach growled.

Predictably, the food had been lousy on the plane thus he'd had very little to eat the entire day. Maybe Jordan would want to catch a quick bite, even late as it was, so he reached for his phone to call him. Thinking maybe Jordan had called or texted him while he was sleeping, he checked his messages first.

Nothing. Hmm, that was strange. His stomach clenched at the thought that something might've happened to Jordan while he was away. Maybe the drugs…shit no. He would've heard something, right? Without stopping to think, he hit the button for Jordan's phone. It went straight to voicemail. Now more than a little concerned, he scrolled down to the lesser used landline number. It rang three times; then finally, someone answered.

A dog barked in the background, and Luke

couldn't help but smile. He'd missed Sasha too.

"Hello?"

That didn't sound like Jordan's voice. "Uh, hi, is Jordan there?"

"Who's calling?"

The voice sounded familiar, but he still couldn't place it. "It's Luke."

"Oh, hey, Luke, it's Drew."

Luke relaxed. Right. Drew. Why wouldn't he be there? Jordan and he were best friends, and even though their friendship had been strained, Luke was glad Jordan still had his friends in his life to support him.

"Is he there? I got back a few hours ago." Wow, he was smooth. Could he sound any more like a bumbling idiot?

"Yeah, sure, hold on a sec." Luke heard Drew call out. "Jordy, Luke's on the phone." Luke could only make out a low murmur of voices; then Jordan came on the phone.

"Hello."

The curt, almost unfriendly tone of Jordan's voice surprised him. "Hey, Prep School, didn't you get my text before? I got home earlier and fell asleep for the whole afternoon."

He laughed, then stopped as he realized he was laughing solo. "What's the matter? Is everything all right?"

"Everything's fine."

Yeah, right. Ice cubes radiated more warmth than

Jordan right now. "Bullshit. What's wrong with you?"

"Nothing. Thanks for calling, but I'm a little busy right now."

"But—"

Click.

What the fuck?

"Son of a bitch." The walls echoed with his angry growl. "That bastard hung up on me. Who the hell does he think he is?" He picked a pillow off his bed and threw it across the room, unable to fathom why Jordan would be angry at him. Luke stormed across the room and picked up the pillow to place it back on the bed. Since everything looked better on a full stomach, he decided to bring the mountain to Mohammed.

A little more than an hour later, he waited on the top step of Jordan's brownstone, a bag of Magnolia Bakery cupcakes in one hand, the other holding takeout from his favorite Italian restaurant. He pressed the bell and waited. A grin spread over his face as he heard the frantic barking of Sasha and Jordan pretending annoyance, shushed her. The curtain covering the glass part of the door parted, and Luke met Jordan's eyes. The curtain fell back.

When the door didn't open after a moment or two, Luke rapped on the glass. "Come on, Prep School, let me in."

Another few heartbeats, then the door opened. Sasha jumped up on him, whining and licking whatever part of him she could reach. Luke couldn't help but laugh as he made a fuss over her, then followed her into the house after kicking the door closed behind him.

Faint moonlight streaming in through the kitchen windows outlined the silhouette of Jordan's body standing by the center island. As Luke walked down the hallway to join him in the kitchen, he had the chance to admire Jordan's broad shoulders, tapering to a narrow waist and slim hips. Muscles that hadn't been there before now rippled slightly under his tight white T-shirt. Luke's entire body hardened as Jordan tipped his head back, draining his drink.

"Jordan." With a muttered curse, Luke dropped the bags on the island and pulled him close, his mouth hungry for a taste of Jordan's lips. It was as electric a feeling as before, their mouths coming together in a clash of lips, tongues, and teeth. He palmed Jordan's firm ass as he rubbed himself against the tight body he'd dreamed about these past weeks, lying alone in his hotel room. He could feel the thick length of Jordan's erection through the thin sweats he wore. "Damn, I've missed this."

It took him several moments to realize that Jordan had stopped responding. He wasn't hugging Luke back, and after that heady kiss, his lips had gone hard and unyielding. Luke pulled back, confused at Jordan's withdrawal.

"What's the matter with you? Is anything wrong? I thought you'd be glad to see me." His knuckles brushed along the fine bones of Jordan's cheek. Jordan shivered in response but stepped out of his arms to circle the center island in the kitchen, placing the wide slab of granite between them like a great divide. He dropped down onto one of the stools and splashed some vodka into his glass. Straight vodka, Luke noticed.

"I'm fine. Why wouldn't I be?" His tone, in direct contradiction to his words, spoke volumes. It came out cold and clipped, not at all the way you sounded when you were happy to see a person after he'd been gone for so long. With the practiced ease of a long-standing drinker, Jordan downed half the glass.

"Well, for starters, I texted you hours ago, and you never responded. Then earlier when we talked, you hung up on me." Luke busied himself by taking out the food—baked ziti and chicken parmigiana—from the bags, arranging it on plates as he spoke. "I brought us some food and dessert. I figured we could catch up." He grinned, hoping Jordan would smile back at him.

No such luck. Those pale blue eyes remained as flat as when he'd first seen him months ago.

"I'm not into playing games, Lucas, nor am I here for you to have a quickie whenever you want your itch scratched." He picked up his glass and drained it, but Luke saw the slight shake in his hand.

"Are you okay? You're trembling."

Jordan slammed his glass down with such force Luke couldn't believe it hadn't shattered. "Don't play this bullshit with me. You leave and all I get are e-mails or calls asking how I physically feel from the withdrawal. Have I given up the pills? Not one single time did you ever call simply to talk. You're the first man I've touched since Keith. Do you know what it meant to let you into my bed?"

Damn. With hindsight, Luke now understood he should have made the time to talk to Jordan about things other than the center or his drug use. "I'm sorry. I should've realized it." Even to his own ears, that sounded like a fumbling excuse.

"The only thing you care about is the drugs. Now you walk in here and expect what? A quick fuck?" He pushed up off the stool and advanced on Luke, his blue eyes now alive, blazing with anger. "For the record, listen well. No one uses me."

"That's not true. You couldn't be more wrong." Luke defended himself, shocked by the anger and hurt on Jordan's face. "I wished I could've called more. I tried as best I could, but I was busy. I was running from early morning until late at night." Never in his wildest imagination had it occurred to him that Jordan might be hurt by Luke's constant questioning about Jordan's withdrawal. Luke thought he was showing concern for Jordan when he asked about the drugs. Didn't that show he cared? Then again, what the hell did he know about this relationship thing? Luke never had anyone who gave a damn where he was and what he was doing. "I'm not playing games. I-I didn't know it mattered to you, that I mattered. I've always been on my own."

Jordan's anger deflated. He turned away and braced his hands on the top of the island, head bent, but his shoulders remained tight with anger. "I'm sorry I snapped. I guess it's that you're the first man I've been with since—"

"Since Keith, yes, I know." Luke walked up to Jordan and slipped his arms around him, laying his cheek on Jordan's head. "I should've been more sensitive to that fact, and I'm sorry." He kissed the top of Jordan's head, inhaling the unique scent of his warm skin and aftershave. Intoxicating. His senses reeled, desire spilling through his veins like water rushing into a dry riverbed. The hard ridge of muscles on Jordan's stomach clenched underneath Lucas's splayed fingers.

A shudder passed through Luke's body as he nuzzled the heated space where Jordan's neck curved to meet his shoulder. "I'm sorry. I've thought of nothing else these past days, knowing I was coming home and you'd be here." With frantic hands, he pulled off Jordan's T-shirt, revealing his pale, golden skin, then turned him around so they were finally face-to-face. "You've been working out, Prep School, huh?" He touched the soft flesh of Jordan's shoulders with his fingertips and traced the defined swell of muscles that hadn't been there a month earlier. Luke's fingers dug into Jordan's bicep to yank him closer so their lips were but a breath apart. "I feel the difference. Your body's harder than it was before."

"You have no idea." Jordan gritted the words out before thrusting his hips forward.

Luke staggered slightly, then planted his feet wider to stand firm. The heaviness of Jordan's erection continued to rub against Luke's own straining cock. "So am I forgiven?" Their gazes locked, his own need reflected in the fire kindled in Jordan's eyes. "Say it, so I can give you what I know you want. I feel it, right here." He reached down between their bodies and cupped Jordan's cock. It swelled further beneath the thin fabric, which grew damp even as he held him. In one swift move, he yanked down Jordan's sweatpants and, without breaking their intense eye fucking, took Jordan's now-exposed cock in hand and began to stroke.

It came as no surprise to him when Jordan reciprocated by unsnapping Luke's pants, letting them fall to his ankles. "I'm sorry too. I'm pushing too hard. We need to get to know each other better." A wicked smile curved his lips. "How's this for a start?"

Luke's breath caught as Jordan took their cocks into his strong yet elegant hand. He collected the wetness seeping from the tips and spread it over their shafts, all the while continuing the friction, which soon had Luke swaying on his feet, his head buried in Jordan's neck. "God, Jordan, what you do to me."

Frantically, they both stepped out of their pants and kicked them away, then Jordan continued the stroking and rubbing of their cocks together and whispered in Luke's ear. "You matter more than I can say, so I'm going to show you. I'm going to make sure you'll never be able to forget me again."

Before he could stop himself, Luke blurted out, "I could never forget you."

Jordan's hands faltered, then proceeded to perform wicked twists and turns, his fingers dancing and stroking up and down the lengths of their hard shafts. Luke knew it was only a matter of time before he blew up and incinerated. The heat of their bodies and the sounds of their naked skin, slick and wet, set his blood on fire. "Oh God." His breath rasped in his throat as his body tightened, and his cock began to throb.

"I didn't know where I stood." Jordan's lips rested against the corner of Luke's mouth, planting small kisses on his lips. "If what you said is true, it means everything to me."

Unable to speak with the conflicting emotions running through his mind, Luke bent and captured Jordan's soft, yielding mouth. Everything melted away: his fear of commitment, the self-imposed loneliness, and the walls he'd built so strong and high to keep everyone else out. Nothing else mattered but this man and how right he felt in his arms.

The scent of Jordan, mingled with the warmth of their bodies and the sharp tang of sweat and sex, melded together into a concoction he didn't mind being addicted to. The kitchen walls swam before his eyes as his vision blurred. Strong hands continued to massage his cock and his balls. That soft skin over his hardness felt tender, each touch sending waves of aching pleasure through him.

His orgasm barreled down on him, splintering him, and he came apart, jetting streams of creamy ribbons overflowing onto their stomachs. Unable to stand, he sagged into Jordan's arms. To his shock, tears rolled down his face. He found himself gasping for breath.

"I've got you, Lucas. Let go of everything and hold on to me. I won't let you fall." Jordan held him, slipping his arms around his waist, heedless of the sticky mess that lay between them.

"I'm okay. I didn't know. I didn't..." Embarrassed at his outburst of emotion, he tried to pull away, but Jordan refused to let him go.

"What didn't you know?"

How could he put it into words? All the sex forced on him at such a young age had crushed his dreams. The nights spent with those anonymous truckers had shattered his illusions even further about sex and love. Sex for him revolved around the moment, the hard flash and burn, the want and need that came and went with the wind, leaving no mark of remembrance. And love? There was never any thought or mention of the word. Love wasn't present in the dirty back roads and dimly lit truck stops where Luke had been shaped into the man he'd been for the last ten years.

"I've never been with someone I've wanted as much as you. And even now, now that we've had sex, it's not enough. I...I want more. I want to be with you again and again, and it fucking scares me to death because I don't know what to do." He sank into a chair, his legs still wobbly.

"What we do is take it as it comes, one day at a time. I want to be with you too, and believe me, that scares me almost as much."

"Are you sorry for what's happened between us?" Although it hurt his heart, Lucas needed to know. "Because of Keith and it being too soon?"

To his relief, Jordan smiled and bent over to kiss him on his mouth. "No, I'm not. It's more than two bodies having sex for me, and I think for you as well. But we don't have to go there yet."

Once again Jordan kissed him, a sweet brushing together of their lips. He smoothed back the curls that Luke could never keep out of his eyes. "I count myself lucky beyond words to have found you, but no one knows where time will take us. For all those months after Keith died, I lived in a black void, unable to move forward. And while I'd never give up what I had with him, I think it's time for me to live again."

Jordan played with his hair, winding the curls around his fingers. Luke never would've suspected the man could be as gentle and loving as he was right now. The facade of pride and arrogance had to be strictly for show, for work purposes.

"I don't think anyone should ever make you try and forget him; yet, selfishly, I'm glad you want to move ahead." Luke gulped. "With me."

This baring of souls was hard. It was easier to stay home every night in his apartment and watch television, pretending his loneliness didn't exist, venturing out only for occasional, hurried sex to satisfy a physical need, nothing more. But now he'd had a taste of what he'd missed all these years. Companionship, family, friends.

Love.

Luke's thoughts came up short. It was way too soon for that emotion to rear its ugly head. He went searching for his pants and pulled them on. Jordan handed him a warm, damp dishtowel to wipe himself up with. "Thanks. How about we have that late dinner now? We'll have to reheat the food, but it'll still be good."

Jordan nodded, and side by side they puttered about in the kitchen, Luke learning where everything was kept, taking orders from Jordan about what to do. He was surprised at Jordan's adeptness as he watched him chop greens and prepare a salad, complete with homemade dressing. "Hey, Prep School, I thought you'd only know how to make a reservation. When did you learn to cook?"

"I always enjoyed it. Frees my mind after a stressful day." Jordan swept the vegetables from the cutting board into the large bowl and mixed them with the salad greens.

There was something sensual about the way he handled the knives, a strength and sureness that Luke understood came from Jordan's surgical abilities. It mesmerized him, and he didn't even realize it until Jordan snapped his fingers in front of his face.

"Lucas, *Lucas*, what's going on? I've been speaking to you, and you're in a daze."

"Hmm, what? Oh, sorry." Not really. He'd been thinking how quickly they could eat and then maybe go upstairs. To bed. "What is it?"

Jordan had already put away the knives and set the salad on the table. All that was needed was for the food to get hot enough. After wiping his hands on a dish towel, Jordan sat next to him and took his hands. "Tell me what happened between you and Ash. Talk to me. Let me in already. Doesn't it get lonely living in the dark? Are you going to spend the rest of your life in the shadows?"

Luke tensed, but Jordan held tight, forcing him to stay, not run and hide from the past like he normally did. If anyone could understand, maybe it was Jordan. The honesty and tenderness in those blue eyes were for him. It hit him then that maybe he didn't need to face life alone anymore.

Did it make him weak that he'd do anything for Jordan, to see him happy?

Chapter Fourteen

LUCAS PUSHED AWAY from him to stand by the large back windows and stare into the black of the night. "He left us. He left us alone with a monster, and he knew it. I can't ever forgive him for that. It doesn't matter that I almost died, abandoned in a hospital. Left to live on my own, not even eighteen years old. That wasn't the worst part even, if that makes any sense to you. What hurts the most is that after he left, Ash never tried to find out what happened to us. And when I lost Brandon, I had no one. I didn't care anymore. I still don't." Lucas stood shaking, his hand trembling on the window.

"Did your foster father ever touch you, force himself on you? Talk to me. You know I'll never judge you." The pain in Lucas's face shredded Jordan's heart.

"There were some strange looks he'd give me every once in a while, lingering glances that creeped me out. But nothing physical from him; he saved that for our foster mother, beating her whenever he felt like it. I'd heard talk that Munson liked young boys, and that the police even talked to him about it. But you know small towns. Nothing ever came of it, but I knew after that to watch out for Brandon since he was so young."

"Lucas." Jordan touched his shoulder, but Lucas flinched, his handsome face dark and grim with anger.

"You asked, remember?" Lucas spat out. "Well, there it is. I'm positive Ash knew what that man was capable of. I'd bet my life it's why he left in the first place. How do you leave and turn your back on people you swore to love and protect?"

Jordan's heart shattered as Lucas wrenched away from him and stalked to the opposite side of the room. Despite numerous protests to the contrary, Lucas did still care. After almost a year without his friends, Jordan knew the opposite of love wasn't hate. The two emotions were too entwined to be separated. No, the opposite of love was indifference. Nothing was worse than a person who simply didn't care enough to have any feelings at all.

Lucas rounded on him, anger dripping from his words. "And who are you to talk? You cut your friends out of your life."

Jordan smiled. "Not anymore. We made up while you were gone. They were here earlier, and we had a long talk." It felt so good to say it, and earlier this evening, when Drew and Mike were over, it was like old times. They'd caught up on each other's lives, and Mike told them he planned to ask Rachel to marry him. He was so obviously in love with her, and Jordan couldn't have been happier. His friend deserved every bit of happiness life had to offer after almost dying in Iraq. And Rachel was perfect for him. Sometimes you didn't see what was best for you, even when it had been with you all the time.

However, the reason why he'd asked them to come over, the help he'd wanted from them to kick the pills, that topic he'd never found time to bring up. Truthfully, he was ashamed and embarrassed. He'd always been the strongest, the one they turned to for help. Plus, it wasn't the right time, with Mike talking about marrying Rachel.

You're such a chickenshit. You know if Lucas finds out you're still taking the pills, he'll never forgive you for lying.

It wasn't as though he'd lied outright. He *was* trying to quit and had cut down, although taking five pills a day instead of eight wasn't exactly telling the truth. And the fact that he was drinking more to compensate for the loss of those three pills—well, he didn't need to go into it. Life seemed back on track now. He and his best friends were cool, and now he had a relationship to build.

Surely he could cut down on the pills. He had no reason to be anxious anymore.

Lucas brushed his knuckles across Jordan's jaw. "So you and Drew are back to being best friends. I admire your friendship. I hope he knows how lucky he is to have someone like you care about him."

"We're lucky to have each other. He thought I hated him. I never could. I mean, it's Drew. Who could hate him?" His gaze held Lucas's. "But that's what happens when you let things fester and don't talk it out."

Lucas bent over the island, bracing his hands on the granite. "I'm happy you're friends again and you have your support system back. But where does that leave me with Ash? I don't want to see him or talk to him."

"Shh." Jordan took Lucas's stiff, unyielding body into his arms and hugged him until he felt the tightness relax and the muscles under the thin T-shirt soften. The touch and feel of Lucas, where before it was only an impossible dream, now breathed life back into the frozen part of Jordan's heart. Warmth and desire seeped through him as he pressed his cheek to Lucas's, enjoying the scratch of his late-evening stubble. Feeling more alive than he had in what seemed like forever, he slipped his hands into the thick silk of Lucas's hair, massaged his scalp in an attempt to soothe him. "We'll work it out; I promise. Right now I don't want to think of anyone else but you and me."

Like a big cat stretching in the sun, Lucas rubbed his head against Jordan's palms. "I think I like the sound of that. You and me. I've never had to think of anyone else before, so you'll have to teach me." He wrapped his arms around Jordan.

A promise of a lifetime. An emotion he didn't dare dwell on yet took root within Jordan, planting seeds of hope and courage. Keeping Lucas's trust was of the utmost importance in their relationship. Even Keith had never needed him like this. Jordan had always been the dependent one in their relationship, the one who required "fixing," but with Lucas, both of them were damaged to some extent. "We'll teach each other." He kissed Lucas and closed his eyes for a moment.

Please give me strength to kick this thing. Don't let me screw this up.

With reluctance, he pulled out of Lucas's embrace. "How about we eat now? Then we can have our coffee and dessert upstairs." Instant desire sparked in Lucas's eyes, kindling an answering fire within him.

"How about we go upstairs and leave everything?" Lucas advanced, caging him between his arms against the large granite island. At the first touch of Lucas's lips on his neck, Jordan moaned, the licks of Lucas's tongue creating a delicious friction. At a sharp nip from his teeth, Jordan hissed and dropped the cutlery he held in his hand. His cock stiffened, and all reason fled his mind.

"What? Yeah, let's go."

Lucas roughly yanked him against his hard, broad chest. "I like it when you're agreeable, Prep School. Come on, then." Lucas led him out of the kitchen after turning off the oven. They walked up the stairs, but with Lucas massaging his shoulders and kissing the back of his neck, Jordan's legs felt anything but steady. The heat from Lucas flowed off him like waves.

Jordan halted at the doorway to his bedroom.

Lucas sighed and placed a restraining hand on Jordan's shoulder. "If you don't want—"

Exasperated, Jordan snapped. "Okay, look, you need to stop thinking that every time I hesitate a moment, I don't want you or I'm changing my mind." He saw a hint of a smile on Lucas's lips but continued. "I want you, goddamn it. And when we're together in this bed, there won't be anyone else with us. Not Keith, not Ash. No one. Understand?"

Lucas nodded and smiled, curling his hand around Jordan's bicep. "I never doubted that. I'm smiling because you're a totally different person when you let yourself go."

"Is that good or bad?" Jordan held his gaze.

Lucas's mouth covered his in a soft, sweet kiss. "It's good. So very, very good. It makes me wonder what else you've got hidden inside you."

That slow, sexy murmur in his ear nearly undid Jordan. How long had it been since he was held? They stood, two seemingly lost souls who'd been bent by the storms in their lives, yet both found the resiliency and strength to survive and not become broken beyond repair.

Jordan tugged him into the bedroom. "If you'd come in I'll show you."

"You're also hot when you're annoyed." Lucas's lips skimmed Jordan's cheek, stopping at the shell of Jordan's ear. "Makes me hard."

Suddenly the room pulsed heavy with sex. The air steamed thick with promise, and everything they did, removing clothes, kissing with increasing hunger and passion, and running their hands overheated skin, moved in slow motion, ending with the inevitability of their naked bodies entwined together on the bed. By the time Jordan lay beneath Lucas's hard, muscled body, his thick, straining cock brushing against Jordan's belly, he physically ached with the need to feel Lucas deep inside him.

"Lucas." He found it hard to breathe and could only whisper. "Please."

Lucas's eyes glinted bright with desire, the green-gold sparking in the glow of the dim lamp left burning. "Don't deny me the right to touch and taste you. I feel like I've waited all my life for this. I'll be damned if I'll be rushed." Holding onto Jordan, he rolled onto his side, flinging his leg over Jordan's hip. With a slight move, Lucas flexed and brushed their cocks together, and they kissed. The passion simmering between them burst over Jordan, clean and bright as the wet warmth of Lucas's mouth possessed him. As their tongues tangled and slid, their eager hands rediscovered the dips and curves of each other's bodies, caressing hard bone and soft skin.

Jordan moaned into Lucas's mouth and rocked his hips forward, greedy to keep that friction going. He sucked on Lucas's tongue while Lucas's hand insinuated itself between their bodies, his thumb swirling over the heads of their cocks, picking up the precome leaking from them both. Well lubricated, Lucas slicked his hand up and down their shafts, the softness of their skin hiding the hardness within.

Jordan bucked against that teasing, rubbing hand, which continued to torture him. The longing and need to feel Lucas inside his body engulfed him, and he wrenched his mouth off Lucas's. "Damn it, fuck me already." Pride flew out the window, and he no longer cared how desperate he might sound. Every sensation, every breath he took centered around getting Lucas's cock inside him. He wanted the sting and burn of the initial invasion and craved the ultimate pleasure of having Lucas sink into him. Desire throbbed hot and liquid within his blood, warming him, wrapping itself around his body.

A violent tremor ripped through him, and he twisted under the movement of Lucas's fingers. "Get a condom and lube from the drawer. Now." His voice rasped, harsh and choking.

Lucas chuckled, but it sounded thin and strained. "Always demanding, aren't we?"

Jordan heard the scrape of the drawer and the crinkle of foil as a condom package was ripped open. After their last night together, Jordan had bought a box of condoms, anticipating their use. His body clenched at the thought of Lucas inside him. *Please, please let it be good for him. He needs to know it's him I want.*

"Lucas, look at me."

He immediately fell into that hot, fierce gaze. But he saw a flash, only for a second, of the uncertainty and apprehension he feared would still be there. "You have to know. It's you I've been thinking of. It's you I want. Only you. I wouldn't trade this moment to be with anyone else." He spread his legs wide, offering himself up to the man who had somehow broken into his heart like a thief in the night, stealing it as easily as if he'd been given it willingly. "Now get inside me."

"Who would've ever thought the ice king, Dr. Peterson, was such a talkative and bossy lover?"

Jordan decided if he survived the sex, he might kill the man. "If you don't shut up and fuck me now, you'll never find out." He didn't get a chance to argue further as Lucas once again took possession of his mouth, plunging his tongue inside and stealing his breath away. Lucas's mouth seemed to be everywhere; nipping at his jaw, kissing down his neck, and finally coming to rest at the base of his throat. Jordan felt Lucas's lips curve in a smile against his skin.

"Here I thought you were the quiet type. And I like you all bossy and authoritative. Your eyes get dark, and your whole body gets aggressive." Lucas's lips continued their assault, sucking at Jordan's nipples, pressing more kisses to his neck, and finally returning to his mouth, where he took hold of his bottom lip and tugged. "I wanted to bite and lick you from the first time you walked into my office. Skinny and sad as you were, I haven't been able to get you out of my mind from the beginning."

A thrill shot through Jordan's body, and he nipped Lucas's earlobe, then sucked it into his mouth as their cocks rubbed together. A ripple of lust coursed through him, but it went deeper than that. He'd been fascinated with Lucas since they'd met. Something about his darkness and vulnerability struck a chord within Jordan and his breath caught watching those hazel eyes ignite. Lucas reached between them and used his hand, slick with lube, to wet his sheathed cock. He trailed a slippery finger from Jordan's balls down to his opening, teasing the outside rim.

Liquid trickled from the head of his cock, and Jordan though he might explode with lust. "Lucas. For the love of God, please." His moans drew another low laugh from his lover.

"Easy, Prep School." The tip of Lucas's finger circled Jordan's hole, dipping in and out, stretching him. "Let me make it perfect." Lucas continued the evil twist and pull with his fingers as he whispered, hot and damp in Jordan's ear.

Finally, the head of Lucas's cock breached his entrance, and without waiting for him to set the pace, Jordan shifted and hooked one leg around Lucas's hip, slotting his cock up inside. That initial sting of entry, the feeling of fullness, the drag inside his body, all that marvelous heated friction created sensations he'd believed lost to him forever. Jordan gasped aloud. Insatiable hunger rose within him, and the initial thrust of Lucas's cock so deep inside him had Jordan clawing the sheets off the bed.

Everything Jordan had imagined proved true. Sex with Lucas proved uninhibited, wild, and limitless in its passion. The atmosphere around them rose thick and carnal, and the sounds of their lovemaking—the grunts, whispers, and moans—resonated in the dimly lit bedroom. His balls drew up achingly hard and tight, and deep within his belly the lick of fire turned into an inferno.

With one hand Lucas braced himself, and with the other he grasped Jordan's aching cock, stroking and sliding his hand up the straining shaft. Lucas whispered in a slow, sex-draped drawl, "Come on, darlin'. Come all over me."

Possessive heat engulfed Jordan. Lucas continued to pound into him, then kissed him, plunging his tongue deep into his mouth. He sucked Lucas's slick tongue eagerly. Unable to control the sensations rolling through his body, he wrenched his mouth away to thrash his head back and forth on the pillow. "Fuuck, Lucas, yeah, right there, now. *Oh God.*" He heaved off the bed, digging his heel into the small of Lucas's back as if to thrust Lucas as hard and deep into his body as possible. His orgasm thundered through him, his body vibrating from the incessant pumping of Lucas's cock. Stars burst before his eyes like fireworks, and he'd never felt more alive. His cock splashed streams across his belly, hitting his chest.

Lucas remained wonderfully hard and hot within him. Never a selfish lover, Jordan met each thrust, squeezing himself around Lucas's cock, clutching and milking it until Lucas let out a howl and, with one last snap of his hips, sank himself deep inside Jordan. He climaxed, his hands bruising as they dug into the meat of Jordan's shoulders. With a groan, Lucas collapsed, gasping for air, his face buried in Jordan's neck.

Jordan wrapped his arms around Lucas, clinging to him. Exhausted as Lucas must've been from his travels, he still tried to respond, and pressed a clumsy kiss to the corner of Jordan's mouth. Jordan couldn't help but smile as he hugged Lucas's large, sweat-slicked body close, kissing his shoulder. Shattered and sated by the incredible lovemaking he'd experienced, Jordan's body still hummed, alive with sensations he'd missed for a year. Reveling in his soreness, Jordan stretched underneath Lucas. He'd almost forgotten the bliss of being so thoroughly well loved. He closed his eyes and continued to hold on.

At one point in his darkest despair, he'd lived like the walking dead, knowing the only way he'd ever come to life again would be if Keith returned to him. But that could never be, no matter how he wished and dreamed it to happen. Keith was gone, and he wasn't ever coming back, except in his dreams. What was real, present to his touch, was the absolute vitality of Lucas. So having cried an ocean of tears, in his heart and head, he bid a final farewell to Keith, knowing his former love would be happy Jordan had once again found joy. The sorrow of the past could no longer prevent him from living for the potential of a future.

Lucas rolled on his side and pulled off the condom, knotting it, then tossing it into the wastebasket. His eyes heavy-lidded with sleep, he pulled Jordan close to his broad chest. "Go to sleep, Prep School, and stop thinking so much. You're gonna need your strength for later."

Finding comfort and a sense of home in Lucas's arms, Jordan fell asleep, pushing aside the nagging thought that he still hadn't given up his pills.

Chapter Fifteen

Today was the day. The opening of The Keith Hart After-School Community Center had arrived. The result of months of meetings and phone calls and more meetings and many late nights now revealed itself in the final product.

Luke didn't mind those late nights now that they were spent with Jordan. He shifted in his seat and checked his watch for the third time in half an hour. Restless and fidgety, Luke paced the open space between his desk and the conference table, only pausing once to gaze in the mirror to make sure he looked okay.

Charcoal-gray suit, light blue shirt, and his favorite cartoon tie. He grinned at his reflection, thinking back to the first time he and Jordan had gotten dressed for work together, and Jordan seeing his collection of cartoon ties.

"Who'd have thought that under that dark and serious frown, you're really a big kid at heart?" Then Jordan had kissed him, undoing the tie and the shirt, and made them both extremely late for work.

"I'm smiling too, looking at you."

Jordan's teasing voice broke into his reverie. He spun around to see his smirking lover leaning, with that negligent grace he possessed, against the doorframe. Valerie gave him a big smile as she passed by him.

"Come on in and have a seat. We have time." His gaze took in Jordan's sinewy body, and a fresh wave of lust rolled through him, remembering how he'd woken up this morning. Nothing compared to Jordan's hot, wet mouth on his erection, coaxing him to completion with small sounds and wispy, tickling touches.

Kicking the door shut behind him, Jordan then stalked over and grabbed him around the neck, crushing their lips together and thrusting his tongue into Luke's mouth. They stayed that way until Luke's phone buzzed, the loud noise jarring in the silence, causing them to spring apart.

He wiped his mouth on his sleeve and, still panting, answered the phone. "Conover." It took a second for his racing heart to steady itself.

"Mr. Conover, I'm sorry to interrupt, but Wanda Grant is on the phone for you." In an effort to break out of his shell, Luke had told Valerie he and Jordan were in a relationship. It only made sense, since she knew more about him than anyone else, considering how much time they spent together. His revelation opened the floor for her to confide in him that her brother was also gay, but they hadn't had a chance to have any further conversation.

"Wanda. Are you and everyone else set for later?"

Wanda and her staff had worked tirelessly to make Keith's dream become the reality he'd never get to see. From the corner of his eye, he caught Jordan frowning at his phone, then shutting off the screen with an almost angry jab of the button.

"Baby doll, we are more than ready. Everyone here is so excited about working there and helping out." A note of pride crept into her voice. "I always knew you'd do great things."

A slow burn heated his face. "I didn't do anything, really. It was all because of Keith, and then Jordan's helped so much."

"How *is* that fine-lookin' man of yours?" Wanda had been overjoyed when he confided in her how he and Jordan had taken a step toward a relationship. They'd had her over for dinner several times at Jordan's town house, and the two of them had hit it off so well she'd even shared her secret for her famous peach cobbler with Jordan. Sometimes Luke wanted to pinch himself to make sure life actually was as good as it seemed, and yet he couldn't shake the fear that it would all vanish and he'd be left alone once again. After coming out from the shadows, he didn't know if he could survive it.

"Jordan's good, waiting impatiently here for me, as a matter of fact. We're going over to the center a little early to make sure everything is set up the way it should be."

At the mention of his name, Jordan glanced over his shoulder and raised a brow. "Who is that?"

Luke covered the mouthpiece. "It's Wanda. She's asking about you."

A smile broke out across Jordan's face as he crossed the room. "Let me speak with her." He plucked the phone from Luke's grasp before Luke had a chance to answer. "Wanda, how are you? I'm sorry I missed you the last time I stopped by."

Luke leaned his hip against his desk, contemplating his lover. Jordan's outlook on life, the gentle, loving side of him he rarely showed the public, coupled with his devastating looks and natural self-confidence, made him impossible to resist. These past few months showed Luke the world he'd missed by secreting himself at home, hiding out and immersing himself so deep in his work that life passed by without him ever noticing.

Jordan laughed, throwing his head back with abandon, his cheeks flushed and blue eyes sparkling. Luke couldn't help comparing him to the emotional wreck he'd been when they'd first met, right here in this office. Thank God Jordan had come through his darkness with little lasting trauma. His strong will and determination had made his addiction to pills short-lived. For the life of him, Luke couldn't understand how someone could get addicted to drugs, especially a person as strong and confident as Jordan, but it no longer mattered.

"Where's your mind at, that has you so lost in thought?" Jordan's voice penetrated his musings. He jerked back to awareness and the heat of Jordan's body pressing up against him. Luke slipped his arms around Jordan's waist and pulled him closer.

"I'm thinking about what used to be and how happy I am that I'm no longer that man." He cupped Jordan's jaw in his palm to stroke the angled line of his cheekbone. "And how you were the reason for the change."

Unusually serious, Jordan shook his head. "No, it wasn't me. No one can make anyone change. You have to want to do it and be ready to embrace it. I was merely lucky to be there at the right time; that's all."

Luke eyed Jordan with curiosity. "You don't believe people change because they know it will make someone else happy? That they want to better themselves because the person they care for would be happier?"

Jordan's face pinched tight.

"But then it's not real. It's never right to change because it would make someone else happy. That's not being true to yourself; it's for the wrong reason. You can only ever really change for you."

It was on the tip of his tongue to question Jordan further when the phone rang again. Luke hit the speaker button.

"Mr. Conover, Dr. Drew Klein is on line two."

"Hold on a minute, Valerie." He hit the Hold button and Jordan's eyes flickered. "Are you going to take that? I'm sure I know what this is about, don't you?"

He most certainly did. Drew had been practically begging Jordan to arrange a meeting between Ash and himself, and he'd flat-out refused. He'd bet his last dollar Ash hoped that tonight they could talk, and would think nothing of using the event to further his own selfish needs.

Jordan's thin smile unnerved him. "Even if I asked, no, begged you to try with Ash, for me, because it would make me happy, would you do it?" His finger hovered over the Hold button on the phone.

Luke couldn't keep Jordan's gaze. He shook his head and stared out of the window. "It's not the same thing."

"That's what I mean. You can't because you aren't ready in your heart." Luke pushed the button, and Drew's voice came over the speakerphone.

"Hello, Luke? Are you there?"

Luke sighed. "Yeah, I'm here and so is Jordan. You're on speakerphone."

"Hey, Jordy, I tried calling you first, but your phone is off for some reason. Look, guys, the reason I'm calling is that I was wondering if, after the celebration tonight, the four of us could go somewhere and talk."

Jordan raised his brow and gave him a pointed stare. Luke's jaw clenched so tight he thought his teeth might crack.

"Jordy, Luke, are you there?"

Drew's anxious voice stabbed an arrow of regret through Luke, but he knew his answer. "I'm sorry, Drew. The three of you can meet, but I'm not going. I told you all before, I've got nothing to say to him."

"Luke, look—"

"No, *you* look." Heartsick and exasperated, Luke couldn't help but lash out, even though it wasn't Drew he was angry with. "I don't want to talk to him. I don't want to hear his excuses and stories about what happened. I'm glad you two are happy, but leave me alone." He strode past Jordan. "I'll wait for you by Valerie's desk."

The door closed behind him with a soft *snick* of the lock. He didn't even realize how affected he was until Valerie put her hand on his arm and offered him a glass of water.

"Come sit down." Her warm eyes held no judgment.

Luke drained the glass and handed it back to her. "I'm fine. I'm waiting for Jordan to finish up with his friend; then we're off to the Center."

"It's going to be a wonderful place. My brother's even heard about it where he works."

"He's a psychiatrist, right?" Valerie had told him her brother ran a clinic somewhere in the city.

"Yes. Tash works with people who struggle with their identities as well as those who've been abused or have addiction problems."

Luke shuddered. Not a fun job. "Tash? That's an unusual name."

She laughed. "It's Sebastian, but when I was a baby I couldn't pronounce that monstrosity and called him Tash. The name stuck."

The door to his office opened and Jordan walked

out, calm and unruffled. "Ready to go?" He smiled at Valerie.

Only Jordan could sail through the awkwardness of a conversation between his lover and his best friend and emerge cool as ice.

"Yeah, I guess." He tried to catch Jordan's eye, but one thing he'd learned these past few months together was that Jordan was as good at evading issues as he was. "We'll see you later tonight at the Center."

"I wouldn't miss it, gentlemen." Valerie smiled a farewell.

They walked to the elevator banks.

"You do realize that Ash is coming tonight to the opening?" Jordan eyed him as they stood waiting.

It wasn't ever a question in his mind. "Yeah."

They rode down the elevator in silence.

TEARS STUNG JORDAN'S eyes as he watched the sign placed on the building. "The Keith Hart After-School Community Center." He whispered it to himself, waiting for the usual pain to slash its way through his body. Surprisingly, though, it didn't happen. A warm steadiness, a sort of peace descended over him. It reminded him of Keith's embrace. And now, of Lucas's touch. He raised his eyes to the sky. One thing he'd never been was a religious person. It had nothing to do with his homosexuality being accepted or not. As a physician, he saw things too clinically and scientifically to believe in a higher power.

Yet today seemed different than all the days prior. The clouds continued their lazy hang, puffing along in a slow-motion samba against a sky that looked a little bluer. He leaned back, face upturned toward the heat. It was the culmination of a dream—one Keith had spoken of often. One they planned to work on together, but Jordan carried on alone.

A gentle breeze ruffled his hair. The warming fingers of the late-afternoon sun caressed his face. Keith's presence was overwhelming.

"I feel him too."

Startled, he dropped his gaze to stare wide-eyed at Lucas. "You do? I thought—"

"No. He's here to tell you how proud he is of you and what you accomplished."

Not alone. Not anymore. He held the back of Lucas's neck and dragged him in for a swift yet devastating kiss. "We accomplished it. I never could've done this without you."

Bits of green and gold glittered in Lucas's hazel eyes. "Thanks, Prep School."

Feeling around in his pocket for a minute, Jordan pulled out the key. "Success." He opened the front door and turned on the lights.

The construction crew had gutted the entire space and painted it a bright and cheerful yellow. The floors were a shiny, easy-to-clean laminate with colorful rugs scattered about. Ten rooms with glass windows and doors were set along the back wall, each outfitted with a bookcase, desk, and computer workstation. The large and airy main room had round tables with chairs set about. Shelving was built along the wall, holding every type of board game, as well as art supplies. Pictures of happy, smiling children and familiar landmarks from all around New York City hung on the walls.

A full library, complete with all the classics as well as fairy tales, mysteries, and romances, occupied the second, somewhat smaller room in the back. Plump-cushioned low sofas and chairs waited for kids to lie all over them. All of Jordan's friends had spoken to their local libraries, and they'd agreed to have one of their staff come by for weekly readings.

"What did you and Drew talk about after I left the office?" Lucas dropped into a chair at one of the desks set up for quiet reading.

Jordan sat next to him, smoothing his hand over the shining surface of the new bookcase. "He wanted to plead his case for Ash with me, to get to you. Ash is desperate to talk to you, and Drew loves him, so he'll try to do anything to make it work." In his heart, Jordan wanted Lucas to make up with Ash, but it was a decision Lucas had to make on his own. It had to come from Lucas's heart, not Jordan's. "Are you certain you won't meet with Ash, even to merely hear his story?"

"Forget about it. He has his relationship; I have mine. He needs to let it ride and stop trying to make up for a past he can't change." Lucas's arm came around Jordan's shoulder in a slow slide, pulling him close to his side. "I admire your sense of friendship."

The warmth of Lucas's mouth pressed against his, heating his blood. They stayed that way for several minutes, their leisurely kisses intensifying until Jordan dragged himself away, gasping for breath. The steady thump of Lucas's heart soothed him. "He's like my brother. I can't imagine my life without Drew in it."

"I can't imagine my life without you, Prep School. You mean more to me than I ever thought possible."

Lucas's quiet declaration nearly undid Jordan. He cared so much for Lucas, but the deception he'd created of his life tore him up inside. He desperately wanted to give the pills up; lying to Lucas, to his friends went against his nature. Guilt chased its tail around his heart. In the two months since Lucas had come home from his European trip, Jordan had cut down on the pills but hadn't been able to let them go completely. The kid he'd bought from kept pressuring him to buy, and Jordan resisted, but even as he sat, his hand shook slightly. Whether it was from emotion or the pills, he didn't know anymore. When had he lost control of himself, sliding down this never-ending slope of lies?

A pill would be so easy right now. His blood sang for it. Like *The Tell-Tale Heart*, the little yellow lifesaver pulsed in his pants pocket, though he tried desperately to ignore it.

Chapter Sixteen

SOMETHING WAS WRONG with Jordan. Maybe it was the emotion of the evening as he worked the crowd, shaking hands and thanking everyone for coming, but Luke didn't think so.

"Is he okay?" Jerry stood at Luke's elbow, drink in hand. Lines of concern deepened the grooves in his already weathered face. Luke liked Keith's former partner and counted himself fortunate the man accepted him in Jordan's life. "I don't like the way he looks."

"You noticed it too?" Lucas glanced over again at Jordan. The same charming smile flashed white but failed to reach his eyes. It looked false and forced. Everything about Jordan seemed unnatural tonight, as though he was putting on a show and wanted everyone to see how adept he was at playing his part.

"I noticed he's drinking way more than he used to, and he's strung tight as a wire." Jerry's eyes narrowed. "How much has he had to drink, by the way?"

Luke thought for a moment. "I know this is the

second one I've seen him drink."

Jerry's gaze turned speculative as he took a sip of his club soda. Luke knew though he was off duty, the detective still carried his weapon and wouldn't drink any alcohol. "That, Luke, is a very interesting way of answering my question. I take it to mean that though you've seen him drink two drinks, you believe he's had more than that. Am I correct?"

Luke squirmed under the man's shrewd stare. He didn't want it to seem as though he was betraying his lover, but Jerry had been a good friend to both him and Jordan and truly had Jordan's best interests at heart. "I couldn't say for sure, but maybe." He pushed the hair off his face and rubbed his eyes. "Something's going on with him tonight; most likely he's a little overwhelmed with the project's completion. It has to be hard for him to see it finally come to life without Keith."

At that moment Drew and his grandmother approached, and he couldn't help but return the elderly lady's smile. After they greeted Jerry, who left to rejoin his wife, Esther slipped her arm through his and squeezed.

"Lucas, sweetheart. You look wonderful. And this place." Her gaze scanned the room. "What a wonderful tribute to our darling Keith." Tears threatened, then receded, leaving her eyes glittering with sadness.

"Let me get you a drink, Esther. Some water or a club soda perhaps?" He kept his steps slow and short to match hers as they walked to the table set up for refreshments.

"Lucas. I might be old, but I'm here to celebrate. I want a glass of champagne."

"Nana." Drew stood behind them. "You know you aren't supposed to drink."

Luke handed her a club soda with lime as she grumbled about overbearing grandchildren.

"Hello, Luke."

His stomach clenched at the sound of Ash's quiet voice. "Esther, I'm sorry, but I need to check on something. I'll see you later." He bent down and gave her a kiss. "Enjoy yourself, Drew." Without ever turning around, he blindly walked away. Sweat dampened his face and neck, and he felt curiously light-headed. As he passed by Wanda, who was busy chatting with the commanding officer of the neighborhood precinct, he stopped and whispered, "I'm gonna step outside. I need a little space."

She glanced over his shoulder and, with a sad little smile, nodded. "Okay, baby doll."

He pushed open the glass doors, the night air cool as it hit his face. The rough brick dug into his back as he leaned against the wall, but he enjoyed the discomfort. It made him feel less guilty about the shitty way he'd treated Ash these past months.

Even though he'd been prepared tonight to see him, hearing Ash's voice again ripped him up inside. He'd yet to fully explain to Jordan what had happened before he'd left home and why he blamed Ash. Jordan would raise his brow in that irritatingly arrogant way he had and shake his head in disappointment. Luke knew

Jordan wanted him to make up with Ash, but he couldn't take that step. Bile rose in Luke's throat at the thought of telling Jordan about his past.

God, he wanted to hold Jordan. Right now. They hadn't been separated since that first incredible night they'd made love. To be able to touch Jordan and hear his breath quicken with desire every night was a gift and everything faded except how Jordan tasted, smelled, and sounded. Each night they made love brought Luke to the brink of saying words he never thought he'd utter.

Sex, life, everything was different when you cared about the person you were with. He'd never understood that before. The guys in the office joked about the women they were sleeping with, describing the sex in intimate detail, but once they became serious with them, the talking stopped. Their expressions changed when they spoke of their women then, softer, gentler. More intimate. As if they held a secret.

Never having had a relationship with another man, Luke couldn't appreciate the sentiment. Until now. Now Luke recognized the details about Jordan that made him so special and held them close, not willing to share them with others. It made them more intimate. The kindness and empathy Jordan displayed when dealing with patients. The curve of his lips when he smiled and greeted Luke with a morning kiss. The cries of passion as Luke thrust into him, first gently, then deeper as they made love. Jordan holding him, clasping him tight within his body until it became impossible to tell where Luke began and Jordan ended.

Even the arrogant tilt of Jordan's head and the sardonic lift of his brow fascinated Luke. Jordan's comforting strength to hold on to tonight, to be able to face down Ash. Even though Jordan wanted him to forge some kind of relationship with Ash, if he chose not to, Luke knew Jordan would remain by his side and defend him.

Several weeks ago, he'd confided in Jordan a little more about Ash's abandonment and what it had done to him. How losing Ash had destroyed the plans they'd made of always being a family. It tore him up inside to relive even that small portion of hurt and devastation, but he'd wanted Jordan to know part of the truth. Together he and Jordan were building a fortress of trust and security, one that would provide a sanctuary from whatever resided out there in the world, ready to attack them at any time.

The sum of all parts that made up this complicated, infuriating, yet mesmerizing man named Jordan was so much more than he could ever have imagined as a lover, as a friend, as…it hit him then, with a clarity he'd never thought he'd have the opportunity to experience.

He was in love with Jordan.

Unwilling to go back inside, Luke paced the side-walk, certain a goofy grin was plastered on his face to match his cartoon tie. If he'd had a normal upbringing, Luke supposed falling in love was something he would've seen coming like a freight train barreling down on him, full speed. Luke waited for the fear and anxiety to hit him, but it never materialized.

He was in love. And with that knowledge came the realization that he wanted it all—the whole television-family kind of life. Lazy Sunday mornings spent in bed, then getting up to read the papers, eat bagels, and walk the dog. Saturday nights meeting friends for dinner, then going home to make hot and passionate love. Going for ice cream in the summer and hot chocolate in the winter. He wanted the whole fucking fairy tale he never thought he'd get.

Not here, though. He couldn't tell Jordan here. It was Jordan's night and, in a way, Keith's as well. But tonight, when they lay together in bed, Luke planned to whisper it in Jordan's ear as he slid inside Jordan's heat.

"I love you." He whispered it, to hear how it would sound out loud.

The doors opened, and Wanda came outside. "Luke? Baby doll, you out here still?"

Hopeful the dark hid his flaming cheeks, Luke answered back "Yeah, Wanda, over here." He stepped under the fuzzy glow of the streetlight so she could see him better. "I was getting some air." As he came closer to her, he saw the worried expression on her face. "What's wrong?"

"Did you see Jordan come outside? Some of the people from the shelter wanted to thank him, but we can't find him."

"I saw him before I came out here. I haven't seen

anyone walk through the doors since I've been here." He put his arm around her shoulders. "Let's go back inside. Maybe he went to the restroom."

They walked back into the center, and Luke quickly scanned the room but didn't see Jordan's tall, lean form anywhere. His friends were all standing about in a circle, with Esther in the center, sitting like a queen in her chair. Near the doors that led to the library, he spotted Jerry.

"I'm going to go talk to Detective Allen, Keith's partner." He smiled down at Wanda, trying to reassure her. "I'm sure everything's fine. Don't worry." He patted her shoulder and threaded his way through the groups of people clustered about the room until he reached the older man.

"Jerry, can we talk a sec?" He jerked his head to the corner of the library, where it was a little quieter. The detective followed him and leaned against a wooden bookcase.

"What's the matter? You look concerned."

"When did you last see Jordan?" Luke raked his hand through his hair. "Wanda hasn't seen him in a while, and he's not anywhere inside." An uneasy tendril of dread threaded its way around his spine.

Jerry's demeanor switched from relaxed to alert in an instant. "Come with me, and we'll search." He led the way out of the library and straight to the back of the large main room. They walked the entire periphery with no sign of Jordan. After looking in each computer room and even the men's room, they decided to look out back, in the narrow courtyard behind the Center, where the deliveries were made. It hadn't been more than fifteen minutes since he'd spoken with Wanda.

When Luke pushed open the heavy door, he expected to see the alley empty. Flares of light cut through the darkened space, lit by a necklace of halogen lights strung up and nailed against the building. A few plastic garbage pails lay haphazardly strewn along the concrete pavement. Luke's eyes widened at the sight of a teenage boy, his baggy jeans ripped at the knees, the oversize black hoodie he wore dwarfing his skin-and-bones figure, standing with Jordan by the chain-link fence. The two of them argued in strident, angry voices.

"Jordan? What the hell is going on?" Luke called out, fearful for his lover's safety.

The kid spun around, eyes spitting fear. "Who the fuck is this, man? You call the cops on me, you motherfucker?"

Jerry stepped forward, showing his badge and shield. "Police. Halt. Show me your hands."

The kid tossed something down on the ground and scaled the iron fence like a spider, then dropped to the sidewalk below. The beat of his running footsteps receded into the dark of the night. It took only a few long strides for Jerry to reach Jordan's side. Jerry shoved his badge back into his pocket and bent down to pick up the clear plastic bag that lay at Jordan's feet.

"Jordan? What's going on?"

Between the rushing of blood in his ears and the

pounding of his heart in his chest, Jerry's words echoed as if from far away. Luke could barely move, as if he walked through sticky molasses. By the time he reached Jordan and Jerry, the two men were in the middle of a vehement argument.

"I didn't know what he had in the bag, Jerry. I swear."

"What were you doing out here? I thought you'd be inside with your friends and everyone else who came to see the center's grand opening." Jerry stood, arms folded, glowering at Jordan.

The door opened, and Luke glanced over his shoulder to see Drew, Ash, and the rest of their friends streaming into the alley. Dismissing them from his mind, he slid his arm around Jordan's shoulders. "Hey, Prep School. I was worried about you."

Jerry thrust a plastic bag into Luke's face and shook it. Pills, little yellow ones like Jordan had sworn he'd given up, rattled against each other. "Do you know why Jordan would be interested in these?"

Luke blinked, astonished at what he was looking at. "Jordan?" He reached over and plucked the bag from Jerry's hand. "These aren't yours, right? Tell Jerry. You gave the pills up."

Then Luke saw it. The slight hesitation, a slip of the mask Jordan wore, revealing the ugliness of his addiction underneath. Jordan's gaze skittered away from Luke's demanding glare.

Jordan licked his lips. "I've been trying. I wanted to tell you. It's been so hard, but—"

Luke crushed the bag between his fingers. "But what? You figured I'd never find out? That you could continue playing me and everyone else around you like a fool, risking not only your life but the lives of patients as well?" Luke threw the bag at Jordan's face. "You lying bastard."

"Now, wait a minute." Drew pushed past him to stand by Jordan's side. He draped a protective arm around Jordan, who sank into Drew's shoulder with a shudder. "You aren't being fair to Jordan. Give him a chance to explain."

"Explain what? That he's an addict? You know…" Luke paused and scrubbed a palm over his face before continuing, directing his speech toward Jordan. "I asked you every day about this. We talked about how you'd kicked the pills, and not once in the two months since I've been back—that we've practically been living in each other's pockets—did you think to mention you were having trouble. Didn't you think I'd help you? Fuck it. I can't believe I was so stupid."

"Lucas, please let me explain."

"Now?" Luke snorted with incredulity. "Because you got caught? I should've known better than to get involved with you. You're a selfish, self-absorbed liar."

Ash grabbed him by the shoulder and pushed him hard enough so he stumbled back a few steps. "Stop it, Luke. You have no right to say that about Jordan. If you cared about him, you'd try and help him, not cut him down when he's hurt and vulnerable."

Luke could hardly believe what he was hearing.

Jordan, hurt and vulnerable? He was the one who'd been lied to, the one who'd risked everything. Jordan had everyone: his family, his friends—shit, he even had Ash on his side. Luke had no one, nothing left. Even his heart no longer belonged to him since he'd lost it to Jordan.

"It figures you'd back him instead of me, the brother you claimed to care so much about." Luke shoved Ash backward, then bent at the knees in a fighter's stance, his fists slightly raised. Best to be prepared for anything where Ash was concerned. "I should've known better than to think for a minute you'd stand with me." Unexpectedly, Luke's voice caught in his throat, and he choked.

Fuck. The last thing he needed was to show he cared, even though the ache in his chest made it difficult for him to breathe. Luke's eyes locked with Ash's, and Luke saw not only pain but pity residing in Ash's knowing silver gaze.

"I've always been on your side, whether you believe me or not. You won't give me a chance to talk to you, like now you won't give Jordan a chance. It's what you do, Luke. Rather than deal with the problem, you run away from it and hide."

The fuck he did. And who was lecturing him? The goddamn king of disappearing acts.

Jordan spoke up for the first time. "Ash, I don't need your help." A muscle twitched in Jordan's jaw as he shook off Drew's arm, which had remained around his shoulders. "Lucas, please. I'm not an addict, for

Christ's sake. I caught that kid back here and when I approached him, he tried to sell me that stuff. I'll admit I still struggle with the pills, but I've cut down on them." Jordan grasped Luke's arm and pulled him away from the crowd of people, but Luke resisted.

"It all makes sense now to me, you know? The shaking hands, the shifting moods. You craved the drugs, not me. It's never been me, has it?"

A horrified expression crossed Jordan's face. "That's not true. I've never faked my feelings for you." With a shaky hand he touched Luke's chest. "Don't you know by now what you mean to me?"

Emotions tore through him as he batted away Jordan's arm. "No. I know how the drugs make you think you feel. But you haven't been clean since I met you, right?" He grabbed Jordan by both arms and pulled him up against his chest. "Have you?"

Gone was the image of the sophisticated doctor who cared little of anyone's opinions but his own. All the arrogance had drained out of him, as well as the sense of laughter, which had only recently returned to his eyes. Shadows bruised underneath his lashes, and Jordan's once fine, pale skin creased rough and coarse. Yet despite Luke's furious anger at Jordan, Luke still wanted him and craved the touch of his mouth, knowing how soft and full Jordan's lips were and the warm scent of Jordan's smooth skin. Even now, Luke's fingers clenched around the lapels of Jordan's suit jacket to hold him close, though he wanted to push him away. Luke's heart began to pound in heavy thumps.

"Shit." With a smothered curse, he flung Jordan away from him. "You need to get back inside and pretend everything is fine for the sake of the center. Keith's memory shouldn't be tarnished by your behavior."

His body slammed into the wall, and Jordan's outraged, snarling face crowded mere inches from Luke's own. "Don't you dare speak about Keith." Jordan's hot breath blew damp across Luke's face. "Who the hell are you to lecture me about his memory? Who the hell do you think you are?"

Luke thrust Jordan off him as cold spilled through his veins. Only pride and years of fending for himself kept him from falling apart like a house of cards in the wind. "I'm nobody. Nobody at all." Without a backward glance, he strode out of the alley, back into the center, not stopping until he pushed open the glass-front doors to the street. Luke balled his hands into fists and squeezed his eyes shut. Until the cool air hit the wetness on his face, he hadn't realized he was crying.

Chapter Seventeen

T HE DEAD SILENCE echoed loudly in the darkness after Lucas left. Jordan braced himself against the crumbling facade of the building. The only thing he could concentrate on was not falling to his knees. Jordan's brain couldn't process what had happened with Lucas.

His heart was another story altogether. He'd fucked up badly.

"Jordan?" Drew placed a gentle hand on his shoulder, but Jordan shifted away. Drew meant well, but Jordan couldn't stand any gestures of comfort and well-meaning sympathy.

Drew dropped his hand but didn't walk away. "Are you okay? Can we get you anything?"

For a brief moment, Jordan wanted that bag of pills. The entire lot of them. Would it be so wrong? He could swallow them all and slip away, no longer a burden to his family or friends. Be at peace finally. And Keith, who'd never judged him, would be there, waiting. It was all so tempting. But so wrong. The past few months that he and Lucas spent together had brought him to dizzying heights of passion that reawakened his lust for life. Jordan craved a return to the normal existence he'd once had, but he didn't know how to push his body up past that last rung of the ladder to finish his climb out of hell. The flames had already consumed his life by taking Keith, and now his addiction was on the verge of destroying him.

Addiction.

The ground dropped from beneath his feet as his admission shattered the protective shell around him. He was an addict. Lucas had been right all along.

Jordan couldn't stand to think of the pitying glances thrown his way. He drew himself up, stiff and straight. There were still too many people about, and if he didn't play host and seek out each of them, it would be doing a disservice to Keith's memory. The control he was famous for kicked in, and drawing on some remaining vestige of pride and strength, he addressed his friends over his shoulder, avoiding eye contact with any of them. "I need to get back inside to the guests. I've got to speak to the commanding officer of the precinct and then some of the politicians who also showed up." He attempted a smile, but it barely registered on his frozen lips.

Ignoring the cold rush of anxiety that swept through him, Jordan smoothed down his suit jacket and strode back inside. If he dwelled on what had happened outside with Lucas, he'd crumble into dust. More than anything else, he wanted a pill to steady the noise in his head and the uneven pounding of his heart, but gathering whatever shreds of dignity he had left, Jordan reined in his craving. The past few weeks had seen him cut back his pill usage dramatically. Many times when it had been only Lucas and him together, Jordan had thought about telling him the truth about his continuing anxiety and the pills.

But then Lucas would say how proud he was of Jordan, how strong Jordan was to kick the habit. He'd tell stories of people he'd seen become victims to drugs and how he refused to fall into its deadly trap.

"I'm so proud of you, Prep School. You're not another pretty face. You're strong."

And sick to his stomach with guilt and disgust over his own weakness, Jordan would only nod and fall into Lucas's kiss.

How could Jordan let him down and admit he'd been lying to Lucas from the start? The fragile trust Lucas had given by exposing parts of himself Jordan knew Lucas had never told anyone would have been dashed to pieces, splintered beyond repair.

Jordan had gambled on time, but time had run out, and he'd lost.

As Jordan continued to mingle with the people in the room, speaking the rote words of thanks and pleasantries, his mind calculated how long he'd have to give Lucas to calm down before seeing him again. Tonight was done. He knew Lucas well enough now to understand the man's need for space and time away to think. Tomorrow, Jordan decided. Perhaps in the light of day, Lucas would understand Jordan hadn't meant to hold back the truth but rather didn't want to suffer the sting of humiliation by admitting his addiction, his ultimate weakness.

"Dr. Peterson?" A hesitant female voice broke into his self-torment. He blinked and stared for a moment at the young woman in front of him. "It's Valerie, from Mr. Conover's office?" Concern creased her brow. "Is everything all right?"

He swallowed, the acrid taste in his mouth burning a path down his throat. "I recognize you. Yes, yes, of course I'm fine. I'm so glad you could come." A tall man hovered by her side, a serious expression on his pleasant, tired face. Her husband, Jordan surmised. The overhead lights picked out threads of silver in his light brown hair, and Jordan guessed the man to be in his late thirties.

A relieved look crossed her eyes. "This is my brother, Dr. Sebastian Weber. Tash, this is Dr. Peterson, the president of the foundation that is running this center."

"Dr. Weber, thank you for coming." Jordan shook Dr. Weber's hand, surprised at the strength of the man's grip. "What do you practice?"

The force of Dr. Weber's intent stare set Jordan back a step or two, as if he'd been physically slapped. "I'm a psychiatrist."

Wise hazel eyes stared back at him from behind wire-rimmed glasses. "I have patients from all walks of life, fighting battles they never dreamed they'd have to face."

Jordan shifted with uncomfortable awareness, as if Dr. Weber saw behind the mask he offered up to everyone. Pressure built in Jordan's chest as their gazes locked. In Weber's eyes, Jordan viewed sympathy and an uncanny knowledge of Jordan's own internal struggle. For the first time since he began abusing the pills, a flutter of hope, faint yet definite, sank deep into his bones and blood, that maybe he could break free and take back his life.

In a practiced move, Weber pushed his glasses up the bridge of his straight, strong nose. It made him look younger, somewhat sweeter and more vulnerable. His silver-flecked hair and serene smile seemed at odds with his youthful, gangly body.

"Dr. Weber?" An idea came to him, and Jordan knew it was his answer, quite possibly his salvation.

"Please call me Tash."

"Very well. I'm Jordan." Jordan took a deep breath. "Can we talk? Maybe have coffee tomorrow? I have a problem, and maybe you can help me."

JORDAN SAT BY the window in his favorite coffee shop on Ninth Avenue, sipping a latte. Inexplicably nervous, he tapped the tabletop with the wooden stirrer, wondering why he'd thought meeting Tash was a good idea. Last night had been horrible—the worst night of his life other than Keith's death. Lucas's face rose before his eyes, shock leading to pain, anger, and the horror of being lied to. Despite his friends' fury over Lucas abandoning him, Jordan understood why. Why Lucas chose not to stay and talk but ran instead. For the first night in weeks, Lucas hadn't spent the night. Jordan didn't expect to hear from the man. He'd yet to face Jerry's angry questions.

From their talks, trust had been the foundation Lucas built his life on. Lucas assumed Jordan had quit his habit during the time he'd been away in Europe, and Jordan did nothing to prevent him from continuing that assumption. His lie of omission was no different than if he'd spoken it outright to Lucas's face. How easily he'd broken that bond of trust they'd begun to weave. Jordan had no one to blame but himself.

Spying Tash entering the coffeehouse, Jordan waved him over to the secluded corner he'd chosen for them to sit in. He'd picked that spot so no one would be able to hear their conversation or intrude. "Come. I have a table. Get your coffee so we can talk." Tash smiled and ordered his cappuccino, making friendly conversation with the barista as he waited for her to make his order.

Jordan eyed Tash's easy smile, thick brown hair gilded with those silvery flecks, and strong, capable hands, all of which added up to an extremely appealing man—but not for Jordan. The man's lean runner's body, encased in faded jeans and a soft green sweater, wasn't broad and muscular like Lucas's. Jordan recalled the flex and play of Lucas's body beneath his hands the last time they made love. A quiver of desire shot through him. His hand tightened around his cup of coffee, and Jordan wondered if he'd ever again hear the tenderness in Lucas's whispered words of passion.

It had taken Jordan almost a year to gather the broken shards of his life and piece together a framework to do more than exist day to day. No matter how hard he'd pushed them away, his friends refused to allow him to mourn alone. There was no easy answer as to why he thought he could hide his secret dependence on the pills, but for the first time in his life, he was shaken and scared. Broken and alone. He'd locked himself in a cage, unable to set himself free. He needed Lucas, but Jordan couldn't figure out how to push beyond his own betrayal and ask him for forgiveness. At this point, Jordan didn't even believe he was a person worth saving. He fervently hoped Tash could help him, not only with the physical detox of the pills from his body but to understand the psychological breakdown of his relationship with Lucas.

"Good to see you again." Tash slid into the seat opposite him and placed a cup of steaming coffee on the table. "Are you feeling better this morning?"

"Not really." At Jordan's admission, Tash's eyebrows rose.

"And you'd like to talk about it?"

"I would." Jordan twisted his fingers together. How could his life have gotten so fucked up that he'd come to this point of baring his secrets to a stranger? Embarrassed, Jordan began to fill Tash in on his history. "You know I lost my partner last year, right?"

Tash nodded but stayed silent.

"To say I became very angry and depressed was putting it mildly. I directed my anger not only at the world at large, for the senselessness of Keith's death, but at my best friend, Drew, whom I blamed for everything that happened that night. My therapist urged me to talk to him, but I couldn't."

"That's quite a bit to deal with at one time. I can understand why you sought treatment." Tash's neutral voice gave nothing away, and Jordan took another gulp of his cooled coffee and continued.

"The anger turned into anxiety and panic attacks, and my doctor prescribed medication, Xanax. The time came that he wanted me to stop the pills." Jordan swallowed and took a sip of his coffee, not because he wanted it but to forestall what he had to say.

"But you didn't stop them, did you?" Tash's quiet voice held no censure, emboldening Jordan to continue and not lie or obfuscate the truth.

"No. I didn't. I-I told him I didn't feel ready to stop, but he dismissed me, saying it had been eight months. Long enough for me to have worked through whatever issues I had." Jordan forced himself to meet Tash's eyes. To his surprise, they held no sympathy, but spit angry green sparks.

"Do you mean to say your doctor told you to basically get over it?" The anger in Tash's voice caused Jordan to blink in astonishment.

"Um, well, yeah. He said—"

"I don't give a shit what he said." Tash's fist banged

hard on the table, drawing the attention of several of the patrons sitting near them. "As a doctor, he knows how hard it can be to stop those kinds of drugs. Telling you to quit cold turkey was the height of unprofessionalism by your treating physician and bordered on malpractice, as far as I'm concerned."

Jordan sat unblinking and began to shake. Tears burned hot behind his eyelids. Finally, someone understood the hell he'd been going through. "I wanted to quit, but I didn't want anyone to know how far I'd fallen. To admit I had such a weakness." Jordan choked out a bitter laugh. "I couldn't do it. Not to my friends and family. They'd always looked up to me. I couldn't let them down."

"It isn't weak to ask for help when you're hurting, Jordan. It takes strength." Tash's anger had subsided to what Jordan now recognized as his naturally unruffled demeanor.

"You don't know me, though. I've always looked out for everyone. Since we were young, I protected Drew and Mike. They needed me."

"Are you sure about that? Or did you need them to make yourself feel important?" Tash sipped his coffee, then placed the cup back on the table. "Let's talk about your best friends. Val told me a bit about them, I guess from what Luke told her, but I'd like to hear it from you."

Jordan shrugged. "Not much to tell. Drew, Mike, and I have been friends since we were little. Mike is with Rachel now, and while it was strange at first, since we've known each other all our lives, I can see Mike is crazy about her and Rachel's a great girl. I'm happy for them."

"And Drew?"

Jordan tensed, and he could hear the note of self-defense creep into his voice. "He's with Ash now. We obviously can't be as close as we once were." He took a sip of coffee, watching his hand shake as it held the cup. "What does this have to do with anything, with me?"

Not bothering to answer the question, Tash asked one of his own. "How do you feel about Drew's relationship with Ash? Any resentment at being replaced as the number one guy in Drew's life?"

"I wasn't—"

Tash continued as if Jordan hadn't spoken at all. "Drew moved on with his life and is happy. Does that bother you? That he's happy with a man you don't like?"

This line of questioning delved a bit too deep for Jordan's liking. "It doesn't matter if I like Ash or not. He loves Drew, and they work. It's that...that..." His shoulders slumped.

"What? Go on, tell me." Tash's hand covered his—warm, dry, and solid.

"I have no one now who needs me anymore. Keith needed me, he always said—to show him the happy, joyful side of life—and he's gone. Drew has Ash, and Mike has Rachel." His voice dropped to a whisper. "I'm superfluous now. If I disappeared, the only one who would care would be my dog."

"Is that what you believe?"

"It's what I know. After Keith died, I isolated myself from everyone close to me. They carried on fine with their lives. I should've disappeared." It all came pouring out of Jordan, his self-doubts and the disappointment. "No one would've noticed, and it would've made everything easier overall. Sometimes I think about ending it, but I'm too much of a coward."

"You aren't a coward. It takes strength to admit these truths not only to yourself but to others." Tash's hand remained on Jordan's, his long fingers curling around Jordan's damp palm. "What we have to discover is why you view your self-worth only as it relates to how others see you, not in your own accomplishments."

Confused by that statement, Jordan couldn't help but question Tash further. "What are you talking about? That sounds like psychiatric mumbo jumbo to me."

Tash laughed, his hazel eyes sparkling with amusement. "I *am* a psychiatrist, remember? The mumbo jumbo, as you call it, is what I do." He gave Jordan's hand a quick squeeze. "You have to learn to define yourself by your own accomplishments. What other people think of you shouldn't matter. You think you're responsible for your friends' happiness, but you aren't."

"But—"

"Uh-uh." Tash gripped Jordan's hand harder. "In this case *I'm* the doctor, and you need to listen to me.

Now this is how it's going to go down. I'm going to get you detoxed and be on call for you 24–7 for the week. Then you'll be in a recovery program, which I run. But none of this will happen unless you admit to yourself first and then your friends that you have a problem. That's the first step in recovery."

Things were happening at a breakneck pace, and Jordan found himself teetering on the edge of losing control. "What about my job, the clinic? I'm letting everyone down because I'm too fucking weak to control myself."

"Jordan. Listen to me. You have an addiction. It's nothing to be ashamed of. But if you don't get a handle on it, you could die. You can't practice medicine while under the influence of drugs. I'm surprised you've been able to do it for as long as you have."

"I thought I could handle it. I made sure never to operate if I took pills beforehand. I wouldn't put my patients in jeopardy." Hot with humiliation, Jordan rubbed his eyes. "I've been trying to cut down, but it hasn't been easy."

"I know." Tash's sympathetic smile had the effect of making Jordan feel worse. "That's the nature of an addiction. You believe you'll be okay and can do it alone, yet the craving never goes away, does it?" The knowing hazel gaze pinned Jordan.

"No," Jordan whispered. "Every time Lucas would tell me how proud he was that I'd kicked the habit, it only made me more anxious because I knew I was lying to him, and I'd end up taking another pill."

"So what do you say? Are you ready to tell everyone? Are you ready to beat this? I have faith in you. I know you can do it."

But Jordan had a few questions of his own. "Why are you taking such an interest in me? We really don't know each other. I only know your sister because she works for Lucas."

The good humor faded from Tash's exceptional hazel eyes, leaving them dark and haunted.

"Let's say I won't allow another person I see drowning get swept away without helping him."

"Sounds ominous."

"It can be," Tash admitted, a sad smile passing over his lips, coming as quickly as it disappeared. "But I know what to look for now, and I won't let you sink. I'll be your lifeline if you let me."

Tash's hand still held his, and Jordan had no desire to let go. There was no sexual desire or hidden innuendo in Tash's touch, merely a refuge from the storm that had been battering Jordan's body and soul for months now. It wasn't until he'd been pummeled so hard he could barely stand that Jordan realized the terrible burden that had been weighing him down.

"I want to be normal again." Jordan's voice caught on the dryness of his throat as he held on tight to Tash's hand. "I'm so ashamed to have allowed myself to sink this low. I've risked my friendships, my career, and now my relationship with Lucas—perhaps the most important thing of all."

"How is that going to be affected by your treatment? Won't Luke be supportive and help you get through it?"

Had he told Lucas from the beginning, Jordan wouldn't have hesitated to say yes. But now, he couldn't be so sure. He shook his head. "I don't know. I might have screwed up so badly that the relationship is beyond redemption at this point." Pain seared his chest as if he'd been branded with an open flame.

"I'd have to believe someone who loved you would stand by you and understand your confusion."

Jordan nodded but was unable to raise his gaze from the floor. Patterns of sunlight danced across the black tiled floor. "Lucas had no parents, so growing up, he looked to Ash as his hero. When Ash left them, it crushed Lucas, and he withdrew into himself." Jordan swallowed against the rising lump in his throat, remembering the pain in Lucas's voice as he spoke of his past. "I still don't understand what happened that he ended up in a hospital, but when the time came for him to be released, his foster parents and remaining foster brother, Brandon, had left town without a trace."

"He's been on his own a long time," Tash remarked, his voice contemplative. "Yet you think he'd leave you right when you need his support so desperately?"

Jordan shrugged and withdrew his hand from Tash's grasp. "It's because he's been on his own for so long. He doesn't need anyone."

Tash huffed out a humorless laugh. "Don't fool yourself, Jordan. We all need someone." His eyes grew slightly unfocused, as if he was looking inside himself and wasn't too happy with what he saw. "There are those nights when the dark is so black and thick, you can't see yourself, and all you wish for is someone to hold on to. So you reach across those empty sheets of silence, groping and grasping, hoping you'll touch something, anything warm and alive. But once again you come up cold."

Jordan stared wide-eyed at Tash, a little shocked at the naked pain on his face. "Tash, are you all right?" Without hesitation, he reached across the table and covered the man's cold, slightly shaking hand.

Jordan's touch must have startled Tash, for he blinked and let out a nervous laugh. "Yeah, sure. I'm fine." But he didn't let go of Jordan's hand, and strangely enough, Jordan didn't mind. It was a solid hand, with strong fingers. They sat in companionable silence.

Before Jordan could question Tash about the detox treatment and the specifics of what it would entail, a shadow fell over their table, blocking the sunlight streaming in from the large windows facing the street. Jordan glanced up, and to his shock, Lucas stood outside staring at their clasped hands, his eyes wide from shock and hurt.

Shit. Jordan pulled his hand away and half stood, ready to bolt out of the coffeehouse, but Lucas had already taken off down the street. To chase after him would be pointless so he dropped back into his chair. Life couldn't possibly get any worse than it was right at this moment, could it?

Chapter Eighteen

P AIN RADIATED THROUGH Luke as he ran down the
street. He hadn't a clue where he was going but
knew he needed to put distance between himself and
what he'd seen. It surprised him that Jordan had moved
on so easily, yet there it was, the irrefutable truth
shoved in his face in the mocking, cheerful sunlight.
He'd been ready to do it, tell Jordan he loved him and
give away a piece of himself for the first time, when all
along he'd been played for a fool.

His footsteps slowed, but he continued to wander
the streets, not paying attention to where he headed. It
didn't matter anymore. He had no place to be and no
one to meet. Why did people look to form relationships
and fall in love? The suffocating numbness choking
him wasn't worth it. He'd rather have remained alone
and not suffered this aching void.

The blare of a car horn startled him, and glancing
up he saw he'd reached the High Line entrance. It ran
all the way up the West Side of the city, from Gan-
sevoort Street in the Meatpacking District to 34th St.,

about a mile and a half. On the weekends, he and Jordan would sometimes come to the elevated, park-like walk, built high above the city streets on the historic freight rail line, and enjoy the view of the city and the beautiful gardens planted. He climbed the stairs and wandered down the pathway, letting the crowds push him along. After about fifteen minutes, he spied an open bench and sat, staring at the skyscrapers until they blurred before his eyes.

His cell phone buzzed, and Jordan's name flashed on the screen along with a picture of the two of them and Sasha, a silly selfie taken at the park. *Fucking hell.* He wasn't some teenage girl crying over a breakup. Time to get a grip and put this mistake behind him.

"What is it?"

Several people shot him wide-eyed looks, walking a bit faster as they passed by, and he realized his words had come out a bit louder than he'd thought.

"Lucas."

The strain in Jordan's voice struck a chord, and for a moment, he softened, worried that Jordan couldn't handle the pressure. But then he recalled Jordan holding the other man's hand, and he once again hardened his heart. "Yeah? What do you want?"

"I, um, I'd like to see you, Lucas. Talk to you." There was a small expulsion of breath, and then Jordan spoke again. "Please? I can come by your place, or you can come over and I'll make dinner—"

"Stop it." The only reason Jordan wanted to see him was because he got caught. "There's nothing to talk about. You let me think you weren't taking the pills when in fact all the time we were together, you were on drugs. How real of a relationship did we even have if you were high all the time?"

"Is that what you think?"

The confident, arrogant man he'd fallen for contrasted sharply with the hesitant, broken voice he now listened to on the other end of the phone. For a moment he let down his guard. "Who was the guy you were holding hands with?"

The phone remained silent, though Luke could hear Jordan's breath. "He's a friend."

"You looked more than friendly to me, the way you two held hands. Who is he? Have you been seeing him while you were also with me?" Luke held his breath, shocking even himself with the question. He'd never before thought to question Jordan's fidelity, but now that he knew Jordan still used drugs...people did things out of character when they were under the influence.

"Fucking hell, Lucas. No." Anger vibrated out of the phone, and Luke pictured Jordan's blue eyes spitting fire. He always liked when Jordan became angry, and despite himself a smile tugged at his lips.

"Tash is only a friend. As a matter of fact—"

"Tash? As in my secretary Valerie's brother, Tash?" Now he knew why the man seemed so familiar. Dr. Sebastian Weber was a sophisticated good-looking man, and gay. Jordan's type. And suddenly, Luke saw clearly how foolish he'd been to think Jordan could love him. Luke was a product of abuse, foster care, and the streets; Jordan, on the other hand, came from the world of prep schools, European vacations, and the best of New York City's glamorous social life. Tash Weber, not Luke Conover, was the perfect partner for him. Add in the fact that he was also a doctor, and the two men had everything in common. Perfect for each other.

"Yes, we met the other night." Jordan started to explain, but Luke had no desire to listen. Wise to the ways of the street, when it came to matters of the heart Luke was as much of a sucker as a tourist right off the bus in Times Square. And suddenly, he needed to speak to the one person in the world who'd always understood him and had never let him down.

"I'm sorry. I have to go." Without waiting for Jordan to answer, Luke clicked off the phone. He stood and, with determined steps, left the High Line.

"BABY DOLL, YOU look awful." Wanda held Luke at arm's length, searching his face with her dark, knowing eyes. "You wanna talk about it?" They were at the Center, where Wanda was in the middle of checking the supplies to make sure they had enough for the kids to do their art projects.

Luke ducked his head like a child waiting to be scolded for doing something bad. "I do, but I feel like an idiot."

"Is it about Jordan?"

Luke looked up sharply. He hadn't ever really discussed his and Jordan's relationship with Wanda. "Um, well."

She grinned. "Oh, come on now. I'm not blind. You and that man had it bad for each other from the start. Every time you saw him, you'd get all grouchy and defensive like a bear. And that poor man's been walking around wounded and lost, waitin' for someone to give him a big old hug."

"I never intended it to be serious. I thought he was safe, that he wouldn't mean anything to me." Luke swallowed heavily. "That I—"

"That you wouldn't fall in love with him. Right, baby?" Wanda took him in her arms.

He held on to her and nodded against her soft, sweet-smelling shoulder. "I think I made a mistake, and I don't know how to fix it."

"But you want to, right? Because you love him."

"How did you know?" He kept his head down and his arms around her, not ready to face her scrutiny.

"Baby doll, I've known since the first day you walked into the shelter that you were lookin' for that special someone. I watched you grow up, and no one was prouder than me when you graduated college and worked your way up and got that job." She paused for a moment, and Luke remained silent. He could hear his heart beating and feel the soothing touch of her hands across his back.

"But when you met Jordan, a switch turned on inside of you. You became interested in life for the first time." She laughed. "Even if you fought and argued, you enjoyed it. He made you come alive, baby. And I understand you're scared about the past. But you gotta let it go. Grab this chance at happiness. Look at what happened to Jordan and his detective. Here one day and gone the next. You don't want to lose Jordan over fear, do you?"

"It isn't that." Luke finally pulled away from Wanda's embrace and led her to a back room they used as a lounge, to take a break or eat their lunch while working. He closed the door and indicated she should sit in one of the comfortable chairs arranged around the rectangular table; then he took a seat. "Before I left for Europe, I found out that Jordan was abusing pills—Xanax. He started taking them when his fiancé was killed, and even though his doctor told him he didn't need them any longer, he continued."

Wanda shook her head, her eyes sad. "That poor man. As if he didn't have enough to deal with."

Luke shifted in his chair. "Anyway, he promised me when I left he'd see someone and kick the habit, but I found out at the opening here the other night that he still took them. He lied to me."

Wanda brushed the tears out of her eyes. "My heart breaks for him. So you're tryin' to comfort him and help him, I'm sure, and he's pushin' you away. Cause from what I've seen of Jordan, he's too proud to let anyone try and help."

He cleared his throat. "Uh, not exactly."

She frowned. "I don't understand."

Luke studied his fingernails for a moment. "I got

angry with him because he lied to me. And it's drugs. You know how I feel about that. I don't even know if it's really me he wants or if he's always high when we're together and it wouldn't matter who he was with."

Wanda snorted. "Honey, you are outta your mind. That man is crazy about you."

"He's crazy about his drugs. That's all I know for sure." He stood and kicked the chair away from him with his foot. "If I were enough for him, he wouldn't need the pills. But I'm not. He denies it but it's probably because he still loves Keith." His hands clenched at his side as all the hurt and pain spilled out of him. "If he loved me, it should be enough. *I* should be enough for him. But I'm not. And I never will be because he doesn't love me more than he loves his pills. Or more than he still loves Keith." He turned his back on Wanda, unwilling to let her see the tears in his eyes. "I won't be lied to, and I don't need to be a stand-in lover for a dead man. I was fine on my own all these years. I'll be fine again."

"Luke, look at me." Wanda pulled at his shoulder. Reluctantly he turned around, his jaw set, eyes narrowed.

"What is it? I know I'm right."

"No, you aren't. I've been around the block more than one time and forgotten more than you'll ever know." She poked him in the shoulder. "Sit back down and listen to me."

Protesting crossed his mind, but in the face of her anger he wisely shut his mouth and flopped back down in his chair. "What?" He sounded like a petulant child, but he didn't give a shit.

"That man has been through hell in the past year, and you were the only thing he counted on. He finally learns to open up and give you his heart, and what do you do at the first sign of trouble? Instead of supportin' and tryin' to help him, you lecture him and act like you're the one who was hurt."

"You don't understand. He lied to me."

Wanda leaned against the desk and folded her arms. "Maybe knowin' you would react this way, he was right not to tell you."

"But Wanda." Luke used his most reasonable tone of voice. "If he was always high, then how do I know that he does care? I don't know shit about relationships. You know that. But I've seen enough people hooked on drugs who'll say or do anything when they're high. I can't and I won't tell him how I feel if he's on those pills."

"You're taking away his hope, baby. Give him something to strive for. If he knows you're there for him—"

"No." Luke cut her short. "I don't want him kicking the pills for me. He needs to do it for himself." Suddenly that conversation he had with Jordan about doing things for the right reason seemed prophetic. No wonder Jordan had become so agitated.

Wanda nodded. "I agree. But at least offer him your support. Let him know you'll be there waiting for him at the end."

The picture of Jordan holding hands with Dr. Tash Weber flashed through his mind. "It may be too late. I may have lost him already."

Wanda sniffed. "Who are you kidding?" Her voice rang out in disbelief. "I tell you what. You go right now to him and tell him how you feel. I guarantee you'll make his afternoon." She grabbed his arm and yanked him out of the chair, a wicked-looking grin on her lips. "Make sure you give him some lovin' and let him know how you feel."

Heat warmed his cheeks. "Wanda…"

She hugged him close. "He needs you now. No matter what you think. And I don't care what you say; you need him too. He makes you feel, baby doll."

For a moment, he clutched her to him, the mother he never had, and let the tears fall. He might be thirty years old but he'd never had the chance to be a child.

"But what if—"

"Shh. I know what you're gonna say. What if he doesn't care?"

He nodded into her shoulder, feeling like that lost eighteen-year-old all those years ago when he'd first stumbled into the shelter. Her warm, soothing hands rubbed his back as if he were that child in need of comfort. "I'm positive that won't be the case, but if it is? Then you'll have to change his mind, won't you? Life isn't ever definite. When you think you have it all figured out, it bites you in the ass, letting you know not to take anything for granted."

He sniffed and pulled away from her embrace.

"Thanks." Luke bent down and gave her a kiss. "I love you, Wanda."

"I love you too. Now go get your man."

She opened the door and pushed him out, laughing. The laughter in his throat died when he saw Jordan sitting at a table with Drew, Ash, and Esther.

Their gazes locked across the room. He had no idea what he wanted until Jordan stood. He truly looked terrible, pale and drawn, as if he hadn't slept all night.

"Can we talk, Prep School?"

The tentative hope flaring in Jordan's eyes nearly broke Luke's heart. He'd never looked as vulnerable as he did right then, so close to breaking. "I'd like that, Lucas."

Chapter Nineteen

I T HAD TO be a good sign that Lucas was willing to talk. The earlier anger in his eyes had disappeared, replaced by caution. Perhaps he'd be willing to listen after all. "I have to go home and walk Sasha. Want to come with me?"

"Yeah," said Lucas. "I kind of miss that mutt."

Jordan leaned over and kissed Esther's soft cheek. "I promise to come see you soon."

"Dear boy." She placed her little hand on his and, to his surprise, stood up and led him away from the group. "Talk to me. You're so hurt, and your eyes are so sad. Please, you need to make this right with Lucas. Finding love one time in this life is a joy. Finding it twice is a gift not many are given."

Stunned into silence, Jordan gaped at Esther. *Love?* He didn't love Lucas.

Did he?

"Yes, I said it." Esther's sweet smile broadened. "It isn't ever going to be the same as before. But it shouldn't be. Lucas isn't Keith. But he gives you strength and courage in a different way, I can see. And you, my dear, give him something he never had."

"What?" Jordan honestly didn't think he had anything to offer. Not any longer.

"A home. A sense of belonging to a person and a place. That young man has been searching all his life for someone to hold on to." With surprising strength, she squeezed his hand. "I think you're the one he needs."

"I never planned for any of this to happen."

A chuckle escaped Esther. "Oh, silly boy. Didn't I ever tell you my own mother's favorite saying? 'Man plans and God laughs.' When it comes to matters of the heart, we have little control. I've known you since you were a little boy and watched you grow up to be a man anyone would be proud to call a friend. You've never been afraid to stand up for yourself."

"But I deceived him. I lied to all of you." Admitting it in front of Esther might have been his lowest point yet. "I'm so ashamed."

"Shame is hard but humbling. Now that you've said it, you must move forward or it will consume you. Do you think we're all perfect?" In a louder voice, she pointed at his friends sitting at the table, who'd made no attempt to hide the fact that they were listening to their conversation. "I defy anyone here to state that they've never done anything they regret or are ashamed of." Esther searched the faces of everyone present. No one dared to contradict her. "Of course not." She faced Jordan once again. "You've been lucky that the strength of your personality and your friendships has allowed you to remain unscathed. Now you must delve deep inside yourself for your own pocket of strength. Find the courage you have within you."

Mindful of her delicate bones, Jordan gathered Esther to his chest. "I love you. You know that, right?"

She smiled though her eyes were shiny with wetness. "I do. And I've always been proud of you—from the first time we marched together in the Gay Pride Parade to right now. Go make it right."

Jordan gave her one last hug, then returned to Lucas. "Ready to go?" He waved good-bye to his friends and gave Esther a kiss on her cheek.

He nodded, and they took off. The Center was located only a few blocks from Jordan's brownstone, and he could hear Sasha barking as he ran up the stairs.

"Quiet, girl. I brought you back your friend." He opened the door and held it for Lucas. "I think she missed you." He laughed as the dog hurtled past him to jump on Lucas, whining and licking him, her stubby tail wagging at a furious rate.

Lucas went on his knees in the hallway, his face receiving a thorough tongue washing from Sasha. He brushed the curls out of his eyes and laughed. A wave of desire swept over Jordan and Lucas glanced up, his hazel eyes mirroring the same raw need.

Jordan dropped next to him. "I'm sorry I lied. I-I was so humiliated." He extended his fingers as if to feel Lucas's face, but hesitated and curled them toward his palm instead, not knowing if his touch would be welcomed. "I still am. I never meant to deceive you. That wasn't why I kept it from you. You have to believe me."

To his shock, Lucas grabbed his hand and held on tight. "I know. Now, I know that. And I'm sorry too. I've spent my life running away from everything instead of facing up to the things that hurt me. I should've stayed to help you. You needed me, and I let you down. You don't leave a person when they're hurting or in pain." Lucas entwined their fingers, and Jordan watched in wonder as Lucas kissed their tips with a tenderness he'd never shown before. "You're not supposed to leave the one you love alone to face their demons."

Jordan froze. "What?" Sasha had finally wandered away, the tags on her collar jingling, mixing in with the screams of laughter from the children playing some game on the sidewalk. Every sound echoed loud in Jordan's ears, committing this time and place to memory. Beams of hazy late-afternoon sun filtered through the sheer curtains on the glass-front doors, burnishing Lucas's chestnut curls into a gilded halo. Jordan gaped at him, transfixed.

"I knew you'd make me repeat it. You want to hear me say it over and over, don't you, Prep School?" A lazy grin spread over Lucas's handsome face, lighting up his usually somber expression. "I'm happy to, but first I have to do something."

"What?" Jordan held his breath. In this day of firsts, he had no idea what Lucas had in mind.

"This." And Lucas brought his mouth down on Jordan's in a gentle kiss as he cupped the back of Jordan's neck. Steadying Jordan. Grounding him. The sweet taste of Lucas's mouth, warm and cinnamony, sparked life into Jordan's blood, resting dormant in his veins since Lucas walked away. Heat spiraled through Jordan as he clutched Lucas's leather jacket, pulling him close, forcing the press of their lips harder against each other. God, how he'd missed this man. And that cage he'd locked himself in sprang open, freeing him finally, from the remnants of the past. Jordan's mind spun in wild circles as Lucas ended the kiss but kept his hand on Jordan's neck, massaging him with those marvelously talented fingers.

Jordan's breath caught in his throat as Lucas's beautiful hazel eyes fixed on him. An uncertain grin flickered over Lucas's lips. "I love you, Jordan. I've never said those words before. It took the thought of losing you for me to realize what an idiot I've been. I know I hurt you and you still love Keith, but is there a chance for us?"

Jordan's heart squeezed at the flash of vulnerability in Lucas's eyes. "You're right; you are an idiot. The chance is gone. It set sail a while ago."

Lucas's shoulders slumped. "Oh."

That toneless, defeated voice broke Jordan. He couldn't tease Lucas any longer. "There's nothing to take a chance on because I love you too. I love you so much it makes my heart hurt. And while you're right in thinking I still love Keith, and a part of me always will, it takes nothing away from the love I have for you." He kissed Lucas's soft mouth. "I'm so in love with you I can't see straight anymore. I wake up in the morning wondering how I got so lucky to have a man like you in my life. When I realized I'd pushed you out of the door because of my cowardice and lies, I thought I'd go crazy."

"You didn't lose me forever; we lost the way back to each other for a while." Lucas traced Jordan's cheekbone with the pad of his thumb. "I wasn't planning on giving up on you so easily if you said no. You're worth fighting for."

Jordan rubbed his cheek against Lucas's hand, reveling in his touch. "I like a man who takes what he wants. It's the way I've always lived my life. I don't believe in holding back."

Their gazes locked, and Jordan was about to suggest they go upstairs to bed when Sasha came bounding into the room, dragging her leash. She jumped on the two of them, breaking the intensity of the moment. It didn't matter, though. Tonight they'd start rebuilding the tenuous bonds of their fragile relationship. No matter what, Jordan was done with the lies and hiding his flaws.

"I actually do need to walk her. Why don't we both go, and we can pick up some things for dinner on the way back." Jordan took the leash out of Sasha's mouth and stroked her smooth, silky ears. What a comfort she'd been to him in the months since he'd found her. With Keith's death and the dream of a child gone, for the moment at least, she'd become the outlet he needed to lavish his affection on. "I'll cook for you, make you something special."

"A celebration, huh?" Lucas got to his feet, a smile lightening his once all-too-serious expression.

Jordan's wish was to keep him looking like this always. Light, happy, and unfettered by the darkness that plagued him from his childhood. "Of a sort. We have a lot to discuss. I'm going into treatment starting Monday, and I'm going to need your help."

They walked out of the house together, Jordan holding on to Sasha's leash as they began meandering down the block with no specific destination. Sasha was of a mind to sniff each leaf and branch, so it promised to be a long walk. After about half an hour, they found a coffee shop with an outside seating area, so they ordered lattes and sat at a table with enough space for Sasha. The waitress was kind enough to bring a bowl of cold water for the dog and then disappear. No other patrons sat near them, and Jordan decided this was as good a time as any to tell Lucas about what he planned to do.

After sipping his latte, Jordan took Lucas's hand. He ran his fingers over Lucas's knuckles, took a deep breath, and began. "Like I said, I'm going in for treatment starting Monday. It's very quick and intense. I'm sure I'm going to go through some severe withdrawal, but I feel this is the best thing for me."

Lucas remained silent, studying their clasped hands, and Jordan grew nervous. "It's too much for you to handle, right? It's fine." Jordan pulled his hand away and picked up his coffee. He couldn't blame Lucas. Why would Lucas want to get involved with someone with a problem like Jordan's? His vision wavered as the frantic beating of his heart and racing pulse made it hard to catch his breath. "I'm seeing a psychiatrist anyway who has already said he's willing to help me and stay with me while I detox."

"Was that the guy I saw you holding hands with today?" Lucas growled. "That's Tash, my secretary's brother, right?"

Warmth rekindled within Jordan as he recognized the possessive need simmering in Lucas's voice. "He's very nice. Kind, considerate, and I know he's dedicated to seeing me through this. It's imperative I have someone with me at all times when I go through the treatment, and he's volunteered."

"The fuck you say, Prep School. If anyone is going to be staying with you, it's me. I'm the one who knows you." Lucas grabbed Jordan by the elbows and yanked him so their lips were mere inches from each other. "I'm the one who loves you. You're fucking mine, and I take care of what's mine." He crushed his lips over Jordan's, and they kissed—hot, wet, and raw, right there on Ninth Avenue.

The sounds of the passing traffic and pedestrian footsteps faded into the background as Jordan fell into the kiss, letting Lucas take control. He'd never shied away from public affection before, but that didn't mean he needed to put on a display for anyone. But that was before Lucas had barreled into his life, taking control of his heart. "Lucas," he gasped, trying hard to catch his breath. "Let's go home. Now."

Lucas sat across from him, eyes heavy-lidded with his rising passion, lips gleaming wet. "I want you inside me."

It would be a first between them, and Jordan stared at Lucas in disbelief. "What are you saying? You've never—"

Lucas's fingers tightened on his. "It makes sense to me. It could only be you. I want you in every way possible."

Could he have gotten any luckier? Out of the hellfire that had been his life this past year, he'd discovered he was stronger than he'd imagined and more resilient. Most important, he'd found love amid the ashes of his heart.

Jordan stood, and Sasha jumped up, eyes bright, ready to be on her way. "Let's go home. We have all night." He took Lucas's hand in his. "There's no need to rush."

They walked down Ninth Avenue and stopped at the supermarket; Lucas waited outside with Sasha while Jordan picked up everything he needed for dinner. It was twilight by the time they headed back to Jordan's town house, the dark lavender-lit sky a brilliant backdrop to the building lights beginning to wink on throughout the city. His street remained relatively dim, as it consisted mostly of town homes and low-rise buildings, and the streetlamps had yet to come on for the evening. He'd almost forgotten the simple pleasure of walking hand in hand through the city streets, and once again Jordan marveled at how lonely and lost he'd been when he woke up only this morning, and now, at the setting of the sun, his life couldn't be more satisfying and complete. He slanted a glance at Lucas and caught his eye.

"What?" Lucas smirked.

Jordan kissed the corner of his mouth. "Nothing."

"That didn't feel like nothing." Lucas slung his arm across Jordan's shoulders. "I have to say, Prep School, you surprised me." They continued walking, Lucas's arm tight around him—a perfect fit.

"I did? How?"

Lucas's hand massaged his shoulder, continuing down his arm. Even through his jacket, Jordan sensed Lucas's touch, strong yet gentle. It was one of the things he loved most about Lucas. To everyone else he presented a tough, brooding man, but when they were together, his main concern was Jordan.

"I didn't think you'd keep up with the gym, but you've done better than I imagined."

"Oh yeah?" Jordan leaned in to whisper in Lucas's ear and heard the hitch in his breath. "If you're good, maybe I'll let you do a more thorough examination after dinner."

Lucas had no response except to tighten his arm around Jordan's shoulder, but Jordan wasn't fooled. The dog pulled them here and there down the block, while they discussed what Jordan planned to make for dinner. A young man rose from a neighbor's stoop and approached them. Sasha growled in warning, pressing her body across both his and Lucas's path.

"What the hell?" Lucas's arm tightened around Jordan. With a sinking heart, Jordan recognized Johnny, his former dealer.

"It's okay, Lucas. I know who this is." No more lies, no subterfuge. "It's the guy I bought my pills from."

"Yeah, I'm his dealer. Whassa matter, Doc? Too fancy to call it what it really is?" Johnny sneered at Jordan, his pale, sharp-featured face twitching, dark eyes darting side to side.

"Call yourself what you want, Johnny. I told you before, I'm not buying what you're selling anymore." Jordan put a restraining hand on Lucas's shoulder. "Don't engage him. It's not worth it."

"Yeah, tell pretty boy here I ain't gonna touch you. I ain't no queer." Johnny's thin lips curled in obvious disgust. "But my boss don't like that community center, and he don't like you hanging around with no cops. He knows what you're up to, and you better not be plannin' on setting me up or nothing."

"Listen you little punk—" Lucas took a step forward, and Sasha began to bark in earnest, but Jordan held on to his arm, holding him back.

"It's all right. Let him have his say, and then he can go." Jordan had no intention of ever speaking with this kid again. He'd hoped after the last time that Johnny would simply disappear. "I told you before, I don't need what you're selling any longer."

Johnny gave him a hard stare, then brushed his hair out of his eyes. "Make sure you keep your mouth shut, and don't talk to the cops." He turned on his heel and ran down the block.

Sasha let out gruff, growling barks at his receding back, and Jordan expelled a loud breath he hadn't even realized he'd been holding. Lucas remained silent by his side, but Jordan knew he'd want to discuss what had happened. He had every right to know. "We can talk, but let's go inside first, okay?"

Lucas nodded, and they walked the short distance to Jordan's front entrance. Sasha bolted inside as soon as the front door opened and headed straight for the kitchen and her dish of dry food, while Jordan hefted the grocery bags up on the wide countertop. "Do you want a drink? There's beer in the fridge or wine on the side table. Stronger stuff is in the living room."

"I remember, darlin'." Lucas opened the refrigerator and took out a bottle of beer. "Want one?" He wiggled the bottle at Jordan.

A shiver rippled through him. Damn, he loved that sexy little drawl that came out only when Lucas was truly relaxed. "No, thanks. I'm going to have some red wine."

"I'll pour it for you."

Jordan began preparing their dinner of steaks, baked potatoes, and roasted broccoli, but became distracted by the sight of Lucas opening the wine. The muscles in his back and shoulders flexed under his shirtsleeves as Lucas pulled the cork out of the bottle, and Jordan envisioned Lucas lying underneath him in bed, naked, spread out, and open to him. His breathing quickened.

"Jordan, *Jordan*." Lucas stood in front of him, holding a glass of red wine, a smirk on his handsome face. "What the hell were you thinking that had you so far away, hmm?"

Jordan took the glass out of Lucas's hand and kissed him. "You'll have to wait and find out, now won't you?" He sipped his wine and returned to preparing dinner. They chatted about inconsequential things as the food cooked. Lucas set the table, and as they sat down to eat, it struck Jordan how comfortable the two of them were together in this house. How definite and real. Waiting for the throb of pain that usually accompanied his thoughts of Keith, it didn't come. Loving Lucas didn't mean forgetting Keith and all they'd shared. The last obstacle that had trapped his heart had been hurdled, and Jordan blinked back tears. The choking fog of despair lifted, bringing fresh white light into his soul once again.

Setting him free.

"You're thinking of him, aren't you?" Lucas put down his knife and fork. "It's okay. I understand."

No, he didn't, and Jordan knew he had to make Lucas understand once and for all. "It's not with regret. It's with a sense of joy, and a little bit of fear as well."

"Why fear? What are you afraid of?"

Jordan picked up his wineglass and stared into its

ruby depths. "Of a happiness that might get snatched away again. Of seeing all the beauty life has to offer, and knowing I'd be missing out if I kept myself shut away." Jordan took a deep breath, then exhaled and spoke from the heart. "Of loving you so much and having you always wonder if I'll ever love you enough."

This kind of talk required him to be touching Lucas, to show him how deep the emotional connection between the two of them really went. Jordan placed his wineglass back on the table. He moved over next to Lucas and slipped his arms around Lucas's neck to hug him close. "I don't want you to live with doubts, wondering if I really want you. You're not a stand-in for Keith, nor am I comparing the two of you."

The pounding of Lucas's heartbeat filled Jordan. "I love you, Lucas. I love you for who you are and who you've made me."

"I didn't change you. I don't want to." Lucas took Jordan's face between his hands. "I said to myself the first time I met you, you'd be trouble for me. Your pride and your damned spirit turned me on like nothing else ever had before."

Jordan grinned. "And here I thought it was my good looks."

Lucas remained serious. "Darlin', you looked like shit that day. I knew I was seeing a man who'd been through hell and back, and I couldn't relate. But I've never loved anyone before and your behavior seemed totally foreign to me."

Jordan knew Lucas could never be happy again

unless he faced up to his feelings about Ash. It was high time he did. "That's not true; you have loved before. And I know you're going to get angry with me, but you still do love him." Jordan refused to look away from Lucas's face, even as it tightened in anger.

"Stop it. I'm not going to talk to him. Ash and I have nothing to say to each other." Lucas pulled away from him and emptied his plate into the wastebasket, then placed it in the dishwasher. "Are you done with your dinner?"

Jordan nodded, watching as Lucas did the same with his plate. He wasn't willing to let the topic go, however. "You're lying to yourself. You know it, and I know it as well."

"Stop it, Jordan." Lucas banged his hands on the tabletop, and Sasha, lying in the corner, picked up her head and whined. "That topic is closed. It's not up for discussion."

"If you didn't claim you hated him so much, I wouldn't care. But the pain and hurt in your voice rips my heart out." Jordan put a hand on Lucas's shoulder, but he drew away. Still, Jordan persisted. "The opposite of love isn't hate, Lucas. The opposite of love is not giving a damn at all. You give a damn. You care so much you won't be able to live a normal life until the two of you sit across a table and hash it all out. I don't know what happened all those years ago. But whatever it is, it's still killing you, eating away at your insides like a parasite, and you're fooling yourself into thinking you can get rid of it like yesterday's trash."

Continuing to glare at each other, neither spoke until the doorbell rang, setting Sasha racing to the front door, barking her head off. Jordan shook his head in despair and went to answer it.

"Jerry, hey, come on in." Jordan held the door wide open. "Sash, quiet down."

The detective stepped into the foyer. "Sorry to interrupt your evening, but I wanted to discuss something with you if you have the time." Jerry's gaze focused behind Jordan's shoulder, and he knew Lucas had come into view. "Oh, sorry, I didn't mean to interrupt. Hello, Luke."

The two men shook hands. "You didn't interrupt anything. We're finished with dinner, and I was about to make some coffee. Want some?"

Jerry nodded, and they all walked into the kitchen. Jordan busied himself with the coffeemaker, while Luke and Jerry discussed the stock market and what the next tech trend was going to be. After they all settled in at the table, Jerry took a sip of his coffee, then spoke.

"Jordan, what can you tell me about that kid you had the confrontation with the night of the community center opening?"

Surprised, Jordan glared at Jerry. "Are you planning on charging me? I don't understand."

Lucas, obviously still pissed off at him for their earlier confrontation, lashed out at him. "Jesus, you're rude. I'm sure Jerry is asking for a reason."

Realizing he was out of line, Jordan apologized. "That was uncalled for on my part. What do you need to know?"

Jerry chuckled. "No need to apologize. I know you didn't mean anything by it." He flipped open the notebook he never went anywhere without and consulted some notes. "It seems that our sources have heard some chatter lately about dealers who've been getting angry with the development of community centers like yours, as well as neighborhood watches and tenant associations banding together to stop the drugs and guns."

Remembering Johnny on the street earlier and his warning, Jordan dismissed any concern. The kid was a small-time dealer, not part of a dangerous drug underground. "He's a teenager who probably got himself in too deep, as I see it. I've only dealt with him, and he never mentioned anyone else."

Lucas interjected at that point. "Wait a minute. We ran into him again tonight, right before we came home. Didn't he say you needed to watch yourself earlier? That his boss didn't like what you were doing with the community center?" He turned to Jerry. "Isn't that what you meant?"

Jerry nodded. "Exactly. That's a threat if I ever heard one. You have to watch yourself. I'm going to ask that a car drive by here every hour to make sure you're safe." For a moment he looked uncomfortable. "Uh, Luke, are you living here now? I'm assuming you two are a couple?"

Jordan grinned as Jerry's face turned red. "We are, but nothing's been decided on that front. Yet."

If Jerry had an opinion, he kept it to himself as he put away his pen and notebook. "I'm happy for you, Jordan, and I know Marie will be thrilled." He stood up and shook each of their hands. "You should both come to dinner soon. I know she'll want to meet you, Luke."

"I'm entering a detox program starting Monday, so I'll be tied up with that, but certainly after I settle everything, we'll come, right?" He raised a brow to Luke, who nodded back.

"I'm glad to hear that. It won't be easy but you're strong enough to beat it."

The unexpected praise warmed Jordan. Perhaps more people had faith in him than he initially thought.

They walked Jerry outside. The night air blew cool but not chilly, and Sasha came with them to sit on the stoop. "Remember, Jordan, don't take any risks and be careful."

Jordan patted the older man on his back. "Yes, I will, Dad. Now go home to your wife already." He watched Jerry walk away down the block, then asked Lucas, "You want to grab her leash? She should have one last walk before we settle in for the night."

"You still want me to stay?"

Surprised at the hesitancy in his voice, Jordan wrapped his hand around Lucas's arm and pulled him close. So close the delicious roughness of his stubble pressed prickly warm against Jordan's own cheek. He inhaled the scent of Lucas—leather, coffee, man. "I never want you to go."

Chapter Twenty

T HEY'D FINISHED WALKING Sasha, and Luke's
nerves hummed in anticipation. What had started
out as a lust-inspired remark, that he wanted Jordan
inside him, had turned into an obsession of thought
and desire. During his traumatic journey to New York,
he'd had no choice but to accept men inside him.
Payment, they'd said, as they grunted and pushed their
way into his uncaring shell of a body. It was the only
way Luke had known how to survive. He'd vowed
never to let anyone inside him, ever again.

All that had changed, thanks to Jordan. Watching
Jordan give Sasha fresh water and settle her in for the
night, Luke leaned against the carved newel post of the
staircase. Jordan had shed his jacket upon entering the
house, and the T-shirt he wore stretched across his back
and shoulders, accentuating the flex of muscles as he
bent over to give the dog one last pat.

Luke's eyes narrowed as Jordan approached him.
"What is it?"

Jordan shook his head and grabbed Luke by the

waistband of his pants, yanking him close. "Do you know how torturous it's been for the last hour, sitting with Jerry, making small talk, when all I wanted was to lay you over the countertop and fuck your brains out until you screamed?"

Fucking hell. In an instant, Luke's dick hardened. The thrust of Jordan's erection prodded him, the thin fabric of his sweatpants no help in concealing his mutual excitement.

"Oh yeah?" Luke licked his lips and took a deep breath. "That sounds pretty fucking hot, Prep School, but I'm kinda looking forward to being in a bed with you right now. 'Cause one time isn't gonna be enough tonight." He tangled his hands in Jordan's blond waves, kissing him, wanting to possess every inch of him. And Jordan, in his usual no-holds-barred manner, gave as good as he got, plunging his tongue into Luke's mouth while rubbing his body flush up against Luke.

Luke finally broke off the kiss, gasping for air. "You're killing me. Let's go upstairs."

Jordan said nothing and held out his hand. They walked upstairs together, and his mood shifted from playful to contemplative. The air hummed with a fine electric charge playing in the background. Every hair on Luke's body stood on end, and his heart thumped madly. With gentle fingers, Jordan touched his cheek, his face a picture of concern.

"Hey, we don't have to do this. It's not important to me who does what in bed."

Luke leaned into Jordan's touch. "I want you in

me. It's been years, and before—" He choked on the words but pushed them out, knowing he had to tell Jordan. It was time to strip himself bare to the bone and show all the ugliness and rot that lay within him. "Before when I did, it wasn't for love or lust or even friendship. It was payment, a means to an end to escape. It meant nothing."

He listened to the silence. Jordan stepped back but didn't break contact, threading both his hands through Luke's curls, forcing Luke to meet his gaze.

Luke didn't want to see the pity, hear the sympathy in Jordan's voice, but what he saw in that pale blue gaze of Jordan's stole the breath right from his body.

No pity, only protectiveness. No sympathy, but rather, anger. No disgust. Instead, Luke recognized love. Acceptance. And pain for him and what he'd experienced.

Jordan kissed him softly on the lips, then drew back. "Oh, babe, I'm not here to judge you. Who am I? I don't know why you ran away, and I won't ever push you to tell me. But only you have the right to control your body. When your choices are stolen from you, it's up to you to decide how and when to reclaim your life."

Luke held Jordan tight, needing the solid warmth of the man to center him and make it easier for him to speak. "My choice is you, and I choose now." He rubbed small circles on Jordan's back, still not believing he had the right to have this happiness and this man in his arms. "God, I want you so bad."

"Those words—you. You mean everything to me. Take off your clothes and get on the bed. I can't wait to have you." Jordan's authoritative tone sent a shiver through Lucas. He wanted Jordan dominant, on top, thrusting inside of him. His body clenched tight.

Without a word Lucas stripped and lay on the bed. *This is different. You love Jordan.* But still he trembled, fighting to lie still. Someone as perceptive as Jordan would notice the subtle shaking in his arms and legs.

"Talk to me; tell me what's going on in your mind right now." Jordan didn't lie on top of him but curved his pale, nude body into Luke's and held him close. "Let me in."

At least he didn't have to meet Jordan's eyes when he spoke of his humiliation. "When I made my way up north from Georgia, I didn't have the resources to pay. I was young, alone, and so naive. I didn't realize there were people who'd take advantage of me." He swallowed. "Sexually."

He drew in a deep, shuddering breath. Jordan stroked his chest with his steady, warm hands. "Shh. Take your time. I'm here and I promise I'm not going anywhere."

"Don't make promises you may not keep."

Behind his back, Jordan stiffened, his hands ceasing their comforting touch. "Do you think I'd bail on you because of choices you made over ten years ago when you were nothing more than a child?"

Bile rose in Lucas's throat, and he pulled away from Jordan to sit in the center of the bed. The trembling began again. "Jordan, I became nothing more than a whore." Now that he'd said it, the words burst out like water from a dam, breaking free. "I slept with men and used my body to pay my way. I let them fuck me"—his voice dropped until it barely rose above a whisper—"I didn't want to, but I didn't know what else to do."

"You did what you needed to do to survive, all alone and hopeless." Jordan slid his arms around Luke and hugged him tight, nestling himself against Luke's back. "What you've told me only makes me love you more for the strength and perseverance you showed. I'm in awe of what you've made out of your life." The softness of Jordan's lips pressed against his neck.

Maybe it had all been worth it. To have suffered as he did, only to claw his way up and out of that blackness, proved happy endings do exist, especially if a man such as Jordan waited to accept and love him. "Since then, I've never let a man inside me, but now, I can't stop thinking of having you. Feeling you inside me."

"Let me in then." Jordan gently pushed him down on the bed, facedown. "Close your eyes while I taste every inch of you."

Luke complied and stretched out, arms relaxed at his side. He sensed Jordan hovering over him. Heated, wet kisses started at the base of his neck. Only Jordan's lips touched Luke's skin, his mouth traveling down Luke's spine, slow and deliberate. The tip of Jordan's tongue traced each vertebra as he worked his way down Luke's back, licking, kissing, caressing him with such tenderness Luke vibrated from the sensations erupting throughout his body.

Never in his life had Luke felt so wanted. Desire, hot and thick, coursed through him, and he moaned, the sound echoing off the bedroom walls.

"You like that."

Luke smiled at the self-satisfied tone of Jordan's voice. "You know I do." His voice caught in his throat as Jordan trailed his fingers up the crease of his ass. Nervous, Luke shifted, not willing to give in to the buzz of excitement that shocked him with its intensity.

Jordan knew him so well, it seemed, as he whispered, "Turn over."

When Luke faced Jordan, love and tenderness blazed from his eyes. Not since Wanda had stepped in, assigning herself the role of his surrogate mother, had Luke felt as cared for, as protected.

As loved.

Jordan cupped his cheek. "If you don't want to go through with it, I understand."

The only appropriate response was to pull Jordan in for a kiss. "I want you more than ever."

After that, Jordan took control. Luke had never seen him so strong and sure of himself. This was the man Jordan must have always been before death and sadness overtook him. His mouth moved everywhere on Luke's body—kissing his neck, sucking at his nipples and finally, mercifully, enveloping his erection. Warmth and wetness slid over Luke's hardness as Jordan's tongue first sucked and teased the sensitive head of his cock, then glided down his shaft, encompassing him entirely. As Jordan's mouth worked on Luke's cock, his strong hands caressed Luke's abdomen, then trailed down to the juncture of his legs, cupping his balls and teasing the crease of his ass.

It had been so long, and he wanted Jordan so badly, he was unprepared for the ferocity of his body's need to come. "Oh God." Luke couldn't help but cry out as the hard pulls of Jordan's hot mouth, coupled with the light touch of Jordan's fingers, sent him spiraling toward that bright white light where love and passion waited. His body clenched hard, then splintered, racked with powerful shudders. Luke came, and Jordan swallowed down every drop. After giving Luke's cock a final lick and placing a lingering kiss to the head, Jordan sat back on his haunches, looking down at Luke's worn-out body. A smug smile teased his lips.

"How do you feel now?"

A throb of anticipation tightened Luke's belly. "Come on, Prep School." He turned over on his stomach and rose on his arms and knees. "I'm no virgin, but you'll need to go slow at first."

And once again, Jordan began the sweet, languorous kissing up and down Luke's back. He draped himself over Luke, and he planted a heated kiss on the corner of Luke's mouth, then whispered in his ear.

"I've waited what seems like forever to fuck you, and I'm going to take my sweet time now." Hunger spiked throughout Luke's body, but as Jordan's finger, wet with lubricant, breached his hole, a dark memory snaked around Luke's spine.

Every sordid memory he'd buried years ago came rushing back: the yawning darkness of the trucks, their musty, dank smell invading his nostrils as he lay on the different floors. All filthy, all humiliating. The hard press of the anonymous trucker's hand against his back, holding him down. The clinking sound of a belt being undone, and the buzz of a zipper dragged down.

The harsh, burning push inside him. The pain and his tears.

Whether he made a sound or not, he didn't know, but Jordan ceased moving and hugged Luke tight. Entwining their fingers so their hands were clasped tight, Jordan kissed Luke's neck and cheek, whispering softly into his ear, "It's going to be okay, babe. Relax. Remember I love you." Jordan kissed him again and waited.

Luke welcomed the weight of Jordan's body on top of him. It wasn't anything like those men before. It didn't smother him or make him feel trapped. Instead, safety, trust, and faith stole through him. And once he fought past the initial terror, fear, and shame, the earlier hunger and desire roared within him once again. His body ached with a need he'd never experienced.

"Fuck me now. I want you."

And he meant it. Jordan pressed one last kiss on Luke's back and drizzled more lube over his quivering hole. Jordan slid one, then two fingers inside of Luke, and moved them in and out until Luke moaned and rocked his hips back and forth to match Jordan's movement.

"Now, damn it." Luke barely had the capacity to catch his breath and speak.

Jordan pushed his sheathed cock into Luke's willing body, and instead of fearing the invasion, Luke pushed back, sinking Jordan halfway inside. "God, you feel so good." The stretch and fullness mixed in with the pleasure and the sting and burn until he didn't know where Jordan began and he ended. The pull and the push and the slow drag of Jordan's hardness against his sensitized passage sparked an unfamiliar craving within him. A need to be possessed and taken. It shocked and scared him.

A trembling commenced deep inside Luke, like a dark wave threatening to overtake and drag him under. Luke tensed, and Jordan bent over to kiss him, then whisper in his ear. "Own it, Lucas. Control it. I fucking love you. Take everything you need." Jordan continued his push deeper and deeper inside of Luke, and Luke's body began to respond as never before.

Luke's mind emptied of everything but sensation, his body succumbing to Jordan's touch. When he thought the pleasure couldn't soar any higher, Jordan reached beneath Luke and grasped his rigid cock, stroking it with hard, long pulls. Luke shuddered hard, his heart pounding, breathing unsteady.

Jordan stilled, his cock remaining buried deep within Luke. The strain in his voice was apparent as he spoke. "Are you all right? Tell me what you're thinking."

Somehow he managed to dredge up the ability to speak. "I'm thinking you need to move." He reached out his hand, and Jordan grabbed it. "Now."

Jordan complied, snapping his hips hard, thrusting himself deep within Luke's willing body. Trust in their relationship, and having the faith to accept what he'd done and move on, freed Luke to take this step. Jordan opened Luke up to jump headfirst into the love that drenched him as Jordan climaxed, leaving them both shaking and sated; their damp bodies plastered together. Luke loved how every inch of Jordan's pale skin fused to his, connecting them as throbs of pleasure continued to ripple through him.

Jordan buried his face in Luke's curls and nuzzled his neck. "You smell fantastic."

"You're pretty fantastic yourself, you know?" Luke stretched and groaned. Jordan's softening cock slipped out of his sensitive passage, and he hissed a bit. Almost immediately, Luke missed that comforting warmth, even though Jordan remained next to him. Who would have ever thought he'd be a greedy lover? Yet here he was, the compulsion to keep touching Jordan's skin so strong Luke reached out to trail his fingers over the tight, corded muscles of Jordan's thigh simply to keep the physical contact between them.

"Did I hurt you?" Jordan removed the condom and tied it off to drop in the wastebasket, then lay back down next to him. He propped himself up on his elbow to stare into Luke's eyes. "I was worried."

"I know, and you should stop. You didn't hurt me.

I loved it." Luke grabbed Jordan around his neck and pulled him down for a deep kiss. "But how do you feel? Are you ready to start the detox?"

Jordan lay sprawled on Luke's chest and played with his hair. "Yeah. I want to be normal again. I feel like this is a whole new beginning for us as different people. You've finally broken free of your pain, and I'm ready to admit I'm not strong enough to handle my problem, and I can't kick this on my own."

Luke rolled over to trap Jordan underneath him and stared into his face. God, he was so damn beautiful. Even after hot, sweaty sex, with his hair in tangles, a certain elegance about Jordan set him apart from everyone else.

"What are you staring at me for?" Jordan raised a blond brow, a smile tugging at his lips.

"I'm damn lucky." Luke's hand idly stroked Jordan's shoulder, the skin smooth under his touch. "I'm waiting for someone to trip me or smack me in the head, telling me it's all a dream and I don't deserve to be with you or be happy." Self-conscious at his heartfelt declaration, Luke tried to turn away, but Jordan wouldn't allow him to break eye contact.

Staring deep into Luke's eyes, Jordan's honesty shone bright in his clear-eyed gaze. "You're the only thing that's kept me sane all these months. That's why it was killing me, knowing I was lying to you, behaving like a weak, selfish fool."

"Darlin', you are many things, but a fool isn't one of them." Luke's lips quirked in a smile, but Jordan remained serious.

"Stay here with me while I go through this detox. Please? Even if I act like a bastard or say stupid things I don't mean." He squeezed his eyes shut for a moment. "I'm scared, Lucas. I don't know what's going to happen."

It must have taken every bit of courage Jordan had to put aside his massive ego to admit his fear. "Hey, Prep School. I'll always be here for you."

Visible relief flooded Jordan's face. "Thank you," he whispered. "I need you. I need you so much."

He hugged Jordan with a fierce possessiveness. "Don't you worry. Nothing's going to hurt you as long as I'm around."

Chapter Twenty-One

MONDAY CAME MUCH too quickly for Jordan's taste. By nine thirty he'd already finished his second cup of coffee. Ignoring the many phone calls to make, Jordan sat at his kitchen table and chose to think about the incredible weekend he and Lucas had shared. Sasha nudged her muzzle under his hand, and he idly scratched her silky ears. The dog loved Lucas, and Jordan swore she seemed happier when they both walked her and were home with her.

Home. Once again his house felt like a home, thanks to Lucas's presence. Jordan knew he needed Lucas there with him during the nights, when his demons crawled out and made their presence known like an unwanted houseguest. When he confessed his anxiety, Lucas had looked at him strangely.

"You know I'm here for you; whatever you need. But I don't understand what you're anxious about." He kissed him. *"You're a big, bad-ass doctor who doesn't take shit from anyone."*

Jordan contemplated Lucas's remark as he finished

his coffee. While it was true he longed to return to the person he'd once been, he'd changed too much to ever be as dismissive and self-centered as before. It was hard to feel superior when all you were holding on to was the hope of getting through one more day. And your only hope was a small yellow pill.

Doctors carried a natural arrogance around with them. Jordan had never questioned it, as he considered it his due. After all, he saved lives, and as an orthopedic surgeon, he literally put broken people back together again. Setting a shattered bone, piecing together its fragments required manual skill and technical ability, leaving little room for experiment or discussion. It couldn't compare to what Tash hoped to accomplish with him.

Over the past year, he'd discovered that the mind was an unexplored place of fathomless, twisting caverns. Life had become a desert set with minefields, and Jordan had been unprepared for the havoc and grief Keith's death, plus the near destruction of his friendship with Drew, would wreak on him, driving him almost crazy. He'd thought he was stronger than people who'd given in to the desperation. He'd thought he could handle it. He especially never thought he'd become an addict, which proved how much control emotions really had over his mind.

It was part of the reason he decided to go for the seven-day detoxification—a total withdrawal from the Xanax. He'd been weaning himself down and presently only took four pills a day. Still too many, but greatly reduced from what he'd been taking for the past six months. With Tash's professional help during the day and Lucas's love giving him strength at night, Jordan had no doubt he'd overcome his problem. Even now he sensed his resolve returning, flooding his veins with the cocksure attitude that had propelled him to the top of his class and near the top of his field despite his youth.

None of that reasoning helped as he dialed the phone to speak to his boss, the head of orthopedics. Nervous perspiration broke out over his body and his hands shook. How had he allowed himself to sink so low?

"Dr. Springer's office."

God save him from perky people before ten in the morning. "Good morning, Elyse. It's Dr. Peterson. Is he in?"

"One moment, Doctor." Was it his imagination, or did she hesitate?

Before he had a chance to think more about it, the brusque voice of his boss came on the phone. "Jordan? What's the matter?"

He gripped the phone tight and feigned nonchalance. "Why should anything be the matter?"

"Because in the ten years you've worked here, I can't remember the last time you called me. So don't bullshit a bullshitter. Start talking."

He swallowed heavily. "I know I've only come back full-time for a few months now, but, um, I'm going to need a few weeks off. I haven't scheduled any surgeries and…"

"What's the matter, Jordan? Are you sick?"

The surprisingly caring note in Springer's voice caused unexpected tears to rise in Jordan's eyes. *Goddamn it. Get a grip.* "I'm fine…no, I'm not. I'm going in for detox, David. It's a rapid seven-day program, and I'll want the week after off as well, to make sure I'm well enough to return to work. If you still want me."

Silence. Jordan braced himself for what he believed would be his termination due to his drug abuse. He wouldn't fight it, and it would mean he'd never work in a hospital again. The end of his career. Being an orthopedic surgeon was the only thing he'd ever wanted to do since he was in college. His whole body began to shake. What a fucking mess he'd made of his life.

"Do you think we're going to abandon you, Jordan? You've been a practicing physician long enough to know how many doctors face these types of challenges every day."

And Jordan, who believed he'd have to go through this ordeal alone, listened in wonder.

"We take care of our own. Everyone on staff here has been aware of your struggles over the past year, and we all commend you."

"David, I became addicted to Xanax when the struggle became too much to handle. What exactly are you commending me for?" Perhaps he was shooting himself in the foot, but in the ten years he'd known David Springer, the man had hardly been the warm and fuzzy type.

Nor was he now. But his voice, though stern, wasn't condemning or accusatory. "For recognizing you need help. That you had an addiction. This problem has touched almost all of us in this community in so many different ways, whether it be a friend, a family member, or even ourselves. Do you think you're the only one?"

"I didn't know." Before he himself had this problem, Jordan never would have cared about someone else's struggle. "It's not anything I'd ever thought about before—"

"Before you yourself had this problem, right?" Springer chuckled. "I know you, Jordan. You're an excellent technical doctor, but concern for your fellow man was never your strong suit." His voice once again softened. "Sometimes it takes a kick in the ass to show us what really is important in life, doesn't it?"

After hanging up with Springer and promising to keep him abreast of his treatment, Jordan rinsed out his mug and took Sasha out. After a long invigorating walk for the both of them, he mounted the front steps of the brownstone, key in hand when Sasha barked and pulled at her leash. He turned around to see Drew and Ash at the foot of his stairs. Ash was dressed in a suit, obviously on his way in to work, while Drew was his usual more casual self. Hopefully that meant Drew planned to stay for a while and Ash would leave. Even though Jordan had tried to get Lucas to reconcile with Ash, the fact remained that Ash had hurt Lucas so badly he'd been an emotional cripple his entire life, and

Jordan could understand his lover's refusal to resolve their differences. In the war between the two of them, Jordan would always be on Lucas's side.

"Hello, you two. What's up?" They approached, and Sasha met them halfway up the steps, sniffing and licking both their hands. Drew's light green gaze swept over Jordan, assessing him, he thought. "I'm fine, Drew."

Faint pink stained Drew's pale skin. "I know, Jordy. It's been a while since we've hung out, and I thought I could come by, and we'd catch up before I had to go to the clinic."

Ash knelt down to scratch Sasha behind her ears and grinned up at him. "Don't worry. I'm not staying." His smile faded. "Is, um, Luke here, by any chance?"

Jordan almost felt sorry for him. Almost. He had to give Ash credit for never giving up hope that somehow, some way, Luke would cave and talk to him. "No, he left a while ago."

"Oh." After giving the dog one last pat, Ash leaned over and kissed Drew. "Bye, baby. See you tonight."

"Have a good day."

Drew's concentration remained on Ash until the man got into a cab. Only then did Drew face Jordan again with a smile on his lips.

"Things still good between the two of you?" Jordan hoped his tone came across as concerned. Ash had begun to grow on him. Like a fungus.

"Of course." Drew's smile faded. "I love him, Jordan. If you're still hoping he's been some kind of experiment for me, give it up. It's been over a year already, and he's it for me."

"No. No." Jordan put up his hands. "Let's go inside. Tash is coming over, and I need to get ready for him."

Drew followed him silently into the house. Jordan gave Sasha fresh water and indicated to Drew he should take some coffee. "Pour yourself a mug and we can catch up."

Drew poured one for Jordan as well. "Tash is the doctor you introduced us to the night of the center's opening, right?" He sipped the coffee and took a bagel from the plate on the counter. "You don't mind, do you? We ran late, and I didn't have a chance to eat breakfast." He sat and took a knife out of the chef's block to cut his bagel.

"Be my guest." Jordan could only imagine why he overslept, knowing Ash's former reputation as an insatiable lover. He remonstrated with himself, knowing he had to stop accusing Ash of things that weren't true. The man had been nothing but faithful to Drew from the time they'd met, never once reverting to his wild ways. It showed how hard it was to change people's opinions, no matter what the facts were. He'd have to remember that as well in his own life. If he wanted people to know he was no longer the arrogant bastard he'd always been, he had a lot of minds to persuade.

"Yes, Tash is a psychiatrist and will be administering my treatment here, at home. Afterward, I'll be in therapy with him."

"I'm proud of you." Drew put his bagel down on the plate. "It takes tremendous courage to admit an addiction and quit. But I've been reading up on this therapy." He picked the bagel back up, took a bite, and chewed, his furrowed brow evidencing his concern.

"What's the matter, Drew?" Jordan set his mug down on the island and sat.

"I'm a little worried about this drug they give to you, flumazenil. It can have some bad side effects. Are you aware of it?"

Touched by his friend's concern, Jordan hitched his stool closer to Drew's. "Look, I've done my research. I haven't been on the pills that long, so I have that in my favor. But my dosage had been high for several months, so I know I'm going to have withdrawal. Yes, it's not perfect, but I want my life back as quickly as possible. I'm willing to take the risks. It's been hell on earth keeping this from everyone."

"Where does Luke stand in all this? Is he supportive? Because the way he reacted that night at the center opening, I have to admit I was really disappointed in him."

Jordan had no intention of discussing Lucas's reasons with Drew. "He's with me all the way." Jordan took a sip of his coffee. "I love him, Drew."

Drew's eyes crinkled as he grinned. "I could tell. You're finally tolerable to be around. We all owe him one." The smile faded, and he looked sober for a moment. "And I presume he feels the same way?"

Jordan couldn't help the stupid smile he knew broke over his face. "Yeah, he does. I couldn't have made it back without him."

Drew slipped off his stool and hugged Jordan hard. "All I've ever wanted was for you to be happy again. I had such doubts after Keith died. You were so torn up with grief." Always emotional, Drew stopped for a moment to wipe the tears from his eyes. "It's been wonderful watching you come back to life, you know? I couldn't be happier for the two of you, even though I wish we could all settle our differences. Still, it kills me that you didn't come to me for help. You know I'd never judge you."

"I was too fucking proud to admit it. I'm sure you can understand. But I'm over it now. I'm a different person than I was a year ago. Maybe I needed something to kick me in the ass to show me how off the rails I'd gone. All I know is that I'm never going back to how I was before."

Drew raised a brow and grinned, disbelief etched on his face. "Are you kidding? Don't tell me you're going to be nice."

Jordan flipped him off. "Ass. You know what I mean. I know what it's like to be weak and hopeless. I won't ever put down someone else again for feeling that way."

Sasha came wandering in to sit at his feet, and he bent to smooth her short, shiny fur. "It took me a while to move past my guilt as well. Guilt that I could have feelings for someone other than Keith. Sex, yeah. Even though I never believed in sex to get off, it was easier thinking I could do that, rather than ever look at another man or have feelings for someone else. How could I betray Keith and what we had together? But it's not about that. Lucas understands he's not a replacement. I fell in love without even recognizing it happened."

Christ, could he get any sappier? When he sneaked a glance at Drew, his friend had a huge grin on his face.

"What a softie you've become."

"Oh fuck off, D." But they both laughed and sat in companionable silence, drinking their coffee until the doorbell rang, and Jordan knew the hardest fight of his life was about to start. His heart slammed and he trembled. Drew squeezed his arm. "It'll be okay. We're all here for you."

Jordan didn't answer; the nerves had taken control of his body and he struggled not to throw up from fear. Through the sheer curtain covering the glass-fronted door, he could see Tash standing on the stoop, a large satchel in one hand, a cup of coffee in the other.

Here goes nothing. Mustering a smile, Jordan opened the door. "Good morning. Come on in."

Tash smiled back at him. "Good morning." He walked in and placed his bag at the foot of the stairs. "Beautiful place you have here." His gaze swept the room. "Mid to late nineteenth century, I'm guessing."

Jordan nodded. "Yes. It was built around 1880, from what we were able to find out from city records."

"Mind if I wander around?"

"Of course not." Jordan watched as Tash entered the front parlor and gazed up at the tin ceiling.

"Great restoration, too." He looked about appreciatively. "Everything in this room is perfect."

"Thanks."

Drew entered the room, pulling on his jacket. "Are you sure you don't want me to stay? I can reschedule my patients."

But Jordan had gotten himself into this mess and he'd get out of it on his own. He didn't need his friends to see how low he'd sunk.

"No, I'll be fine."

"Call me later then, okay?" He hugged him tight. "I love you. Everything's going to be all right."

"Thanks, D. Love you too, man." He hugged Drew's slender frame. *Thank God for my friends.* "Talk to you later."

Drew shook Tash's hand. "Good to see you again. Take care of this guy. He's a pain in the ass, but I like having him around."

Jordan groaned. "Don't you have work to do? Boobs to lift or something?"

Drew shuddered. "Not anymore. God save me from the ladies who lunch and have too much money and time on their hands."

After Drew left, Jordan showed Tash around the rest of the house. The man certainly knew his architecture, and as they stood in the front parlor, Jordan questioned him on his obvious knowledge.

Tash laughed and pushed his glasses up on his nose.

"Oh, it's only a hobby. I have a carriage house in Brooklyn I spent years renovating, so I'm always interested in seeing what other people have done with their homes." He ran his hand over the carved mantel of the fireplace. "I appreciate when I see a house, like yours, where so much obvious love and thought was put into the restoration."

"Keith and I spent every weekend doing something for this money pit. But I won't deny I love it."

"Why deny it? And it's good you have a comforting place to do the treatment in. Makes things that much easier." He pulled open his satchel and took out a bag of saline, the vial with the dosage of the flumazenil, and the intravenous tubes.

As he worked, Tash talked. "I'm starting you out on a low dosage to see how you react. You haven't been on the Xanax for that long, which is a good thing, so I'm hopeful this will work right from the start."

Jordan clasped his shaking hands together. His heart pounded so hard he hoped he wouldn't stroke out. What a chickenshit he was. He'd taken the drugs with no thought or concern; why did the treatment scare him so much? "How will we know if it works?"

"It's not going to happen overnight, Jordan." Tash put down the vial on the marble coffee table. "You didn't become addicted immediately, so I'm sure you know the treatment won't work after one dose. But after tomorrow, your anxiety level should drop significantly."

"Um, all right. Do I need to do anything?" Jordan

watched as Tash set up the portable IV pole and hung the bag of saline on it.

"Roll up your sleeve and let me go wash my hands."

"Right down the hall to your left."

Tash headed toward the small powder room next to the kitchen. Jordan pushed up the sleeve of his thin sweater and leaned back on the sofa with his eyes closed. Memories of making love with Lucas played in his mind, and a yearning to hold him and be held welled up from within, so strong he almost couldn't breathe. He'd never been so alone as he was at this very moment.

"Hey, Jordan, don't worry. I promise it will be okay." He opened his eyes to view Tash kneeling next to him, a sincere, comforting smile on his handsome face. Jordan couldn't be more thankful to have someone like Tash as his doctor.

"I know." He huffed out a nervous laugh, running his hand through his hair. "Fear of the unknown, I guess."

Tash picked up his hand and squeezed it. "Don't be ashamed. It's normal to be scared. I'd be surprised if you weren't. But I'm going to be with you every step of the way. That's what I'm here for."

Jordan was sitting and staring at their entwined hands when a growling voice broke into his reverie.

"Am I interrupting anything?"

Jordan jerked his hand away and turned around to see a glowering Lucas standing in the doorway. Elation bubbled up inside of him and a wide smile broke across his face as he jumped up and ran over to Lucas.

Jordan threw his arms around him. "What are you doing here? I'm so happy to see you."

After a moment's hesitation, Lucas hugged him back, hard and tight. So tight he almost couldn't breathe, but it felt good to be wanted and needed by this man. "I had Val rearrange my schedule this next week so I can be with you for the treatments. My phone calls will be routed here if that's okay."

"You don't know how much I wanted you here with me." Lucas's heady scent enveloped him, and Jordan couldn't let go, burrowing his face into Lucas's shoulder, digging his fingers into the wool of Lucas's suit jacket. "I was thinking about you."

"Oh yeah?" Lucas slid an arm around his shoulder and raised a brow, a lazy grin tugging at his lips. "What were you thinking, Prep School?"

Jordan pulled him close, loving the hardness of Lucas's body against his. He brushed a soft kiss to Lucas's lips. "I'll tell you later tonight. Or better yet, I'll show you."

Remembering finally that Tash waited to start the treatment, Jordan took Lucas by the hand and brought him to the sofa to sit next to him. "It's great that you're going to be here every day. I'll need all the support I can get."

Lucas shrugged off his jacket then rested his arm behind Jordan as they sat on the sofa. "I'm always here for you. After all, Jordan should have the people around who know him best and care for him, right,

Tash?" He turned a cool eye to Tash, and Jordan wondered what was going on.

Tash rolled up his sleeves his jaw tight. The lightness receded from his face.

"As long as they truly care for him. Jordan will need stability and the knowledge he is loved and cared for. His anxiety levels have to be kept to a minimum." Tash stood. "Are you ready, Jordan?"

Lucas squeezed his shoulder. "You got this, Prep School. Remember what you said to me the other night. Fucking own it and take control."

Jordan nodded and, with an almost surreal detachment, felt the cool swab of alcohol against his skin then observed Tash sliding the needle into his vein, then injecting the flumazenil into the IV. After adjusting the drip, Tash placed a small bandage on his arm at the site of the needle insertion.

"That's it." Tash smiled. "Now relax, maybe close your eyes for a while, and take a nap."

Lucas carefully lay Jordan's head down in his lap. "Here, use me as your pillow."

Jordan rested his cheek on Lucas's solid thigh, settling in with a comfortable sigh. The faint scent of citrus body wash combined with Lucas's underlying heat and musk both stirred and soothed Jordan. He closed his eyes, finally able to believe he'd begun to turn his life around.

Chapter Twenty-Two

"Hey, Prep School. You awake?" Luke smoothed the blond waves off Jordan's brow. For the past hour, he'd been on the phone conducting business, but managed to sneak in to grab quick glances at Jordan as he slept. Poor guy went out not long after the treatment began. From all his tossing and turning in bed, Luke knew how little Jordan had actually slept the night before, and he was loathe to wake him, but Tash said he needed to eat something, as it was already after two in the afternoon.

"Why did you stop being my pillow?" Jordan scrubbed his face with his hands, then frowned.

That was more like it. Jordan was a perfect Oscar the Grouch, and Luke made a mental note to buy him an Oscar T-shirt. "You were out of it, and I needed to make some phone calls for work." Lucas's smile faded. He was so worried about the side effects. He should've known better than to go online and check those medical websites that made you believe you suffered every deadly illness known to man. "How do you feel?"

With some anxiety, Luke studied Jordan as he swung his legs off the sofa and sat up. Luke put a steadying hand on his shoulder, but Jordan shook it off. "No, I'm fine. I'm surprised but yeah, I feel good." He glanced around the room. "Where's Tash?"

"Here." Lucas heard footsteps behind him from the hallway. Tash had a stethoscope around his neck and a blood pressure cuff in his hands. "I had to get these. I need to check your vitals, Jordan."

Lucas held his breath as Tash performed the routine exam.

"Well? Will I live?" Jordan laughed and pulled down his sleeve.

Luke failed to appreciate Jordan's attempt at humor. "Don't joke, Jordan. Christ, you're a doctor. You know anything can go wrong with these treatments."

"I'm sorry. I was only trying to lighten the mood." Jordan placed his hand on top of Luke's, sliding their fingers together.

"I know, but I'm nervous." Luke stared at their entwined fingers. "I don't want anything happening to you."

"He's right, though." Tash folded the blood pressure cuff and put it on the coffee table. "This treatment is still not favored by all doctors and has been known to cause seizures in a small percentage of patients."

"Are you fucking kidding me?" Lucas yelled and dropped Jordan's hand. "I don't remember reading that."

Sasha came running down the hallway, barking her

head off. Protective as always, she ran straight for Jordan, crowding against his legs. He spoke softly to her, rubbing her ears and praising her. She licked his hand while keeping a wary eye on the others. She loved Lucas, but Jordan was the one she adored above all.

After taking several minutes to calm his dog down, Jordan addressed Luke's outburst. "I'm aware of the risk, and I still chose to do this. I need to get this poison out of my system as fast as possible." He indicated the needle in his arm. "I did this to myself, Lucas. I have to do it my way."

Luke remained standing, still unconvinced. "But why take unnecessary risks? That's what I don't understand."

"I'm monitoring him with the utmost care, Luke." Tash spoke up from his stance by the fireplace. "I know you're concerned, and I appreciate that, as I'm going to leave him in your care for a while this evening."

Luke whirled, panic-stricken, fear thumping through his veins. "You can't be serious. I don't know what to do." He paced the floor. "What if something happens? What if—"

"Lucas. Relax. Come over here and sit." Jordan patted the cushion next to him. "It's going to be fine."

"No, no, it's not. I'm not a doctor, for Christ's sake. I'm a financial analyst. What am I going to do if he gets sick, sell his stocks?"

Tash burst out laughing. "Listen to Jordan. Chill out and sit down already, and I'll explain what to do."

Reluctantly Luke returned to the couch to sit by

Jordan's side. He folded his arms. "Go on. I'm listening."

Jordan nudged him with his elbow. "Don't be rude."

Tash dropped into the chair opposite them. "It's fine. I don't blame him for being concerned." He turned his attention to Luke. "I'd never leave Jordan if I didn't think you could take care of him. He's already finished with his dosages for the day, and he seems to have made it through them without many issues."

"But he had some?" Luke glanced over at Jordan, who outwardly seemed relaxed and unconcerned. Who the hell knew what time bomb ticked inside of him?

Tash nodded, and Luke appreciated the fact that the man wasn't sugarcoating his speech. "He's slightly pale, and his pressure is a bit low. Not anything to be concerned about, but it's something to keep an eye on." He took out a different blood pressure cuff from his bag. "This is an automatic blood pressure machine. You'll take it every four hours to see if it stays steady. I'll show you how to use it before I leave later."

Luke never took his eyes off Tash, drinking in every word he said. As far as he was concerned, Jordan's life depended on it. "Okay, I've used them before at the gym." He turned to Jordan and glared at him. "You aren't going to give me a hard time about this, right?"

"No, *Warden*, I promise." Jordan smirked at him, but Luke still wasn't laughing, so his expression turned serious. "I promise, Lucas." Then he grinned, blue eyes dancing. "I always wanted a hot male nurse taking my vitals." He stood up and swayed a bit. Luke jumped to his side and held on to him.

"You all right? Go on, lean on me."

A fine sweat beaded on Jordan's forehead. He attempted to laugh, but from the grimace on his face, coupled with the look of panic, Luke knew things weren't as perfect as Jordan would like. "What's wrong?"

"I think I'm gonna throw up." Jordan gripped his arm. "Shit." He stumbled, and Luke half led, half carried him to the small bathroom by the kitchen. As Jordan fell to his knees, retching miserably into the toilet, Luke smoothed the hair off his face and rubbed his back.

"Take it easy, darlin'. It'll be okay." He patted Jordan's sweat-dampened back, but Jordan rolled his shoulders and pushed him away.

"Go away," he rasped. "Leave me alone." He breathed heavily but wasn't sick again.

"Don't be ridiculous. Let me help."

"I said get out," Jordan lashed out. "Stop hovering over me like I'm an invalid." He kicked the door shut on him.

Wise to Jordan's temper and not wanting to upset him any further, Luke waited in the hallway. Sasha sat by his feet and whined.

"Yeah, I know, sweetheart. But his bark is worse than his bite."

After several minutes of waiting, Luke heard the toilet flush and the water run in the sink. The door opened, and a disheveled-looking Jordan stepped out. Hollow-eyed and worn, he leaned against the doorjamb and rubbed his hand over his mouth. "I'm sorry I snapped at you. I hate people seeing me weak and out of control." Sasha let out a short bark, and gingerly, Jordan squatted down on his heels to pet her.

"I know you do. But you need help, and that's why I'm here and Tash as well. You're going to get through this, but you have to work with us."

Glancing up at him from petting the dog, Jordan flashed a rueful smile. "Bet you didn't think you'd end up as my nursemaid."

"I'm not. I'm your lover, and I care for you. So you're going to let me and your doctor do what's best for you. Got it?"

Instead of letting loose with another outburst, warmth kindled in Jordan's pale blue eyes. After giving the dog one last pat, he stood and wordlessly took Luke's face between his hands and kissed him. Hard. He tasted fresh, of mint and clean water, but his tongue slid inside hot, slick, and needy. They stayed like that for a few minutes until Luke heard a throat clear and then a cough.

Kissing Jordan one last time, Luke opened his eyes. Over Jordan's shoulder, he saw Tash standing in the hallway, a surprisingly sad look on his face. Unexpected sympathy for the man welled inside Luke, making him more generous in spirit than he normally might be. "I think you need to get some food inside you, Prep School. All you had was a bite of a bagel this morning."

Jordan made a face. "I can't even think of eating."

"Luke is right, though. You need something inside your stomach to settle it. How about some toast and scrambled eggs? I can make that for you."

Jordan opened his mouth, then snapped it shut. Luke was certain he was about to protest, but weak as he was, Jordan couldn't take care of himself. "Fine." They traipsed into the kitchen, and after Jordan sat down at the table, Luke and Tash busied themselves getting a light lunch prepared. They talked as they worked, and Luke's earlier misgivings melted away in the face of the obvious concern Tash had for Jordan.

He placed a plate of eggs and toast in front of Jordan. "Here you go."

Jordan placed a forkful in his mouth, then pushed the rest of the food around on his plate.

"Not hungry, huh?"

"Not at all. I'm tired. I want to go to bed."

Luke glanced over at Tash, who was washing up. "Can he go to sleep now?"

Tash nodded. "It's the medicine that's making him tired. Sure. Let's take your pressure one more time, and then you can get into bed."

This time, Luke used the automatic machine, with Tash supervising. After all the beeping had died away, Luke squinted at the numbers and breathed a sigh of relief: 118/78. "That's normal, right?"

Both Jordan and Tash nodded, and he grinned. "Well then, let's go get you into bed, Dr. Peterson."

Jordan's eyes gleamed. "Care to join me?"

Luke's blood warmed. "No, darlin'. You need your strength. Now come on." He slipped his arm around Jordan's shoulders and helped him up the stairs. They entered the bedroom, and Luke was in the middle of straightening out the blanket when the phone rang. He handed it to Jordan.

"Hey, how are you?" *It's Drew*, Jordan mouthed.

His stomach lurched. If so, then Ash was involved somehow. He pretended to fold the blanket, anxious to hear the rest of the conversation.

"Sure, of course you guys can come over. Mike and Rachel too. We haven't all been together in a long time." Jordan gnawed on his lips. "Yes, he will be." His gaze flicked up to meet Luke's. "I don't presume to speak for Lucas. He can make his own decisions." Then Jordan smiled at him. "Whatever he chooses, I'm behind him one hundred percent. Like you are with Ash."

Luke's heart did a funny bounce in his chest. He tried to remember when he'd ever heard anyone say that to him, and couldn't come up with one single time.

Damn, he loved this guy.

Jordan disconnected the call and placed the phone on the bed by the time Luke refocused. "They all want to come over and see how I'm doing. They'll be here around eight."

"Sure, of course. They're your best friends. I don't blame them for wanting to see you." Luke thought he'd kept his expression neutral, but he couldn't fool someone as perceptive as Jordan.

"You don't have to speak with Ash. I can barely stand talking to him myself, so we can commiserate together." He gave a huge yawn and settled back in the bed. "Sure you don't want to join me?"

The simple memory of the naked heat of their bodies that morning and the slide of Jordan's stubbled chin on the back of his neck inflamed Luke, but the sight of Jordan's sleepy blue eyes and drowsy smile pushed aside any thoughts of playtime.

"You need to sleep. I'll walk Sasha and come back. Tash will be here."

"Mhmm." Jordan's eyes had already closed, and Luke doubted Jordan had even heard what he said.

Luke went downstairs and found Tash on his laptop. "I'm going to take the dog out for a while. Do you want anything?"

Keeping his eyes fixed on the screen, Tash shook his head. "I'm fine. I have to answer some e-mails and make some phone calls. Take as long as you want."

Luke whistled for the dog and took her leash off the hook by the front door. He walked out into the crisp sunlight and inhaled an invigorating, deep breath. Sasha pulled at her leash, anxious to get moving. "Okay, girl, let's go." He set off for the dog park.

An hour later, they tumbled back into the house. Luke let Sasha off her leash as soon as they were inside the front door, and she made a beeline for the kitchen. He could hear her slurping the water from her bowl. Cold water sounded like heaven, so he grabbed a bottle from the refrigerator and wandered back into the front room, where Tash stared at his phone, taking notes in a small notepad.

With a satisfied grunt, he dropped into a chair and stretched out his legs. It had been a jumbled, nerve-racking day, and Luke was glad Jordan could sleep. Hopefully when Jordan woke up, his body could better adjust to the treatment. Luke closed his eyes.

"Luke, Luke." From a distance, he heard his name. Blinking and yawning, he stretched, then opened his eyes to see Tash standing over him, silhouetted by the glow of the sconces that flanked the door. The light glowed soft and golden, glinting off Tash's glasses, which he'd pushed up to rest on top of his head.

"Hmm, what time is it?"

"After six. You were in such a deep sleep I didn't want to wake you. I checked on Jordan, and he's still sleeping. I need to run home, feed my cats, and check my mail. I'll be back later tonight. Jordan should sleep awhile longer; then he can eat a light meal."

He could handle that. And the guys were coming over, so he wouldn't be alone in case Jordan needed him. "I can run out for a few minutes, right? Like to walk the dog and around the corner to the store for a little while?

"Sure. He's not ill, understand that. He simply needs looking after, and you're doing fine." Tash slipped the glasses back on and met his gaze. "For a while I had my doubts about you. It hurt Jordan when you left him that night."

"I know. You needn't go into it." His reaction still shamed him, and Luke's anger rose a bit at Tash's lecture. Then Luke remembered Jordan sleeping upstairs and how Jordan had suffered over the past year. "I'm sorry I was short. We've made our peace, and we're in a good place now. He doesn't ever have to worry about me again."

"Well, that's good to know." Jordan leaned against the doorway, his hair mussed and sticking up in several directions, but his eyes shone clear and bright.

Luke jumped out of his chair and rushed over to him. "Why didn't you call out for help? You could've fallen."

Jordan made a face. "I'm not sick; you heard Tash. I feel much better now that I've slept. And yeah, you need to walk Sash and get stuff for everyone else when they come later. I've got nothing in the house, not even beer." He kissed Luke. "Go on, seriously. I feel good and I'm going to take a shower." With Sasha following at his feet, he trudged up the stairs.

Tash had already put on his jacket. "He'll be fine, Luke. Give him some space." He checked his watch. "You're okay with me leaving, right?"

"Yeah. I'll run out now while he's in the shower. It shouldn't take me longer than half an hour." Luke walked Tash to the door. "Thanks for everything." He held out his hand. "I was wrong about you as well. You've been a great friend to both of us."

Tash shook his hand, a rueful smile on his lips. "I'm not that nice. If you hadn't come back, I would have waited until Jordan was no longer in my care, then asked him out." Laugh lines fanned out from the corners of his eyes. "Don't worry, though. I know when I've lost."

Well, damn. Give the guy points for honesty if nothing else. Luke closed the door and sprinted up the stairs, calling out to Jordan. "Hey, Prep School. I'm heading out to the store."

Jordan started the shower and yelled out over the spray. "See you when you get back."

Sasha sat at the foot of the stairs, giving him pathetic doggie eyes. "Yes, I'm taking you for a walk, but you can't come into the store."

Obviously, she didn't care, as she raced to the front door, stubby tail wagging. He snapped on her leash, and they headed outside into the darkening night.

Unfortunately, everyone else in New York City seemed to have picked the same time and place to shop, so it was closer to an hour by the time Luke escaped the supermarket and he hurried down the block, anxious to get back. As they approached the house, Sasha growled and whined, pulling at her leash.

"Stop it. We'll be inside in a moment." Luke, juggling two bags, didn't have the strongest hold on her leash, and with one strong tug, she pulled free and raced to the house, barking her head off. The hair on the back of his neck stood up as he saw her enter through the open front door he remembered locking before he'd left.

"Fuck." He dropped the bags on the sidewalk,

unconcerned about the food spilling out. "Jordan." He pounded up the steps to the house and ran inside. "Jordan, where the hell are you?"

Chapter Twenty-Three

L UKE'S SNEAKERS CRUNCHED on the broken glass in the entranceway. He nearly tripped over himself as he sprinted up the stairs. Following the sounds of Sasha barking and crying, he skidded into the bedroom and stopped short. "Fuck me, no." Jordan lay crumpled on the floor, his face battered and bloody. His arms rested over his head as if he'd tried to protect himself from further blows. Fortunately, Luke could see the subtle rise and fall of Jordan's breath in his chest.

"Hey, Prep School, can you hear me?" He dropped to his knees next to Jordan's too-still body. It was only then that he saw the blood seeping into the rug beneath Jordan's head, and he froze. "Shit, fuck." He pulled out his cell phone and dialed 911, reporting the break-in and that they needed an ambulance. The next call he made was to Tash.

"Hey, Luke, what's—"

"Listen." There was no time for small talk. "There was a break-in while I was gone. Jordan's been attacked, and he's unconscious. I called the ambulance, and they're on their way."

"Okay. They'll take him to Beth Israel, so I'll meet you there."

Luke disconnected and listened for the wail of sirens but heard nothing. "Come on, you fuckers. What's taking so long?" Luke checked Jordan again and let out a relieved sigh to see he still breathed steadily.

He remembered that Jordan's friends were coming and knew he'd have to call and tell them what happened. Since he didn't have Drew's number on his phone, he picked up Jordan's cell phone from the floor and scrolled through until he found it. After only a split second hesitation he hit the Call button.

"Hey, Jordan, we were about to leave. What's up?"

And of course, since this was the worst fucking day of his life in years, Ash had to answer Drew's phone.

"It's Luke. I need to speak to Drew."

"Luke." Ash's voice turned sharp, all humor gone. "What's wrong?"

Fuck it. "It's Jordan. The house was broken into while I was out, and he was attacked." Now he heard the sirens. "Look, the ambulance is here; I have to go. They'll take him to Beth Israel."

"We'll meet you there."

Luke clicked off and ran downstairs. He'd never been so happy to see the red-and-white FDNY EMS truck as he was at that moment. "In here," he yelled as he watched the two EMS techs jump out. "He's upstairs."

After pulling out a collapsible stretcher and a medical bag, they followed him up the stairs to the bed-room. Luke stepped aside as they took over. One of the guys, heavily tattooed and bald, knelt at Jordan's feet; the other, lanky with a thin goatee, stood by his head.

"Is he on any medication that you know of?" This from the tattooed EMS worker, whose name tag read *Caruso.*

"Yeah. He started taking flumazenil this morning. He's being treated for Xanax dependency."

"Okay. Anything else? Who are you, a friend?" The guy with the goatee, Hernandez, was taking notes. "Were you the one who called it in?"

"Yes. I'd gone out to the store. We were having friends over for dinner. When I got back, the dog went crazy and ran up here and I followed her." He swallowed hard. "Is he going to be all right?"

Caruso didn't answer. "Luis, get the stretcher." Hernandez sped out to the hallway, and Caruso snapped on a pair of thin rubber gloves.

After checking Jordan's pulse and blood pressure, Caruso turned to him. "Any other medical issues?"

"No, none."

Hernandez came back in then, and begrudgingly, Luke had to admit they got Jordan on the stretcher and down the stairs within minutes. Except for a few moans, Jordan didn't make a sound. When Luke tried to get into the ambulance, Hernandez stopped him.

"Sorry, sir, you can't come with us. Family only."

Unwilling to hold them up, Luke merely nodded and watched them drive away, the red taillights receding, taking his heart with them.

BY THE TIME Luke arrived at the hospital, Jordan had already been whisked into an examining room in the ER. He jammed his hands into his pockets and nervously rocked back and forth on the balls of his feet as he waited to speak with the woman at the desk.

"I'm sorry, sir, but I have no information on his condition at the moment." She offered him nothing more than a sympathetic smile. "Have a seat, and I'll let you know when his status changes."

Frustrated, he jerked a nod of thanks and stalked back to the row of uncomfortable plastic chairs and slumped down in one of the few vacant ones available. As usual, would-be patients and their families crowded the emergency room. It had been over ten years since he'd set foot in a hospital and the harsh, antiseptic smell remained as familiar as his aftershave, overtaking his senses. It evoked the dark memories of the night he'd been brought in, broken and bloodied after that cataclysmic fight between him and his foster father. Even now, he struggled for air, recalling the days of pain that followed. How alone he'd been when only Mrs. Cartwright from down the road had come by to see him, to tell him his "family" had left in the middle of the night and no one knew where they'd disappeared to.

No fucking way would he allow his head games to

start now. Luke squeezed his eyes shut, willing away thoughts of the past. All his concentration needed to focus on Jordan.

"Luke."

He opened his eyes to see Drew and Ash in front of him.

"I don't know anything. They won't tell me. You could find out though, Drew." Luke jumped out of the chair and grabbed the man by his arm. "Come on. You're a doctor; they'll let you in to see him. Excuse me." He pulled Drew over to the woman behind the desk. "This is Dr. Klein. He's a friend of Dr. Peterson, who I came in with. He can go in and see him, right?"

Drew showed her his credentials, and she nodded. "He's in room three, Doctor. Through those doors and past the nurses' station."

"Thank you." Drew gave her a brief smile, then led Luke back to the waiting area. And Ash. "You wait here, and I'll be out as soon as I can." Drew surprised Luke by pulling him close in a short, hard hug. "Don't worry. Jordan's not going anywhere except home with you." He walked swiftly through the swinging doors, and then Luke was alone.

With Ash.

He expected to have to make excuses not to talk to Ash, but his fears were unwarranted as Ash sat in a vacant seat. A faint yet sardonic smile crossed his lips. "I'm not going to try and speak to you; don't worry. There's a time and a place for everything, Luke. This qualifies as neither."

Feeling as if a small weight had been lifted from his shoulders, Luke collapsed into a chair. "Thank you for that." Jordan's face rose in his mind.

See? You can do it. Remember what I said the other night. I fucking love you. Own it; take control of it. You're stronger than your fear.

As if a switch had turned on inside him, it all clicked into place. Not knowing Jordan's condition, whether he was critically injured, made Luke take stock of himself and his own life. What purpose did his hatred of Ash serve? They couldn't go back. But maybe they could use this tragedy—or he could, at least—to make himself stronger and move on from his anger. He loved Jordan. He was certain of that fact, and if loving him meant putting up with seeing Ash occasionally, it was worth it to keep Jordan in his life.

"Hey, Ash?" Luke almost laughed at the look of shock on Ash's face.

"Yes?" Ash's cautious voice wavered.

"Hopefully, Jordan will come out of this and be home soon." Luke took a deep breath. Although he'd made the decision to put it out in the open between them, the reality of saying it proved harder than he'd imagined. A drop of cold sweat trickled down his back. "I'd, um, I'd like us, along with Drew and Jordan, to get together one night. To talk."

Ash blanched, turning into a marble statue. His pale eyes glittered in the harsh fluorescent light of the waiting room. "This isn't some sort of cruel joke you're playing on me, is it?"

"No." Luke shook his head. "Sometimes it takes a crisis to see what's important." He stared off, unseeing, into space. "Nothing's more important to me now than making sure Jordan is all right. I finally get what you feel for Drew."

Ash's lips curved. "Scary as shit, isn't it?"

Luke joined him in that smile. "Yeah. It sure is."

They sat in silence. Luke remained fixated on the swinging doors where he'd seen Drew disappear. One hour turned into two. Before he'd come to the hospital, Luke had contacted Mike and Rachel, and they'd picked up Sasha to bring her home with them. Rachel had texted him, letting him know Sasha had settled in fine, and that Mike was on his way over to the hospital.

After another half an hour, where Luke thought he'd jump out of his skin every time the door swung open, Mike had shown up, so the three of them sat around together, feeling useless, Luke thought bitterly.

"What's taking so fucking long?" Lucas couldn't stand sitting anymore and paced the small waiting area. "It's been hours already. He must be worse than we thought."

"He isn't the only patient. They probably had to take him for X-rays and then wait to read the results." Mike's attempt to reason with him failed, as he felt no better.

"He's too damn stubborn to let a knock on the head keep him down." Ash flashed him a quick smile. "He's probably being his usual obnoxious self to the nurses."

Luke remained unconvinced. "I have a bad feeling." The doors swung open, and Drew made his appearance, looking worn-out and disheveled, but ultimately all Luke could see was the smile on his face. He ran over to Drew and skidded to a stop in front of him.

"Well, tell me? Is he going to be okay? Is he awake?"

Drew put up his hands. "Whoa. Let me tell you what I know." He waved to Mike and Ash. "Both of you come." He led the three of them to a more secluded section of the waiting area.

"He has a slight concussion and severely bruised ribs. They kicked him pretty badly in his side, so the doctor needed to make sure he wasn't bleeding internally from any ruptured organs."

"Was he?" Luke held his breath.

"No, thank God."

Drew paused and took a moment to rub his eyes. Luke could tell how drained he was, not only physically but emotionally. It struck him then that by falling in love with Jordan, he'd inherited an entire family in Mike, Rachel, Drew, and Esther. Funny how that didn't seem to rankle him as much as it had before.

Ash put his arms around Drew, and Drew sank back into the larger man's embrace. The tenderness between them went beyond anything physical. It spoke in the way Drew relaxed against Ash's chest and the brief brush of Ash's lips in Drew's hair. Something about the unassuming Drew Klein had so ensnared Ash he'd completely turned his life around and, more importantly, fallen in love.

Now the same thing had happened to him. Jordan completely shocked his senses, giving him something he never thought to have. A second chance. A home. They'd both been burned so badly, so hurt and beaten down by what life had thrown in their paths, that they'd scarcely recognized when the real thing hit them in the face.

"Is he awake? Can I see him?" Luke bounced on his feet, nervous and dancing as if he stood on the head of a lit match.

"Yeah. Tash is back there with him now." Drew kissed Ash and took Luke by the elbow, leading him through the swinging doors. "You won't be able to stay long, but I know he'll be happy to see you."

Luke swallowed hard, breathing through his mouth, so he didn't have to smell the noxious fumes of ether, antiseptic, and bleach. He kept his eyes trained on the top of Drew's dark head. The beeping of the machines, the moans of the patients, and the blare of the overhead speakers melded together until he could only hear a low whine playing in his head.

Shit. I hope I don't get sick.

They came before a curtained-off area. "He's in here. They don't have a room for him yet." Drew pulled the curtain and stepped aside. "Jordy. Someone's here to see you."

Luke hesitated, then grinned to himself when he heard Jordan's irritable voice. "Who is it? Christ, D. You didn't let Ash in here, did you? My head already hurts."

Peering around Drew's shoulder, Luke winced at the sight of Jordan, pale and bandaged. "Hey, Prep School. How're you feeling?" Black anger welled up inside of him at the thought of anyone laying hands on Jordan, touching him, hurting him. For everyone's sake, he swallowed down the rage threatening to swamp him with bloodlust.

"Like shit. I have a massive headache, my side is killing me, and I'm freezing." The smile Jordan aimed his way belied his complaints. "But I wouldn't mind if you came closer, you know."

As he entered the small space, Luke saw Tash standing off to the side, and acknowledged him, but focused his attention mainly on Jordan. "Try not to talk. You need your rest." It hurt his heart to see Jordan laid out in the bed, on sheets merely a shade whiter than the pallor of his skin.

"Yes, I know. But I need you to rest properly, so come here already." In his typical impatient fashion, Jordan waved his hand at Luke, beckoning him closer. "I'm not going to break. Tell him, D."

Drew rolled his eyes. "Come on, Jordan. Luke and everyone else have been outside waiting for hours. Don't give the guy a hard time. Besides, we can't stay here long. They're going to admit you."

"Why can't I go home? I'm fine." He pointed to his head. "It barely hurts anymore. I can take some aspirin and rest in my own bed."

"Don't be a dope," Luke scolded him. "I can't

watch you properly."

"I'd rather you watch me improperly." His teeth gleamed, but as he attempted to sit up, an inadvertent groan slipped out and he paled.

In a flash, Luke was by Jordan's side, bracing his arm against Jordan's shoulder. His throat tightened. Jordan seemed almost fragile, his bones slight, as though they could easily be snapped by a too-strong wind. "Take it easy. Lie back down."

This time, Jordan merely listened and sank back into the pillow. A light sweat had broken out across his brow, and he closed his eyes. "Shit, my head is spinning and pounding at the same time."

"That's because you probably have a concussion, you idiot," Drew snapped at him. "Now lie back, don't move, and they'll be taking you to your room shortly. You aren't the only one who's exhausted. We've been worried sick for hours, especially Luke."

Impressed by Drew's out-of-character behavior, Jordan's easy compliance with Drew's orders surprised Luke. Sometimes the quiet ones fooled you, he mused, giving Drew a respectful nod of thanks.

"He'll bully you if you don't push back, you know." Drew hugged him as he prepared to leave. "Don't let him tell you what to do. He thinks only he knows what's best for everyone." He returned to the bed where Jordan lay with his eyes closed, his breathing light but steady. "Stop giving everyone a hard time. Listen to the nurses and hopefully you'll only be in here a day or so." Drew bent down and kissed his cheek.

"Try and rest and I'll see you later. I love you."

Jordan opened his eyes. "Thank you. I love you too." He swallowed hard. "And thank Ash for me. I know he's been out there waiting as well."

Surprise flared in Drew's light eyes, but he simply nodded and gave Luke's shoulder a squeeze before leaving. Tash had left several minutes earlier when it became apparent that Jordan wasn't seriously injured. The events of the night hit Luke all at once, and he began to fade, but he needed to reassure Jordan all would be well, and he wanted to tell him about his decision to speak with Ash.

Lucas picked up Jordan's hand and kissed it. "I thought I'd lost you there for a moment, Prep School."

Keeping his eyes closed, Jordan smiled. "It would take more than a hard knock to my head to get rid of me." He licked his lips. "Shit, my whole body hurts."

Luke smoothed the hair off Jordan's brow. There were a cup and pitcher on the table next to the bed, and he gave Jordan a drink of cold water. "Drink it slow."

"Thanks. I've been choking all night; my throat's been so dry."

They sat, and after a while, Luke thought Jordan had fallen asleep. Almost dead on his feet, he rose to go home. He bent to kiss Jordan on his forehead. "I love you, Jordan. Don't ever leave me."

To his surprise, Jordan opened his eyes and grabbed his hand. "If I have anything to say about it, I never will. Having you here with me tonight, knowing I have you to come home to, makes the ride all worth it.

There was only one thought going through my mind when they were beating me."

Luke bit his lip, unable to talk as Jordan continued.

"All I could think of was, God, don't let Lucas find me dead. If I'm going to die, I have to be able to say good-bye because I need to see his face one more time." Tears fell from his eyes. "I didn't want to die without you hearing me tell you how much I love you." Jordan's shaking hand clasped his. "Don't ever doubt your place in my heart and my life."

"I told Ash I wanted to talk to him," Luke blurted out, unable to hold himself back any longer. "When you get out of the hospital, I want the four of us to get together."

Jordan's eyes glowed. "I'm proud of you. But are you sure you want Drew and me there? Don't you want to speak alone with him after all these years?"

Unashamed of his emotions, Luke clutched Jordan's hand. "I can't do it alone. Please be there for me." Luke knew he and Ash faced an emotional battlefield and were bound to hurt one another. The history between them had never really been buried, no matter how he'd tried. It remained by the surface, bubbling up every once in a while. For years he'd smothered his pain by shoveling another layer of resentment on top, but the time had come to unearth the demons and put them to rest.

Jordan patted his hand. "If you need me, I'm there for you." His eyes slid shut, and Luke knew he'd fallen asleep almost immediately.

Luke kissed his cheek. "I'll always need you."

Chapter Twenty-Four

"I CAN DO this on my own. I don't need your help." Nothing irritated Jordan more than to have people hovering over him, thinking him weak and lacking. "It's been over a week already. My head barely hurts anymore." He pushed at Lucas's hand on his elbow.

Without missing a step, Lucas tightened his hold. "Well, tough shit. You're getting my help whether you like it or not. Not only are you still recovering from the attack, but you're coming off the addiction treatment, in case you've forgotten."

"Not likely. Christ, Lucas. You're worse than my mother." His parents remained stuck in the mountains in Switzerland due to the snow, but they'd spoken several times over the past few days. After reassuring them he was fine and having a tearful conversation with them about his addiction, he'd introduced them to Lucas. They'd adored Keith, and Jordan knew his mother had despaired of him ever finding someone else to spend his life with. Her tentative efforts to suggest he meet someone new had been met with angry silence and ultimately his disengagement. When he told them about Lucas, his mother burst into tears. Lucas and his parents had, as expected, hit it off.

"Your mom is cool." Lucas smirked, and Jordan rolled his eyes. "Besides she already loves me, and she hasn't even met me yet."

"All right, stud, let's go downstairs before your ego inflates so much you can't fit through the door. You've kept me a prisoner in this house long enough."

Lucas took his elbow and helped him down the stairs, where a chorus of cheers and applause greeted him. Everyone was there: Drew and Ash, Mike and Rachel, Esther and a distinguished-looking elderly gentleman, Wanda, Keith's partner Jerry, and even Dr. Springer. Tash and his sister, Valerie, rounded out the group.

But Jordan only had eyes for Sasha, who, held back by Mike, barked and strained at her collar. Gingerly, as his ribs still twinged slightly at sudden movement, he knelt down and held out his arms. "Come here, girl. Come, sweetheart."

Whining and wriggling across the floor, Sasha crept toward Jordan as if she knew she couldn't fling herself on top of him. When she finally got close enough, she scooted into his arms and gave his face a thorough tongue washing. Jordan stayed there, despite the soreness in his side, giving the dog comfort. It must've been harrowing for her to not only find him hurt, but then to have her life flipped upside down—first staying with Mike and Rachel, and then not seeing him for the past week and a half while he was incarcerated in the hospital. Lucas had insisted that Mike and Rachel could watch her better than he could, so he could concentrate not only on Jordan's recovery from the beating but the continuation of the treatment for Xanax withdrawal. Plus, he admitted not wanting to leave Jordan alone anymore, even if only to walk the dog. Jordan vowed to give her some much-needed alone time with him, complete with extra treats.

Lucas took a steady hold of his elbow as he attempted to stand. The man had an uncanny ability to understand Jordan's moves, maybe even before he knew himself what he needed. "Thanks." He flashed Lucas a smile.

"I think you should sit down." Keeping ahold of his arm, Lucas steered him into the large front room and settled him onto the sofa. The rest of the guests trailed after them and found seats. From his vantage point, Jordan could see past the open, glass-fronted French doors into the dining room, where a spread of food lay waiting to be consumed. Platters of cold cuts, salads and all types of breads and rolls awaited. On the sideboard sat a myriad of desserts, including a large chocolate cake that looked suspiciously like it came from his favorite bakery in the East Village.

"Jordan, darling." Esther came over and kissed him, patting his cheek with tenderness. "Won't you let me make you a plate of something? I baked you those brownies you love so much." Her bright blue eyes shone with love, and Jordan squeezed her hand.

"I'll never refuse your brownies; you know that." The gentleman hovering next to her caught his eye. "I don't believe you've introduced me to your friend." He grinned as her cheeks flushed pink. Did Esther have a man in her life? Over her shoulder, he caught Drew's eye. His friend gave a thumbs up and a wink. He had to blink twice, though, when he saw Lucas and Ash speaking to each other. Perhaps they'd given him a hallucinogenic instead of the flumazenil treatment. Lucas had said he wished to make peace with his foster brother, and to Jordan, they looked downright cordial to one another. Friendlier even than Jordan himself had ever been to Ash in the past.

"Oh, yes. This is Jack Birnbaum. He and I met at the neighborhood senior center. He lives a few blocks away, and we've been enjoying each other's company."

Jordan extended his hand and was pleased to note Jack's firm handshake. "Nice to meet you, Jack."

The man's good-natured expression never faltered as he shifted his attention from Esther to Jordan. "Nice to meet you, Doctor. Esther has told me so much about you, about all of you in fact. I'm glad you're home. Why don't you let me fix you a little nosh while you relax with everyone." His brown eyes twinkled as he whispered to Jordan, "That'll give me a chance to sneak a few cookies in without Esther yelling at me to watch my diet."

Oh, he liked this man already. "Thanks, Jack. I appreciate it."

Esther patted Jack's hand, and he went into the dining room.

"He seems nice." Lucas sat next to Jordan. "Stretch out. You can put your head in my lap."

Jordan complied, almost moaning with delight as Lucas's strong hands began to massage his shoulders. "You have amazing hands."

All around him, he watched as his friends mingled and enjoyed themselves. The food was consumed and the conversation ebbed and flowed. Through it all he remained aware of Lucas's strong hands on his body; whether it was rubbing his shoulders, briefly touching his face, or pressing against his chest, Lucas's touch soothed him with a comforting warmth.

The afternoon passed swiftly, and his friends took their leave, aided, he was certain, by Lucas's constant declaration that Jordan shouldn't overdo it and needed to rest. Surprisingly enough, he felt good. He'd continued the flumazenil treatment while in the hospital for the two days they'd kept him, and for the past week he'd been recuperating at home. As Tash had predicted, the short period of his Xanax dependency worked in his favor. The anxiety had dramatically faded, and he no longer had that tight, fluttering sensation in his chest when he thought about the future or the past. The treatment would continue, however, for another two days.

"I wish they'd all disappear. I want to be alone with you." They hadn't been intimate since he'd been home. Lucas's hot breath drifted past his ear, and Jordan decided to have some fun. He turned his head, which still lay pillowed in Lucas's lap, so his lips grazed Lucas's thigh, right near his crotch. He blew a gentle stream of heated air and laughed as Lucas let out a smothered curse.

"Cut it out." The warning tone in Lucas's voice sent a spark racing down his spine.

"Make me," Jordan dared.

"Later."

Jordan's blood heated at the sound of Lucas's voice, full of promise, want, and need.

A shadow fell over him, and he glanced up to see Jerry standing there. "Hey. Let me talk to Jerry." Against Lucas's protests, Jordan struggled to sit. "I'm fine. Stop coddling me."

Lucas glared, but Jordan ignored him. "I'm glad you came. Any updates on finding the guys who attacked me? I gave my statement to the two officers who came to the hospital."

"I know, but I had a few more questions." Jerry took out his ever-present notebook. Keith had also never gone anywhere without one.

"Go ahead." Jordan settled back against Lucas's chest. "I don't really remember much, unfortunately, but I'll tell you what I can."

It pissed him off to no end that he couldn't re-member more than he'd already told the police. The thought that someone had entered his house, robbed him of the safety and security he'd always had, left him with an eerie, unbalanced feeling. Lucas had said he didn't see anything of value missing, which led Jordan to believe it wasn't simply a robbery. Whoever did this to him meant to send a message. His thoughts flashed back to the meeting on the street with Johnny, and what he'd said.

"Whoever broke in didn't do it to steal from me. They didn't take my wallet, phone, or computers. I think—" Jordan paused to collect his thoughts. "I'm almost certain they did so to send me a warning not to tell the police about them."

Lucas tightened his arms around Jordan, and he winced. "Ow. Lighten up, big guy."

"Sorry." Lucas loosened his hold but didn't let go of him. "That makes sense. That kid meant it when he warned you about talking to the police, Prep School. But it also had to do with the community center. They don't like its message and the influence it's having on the teenagers."

"I agree." Jordan watched as Jerry wrote everything they said down. "Every kid who comes to the Center is another potential client lost to them. Without these kids they have no way to sell their poison." He fell silent.

Ever attuned to his moods, Lucas prodded him in the back. "What is it? Something's wrong."

Unwilling to trust himself to speak at the moment, he shook his head. Jerry's sharp glance and subsequent smile let Jordan know he understood.

"I fucked up so badly," Jordan began. Feeling Lucas tense beneath him, he stopped and put his hand on

Lucas's arm. "Let me say what I have to say, please. It's important I get this out."

"Fine."

Jordan concentrated on Jerry's kind face. "All the time I was feeling sorry for myself and taking the pills, never once did I think of the impact my buying illegal drugs off the streets from kids like Johnny had on my own neighborhood or the city. In a way, I helped perpetuate the culture that allows guns and drugs to thrive here. I aided Keith's killers."

"Now, look—"

"No." Jordan sat up abruptly, ignoring the painful twinge of his ribs. "Don't sugarcoat it. I want, I *need* to help catch these bastards. Not only will I help my neighborhood and the city, but it will go a little way to ease my own guilt for what I did in tarnishing Keith's memory. I was too caught up in my own self-pity to think about how destructive my actions were."

Jerry rose from his chair to sit next to Jordan and slung a comforting arm around his shoulder. "Keith would've been proud of you. You're not the same man you were a year ago, are you?"

"Keith would've kicked my ass from here until next Sunday if I'd ever done anything this stupid while he was alive and you know it. And no, I'm not, thanks to Lucas. Like Keith, he also has the ability to see past my bullshit and call me on it."

"You're a remarkably easy person to read." Lucas began collecting the plates of leftovers that people had left scattered about. "But let me ask you something.

How do you think you can help the police?"

Here came the tricky part. Jordan knew Lucas wouldn't be happy, but it wasn't his choice to make. Not his fight to fight. "I have an idea that it might be Johnny's boss, his supplier. Johnny couldn't have beaten me down by himself, if at all. But get to the bigger guys and you get to the problem. And that'll be through Johnny. He's only a boy, vulnerable and still fixable if we get to him early enough, and he hasn't been too badly damaged."

With deliberation, Lucas put down the stack of paper plates he'd been collecting and walked back over to where Jordan and Jerry sat. "I know you didn't suggest a setup. You can't put yourself in the middle of this. It's too dangerous."

Jordan's temper rose. "I don't recall asking for your permission."

In all the months he'd known Lucas, he'd yet to see him this scared. "This isn't fucking *Law and Order*, Jordan. Things won't necessarily be wrapped up all nice and neat in an hour, with a guarantee to make it to next week simply because you're on the right side of the law."

The heat of Lucas's fear and anger hit Jordan like a fist. Rationally, Jordan knew Lucas was right, and only spoke like that out of concern and love. But he also knew that his plan was the best chance they had to catch these bastards. Appealing to Jerry, he tried to remain calm and neutral. "Don't you agree with me, Jerry? I'm the best shot you've got at stopping these fuckers."

The lines on Jerry's face deepened. He hesitated, shot Lucas a quick, troubled look, then focused on Jordan again. "I'm afraid I'm going to agree with Luke. You're too intimately involved and things could go horribly wrong. Now that you've given us a lead as to who you believe is at least responsible for the break-in and attack, we have reasonable cause. We'll put them under surveillance and hopefully your kid Johnny will lead us to the bigger fish."

"No, but…" Jordan sputtered, indignant that he could be so casually cut out of the loop.

"For Christ's sake, listen to Jerry." Lucas had remained quiet and in the background while Jerry spoke. "I agree that the kid is probably key. But you aren't going to use yourself as bait."

Jordan would've liked to continue the argument, but he didn't have the strength to argue with both of them. He tipped his head back against the seat cushions.

"I think it's time you rested and took a nap. Why don't I help you upstairs?" Jordan heard the steely determination in Lucas's voice and quickly acquiesced. Bed sounded good—great, in fact. There was nothing he wanted more than to lie down with Lucas next to him.

Thank God Jerry also understood. "I'll be in touch, Jordan, and I'm thrilled you're doing better." He shook hands with Lucas and squeezed Jordan's shoulder. "Don't get up. I'll show myself out."

A minute later the door rattled shut and Lucas locked it behind Jerry. Quiet descended upon him, and without him needing to ask, Lucas gave him something for his headache. The two of them sat in the stillness, the afternoon shadows deepening. Sasha padded in to lie at his feet, her eyes never leaving him.

The pain in his head receded, and he sighed. "This was really nice. Thanks for getting everyone together." He kissed Lucas's slightly scruffy cheek.

Never comfortable with praise, Lucas shrugged. "It was nothing. Everyone helped put it together."

"Uh, I saw you speaking to Ash earlier. Care to let me in on what it was about?" Hoping against hope the two men would continue to make headway toward reconciliation, Jordan held his breath.

"We agreed to meet tomorrow night. Here, if that's all right with you."

"Are you fucking crazy?" A huge grin split his face. "What time?"

Beneath him, Lucas's chest rumbled with laughter. "Seven o'clock. I'll be home from work by then."

Jordan smiled, and Lucas cleared his throat. "I mean, I meant…"

"I know what you meant. I'd been meaning to speak with you about this very thing." Taking both of Lucas's hands in his, Jordan knew he made the right decision. "You have every right to call this your home. I want to share my days and nights with you. Would you move in here, with us?" He glanced down at Sasha, who, thrilled at having some attention directed her way, put her paws on his lap and barked twice.

Lucas laughed and hugged him, careful not to squeeze him too hard. "Are you sure you want me, Prep School? I'm a real bastard in the morning, as you've seen sometimes." His hazel eyes glinted, and Jordan's body stirred to life.

"I know what I want." Jordan slipped his hand into Lucas's. "Right now, I want you to take me upstairs and get into bed with me." He could hear the quickening cadence of Lucas's breath, and it matched his own rising excitement. "I want to wake up with you under me or over me. I want you inside me." He pulled Lucas up from the sofa and together they walked out of the room.

When they stood at the foot of the stairs, he grabbed Lucas around the neck to pull him close. His lips rested against the firm line of Lucas's jaw, and Jordan breathed in the light citrus scent of Lucas's aftershave. "I love you, Lucas." Pressed tight against each other, the unmistakable bulge of Lucas's heavy erection prodded Jordan, and his stomach clenched tight.

Lucas's deep voice drawled slow and sexy in his ear. "I love you too. But I want you to be sure. It's only a little over a year since you lost Keith. I'm not going anywhere. I'm right where I want to be."

Jordan took Lucas's hand and started up the steps. "I'm sure of two things right now. I'm sure I'm going to be screaming your name sooner rather than later."

Lucas sprinted ahead of him and tugged at his

hand. "I'm ready for that as well."

They entered the bedroom, and Jordan unbuttoned his shirt, then tossed it carelessly into the chair by the window. With renewed strength, Jordan twined his arms around Lucas's neck, kissing him until they were both breathless and shaking. "And I'm sure I don't want to be without you ever again."

"You've got me, then." Lucas's strained voice shook.

Jordan found himself being walked backward, and his legs soon hit the bed. He allowed himself to be pushed down, and Jordan lay flat on his back, admiring Lucas's broad, muscled chest. "Hurry. I'm so hard for you, I won't last long." He stroked himself through his jeans.

Lucas's eyes gleamed in the fading light. "Keep your hands off. That's mine alone to touch." Jordan's breath caught in his throat when Lucas's fingers brushed the skin of his abdomen. "Lift up for me." Lucas's lips curved in a wicked smile. He popped open the tab of Jordan's jeans.

Jordan didn't hesitate and moaned in relief when his cock sprang free. "Fuck. I want you now. Hurry." Any pain in his side faded with the onslaught of desire flooding through his bloodstream.

Lucas shucked his own clothes, leaving them in a heap on the floor, then crawled onto the bed, caging Jordan between his muscled arms. The brush of Lucas's hard cock against his sent a shiver of excitement coursing through Jordan.

"Patience. I'm gonna give you everything you want and need." Their lips met in a hot, wet kiss, tongues pushing against each other, teeth clashing.

Jordan's head spun.

Desire for Lucas overwhelmed him, and he couldn't control his cries. "Lucas, please." He hungered to feel Lucas's strong fingers wrap around his straining cock, and he reached between their bodies and began to stroke himself, his hand getting wet and slick from his precome.

"I told you no touching." Lucas pulled Jordan's hand off his cock, replacing it with his own. "Your cock, your balls, every fucking inch of your body is mine." Jordan writhed beneath Lucas, sliding his hard, wet cock through Lucas's fist. "You like that, huh? Tell me, Jordan, what else do you want? You want me to suck you?"

Through hazy eyes, Jordan saw Lucas lick his lips. "God, yes." He was almost sobbing in his need to have Lucas's mouth on his dick.

He almost screamed with pleasure as the heated, wet slide of Lucas's mouth enveloped his erection. "Oh fuck, oh God." He couldn't help thrusting his hips, and the juicy, slick sounds Lucas made around him played like music to his ears. As promised, Jordan screamed for Lucas as the orgasm slammed into him and his body convulsed. He opened his eyes to the air shimmering around him, shining and alive with the electricity that seemed to pour off his body in wave after wave of sexual pleasure. His cock jerked and pulsed, sending his seed down Lucas's throat.

Thoroughly shattered to oblivion, Jordan lay gasping, his damp body still quivering with the aftereffects of their lovemaking. Lucas sat above him, a small smile resting on his lips. His cock remained hard and flushed pink, the head wet and gleaming in the rapidly fading light.

A beautiful sight, Jordan decided, and reached up to stroke Lucas's chest. "Come. Lie down next to me. I want to taste you."

Jordan grasped Lucas's thick erection and stroked him with a firm, sure hand, reveling in the needy sounds coming from Lucas. All he wished for was to give this man pleasure.

Ignoring his protesting ribs, and knowing Lucas was too far gone at this point to tell him to stop, Jordan raised himself on his knees and took Lucas in his mouth, the taste of him bursting over his tongue. Lucas's cock filled his throat, but Jordan didn't let that stop him from making love to it, swirling his tongue over the ridged vein while keeping a firm grasp at the base.

Lucas moaned and thrust upward, fucking his mouth. "Oh fuck, what the hell are you doing?"

Jordan couldn't answer. On all fours, he bent over Lucas's body and kept up a steady rhythm. He smiled around Lucas's cock and slid a finger inside his passage, feeling the tight muscle clamp around his digit. Jordan sank in deeper.

Lucas moaned, thrusting against his hand and Jordan shivered, his mouth tightening around Lucas. He sucked and swallowed, teasing and fluttering with his tongue, and within minutes, Lucas came. Jordan swallowed, then collapsed on the bed, his trembling legs no longer able to hold his weight.

Gutted and shaking, he lay next to Lucas, their damp bodies barely touching. Night shadows flickered across the moon, playing patterns across their naked bodies. His eyes fluttered shut and before he fell asleep Lucas entwined their fingers and pulled him close.

Chapter Twenty-Five

OF ALL THE days to be late, it had to be this one. The entire downtown line was delayed because of a sick passenger, and Luke had zero sympathy. He didn't have a seat, the train was overcrowded with people, and the air-conditioning blew lukewarm air, sending the aroma of whatever the guy leaning against the pole was eating, drifting past his face, making breathing almost unbearable.

Finally, with a lurch and a squeal, the train started up again. It was only two stops until he reached the 18th St. station, but in New York City travel time, that could take five minutes or a half an hour. By the time he emerged from underground and stopped to heft his backpack further up his shoulder, the sun had set already. Luke checked his watch and grimaced at the time. Almost seven thirty. He should've been home an hour ago. They'd asked Ash and Drew to come by at seven. His stomach cramped, as it had been doing all day. He'd barely been able to choke down any food, thinking about tonight.

Him and Ash, together. Talking to each other for the first time in almost fifteen years.

What the fuck had he been thinking? What would he say to Ash, and more importantly, what the hell did Ash think he could say to Luke that could ever make up for leaving? He drew in deep breaths, thinking somehow his mind would miraculously clear and his heartbeat would slow down instead of banging around like an out-of-control conga-line drummer.

He turned the corner on his street, forcing himself to push forward. The taste of dread lay thick in his mouth and throat. *Fight through your fears. Own and control it.* That's what Jordan had said to him, and he'd used that as a mantra. *Goddamn it.* His grip tightened on the strap of his backpack.

He wasn't afraid of Ash; why should he be? It wasn't Luke who left, slinking out in the dead of night, pretending he'd come back for them. All those weeks of waiting and hoping, seeing Brandon's face light up when the mail would come, big eyes bright with hope, only to fall and crease in disappointment as he bravely held back the tears when no letter from Ash came. Ever.

No, Luke wasn't that scared kid any longer, and he wasn't alone. He had Jordan and Wanda. Since he'd known he wouldn't be able to eat lunch today, he'd gone to the shelter to talk to Wanda. To say she was thrilled with the news that he was moving in with Jordan was an understatement.

"Baby doll, I knew he was the one who was gonna get

under your skin and find a home there." She hugged him long and hard, smothering him with vanilla-scented kisses and love. "Both of you needed someone so badly, but I was afraid you'd shut the door on him like you did everyone else."

His heart squeezed as he looked at her loving face. "I tried," he admitted, recalling his attempts to forget Jordan. "He's very persistent." And ultimately unforgettable. Jordan lived his life the way he came after Luke; unashamed, unafraid, and unapologetic for his actions, whether they were right or wrong. What was it Ash had called him once? A proud and arrogant bastard. Perhaps, but underneath it all was a man who loved deeply and fiercely. A man who was unswervingly and unflinchingly loyal. A man who cared for the unwanted. Luke counted himself lucky to be the one who got to see the side of Jordan few ever did. A tender, caring man who took in a homeless dog or sat with a child from the shelter, helping her with schoolwork because her mother had to work late.

He took Wanda's calloused, gentle hands and kissed them. "Life is mysterious. We think we're in control, but we're only holding on for the ride, trying not to lose our grip."

"Your man holds on to you tight. He loves you so." She wiped her eyes. "Now it's time for you to make up with that brother of yours." She held up her finger when he tried to stop her. "Promise me you'll listen to what he has to say. You may be surprised," she said with a smile. "Like you said, life is mysterious."

He opened the front door, and Sasha greeted him.

He bent down to pet her, then straightened up and listened. Again his gut twisted as he heard laughter coming from the kitchen. *Shit, fuck.* Closing his eyes and counting to ten, he took a deep breath and headed to the back of the house. By the time he entered the kitchen, he'd managed to at least put together an outward appearance of a man in control. Meanwhile, on the inside, his teeth bit down on his inner cheek until the pain made him focus on the scene in front of him.

"Hello, everyone. Sorry I'm so late, but the trains were really fucked up tonight." Without looking at either Drew or Ash, he instead concentrated on Jordan.

Jordan's eyes lit up, and he slid off his chair to greet him. "There you are. I was getting concerned. Come on and sit down. Drew and Ash brought sandwiches, and I've got a beer waiting with your name on it." They kissed, and he sank down in the chair next to Jordan and took a long, grateful swig of his beer. While it tasted great, it unfortunately did little to quell the nerves playing havoc with his system. Underneath the table, Jordan squeezed his thigh, leaving his hand to rest there, offering comfort and support.

Showtime.

"So." He placed his beer bottle on the table and, with a calm he didn't feel inside, stared at Ash. "Why don't we get this over with?"

Ash's mouth tightened. "Is that all this is to you then? Something to check off your To-Do List?" He pushed Drew's hand off his shoulder. "Don't. I'm fine." Anger seeped out of his words. "I've waited years to talk to you. Now that the time has come, I won't let you rush through it."

What a joke. "You don't get to make the rules. Maybe when I was young and naive, I let you be in charge. Those days are gone. Long gone." If Ash thought he was in control here, he'd find out soon enough how wrong he was.

"When we were kids, I looked up to you—worshiped you. You were my older brother who could do no wrong. *My family.* Then you walked away without a backward glance. You knew we were too young to come with you when you asked me to. You had no trouble forgetting who you'd left behind. So no. You gave up any right to tell me what to do when you forgot about us."

With each word, Ash shook his head with increasing ferocity, his breath expelling in quick, hard bursts until he interrupted Luke with a harsh cry. "It's not true. I swear. I never forgot. I searched for you, and even though you changed your name, I never gave up. Never. I still haven't given up on Brandon." His hand slammed down on the table. "I won't let you dismiss me now."

"Maybe you should have thought about the reason why I changed my name." Luke's voice shook. "Maybe I didn't want you to find me." Luke dug his nails into the scarred wooden top of the table. "You left and never looked back. You didn't fucking care."

Something dark flickered in Ash's silvery eyes.

"That's not true."

This dancing around the elephant in the room was getting them nowhere. "You haven't got the guts to admit it to me; that's fine. I'm not even angry anymore because I've finally gotten what I've always wanted." He took Jordan's hand and held it. This man was his rock. His family. Ash, however, still needed to hear the ugly truth.

"It doesn't matter anymore because I have Jordan. But when you go to sleep at night, I hope you can admit to yourself what you did to Brandon and me. That you left us alone with a vicious drunk and a physical abuser who also liked to touch young boys."

Ash visibly flinched. Luke pushed ahead with his gruesome story. Perversely, he wanted Ash to hurt and to hear from Luke's lips the carnage he'd left behind.

"He left me alone for two years after you left. Every once in a while he'd look at me funny or make a strange remark to me. I ignored it but made sure to always look out for Brandon. But one night he came into my room and tried to touch me. I screamed so loud Mom—Mrs. Munson—and Brandon came running into my room. I told them to leave, get out. Go to Mrs. Cartwright down the road." He blinked to try and forestall the rush of tears at the memory, but it did no good. "So they left and I remained alone with that bastard. He laughed at me, thanking me for getting us alone together."

Memories of that night flooded his mind. For over twelve years he'd kept it bottled up, but now the doors were flung open and evilness waited, ready to be revealed in all its ugliness.

"He tried to pin me down, but I went berserk, punching and kicking him. When he pulled out his gun, I thought that was it. I was going to die."

"Lucas." Jordan breathed. "You don't have to do this. It's over now. He can't hurt you anymore."

Luke's laughter caught in a sob. "It's never going to be over. Don't you see? It's like a brand, burned into my mind. Every time I close my eyes I see him, that monster." Like a movie playing in his mind, Luke heard the sickening thuds of Munson's boots against his flesh and recalled the excruciating pain as the man kicked him with his steel-toed boots, all the while holding the gun over him. Luke barely felt Jordan put his arm around him, holding him, soothing him. Loving him.

The pain receded as, for the first time in years, he cried for the child he'd been.

"I love you, Lucas. And I'm so proud of you for this. You've beaten your demons. You're in control." Jordan gently touched his lips to Luke's, and he kissed Jordan back like a drowning man breaking the water's surface. Needy, desperate, and gasping.

Several minutes passed before he regained his self-control. After he'd dried his eyes and taken a cold drink of water, he watched as Drew murmured something in Ash's ear. Oh no. Ash wasn't going to be stroked by his boyfriend and made to feel better. Luke wanted him to feel what Luke had gone through, smell the fear and the blood and sweat, as if Ash had been in that very room when he and Munson were fighting to what seemed like the death. Because Luke had no doubt that if he hadn't passed out that night, he'd have died. Munson must've gotten scared and fled when Luke failed to move and respond.

"Do you know that was the last time I ever saw Brandon? I never got a chance to see him or say good-bye. At some point I passed out from the pain, and when I woke up, I was in the hospital. Later on they told me someone had called the police, saying I'd been hurt during a break-in at the house. I was alone, unconscious, and the Munsons had taken Brandon and disappeared. I never saw any of them again. By the time I recovered and was discharged, they'd left town, and no one knew where they'd gone."

Ash's eyes looked like holes in his white face. "I—"

"No. Not you. Me, Ash. This has nothing to do with you. I was the one left in a hospital, not even eighteen, abandoned, alone with no one who cared. I was so fucking scared. Everyone and everything I knew had been ripped out from under me, and I had no idea what I was going to do or where I would even live. I had no money, no home. Nothing."

The humiliation of those days came rushing back on him. The first place he'd gone to after sneaking out and running away from the hospital was the only place he remembered as home. The social workers at the hospital had to be wrong; the Munson's couldn't have left. But it was true; the house sat dark and abandoned.

The Munsons and Brandon had vanished without leaving a trace of where they might've gone. He'd sat on the broken-down steps of the wooden porch and cried like a baby. After a while he'd wiped his eyes and his nose, and with everything he owned in his backpack, he'd headed down the road to the highway. And as he walked, he'd left himself behind. Lucas Carini was no more. Luke Conover, a name he picked from a phone book, was born. And that person would never get hurt, would never care about anything except making sure no one would ever hurt him again.

Feeling the weight of Ash's stare on him, Luke glared back. "Do you remember what we used to talk about at night, or did you forget that too?" The memories of the two of them lying in their beds, sharing their dreams of glory, wrapped themselves around Luke. He'd wanted to be a baseball player, and Ash had wanted to travel the world. "We were going to make it out of there. Have families and share our Thanksgivings and Christmases together. It was supposed to be us against the world, but first we'd take care of and protect Brandon. He was ours, never theirs. But somewhere along the line you forgot us, didn't you? We weren't enough for you."

"No, no. It wasn't that, never that, Lukie, please believe me."

It almost choked Luke to hear the silly, teasing nickname. His anger rose, and that, along with the hurt and disappointment ricocheting through him, almost broke him. "Don't call me that." He lashed out as the traitorous tears stung his eyes. "That was from another time when you loved and cared about me. When you promised to always be there for Brandon and me. You gave up that right. But you knew what Munson was and you still left, didn't you? What happened, Ash? Did he come to you one night, and you freaked out so badly you ran away?" Ash shook his head, but Luke ignored him. "I looked up to you, and it broke me to my knees to know you cared so little. I thought you were my real brother. I wanted you to be. And Brandon." The tears rained down Luke's cheeks. "He was innocent; a little boy who adored you. I thought we were a family. But you didn't love us like that."

"That wasn't it. You don't understand."

"Then make me, goddamn you." He slammed his hand so hard on the table that Sasha yelped and ran out. "Make me understand how you could say you loved us and yet leave us there. Make me understand how I was left alone to protect Brandon from that bastard."

"You want to understand?" Ash thrust his chair hard behind him, teetering on two legs before righting itself. His teeth bared in a snarl while tears dripped down his cheeks. "Fine, yeah, I'll tell you. I knew. That's right." He braced his hands on the table, leaning across into Luke's stunned face. "I fucking knew what he was. How? Because I let him touch me instead of you. I let him fucking rape me instead of you."

Tears poured down Ash's face as Drew slid his arms around Ash's waist. But Ash never took his eyes off

Luke, who sat, breathless and reeling from shock and horror. "Every time he touched me, I wanted to die. But I held on so he wouldn't *ever* do to you and Brandon what he did to me. For years that bastard came to me with a sick smile and told me if I didn't let him fuck me or if I didn't blow him, he'd make you do it." Ash closed his eyes for a moment, more tears spilling out from the corners of his eyelids, wetting his cheeks. "He said he'd take Brandon too. So I had to let him. I couldn't let him touch you, and Brandon was just a little kid. After a while, I was a body, a shell. It wasn't me he was having sex with." He swallowed hard. "It was something he did to someone else."

Luke could barely breathe. "Ash, stop. You don't have to—"

"Oh yes, I fucking have to, don't you see? That bastard stole everything from us. Our childhood, our innocence. Our dreams." Ash dropped his head in his hands. "He stole my life."

The world could explode right outside, and Luke wouldn't notice. He bit down and tasted the metallic tang of his own blood. Without even realizing what he was doing, he walked around the table to Ash and grabbed one of his hands. Ash's palm, clammy and cold, shook in Luke's grip. They locked gazes, and Luke fell into the wasteland of Ash's eyes.

"For all these years it's eaten me alive inside, the guilt, the hatred I have for myself." The short, smooth nails of Ash's fingers dug into Luke's skin, but Luke made no protest. The only thing that mattered now was hearing Ash's story. Luke concentrated on the movement of Ash's lips as the rest of the room spun away.

"You didn't know; how could you? I never wanted you to. But there comes a time, a breaking point. I couldn't take it anymore. I swear I tried to be strong, to stay and watch out for you and Brandon, but I was dying inside." He pulled Luke to sit next to him, and Luke willingly sank into the chair. The truth could sometimes be more devastating than what the imagination dreamed up. Never in his wildest dreams had he thought Ash had been a victim.

"I wanted so many times to end it all, and almost succeeded, but then I found Drew. He forced me to get into therapy. Over the past year I've begun to see maybe it wasn't all my fault. That sometimes outside influences force a person's hand to do things they never imagined. And that maybe I also deserved that happy ending other people always got." Ash looked down at their entwined hands. "And I didn't want to die, really, without ever finding out that maybe you would forgive me."

Drew slipped his arms around Ash. "Ash still needs to learn to forgive himself."

Dread filtered through the fog in Luke's brain. "What do you mean, you tried to end it all?" He caught the quick look between the two of them. Jordan appeared at his side, but Luke barely registered his presence. "Tell me," he begged Ash. "Please."

Jordan's hands came down on Luke's shoulders,

and they shared a glance. "Do you know what he's talking about?"

Jordan shook his head. "Not a clue." He bent to whisper in Luke's ear. "Considering his fragile state, do you think you should continue?"

"Did I hear correctly? Dr. Jordan Peterson expressing sympathy toward me? This truly is a night of firsts." Ash's sad, weak smile was a shadow of its usual devil-may-care self. "Lukie, sometimes things are better off remaining buried in the shadows. I'm sure you have things in your past you want to forget."

Several beats of silence passed before Luke spoke. "I whored myself when I got out of the hospital." Luke blurted to the stunned faces around him. Jordan's grip tightened on his shoulders.

Never taking his eyes off Ash's devastated face, Luke patted Jordan's hand. "It's okay. Let me speak." He stood, continuing to hold Ash's hand. "I'd like to go into the living room with Ash if that's okay. Give us a little time to sort things out together." He kissed Jordan's cheek. "I love you."

"I'm so proud of you." Jordan gave him a brief, hard hug. Luke, still holding Ash's hand, walked with him in silence to the front of the house. He sat on one end of the sofa and Ash at the other. For several minutes, Luke stared at his brother. No matter the years that had passed and the anger he'd nurtured and lived on these years, this man was his blood as if they had been born to the same mother.

As he relayed his story of hitchhiking up to Washington DC and what the truck drivers made him do, Ash sat, a frozen silent statue, the horror in his eyes betraying his tightly held emotions.

"Luke," Ash breathed. "I'm sorry. I wish it was me. It was all my fault this happened to you."

Before tonight, Luke would've agreed. But after hearing the devastating story of Ash's own years of abuse, Luke finally understood why Ash had to leave. A breaking point. The point of no return. And Ash had been a child as well when all this happened to him. He'd hidden it so well; Luke never suspected a thing. But then again, they all had their secrets.

"Remember the summers when we used to go fishing in the creek down the road?" It had been a treat to get away from the heat of the house and spend a day in the cool shade of the trees. He and Ash would take their makeshift fishing poles and a basket of peanut butter and jelly sandwiches and spend afternoons with their toes in the icy running water. They talked about being gay in a small town and how they had to hide it from everyone at school.

"Yeah." Ash leaned back and toyed with the sofa cushion tassel. His eyes had that faraway look, of another time and place. "I remember every minute. I taught you everything I knew." Those fathomless bright eyes turned to him. "The only good in my life came from you. You and Brandon. When I left, I tried to tell the police, but they wouldn't listen to me. I was merely another gay runaway kid. And of course, since Munson was a cop, why would they believe me—a homeless kid nobody cared about. Once I had the resources, though, I never stopped looking for you."

That Luke could believe. For years he'd known someone was trying to find him, even as far back as him living in the shelter. Wanda had told him of people asking questions about a Lucas Carini.

"My investigator is still out there searching for Brandon. I can't rest or forgive myself completely until I know what's happened to him." Ash wiped the tears off his cheeks.

"Tell me about Drew."

It was as if a hand had come by and smoothed away the tension and worry from Ash's face. All the harsh planes and furrows softened, and he transformed into a different person. "Until I met Drew, I was drifting through life, screwing everyone I met. He saved me. There's no one else like him." The lightness faded from his eyes. "If I hadn't met him…" Ash shook his head but said no more.

The feeling of dread returned from their earlier conversation. "You said before you wanted to die. Did you try and kill yourself, Ash?" Even in his most desolate times, Luke had never thought to end his life. Perhaps his anger had kept him alive.

Shooting him an unreadable look, Ash hesitated a moment, then reached down and unbuttoned his shirtsleeves. With growing horror, Luke watched as Ash rolled up the cuffs and revealed the twisted, ugly scars of his past.

"Asher…" The words caught in Luke's throat at the

pain and heartbreak for his brother who had, unbeknownst to him, suffered so much guilt. He left his seat to join Ash at his end of the sofa. "Why?" The marks, though ugly, weren't new, thank God. They twisted around his wrists and forearms in snakelike patterns, weaving around in thin white lines. Some, however, were thicker and told a deeper story of the torment Ash had lived through all those lost years.

"It was the only control I had over my body, the only thing Munson couldn't take from me. I decided what to do." The words came out in a heartbroken whisper. "And when I'd think of you and Brandon and how I'd failed you, I wanted to hurt myself as punishment for my cowardice and shame. It doesn't matter anymore. In therapy I've learned to stop blaming myself for what I couldn't control and to control what I can but never hurt myself in the process. Because I'm worth something."

"Oh, Ash." Without thinking, Luke put his arms around his brother for the first time in years and let go of the chains around his heart. In order to love Jordan the right way, he needed this reconciliation with Ash. It was time for him to forgive. Let go of the pain and anger he'd lived with for so long. Let go of the shame of his birth and childhood. There'd been so much damage done to them that they'd had no control over. Who was he to decide who should be forgiven and who should be held up for blame? He wasn't God, that was for certain. And he'd made enough mistakes in his own life that not only did he ask for forgiveness, he expected it.

Who was he to deny Ash that same right?

That list he'd made all those years ago of past hurts and pain that had dominated his life had little meaning. The memories of the abuse they'd endured would always be there, but together, he and Ash could lock it away in its rightful place as a reminder of where they'd come from and how far they'd moved on.

"You are so worth it. We both are. I'm sorry we both suffered. We aren't the same kids we were back in Georgia, and thankfully we don't ever have to go back to those days. Whatever we do now, we have the chance to make it right." He took Ash's hands in his. "Let me help you search for Brandon. It's killing me to think he's alone. The three of us always promised to stick together, no matter what."

"All for one and one for all, remember?" said Ash with a shaky laugh.

The Three Musketeers. That's what they'd called themselves when Brandon came to live with them. Luke smiled at the memory. "I carried that book for years with me. I never forgot it. And I never forgot you."

Serious once again, Ash looked him straight in the eyes. "We can still do it, can't we? Become the family we'd always dreamed about?"

When he was a boy, Luke had often cried at night, wishing he had a mother to hold him and kiss him when he had bad dreams. As he grew older, he'd learned some nightmares were beyond the help of a mother's love. But family wasn't always made up of blood. It wouldn't come easy, this reconciliation. Ash's battle with guilt was a daily fight, and Luke still struggled with his own shame and the need to hide behind his walls. Yet the yearning to reconnect, to forge those bonds of brotherhood they'd sworn to so long ago, that's what he would focus on and work toward. And now they had the search for Brandon as the starting point to help rebuild their broken relationship. How many people got a second chance?

A noise from the hallway drew his attention. The soft light from the chandelier gilded the gold of Jordan's hair and Drew's pale skin as they stood in the doorway. Sasha sat at their feet. The loving look Drew gave to Ash and the fiercely proud smile Jordan wore were all he needed.

"I think we already have that covered."

Chapter Twenty-Six

I F THERE WAS anything better than a warm bed on a cool morning, Jordan hadn't found it yet. With a sleepy sigh of contentment, he hooked his foot around Lucas's hairy calf to tug him closer. Lucas's warm arms encircled Jordan.

"What's the matter, Prep School? Didn't get enough of me last night?" With his face planted in the curve of Jordan's neck, Lucas's words came out muffled, but Jordan grinned at the petulant growl that filtered through. Lucas hated waking up early. Unfortunately for Lucas, Jordan, having gone through internship and residency, had never learned to sleep late, and he was nothing if not a greedy son of a bitch. He wanted Lucas, and he wanted him now.

"No." Jordan pushed his ass into the heat of Lucas's thighs and bumped up against his thick early-morning erection. Now that Jordan had come off his Xanax dependency and was clean for the first time in almost a year, his body hummed and sensations burned through his bloodstream, lighting a trail of fire in their wake.

The landscape of his existence had changed from a dull gray to one of color, light, and sound…as if dipped in an artist's palette.

"I'm alive and so are you. We're going to be all right." Forgetting for a moment how much he wanted Lucas inside him, Jordan turned around to talk to him face-to-face. "We're like people who've survived some terrible disaster. For a while we walk around shell-shocked, disbelieving it could happen to us."

Lucas's arm tightened around him, but he said nothing.

"Sooner or later, though, we wake up and look around us, wondering what went on in the world while we took a hiatus from life and mourned. It's like after a fire, you know?" Jordan played with Lucas's silky hair, winding the curls around his fingers. "You go back and tentatively pick through the ash and debris, trying to piece together what remains of the life you left behind. You hope and pray there's enough left to keep your memories alive."

"Sometimes, though, it's best to let the past remain where it is and try to make a fresh start. Not all memories are pleasant," Lucas said.

How he loved this man. Jordan traced the line of Lucas's cheekbone with his fingertips. The throwaway children became discarded adults, with only the strong surviving. And strength, as he'd learned over the past year, took the shape of many different people. Like Drew, who'd faced a life change and embraced it head-on, giving Ash all his love and his heart to help him.

And Ash, who'd discovered he was stronger than he thought and a man worth more than anonymous, hurried sex. A man worth loving.

And Lucas. Strong, silent Lucas, who'd struggled with his shame and shut out the world, fearing its judgment.

"Do you know what the best thing about memories is?" Jordan kissed Lucas, burying his face in Lucas's neck, inhaling his intoxicating smell. The swell of his cock brushed against Lucas's already healthy erection.

"What? And this better not be a long answer." Lucas rolled over and straddled him, hazel eyes gleaming in the morning brightness. "I have to go to work, and I want you now." He bent over and began trailing his tongue down Jordan's neck and chest.

"Every day"—Jordan gasped, arching under the wetness of Lucas's mouth—"you get to make new ones. Like we do." He writhed as Lucas licked the head of his cock. "Oh God."

"Time to stop talking." Lucas lapped along the veiny ridge of Jordan's cock and slid his mouth down, engulfing him. He drew hard and tight along Jordan's length, sucking hard until Jordan hit the back of his throat.

"Lucas, fuck." Jordan's whole world spun to a pinpoint of color, whirling like a crazy kaleidoscope behind his tightly shut eyes. "Please, please," he begged.

And Lucas, who knew him better even than he knew himself, understood what he craved and demanded. For the first time since they'd become lovers, it was them alone in their bed. No drug running through Jordan's bloodstream, whispering like a dark lover, sinking its fangs into his mind. His heart no longer rocketed about in his throat, and his skin didn't drip with sweat and fear.

And Lucas? He walked without pain, free of the self-loathing and humiliation that had taunted him like an evil clown from the recesses of his mind. He'd revealed his shame and was still loved.

As Lucas entered Jordan, his heated breath whispering across Jordan's face, they moved together, their bodies offering and accepting. The burn of the fullness and stretch completed Jordan, pleasure curling around his spine, building to a crescendo of want and need that sent him spinning off into a blinding golden haze. Lucas's heavy hands pinned him to the bed, sinking Jordan into the softness of the mattress as Lucas drove himself deeper and deeper.

They'd stopped using condoms after they'd both been tested and knew the commitment they had for one another was permanent. Nothing compared to the delicious drag of skin against skin, the slick, wet sounds of their bodies joining. There were sure to be marks on his body as Lucas slotted himself deeply inside Jordan, but Jordan welcomed them. They made him feel alive.

And when Lucas hit the spot over and over again inside Jordan that sent him whimpering, his head thrashing back and forth on the pillow, Jordan lifted his hips, urging him on. Lucas slid his arms around him and held him close. Always in control at work and in public, in the bedroom Jordan became a shameless beggar for touches, kisses, and words of love. The vulnerability and softness he hid from everyone, friends and family included, belonged solely to Lucas, and Jordan gave of it freely and without limitations. Jordan did nothing by halves; he loved with his whole being.

"Fuck me; come on, Lucas. God, I can't take it anymore." Jordan grabbed on to Lucas's sweat-slicked shoulders, thrusting his pelvis upward, pressing his knees up to his shoulders. They rocked together, heaving their bodies toward that ultimate goal. Jordan grasped his cock hard as Lucas slammed into him.

"Fuck, I'm coming." Jordan moaned, and his cock pulsed, milky white jets streaming out, landing on his abdomen and chest.

Lucas groaned. "Damn, that's fucking hot." He continued to thrust into Jordan, probing deep and hard. With each stroke, Lucas's pace increased, and Jordan watched as Lucas's face contorted into a silent scream of pleasure. Deep inside him, Lucas's cock stiffened and swelled as he came. Jordan tightened his muscles, clamping down on Lucas, clutching his cock. Jordan loved the sensation of the liquid heat inside him as Lucas came. It was the best feeling in the world, to be filled up by the man you loved.

"Shit, that was amazing." Lucas collapsed on top of him, breathing hard. "If I have to get up, I might as well start my day off the best way possible." He pressed his mouth to Jordan's, and they shared a heated kiss that blazed through Jordan. They stayed that way, kissing and touching each other as they came down from the high of their lovemaking.

Jordan toyed with Lucas's sweaty curls as they lay together. "Too bad you have to work on a Saturday." He rubbed his face against Lucas's shoulder. "We could spend the whole day in bed like this."

Groaning, Lucas slid out of him and rolled over on his back. "What are your plans?" He scratched his chest and gave a huge yawn.

"I have to call Tash to set up my therapy; then I'm going to the center. I need to spend some time there with the kids and the volunteers. I want to know about the gun collection project." Jordan folded his arms behind his head and frowned, staring up at the ceiling. "I feel I've let the project down because of my own personal issues."

"Hey. Look at me."

Jordan complied, and Lucas stroked his cheek. "You were going through one of the worst periods of your life. A weaker man wouldn't have been able to face his fears and addiction and come out of it stronger than before." A grin flickered over Lucas's lips. "Damn, I don't know why I'm building up that massive ego of yours. That's never been your issue." He broke out into a full-fledged laugh as he got out of bed.

Jordan lunged at him, but Lucas was too quick and sidestepped away. "Uh-uh. I can't be late. I have a lot of catching up to do if I want to leave early and not be stuck there the whole day." He walked toward the bathroom. "Of course, feel free to join me in the shower. I can always use you to wash my back." Lucas grinned over his shoulder and gave Jordan a wink.

"Massive ego? What's the matter? You can't handle the truth?" Throwing out the line from one of his favorite movies, Jordan nevertheless scrambled out of bed to join Lucas in the shower. He wasn't crazy; a wet and naked Lucas was the best way to start his morning.

Lucas left without breakfast, hurrying out the door with his ever-present coffee thermos in hand. Today was Oscar the Grouch tie day. Jordan loved that playful side of Lucas and vowed to call the detective Ash had hired to see if there was any news on Brandon. There was nothing he wanted more in the world than to reunite Lucas with his younger brother. Hell, he could even admit wanting to do it for Ash as well. Now that he knew Ash's horrific story of abuse, he understood why the man had once behaved as he did. Sex without emotion was meaningless and heartbreaking.

Thank God Ash had found Drew, for Jordan now knew without a doubt, having undergone therapy himself, that Ash would have eventually succeeded in taking his own life. With Drew by his side, loving him and standing strong, Ash would make it. There had to be decency in Asher Davis for him to recognize the pure and inherent goodness in Drew and love him as deeply as he did.

Jordan dressed, then, after downing two cups of coffee and some oatmeal, took Sasha for her walk. He'd come back and closed the front door behind him when his phone rang. Seeing on the caller ID that it was

Jerry, he smiled as he answered. "Hey, Jerry, how's it going?"

"Good." Jerry sounded official and rushed. "Listen, we've had a break. That kid you used to buy from, Johnny, was picked up last night on a breaking and entering. He can't make bail, so he's being held until he can come before the judge. We're gonna interview him now and ask him questions on your assault."

Strange as it might seem, Jordan felt sorry for the young kid. After all, he hadn't forced Jordan to buy the drugs. "Take it easy on him. He wasn't the one who beat me up." Thinking back to how Lucas and Ash had to survive when they were that age, Jordan could only hope Johnny could get some help making better choices. "Why don't you let me talk to him later on? Maybe I can help."

"I don't know, Jordan. That's kinda unorthodox." There was reluctance in Jerry's voice, but Jordan sensed he could be persuaded.

"Look, think about it. I'll be at the Center today. Call me either way."

"How's everything going for you?"

"About as well as can be expected. It hurts still, but the anxiety lessens every day. It's a struggle, you know?" The craving didn't magically disappear. Every now and then something triggered, and the desire to take a pill rushed through his blood. But those times were becoming less and less frequent, and now that he was clean, there was no fucking way he'd ever do this to himself again. He'd rather remain in therapy for twenty years than take drugs.

Jerry grunted. "Well, I'm glad you got the help you needed, but you should know you could always come talk to me. You and Keith were like sons to me and Marie." He hesitated for a moment. "So it's permanent with you and Luke, huh? He seems like a nice guy."

Jerry had suffered too. He and Keith had been partnered for the five years after Keith had made detective. Jerry had confided in Jordan he was thinking of retiring this year. Too much death and tragedy. He wanted to enjoy his life.

"Yeah, it is. Lucas is a good man, Jerry. I hope you and Marie get to know him better."

"We want you to be happy. And I can see you are for the first time since Keith died. So for that, I'm grateful to Luke." A bit of humor crept into his voice. "And if he does something bad to you, I can always arrest him and lose the key."

They shared a laugh and hung up after Jerry agreed to call Jordan later about Johnny.

With a final pat and several treats, Jordan left Sasha and headed for the Center. It was only a few blocks from his house, and as it was a cool late fall day, he enjoyed the walk. With pride, he entered the space, noting it was already more than half full at only ten thirty on a Saturday morning. He found Wanda sitting in the back.

"Hi." He bent and kissed her cheek. "Busy this morning, huh?"

"Hi, baby. Yeah, it's packed." Wanda smiled, then

looked behind him. "Where's your man?"

Jordan laughed. "He had to work this morning. All the time he took off taking care of my problems cut into his own work. So he's putting in some extra hours."

"Hmph. They work him too hard there."

Jordan knew how Wanda disliked the crazy hours and competitive world Lucas lived in, but the fact was Lucas loved it and was damn good at it. "It's his life, Wanda, and he's his own man. Besides"—he took her hand and sat with her at one of the empty tables in the back—"it won't be like this forever. If he makes partner in a few years, he can slow down."

"And how are you doing? Okay now?" She searched his face. "No more secrets and problems, right?"

Heat rose in Jordan's face, but it was a fair question. "I'm getting there, and no. No more secrets. I'm done with that and so is Lucas."

"You're ready then, to make a commitment with him. It's not too soon for you? I know you think I'm a nosy lady, but that's my baby, and I don't want to see him hurt again."

Fair enough. And it wasn't like Lucas hadn't gone through the third degree with Drew's grandmother. "I never expected it, to be honest. But sometimes it sneaks up on you and knocks you down." Over the past year, he'd been flayed to the bone, his skin stripped and bloodied. The last thing he expected to find in the darkness was love. "Maybe all we've had to slog through, the tragedies and triumphs, will make us appreciate what we mean to each other. I'll never let him down, Wanda." Jordan handed her a tissue as he watched her eyes fill. "He gave me back my life."

Tears trickled down her cheeks as she sniffled into her tissue. "All I've ever wanted was for that boy to be happy and find someone to love who'll love him back. He was so lost, even though he tried to pretend everything was under control."

"Making up with Ash helped the most."

She crumpled the wet tissue in her hand. "Thank God for that as well. He needed to do that. And I pray every day they find their youngest brother."

He patted her arm. "I hope so too. Now where's Troy?" He looked around the room for the big man from the shelter who ran the gun collection program and acted as their liaison with the police department. He spotted him by the computer room, and when Troy caught his eye, Jordan beckoned him over.

Jordan made Wanda promise to come by for dinner in the next week and said good-bye, then hastened over to meet Troy halfway. "How's it going, man?" They exchanged the obligatory handclasp and back slap.

"Good, good. We got lotsa my guys on the street sayin' that they're down with this, 'cause you're helping the kids." He shot Jordan an unreadable look. "It's all about the kids."

"Always, Troy. The longer the kids stay out of trouble, the better chance they have of making it through school. And an education is the most im-portant thing to help get people out of the shelter system. So what're the numbers looking like?" They walked as they talked, heading to the office in the back. Jordan unlocked the door and flipped on the light switch. He took a seat behind the desk and logged on to the computer. Troy stood behind him.

"Pull up a chair; make yourself comfortable." After Troy got settled, Jordan opened the database they'd set up to track the gun-turn-in program. A few more clicks and he turned to face Troy with a wide smile.

"This is fantastic. Troy, you didn't tell me you brought in fifty guns in the past month. Way to go." His good humor faltered when Troy failed to return his smile. "What's wrong? Did I get the number wrong?"

"Nah, man." Troy shook his head. "It's right, but it's so useless, you know? Does it really matter if we bring in fifty when we know there's hundreds more out there?" His dark eyes searched Jordan's face. "Is this doing anything, really?"

Jordan toyed with a rubber band for a moment before shooting it across the desk. "Do you vote, Troy?"

"Yeah, sure. I couldn't wait to turn eighteen for that."

"Well, a lot of people don't. They think their vote doesn't matter, so they stay home; then they wonder why things don't ever change. They continue to complain, but they don't participate in the process to make the change happen." A wry smile broke over Troy's face as Jordan spoke, and he knew the man understood the point he was trying to make. "A single vote, in and of itself, doesn't matter, but when you partner it with everyone else's vote, it gives you power. Strength in numbers. So one vote, one gun—it all adds up."

Troy sat a moment. "I never thought of it that way, Doc. You're all right, you know?"

"Yeah, I like to think so." Jordan laughed.

"I don't know many gay guys." Troy's gaze focused anywhere but on Jordan's face. "Um, but I think you and Luke are cool."

"Thanks." His phone rang, and once again it was Jerry. He held up a finger to Troy. "Hang on a sec, I have to take this call."

"Jerry. What's up?'

In the background, Jordan heard the once-familiar sounds of the hustle of the police precinct as Jerry spoke. "Listen, Jordan. Johnny wants to talk to you. Like I said before, it's a little unorthodox, but we're anxious to find out who his supplier is, so we're willing to go the extra mile, so to speak."

Jordan checked his watch. "I'm finishing up some stuff here at the Center, but I can be there in say, an hour or so? Does that work for you?"

"Perfect." The relief in Jerry's voice was evident. "We really appreciate it."

"No problem. I want to catch the guys who did this too. Plus, I'd like a shot at helping Johnny, if I can." Jordan studied the pictures on the wall of the smiling kids and came to rest on the one of Keith taken on the day he was awarded his detective shield. "It's the least I can do."

Jordan spent another half hour going through the rest of the gun program numbers with Troy. Wanda had promised to look after a little girl until her mother returned, but the child looked so sad Jordan took her in his lap and read her a story and helped her draw a picture. When he said good-bye to everyone, she tugged at his jacket and gave him a hug around his leg for a moment before running to the back and hiding behind Wanda.

His eyes burned, and he surreptitiously wiped a few errant tears away before they streaked down his face. Until then he hadn't realized how much of an impact the Center made on his life and others.

Jordan walked the few short blocks to the police station. When he pushed open the front door, the familiar scent and sounds of the precinct he'd once known as well as his own home assailed him. Several of the clerical staff jumped out of their seats to hug him and make a fuss over him.

Jerry pulled him away from the well-wishers. "Okay, everyone. Let Jordan go. He's here to help me. You can talk to him later." They walked to the back of the precinct, and Jerry briefed him as they passed police officers waiting around for prisoners to be processed. He knew many, if not most of the officers and detectives, and exchanged greetings with them as he and Jerry passed by on their way to the interrogation room.

"How did you guys pick him up?" Despite the fact

that Johnny had supplied him with his Xanax, he couldn't hold it against the young kid. Jordan's own desperation had driven him to take the drug in the first place. What had Johnny seen or done to force him into the dark brutality of drugs, guns, and the street?

Jerry snagged himself a cup of coffee from a machine and offered one to Jordan. "He's not too bright and got stuck with trying to steal too many things at once. Funny enough, though, it's the first time he's ever been picked up."

Jordan sipped the hot coffee slowly. "So his record's clean? That bodes well for a reduced sentence or even no time with probation and community service, right?"

Jerry nodded. "If you can get him to talk and tell us who his supplier is, we can work out a deal with the DA and guarantee no prison time. We've already read him his Miranda rights, and he understands them. He doesn't want to talk to the legal-aid attorney, at least not yet." Jerry finished his coffee. "He only wants to talk to you."

They came to a stop before a gray steel door. "I'll see what I can do," said Jordan. He drained the coffee cup and tossed it in the trash. "We could always use more help at the center, and he might fit in perfectly at Drew's clinic as well."

Jerry put his hand on the doorknob. "Do your best, but I don't expect miracles. Kid's a product of his environment, after all." He opened the door. "Johnny, I brought someone to talk to you."

Jordan shot Jerry a look and sidled past him into

the room. At a utilitarian steel table, Johnny sat slumped in his chair, trying hard to look cool and nonchalant, like he spent all his free time hanging out in police stations. In reality he looked exactly like what he was—a skinny, scared street kid with greasy, too-long hair and outgrown clothes that had started out as hand-me-downs from Goodwill or the trash bin.

"Hey, Johnny." Jordan stood by the door with his hands shoved into the pockets of his jeans.

At the sound of Jordan's voice, Johnny's black, fiery eyes, normally sneering and challenging, stared back at him, fearful and dubious. The thin lips, usually twisted in a snide little grin, quivered like those of a broken-hearted child. "Doc. You-you came?" The disbelief showed on his face.

"You asked for me, right?" Jordan nodded to the guard in the corner, then slid into the chair across the table. "Why did you want to talk to me?"

Johnny stared everywhere but Jordan's face. "I…I don't know." His skin tinged pink. "You were always nice to me, and I kinda thought maybe…"

"Maybe what?" said Jordan gently. "You weren't that nice to me the last time I saw you."

Flushing a deeper red, Johnny bit his chapped lips, not even registering that he'd drawn blood. "I know. But you gotta understand. Selling's all I know. And…and Donovan, he's given me a place to stay and shit."

"Donovan?" Jordan's heart tripped. Finally a lead. Not wanting to scare Johnny off, he clamped down on the spurt of excitement that bubbled up in his chest. "Who's he, the guy you work for?"

Realizing he might've given away too much information, Johnny's eyes darted from side to side. "Uh…"

"Look. Johnny, you help us and we'll help you. That's the way it works." Jordan knew he probably shouldn't have said it that way, but to hell with it. This shit needed to stop now. "You have to come clean about the drugs and the guns. That man you're working for is killing people all over this city. I lost someone I loved because of illegal guns. If you tell us what you know, the DA will probably let you off with probation and community service, and I can get you working at the Center or at my friend's medical clinic." He stood up and folded his arms across his chest. "If not, then I'm out, and there's nothing more for me to say."

Jordan held his breath. When no answer seemed to be forthcoming, he spun on his heel and walked toward the door, disappointment flooding through him.

"Doc?"

At the door, Jordan stopped, a huge wave of relief washing over him. "Yeah?" He strode back to the table and sat down.

"Okay. Call the cops in, and I'll tell them what I know. It ain't much but…" Johnny shrugged and picked at a bloody cuticle.

"Thank you. You have no idea how much this means to me." He nodded to the guard.

"Tell Detective Allen to come in, please. The young

man wants to talk."

Jerry and his partner came in to question Johnny, and Jordan left the interrogation room. This part wasn't his job. The chatter of the precinct faded into the background as he passed by the Wall of Heroes—pictures of police officers who'd fallen in the line of duty. There were men and women who'd died on September 11, and Jordan said a silent prayer for them. The last picture was of Keith.

"Hi." Jordan reached out to touch the photograph. "I'm making it. Day by day, but it's happening. And that kid in there? He's going to make it too, because of you and your generous heart. I promise."

His phone buzzed with a text, and he smiled when Lucas's name flashed on top.

Hey, I'm finished at work. Lunch?

Still staring at Keith's picture, Jordan texted back.

Love to, but I have someplace I'd like to take you after. Meet you at home.

He glanced back up at the picture. "See you later."

Chapter Twenty-Seven

MAYBE HE'D MADE a mistake by taking Lucas here, but Jordan didn't think so. The usual construction and tractor trailers hampered the drive into Brooklyn, but for once, he didn't let it bother him. They'd had a nice lunch at one of their favorite cafés in Chelsea, and after expecting to spend the day alone with only the dog, having Lucas home early was a bonus.

Lucas's warm hand covered his as he gripped the steering wheel. "You okay? You're so quiet."

Jordan's mouth quirked up in a smile. "Hey, I can be deep sometimes." His smile faded. "I was thinking of Johnny and all that he's going to face in the coming months."

Jerry had called during lunch and said the information Johnny had given them was going to help them to get a better handle on this Donovan person. It seems he'd originated outside of Philly and only came to New York around a year ago, but brought his people with him to expand his little operation. To look at the man, you'd never know he was a monster who used kids to do his dirty work. He was older and wore an aura of respectability around him as a businessman in the community. In fact, he owned a diner in downtown Brooklyn, and according to Johnny, that's where he ran his business. Jerry promised that Johnny would in no way be connected to anything that went down.

"I'm glad you're getting the kid some help. Working with Wanda and in Drew's clinic will help him. Maybe he'll even get his GED."

Traffic started moving again, and Jordan made the turn into Greenwood Cemetery. The cemetery itself had become somewhat of a tourist attraction since many famous people were buried here, and Jordan had a bit of trouble finding a parking spot. Finally, he parked the SUV and they walked down the grassy path together. Keith's was a simple monument—a gray granite headstone with his name, dates of birth and death, and the phrase, FOREVER IN OUR HEARTS.

Jordan knew Keith would never have wanted any mention of dying a hero or anything ostentatious or flowery. Lucas took the bouquet of lilies they'd brought and laid it on the bench nearby, then stepped back.

"Do you want some time alone? I can wait over by the path."

There was sorrow and not a little pain in Lucas's beautiful hazel eyes. Jordan held out his hand, and after a slight hesitation, Lucas took it.

"I've had enough moments alone to last me a lifetime. Over the past year, I wondered how it was possible for me to be surrounded by people yet be so impossibly lonely. Every day I died a little bit more, wanting what I could no longer have and pushing away everyone who loved me."

He took both of Lucas's hands in his. "I wanted you here with me because Keith should see I'm happy and recovered." Lucas tightened his grip on Jordan's hands. "I've learned to be a survivor, and it taught me that no matter how hard the fight, it's afterward that the real work begins."

"You're much stronger than I ever imagined when we first met. Whenever Keith spoke about you, I thought you were a pretty, rich snob, and I always wondered what he saw in you. He told me of your generous spirit and kind heart, but I guess I didn't believe him." Lucas rubbed his thumb over Jordan's fingers. "I prejudged you on your looks and background, and I was wrong. You surprised me."

"I surprised myself," admitted Jordan. He searched Lucas's face. "You became my strength. Even when I pushed you away, you came back at me, refusing to let me wallow and drown in self-pity. I owe my life to you." Jordan walked over to Keith's headstone and dropped to his knees. He ran his hand over the carved letters. "I loved you hard and with everything I had, babe, but it's not fair to Lucas. It's time I let you go. Let go of the past."

"No." Lucas knelt beside him. "You don't need to forget the past in order to live the future. Before I met and fell in love with you, I never believed I'd find love, or deserved it. I have no doubts about you or us and the commitment we have to each other. Even knowing how much you and Keith loved each other, I also know there are only two people in this relationship. You are who you are because of everyone who's touched your life. I wouldn't have you any other way."

How lucky could he have gotten in his life to be loved by two such very special men? "I do love you, Lucas. You're stubborn and too walled up sometimes, and you work way too damn hard, but you get me like nobody else. Never doubt for a moment you're the only man I'll ever want."

"I love you too. You're opinionated and impossible, with an ego as wide as the sky, but I wouldn't have you any other way." Lucas rose and placed his hand on the headstone. "Bye, Keith. I miss you, buddy."

Jordan kissed his fingers, then touched the engraved letters of Keith's name. "Forever in both of our hearts, babe. See you soon."

Drew once told him that in the Jewish tradition, when you visited someone's grave, you put a small rock on top of the headstone to signify you'd been there to pay your respects. He and Lucas each found a small stone and placed them next to each other on top of Keith's grave.

He brushed the curls off Lucas's forehead and kissed him. "Let's go home." Hand in hand, they walked back to the car and drove away.

Keep reading for a sneak peek of Embrace the Fire, Brandon and Tash's story, coming March, 2017!

Embrace the Fire

Chapter One

Seven years earlier

IN A FUTILE attempt to shield himself from the pouring rain, Brandon Gilbert lay huddled in a doorway near the Port Authority Bus Terminal in midtown Manhattan. Thoroughly soaked and shivering, he squeezed into the corner of the large, now waterlogged cardboard box. The once protective box sagged over his head, allowing the cascading water to run like a river down his back. At six feet, Brandon had a hard time finding any place to keep dry, and it seemed at this point the battle had been lost.

Why he'd thought coming to New York City was a good idea, he couldn't remember. Perhaps it was the anonymity he needed, or the fact that he could reinvent himself, now that he had papers and a new identity. But nothing had prepared him for the stark loneliness of this huge city; he had no steady source of food or shelter, hardly anyone to talk to day after day.

Brandon shifted in the box, and a fresh torrent of rainwater poured over him. The dank smells of the city coupled with the uncaring stares of people as they rushed by caused unwelcome tears to spring to his eyes. It wasn't supposed to be like this. He and his foster brothers were going to stay together, take care of each other. The three musketeers, that's what they'd laughingly called themselves.

Until Ash unexpectedly disappeared, leaving Brandon and Luke behind, never to be heard from again. Then in a night of frantic upheaval he still didn't understand, Brandon found himself on the road to a new life, ripped away from the only person he knew truly loved him—Luke. Where was Luke? Brandon remembered long ago how his brother had dreamed of coming to New York City to live, so when he first got to the city, he'd foolishly tried to locate him. He went looking for a phone book but couldn't find any. The few times he'd gone to the public library to use their computers, he'd searched for *Luke Carini*, but there were no listings with that name. Discouraged, he'd stopped.

And now he was alone. Not a single person who cared about him, plus he could never go home again. Why was he even bothering? If he was smart, he'd go to the river and jump in. No one would notice or care.

A tall silhouette holding an umbrella loomed in front of him, cutting off the dim light of the gray, dripping skies. Terrified, Brandon shrank back farther into the dark corner of the doorway.

"Don't be afraid. I'm not here to hurt you." The figure squatted in front of Brandon, and the face of a middle-aged man came into view. His smile radiated warmth and peace, emotions almost alien to Brandon.

"What do you want?" Brandon clutched his thin jacket around him. "I don't have any money or anything." At that moment a gush of water sluiced down over his face. In his eighteen years, Brandon had never felt so alone and lost.

"I don't want anything from you, except your promise to take my help. I'm with an organization that helps runaway youth." The man's calm smile miraculously settled Brandon's racing heart. "You have no place to go, am I right? Let me take you someplace where you'll be safe and secure."

"Who are you?" Though hope flared hot and bright in Brandon's chest, he knew enough to be wary of men offering help.

"My name is Gabriel, Gabriel Heller. I'm a New York City schoolteacher, and I volunteer on the weekends with the Department of Homeless Services." He pulled out an ID and a pamphlet and offered it to Brandon. "Here, see?"

With some trepidation, Brandon took the laminated card and the pamphlet the man offered after brushing a hank of wet hair out of his eyes. The identification checked out as the man had stated. Gabriel Heller worked for the Department of Education. A teacher. Brandon bit his lip as he read over the mission of the organization and how they planned to help.

"Here." He handed back the items, his thoughts

racing.

All his life, Brandon had wanted to be a teacher; school had been the only outlet he had to escape his home life. Teachers had been his saviors, and until that last, horrible night with his foster father, his plan had always been to go to college and get a job teaching young inner-city children.

"So, have I passed the test? Will you come to the shelter with me?" Gabriel's lips curved in a wry smile. "This isn't a night fit for even a New York City rat to be outside. I'll set you up with a social worker and get you a place to stay. What's your name?"

A yearning Brandon had thought dead burst to life, almost choking him with its intensity. Things like this, good things, never happened to him. "Randy. My name is Randy." Close enough to his real name, Brandon, Randy was the name he'd chosen when he ran away, making sure no one could find him.

"Okay, Randy, come on. I'll get you out of those wet clothes, give you a hot meal, and a place to sleep." Gabriel stood and held out his hand. "You don't have to figure out the rest of your life tonight."

The force of the pelting rain lessened, and the gray of the sky shifted to a lighter haze. Brandon stood and pulled off the wet strips of cardboard clinging to his hair and body. "I don't have any money to pay, and I don't take charity." Some vestige of pride he'd thought long gone, emerged. "I'll work for whatever I have to."

A smile crept over Gabriel's face. "How old are you?"

"Almost nineteen."

Brandon heard Gabriel sigh. "What's wrong?" Was he too old? Now that the chance was in front of him, so close he could reach out and brush it with his fingertips, Brandon wanted it. Desperately.

"I don't suppose you have your high school diploma?"

"Yes, I do." His chin lifted. "I was going to go to college." He slanted a quick look at Gabriel through the wet strands of hair that hung in his eyes. "I wanted to be a teacher too."

They'd reached the van Gabriel had left parked down the block. Another man waited behind the wheel.

"Antonio, this is Randy."

"Hey, man. No night to be outside. You don't know how lucky you are Gabriel found you. He's a life changer."

Brandon's eyes met Antonio's in the rearview mirror. Something tight loosened in his chest, allowing him to return the smile. "Yeah?"

Antonio nodded. "Yeah. Last year I was in your shoes: no home, no job, and no place to go." He started the engine and put the windshield wipers on to clear the windows. "Today, I got a place to live and a job helping Gabriel getting guys like you off the streets. I'm even going to college now." His voice rang with quiet pride.

Gabriel slid into the seat next to Antonio, and they took off downtown. "I'm glad you came with me, Randy. You have the opportunity now to help yourself and hopefully help others in the future." White teeth flashed in the dim interior of the van. "The first step is the hardest, isn't it? But it's all worth it in the end."

The warmth of the heater finally began to penetrate his wet clothes, yet Brandon shivered. The enormity of the second chance he was being offered overwhelmed him. If these men had faith in him, there was nothing he couldn't accomplish. Could he do it? Could he start over again and achieve his dreams?

As Gabriel spoke, Brandon forgot his wet clothes and empty stomach and listened.

Join my newsletter to get access to get first looks at WIP, exclusive content, contests, deleted scenes and much more! Never any spam.

Newsletter: http://eepurl.com/bExIdr

About the Author

I have always been a romantic at heart. I believe that while life is tough, there is always a happy ending around the corner, My characters have to work for it, however. Like life in NYC, nothing comes easy and that includes love.

I live in New York City with my husband and two children and hopefully soon a cat of my own. My day begins with a lot of caffeine and ends with a glass or two of red wine. I practice law but daydream of a time when I can sit by a beach somewhere and write beautiful stories of men falling in love. Although there are bound to be a few bumps along the way, a Happily Ever After is always guaranteed.

Website:

www.felicestevens.com

Facebook:

facebook.com/felice.stevens.1

Twitter:

twitter.com/FeliceStevens1

Instagram:

instagram.com/FeliceStevens

Other titles by Felice Stevens

Through Hell and Back Series:
A Walk Through Fire
After the Fire
Embrace the Fire—Coming March 2017

The Memories Series:
Memories of the Heart
One Step Further
The Greatest Gift

The Breakfast Club Series:
Beyond the Surface
Betting on Forever
Second to None
What Lies Between Us
A Holiday to Remember

Rescued Hearts Series:
Rescued
Reunited

Other:
Learning to Love
The Way to His Heart—A Learning to Love Novella
The Arrangement
Please Don't Go

Made in the USA
Columbia, SC
08 October 2023

24160962R00215